Praise for Lee Harris's Manhattan Mysteries

"Harris's characters are gritty and realistic. . . . This author draws readers into this top-notch novel [*Murder in Alphabet City*] with a mystery that's as compelling as the relationships between the players. In the subgenre of police procedurals, this is one of the very best."
—*Romantic Times*

"Lee Harris brings to the police procedural terrific New York moments, intricate plotting and characters as real as if they were in the next room."
—*Mystery Scene*

"A very dynamic and exciting police procedural . . . Lee Harris can always be counted on to give her fans an exciting mystery."
—*The Midwest Book Review*

"Lee Harris . . . gives us a new detective and a grittier neighborhood in *Murder in Hell's Kitchen,* but her storytelling skill remains top quality."
—Tony Hillerman

"Lee Harris is a good writer and she has a winner here."
—*Mysterious Women*

"Harris knows a lot about cops and a lot about women and she knows how to plot a good mystery. *Murder in Hell's Kitchen* is so believable I kept expecting to read more about the case in the morning papers."
—Stephen Greenleaf

By Lee Harris

The Manhattan Mysteries

MURDER IN HELL'S KITCHEN
MURDER IN ALPHABET CITY
MURDER IN GREENWICH VILLAGE

The Christine Bennett Mysteries

THE GOOD FRIDAY MURDER
THE YOM KIPPUR MURDER
THE CHRISTENING DAY MURDER
THE ST. PATRICK'S DAY MURDER
THE CHRISTMAS NIGHT MURDER
THE THANKSGIVING DAY MURDER
THE PASSOVER MURDER
THE VALENTINE'S DAY MURDER
THE NEW YEAR'S EVE MURDER
THE LABOR DAY MURDER
THE FATHER'S DAY MURDER
THE MOTHER'S DAY MURDER
THE APRIL FOOLS' DAY MURDER
THE HAPPY BIRTHDAY MURDER
THE BAR MITZVAH MURDER
THE SILVER ANNIVERSARY MURDER

MURDER IN GREENWICH VILLAGE

A MANHATTAN MYSTERY

LEE HARRIS

FAWCETT

BALLANTINE BOOKS • NEW YORK

Murder in Greenwich Village is a work of fiction. Names, characters, places, and incidents are the products of the author's imagination or are used fictitiously. Any resemblance to actual events, locales, or persons, living or dead, is entirely coincidental.

A Fawcett Books Mass Market Original

Copyright © 2006 by Lee Harris

All rights reserved.

Published in the United States by Fawcett Books, an imprint of The Random House Publishing Group, a division of Random House, Inc., New York.

FAWCETT is a registered trademark and the Fawcett colophon is a trademark of Random House, Inc.

ISBN 0-345-47596-8

Cover illustration: Matthew Frey

Printed in the United States of America

www.ballantinebooks.com

OPM   9   8   7   6   5   4   3   2   1

In loving memory of
DJL

ACKNOWLEDGMENTS

Many thanks to James L. V. Wegman for contributing his time as well as his knowledge and expertise. This book has benefited greatly because of him.

The city is the teacher
of the man.

—Simonides of Ceos
(556–469 B.C.E.)
Plutarch: Should Old Men Govern?

1

THE WHIP HAD gotten his gold leaf. By virtue of commanding the Cold Case Squad at 137 Centre Street, which since its formation the previous fall had cleared at least three tough cases spectacularly, Capt. Francis X. Graves had been promoted to deputy inspector. Det. Jane Bauer, whose team of three detectives had been responsible for two of those cases being put to rest, learned of Graves's good fortune on her return from her first trip to Paris in March with the man she loved illicitly and passionately, a deputy chief. Her partner, Gordon Defino, had also been promoted from third-grade to second-grade detective, and deservedly so. The third member of the team, Sean MacHovec, had earned a bump to second, but was living under a cloud because of an incident at the end of the last case, and had not received the promotion.

With all the changes, returning to the job after only a short time away was jolting. But the squad was doing its job and although not a permanent fixture, would continue its work, sparing the detectives a return to ordinary precinct squad activity. Results paid off. Jane herself had been moved up two grades to first after their first case.

Spring had been splintered. Jane had to appear in court for a long-delayed trial, thus requiring a refresher on the case. It was a nasty one, with ornery activists on both sides trying the patience of the judge and luring the various media to the courthouse, inside and out. As Jane's testimony came to an end, Defino was called to do the same on an old case of his. Graves was worried: his best team out of commission for weeks. With his ambition, he needed a steady stream of results.

When the trials and vacations were out of the way, Mac-Hovec returned from his temporary transfer to another team, which appeared devastated to lose him. Defino would have liked to have seen the last of him, even if not as strongly as the day they met. Today was a fine day in May with the smell of spring in the air, as the team sat in the whip's office to receive their new assignment. Deputy Inspector Graves, a handsome, articulate man who frequently played police spokesman before the TV cameras, looked more gorgeous than usual, and happier. Something about a gold leaf on his shoulder.

"I see you're all looking good," he began. "Well rested, I hope. We've got a biggie here."

"Less work than painting the house," MacHovec said. He, too, had taken vacation time.

"Maybe not this time. You folks remember the Micah Anthony hit?"

"Oh, shit," Defino said under his breath.

Jane seconded the sentiment. "The undercover cop. That was a long time ago, Inspector."

"And the case is still open," Graves said, "as you know." The file on the desk in front of him was the tallest Jane had ever seen. It represented the work of team after team of angry investigators, angry that one of their best had been gunned down by an anonymous shooter who had left no clue to his identity, and had covered his tracks so well that he might have dissolved into the mist.

"Well, we did good twice," MacHovec said in a you-can't-win-'em-all tone of voice.

"Do good once more," Graves countered dryly. "I don't know who can heft this thing. Annie put it in three separate jackets so you don't break your arms on day one." Annie was the police administrative aide, and probably couldn't have hefted the whole file herself.

"That it?" Defino asked.

"That's it, Detective. I don't have to tell you how important it is to clear this case."

"No, sir." Defino stood, crushed his empty coffee cup noisily, and took the top third of the file.

MacHovec followed, leaving Jane the bottom third, the beginning of the case, the call to 911, the first officers on the scene, and the desperate, unsuccessful attempt to save the dying cop.

"And I was looking forward to coming back," MacHovec said, dropping into his desk chair. "This is a dead end. I should've stayed home and given the house another coat."

Defino, dropping his cup in the trash basket, concurred. "I remember when the call came in. I was on midnights that week, twelve to eight, riding in an RMP with my partner, Pinkie. Long time ago."

"You sound like a couple of dreamy high school girls," Jane said. "I was in the Six that night making a good collar. The desk sergeant told us about it when we brought the perp in. Let's get going before you guys start crying." Newly in the Six at the time, she remembered, and newly in love with Lieutenant, almost Captain, Hackett. Defino was right—a long time ago.

It had been a headliner in every paper, even the *Times*. Det. Micah Anthony was six-one, thirty, black, and a former amateur boxer who worked with poor kids on his days off. He left a wife so beautiful that she was photographed from all possible angles, her skin several shades lighter than her husband's, and her belly big with their first child, a boy born three months after his father's death.

Micah Anthony's family was strict and religious, every child with a name from the Bible. His father worked as a janitor in an office building in Manhattan and his mother taught in day care. One child in the family had died of a gunshot wound years earlier, before the term "drive-by" had been coined. After the killing, Micah made up his young mind to be a cop.

The family lived in Harlem, in a ratty walk-up that they often talked about leaving but never did. Micah was the first to make the move. With a regular paycheck from the job, he found an apartment in the West Thirties, a walk-up like his family's, but in better condition. While living there he met his future wife and married her. They worked for a few years before she became pregnant: she as a model, bringing in enough income that they had a deposit down on a house on Staten Island at the time of his death. A month after the funeral, she moved in, telling reporters it was what they wanted for their child.

After the baby was born, she stayed out of the news for a year, then took up causes for cops, for black cops, and for the kids her husband had coached. Even now, about ten years later, her face and her name appeared occasionally on the news or in a small piece in one of New York's daily papers.

All this Jane knew without reading the file. Every cop in New York knew it. As an earlier generation could pinpoint exactly where they were when JFK was shot, cops of Jane's vintage knew where they were when Micah Anthony was hit. He had been working undercover, investigating the movement of handguns into and within the city, infiltrating a group of "businessmen" who were buying and selling the weapons. He had phoned in his location at ten thirty that evening after a crucial meeting in a house in the West Fifties, about as far west as there were buildings, and said he was going home. A few minutes later he called his wife from the same phone to tell her the same thing. Their apartment was about a mile south of where he stood to make the calls, but he never got home that night. At two the next morning, two shots awoke residents of Waverly Place just west of Washington Square Park in Greenwich Village, a historic and arty area of downtown Manhattan. Three calls came in to 911 almost at the same moment reporting the shots, and radio cars from the Six screamed to the scene. Micah Anthony did not survive the night.

The bottom line was there was nothing: no DNA, no prints, no shells from the Colt .357 Magnum, no marks on the body, no car reported to have torn away from the curb. Anthony had no connection to the Village. His family lived in the middle of Harlem, seven or eight miles north of where he was shot, and they hadn't seen him for a couple of weeks.

His old friends hadn't seen him; his wife had barely seen him and had worried daily about his safety.

Reluctantly, the detectives on the case speculated that he had a girlfriend in one of the brownstones on Waverly Place, someone he had visited after making his last two phone calls, although the medical examiner found no evidence of recent sexual activity. Perhaps the shooting was related to a lovers' dispute, not his police work. A meticulous canvass of the neighborhood with attention to the young women who lived there turned up nothing, and his wife, Melodie, not really a suspect, was at home when the police came to her door. A record of calls from her telephone indicated she had made several to her husband's lieutenant during the night, fearful for his safety when he failed to return home after calling her.

It was a case with one body, two bullets, and no leads. The three men Micah Anthony had spent a couple of hours with at the crib in the West Fifties were hauled in, questioned "continuously and roughly," said their attorneys, and indicted for possession of guns found in the apartment but not for his murder. The evidence was not strong enough for a solid case, and two of them walked, disaster following disaster. From what Jane remembered, every human being who had touched Anthony's life was questioned, down to his kindergarten teacher. What, she wondered, would be left for the three of them ten years later?

"His wife remarried," Defino said, his voice breaking the silence and their concentration.

"When?"

"Two years ago. They always mentioned in the follow-up articles that she hadn't. She was one good-looking gal."

"I remember," MacHovec said. "Who'd she marry?"

"Some guy named Harwood Appleby. Looks like plenty of money there. Why'd she wait so long?"

"Because she loved her husband," Jane said with irritation. "Because the shock of Anthony's death knocked her for a loop. She had her husband's baby and she couldn't see how to start over with someone else."

Defino looked at her with skepticism. "Just asking."

"She still live on Staten Island?"

He turned a couple of pages. "Yeah, but he has an apartment in the city. Maybe she wants the kid to go to the same school."

It sounded reasonable. "I'm reading from the beginning. What a downer this case is."

"It'll be worse when we give up," MacHovec said.

Silence returned. Jane started through the file, bottom up. She made notes of the names: the uniforms who responded to the calls, the first detectives on the scene, the crime scene people, Micah Anthony's lieutenant, and everyone else he had contact with on the job. All these people would have to be requestioned. To her left and right her partners were doing the same thing, scribbling on pads. At noon Defino asked if she wanted lunch.

"Let's do it before I start seeing double."

They got up and left. MacHovec always fended for himself, often bringing a brown bag, sometimes going for a bite from the hot dog stand. The day was spring at its best and neither had a coat. At one of their usual places they ordered their usual choices.

"That gold leaf has Graves believing he's invincible," Defino said.

"Maybe he is, but the question is, are we? That was the cleanest shooting I ever heard of. We can take six months and recanvass and reinvestigate and end up with just what we have here."

"Zip."

"I want to start with the wife, Gordon."

He looked up from his pasta-based dish. "Any reason?"

"Maybe I'm tired of doing things the right way. We can go to Waverly Place anytime. Nothing's going to change. You pick up anything that developed in the last few years?" Defino was working on the most recent third of the file. The original detectives on the case would make some phone calls every six months and leave a Five, the Detective Division 5 form used to record new information and interviews, in the file.

"They're still comparing slugs from new cases. They

don't have much else to go on, no prints, no DNA. And they ask the right questions when they collar a possible shooter. Not that it does any good."

"Somebody out there knows something," Jane said. "If we ruffle some feathers, maybe he'll come out of hiding."

"I think I'll double my life insurance." Defino said it with the practiced certainty of a man who understood consequences.

"Finish your meat sauce. I want to get started."

MacHovec made the call. Mrs. Anthony, now Appleby, was home on Staten Island and agreed to talk to the detectives, but not there. She gave him an address on Sutton Place and said the next day at ten would be fine. She would go into Manhattan after seeing her son off to school.

"Looks like you guys rack up all the goodies," MacHovec said, passing the address to Jane. "I'm not sure I've ever set foot on Sutton Place."

"I'll wear a new tie," Defino said.

They worked quietly, accumulating pages of notes. About two, Defino said, "The wife's the last person who heard from him; the lieutenant's the second-last. Let's talk to him up front."

"I've got his name here somewhere." Jane ran her finger down a now long list of names. "Harold Bowman. No idea where he's working now. Sean?"

"On it." He had the number and location in a minute and then Bowman, now a captain, on the phone. After a few seconds of talk, he asked if they could get up there that afternoon. Bowman was over on the East Side in the One-Seven, a quick subway ride uptown on the Lex from Centre Street. They nodded and he set it up.

Defino sprang from his chair. Anything was better than sitting at a desk and reading old interviews.

Captain Bowman was mid-fifties, graying, putting on weight, and nearly buried in paper. A chair next to his desk held the overflow stack that would not fit on his desk. He welcomed the detectives and made a call for coffee. "Micah Anthony," he said when he hung up. "I haven't seen you two before."

Defino explained briefly.

"Well, maybe new faces will do the trick. You probably want to know what our last phone call was about."

"We can start with that," Jane said.

"It's in the file. I've read it off so many times in the last ten years, I know it by heart. As soon as I heard the news that night, I wrote it down as I remembered it. It wasn't a long conversation. Have you read it?"

"I have."

"Then I can't help you. I'd just read it off to you." He opened a drawer and found an eight-and-a-half-by-eleven sheet of paper and passed it to Defino, who went over it quickly.

"He didn't tell you much."

"He didn't have to. I knew where he was, I knew why he was there, I knew what they were going to talk about. He said he had a lot of paperwork and I would read that when he got it to me. As far as I knew, he went home after he called me."

"Did he call from a cell phone?" Jane asked.

"No. He owned one, a big clunky thing. We didn't issue them at that time—remember, this was ten years ago—but he wanted one, although he kept it off most of the time so he wouldn't be bothered by embarrassing calls. Our arrangement was to use a landline if at all possible. He called me from a pay phone on Tenth Avenue near the crib where the meet was. They found the phone the next day."

"And then he called his wife."

"That's what we learned."

"He wasn't far from home when he made the calls, maybe a mile. Would he have taken the subway, a cab, or maybe walked?"

"He could have done any of those three things," the captain said. "In my opinion, he would have walked. He was an athletic guy, as fit as anyone I've ever seen, and he could do that mile in fifteen minutes easy, ten if he jogged. The subway . . . well, by the time he got to a station, waited for a train, rode down to Thirty-fourth Street, and walked to his house, he might as well have walked the whole way. If he took a taxi—and it's not out of the question; he was tired and he hadn't seen his wife for a couple of days—they never found a record on a trip sheet."

"Was it just a coincidence that the meet was so near where he lived?" Defino asked.

"Far as I know, yes. These guys had a place on the East Side, but the lease had expired and they found the new one on West Fifty-second. When they were arrested, only three guns were found, samples of the goods so the buyer would know they could deliver on the order, but enough for a charge of possession."

"How many people knew about the operation?" Jane asked.

"We kept the number down. I knew, obviously. The PAA knew something undercover was going on, but she didn't know the details or the players. She never met Micah, by the way. We didn't give her things to type up. He did that himself. And then there's his wife."

"What about the wife?" Defino asked.

"I don't know what he told her; I only know what she said she knew, which was that he was working undercover on a special assignment, that she shouldn't worry, and everything would be all right. He called her right after he called me; they verified that. It was a short call: 'Honey, I'm coming home.' That was it. I still call her once in a while. She remarried last year, maybe the year before; time goes by faster than I can keep track. She's a stunning woman: smart, knows how to make money. This guy was after her to marry him for a couple of years. She told me . . ."

They waited.

"OK, you're the investigators; there's no personal secrets in a homicide case. She told me she didn't feel she could be intimate with another man after Micah. I guess she changed her mind. And if you think Micah went down to the Village to see some babe, you won't find one. He was crazy about Melodie. They were a nice couple, expecting their first child, waiting to move to a new house. The Six looked in every bedroom down there for a girlfriend. There wasn't any and no evidence of recent sexual activity in the autopsy."

"Lovers don't always meet to have sex," Jane said, wondering if she was the only one in the room who knew that from personal experience. From the looks on the men's faces, it appeared to be so.

"It was eleven at night; he'd worked hard all day," Captain Bowman said. "He hadn't seen his wife for a few days. If he had a girlfriend, you think he went down there to play patty-cake?"

She let it pass.

"But there was no girlfriend," Bowman said. "I'm sure of it."

"You said the PAA never met Anthony. How did that work?" Defino asked.

"I'll lay it out for you." Captain Bowman pushed himself back from his desk, nearly hitting the wall. Space did not come cheap. "We were OCCB at One PP." That meant the Organized Crime Control Bureau at One Police Plaza. "Micah was a UC detective, working in deep undercover operations. The last one was guns. You know that. He had no actual assigned command or a real office. On paper he was part of a task force we called WRAP, Weapons Reduction and Purchase, just so we'd have a name for it. We talked by phone when he was able, mostly for his protection. I wanted to know he was alive. Once in a while we'd meet, sometimes in New Jersey, once in Connecticut, once or twice upstate or out of Manhattan, never the same place twice. His paychecks went directly to a bank. He received city money that he signed for to do his work, flash money or buy money, depending on what he was doing at the moment. Before his last assignment, he had a great record of arrests. He was never present, you understand. That would have blown his cover.

"He was fantastic at his job. He could have gotten an Oscar for the parts he played. He gave us a steady flow of intelligence information no one else had been able to get. There were hundreds of guns involved in the last buy that never took place. When we raided the crib after his death, we found just the three guns, including a long-range rifle."

"Three," Jane said.

"Right. We traced them to weapons stolen from an armory. We never found the guns Micah was buying."

"Maybe they didn't exist," Defino said.

"They existed, all right. The number and type of each weapon Micah was told he could buy exactly coincided with the number of weapons of those types stolen from the armory. We just don't know where the hell they were hidden."

"And you still don't know ten years later?"

"Right. They could have been in another apartment, loaded on a ship to Timbuktu, or buried somewhere. New York's got a lot of parks and dumps. But not one of those stolen weapons has ever turned up, and we've made a lot of busts with guns in the last ten years." He tasted his coffee, which was cold by now, and pushed it away. "That's it, Detectives, the Micah Anthony story. We gave him an inspector's funeral, a pension to his wife, and life went on. I still haven't met another guy like him on the job." He looked at his watch pointedly.

They thanked him and left their cards, and he said they could call anytime they wanted to.

"How many guns were involved?" Jane asked as they were about to leave.

"Two hundred twenty-seven." He said it as though the number had been engraved on his brain. Ten years later he didn't have to look it up. The amount of money involved in a buy like that would be in the eighty-thousand range.

Out on the street they turned toward Lexington Avenue.

"I'd like to crack a case like this," Defino said.

"That makes two of us."

2

JANE TOOK HER third of the file home with her. She had been walking or jogging to and from work in good weather for several months, but the weight of the file pointed her toward the subway. It was still necessary to walk at the other end, as she lived in the West Village, out of range of the subway. As she walked, she thought about whom she knew from her twenty years on the job who might have an insight into the Micah Anthony homicide, but she came up with no one. A man who worked as deep undercover as he did didn't have pals he said hello to on the job, didn't go for a beer with the guys after work, and didn't tell tales out of school.

She got home and listened to her messages. Her father had called and she called him back, telling him about the new case so he could experience it vicariously. He was retired and living in the Bronx in the same apartment she grew up in. His health had improved in the last few months, the heart medicines working, and he was getting around more, although she worried about him and his friend Madeleine using the subway, not to mention walking from his station to their building after dark.

After dinner she sat with the file. Listening to Captain Bowman, she had felt a tingle of excitement replacing the initial disappointment of working on a case that no ordinary mortal could clear, and that her boss wanted cleared. The thought of recanvassing the area where Anthony was found after ten years left her cold. Even the next day's interview with Anthony's widow would probably be so routine, so full of practiced rehashed statements, that it would lead nowhere. They needed an angle, something different, something that would get them into Anthony's skin, but she didn't see how to do it. They would have to find the men in the crib. One of them could easily have followed Anthony into the street, even overheard his conversations at the pay phone, then taken him by car to the street where he was shot. But what had happened during the three hours between Anthony's kidnapping and his murder? Had he gone willingly with his captors? They had not beaten him. No bruises or abrasions were found on his body. If they had handcuffed him or tied him up, they had managed to do it without leaving marks—not a likely situation. It looked as though he knew his captors, or they had contacted him to meet them and he had gone there willingly. But if the latter were true, they had not reached him on his cell phone or through his pager. That information would have turned up in the initial investigation. And if the people he had just left had told him to go somewhere, he would not have called Bowman to say he was done, or his wife to say he was on his way home. Someone had gotten to him after the phone calls.

None of this qualified as original thinking. In a case as old and important as this one, someone on the job had suggested almost every possibility, explored it, and come up with nothing. This time around, they had to do something different.

Her phone rang while she was trying to think what that different approach would be.

"How are you?" Hack said.

"Hi." She smiled at the voice. "Where are you?"

"Driving home. I spend more time driving than working these days, and I'm putting in lots of hours."

"We've got a new case."

"Tell me." In his old assignment at One PP, he often knew it before she did. Now that he was a deputy chief and working in the Bronx Borough Command, his knowledge of and influence over her job was close to zero.

"Micah Anthony."

"Oh, shit."

"Listen to Graves, he really thinks we can do it."

"Don't give up your day job."

He was the red meat of her life, what kept her going and what would destroy her if she lost him. It had started ten years ago when he was a lieutenant, almost a captain, and she had just gotten her gold shield. Their attraction was as strong as a ton of magnets, and she had not struggled against it or thought about consequences. He understood consequences, but didn't care. They were careful—very careful—and kept it secret. He had told her a thousand times that he would leave his wife if she would marry him, but she refused. An adopted child who had given up her own accidental child, she wanted his daughters brought up by two parents.

She knew, because he had told her and she believed him, that sex with his wife had ended years ago. The intimation that his wife did not miss it filtered into an occasional conversation. It was likely that she knew something was going on, but it was more important to her that it remain secret than that it end. Jane and Hack did not talk about it.

Although cops did not discuss such intimacies in her presence, Jane knew that Irish cops, now mostly Hack's generation, complained about BIC wives, Bronx or Brooklyn Irish Catholic. But the initials were a euphemism. To those who used them, they meant Born Ice Cold.

Jane was a Bronx Catholic, if not Irish, whose misadventure in her late teens left her parents almost paralyzed. That they had supported her was the reason she had turned into a confident, functioning human being. And she wasn't ice-cold.

She and Hack had gone to Paris in March, her first trip out of the country. He had picked the time so that she would celebrate her birthday in that city, and so that they would celebrate ten years of being together. Now they had started another year.

"If I had one," she said, responding to his comment about a day job. "Defino and I talked to Captain Bowman this afternoon. He was Anthony's contact at OCCB."

"Harold Bowman. I remember him."

"He still stays in touch with Anthony's widow, and he's sure Anthony didn't go down to the Village to see a girlfriend."

"They looked into that pretty thoroughly." A horn sounded at his end.

"His reason is that the autopsy showed no evidence of sexual activity. So I said—"

"Let me guess. You said maybe they met to have a nice long conversation on world affairs. Did he laugh you out of the room?"

"Not quite, but you're about to."

"Jane, Harold Bowman had a little something going once that I knew about. He didn't go to see her to improve his mind or eat her cookies. And if Micah Anthony visited a woman that night, it was for what he wasn't getting at home."

"He didn't visit a woman. He told his wife he was on his way home. Hack, before you start breaking up, I don't want to do this case according to rules."

"Then you'll lose your job. Original thinking isn't part of your job description, or Graves's. He'll forget all the good things you've done."

She ignored him. "I want to get inside the stuff that Anthony was doing."

"How?"

"I don't know yet."

"My battery's low. You're getting fuzzy."

"Look at that. Five minutes together and no sex."

"How can you be sure?"

She laughed, but the voice in her ear was gone.

Sutton Place, Jane always thought, was short and to the point. Along the eastern edge of Manhattan in the expensive Fifties, it was a few blocks of superexpensive real estate, apartment houses and town houses fitted with the amenities required by the wealthy.

Jane and Defino walked east from the Fifty-third Street exit of the Lex. The building was on the east side of the street, which meant the apartment might have a view of the East River and a daily sunrise for those whose schedules

awoke them early. It turned out she was right. The door-
man checked their shields, matched their photos to their
faces, then called upstairs and directed them to the elevator.
The door was on the river side of the building, and once
they were inside the view from the living room was superb.

Mrs. Appleby was as beautiful as her legend promised,
and gracious as well. Coffee was already made, and she
served it in fine porcelain cups with a coffee cake that she cut
with a silver knife. When she turned to pour for Defino, Jane
looked at her profile and thought she might be pregnant.

"We understand that you've answered a lot of questions
over the last ten years," Jane said when they had been served.

"Not a lot of questions, just the same group of questions
over and over. My answers haven't changed, but I know you
have to ask them. I'm certainly willing to cooperate. It hurts
me that the people responsible for Micah's death are still
free. I will do anything to help put them where they belong."

"We know the gist of the last two phone calls," Defino
said. "We talked to Captain Bowman yesterday and we're
reading the file."

"Then that's a question I don't have to answer. I suppose
the other thing you want to ask me is about the girlfriend. I
know wives are the last to know about those things, so
whatever I say doesn't count for much, but I don't believe
there was another woman in his life." She smiled. "Except
for his mother."

"Captain Bowman agrees with you," Jane said.

"He's a dear man. He felt this as deeply as I did."

"Did your husband tell you what he was involved in?"

She inhaled deeply. "He was undercover. He worried
about my safety. He told me what he was doing was dangerous, but if I was ever in a situation—that's what he called it,
and I understood it to mean where my life was being
threatened—I could give a phone number to the person
threatening me. I kept it with me all the time. I believe it led
to someone at OCCB, but I never called it so I don't know.
And I was never in a situation."

"Did you know it was about selling guns?" Defino asked.

"Only after he died."

"What's your scenario of what happened that night?" Jane asked.

"Someone was waiting for him when he left the house on Fifty-second Street. Whoever it was followed him and waited while he made his phone calls. Then he told Micah something had come up and they had to go wherever. The person had good ID and Micah went with him." She paused to sip her coffee. "It had to be someone he trusted." Although she didn't say it, the possibility that it might have been a cop hung in the air.

It was one of the possibilities Jane had turned over the night before. A cop would trust a cop if he had a good story. "Do you mean a cop?" she asked.

"Someone he trusted," Mrs. Appleby repeated. "Law enforcement isn't out of the question. I'm sure it's been on the minds of all the investigators when they couldn't come up with a suspect. But it wasn't Lieutenant Bowman. And no one in that office knew Micah's name or what he was doing. Or so I've been told."

"It could have been the people your husband had just seen," Defino said.

"It could be, yes. They were arrested and tried and nothing much came of it. I'm sure they knew more than they said, but the evidence wasn't there. I don't know where to look, Detectives. I hope you do."

"When he called you to check in with you while he was working, did he tell you where he was calling from?"

"Sometimes. He'd say, 'I'm up in Harlem. Give me half an hour,' or 'I'm on Tenth Avenue near Fifty-second. I'll see you soon.' That's what he said the last night."

"When did you call Lieutenant Bowman?" Jane asked.

She made a sound with her lips closed. "About midnight, maybe a little earlier. Micah was still alive at that point, something that has always bothered me. I knew he was in trouble; I just didn't know how big the trouble was. I was trying to find him and he was trying to save his life and it just didn't work."

"Did you call his cell phone?"

"I tried several times but he had turned it off."

"Was that usual?"

"Yes. He used it mostly for outgoing calls. And I wasn't supposed to call him. It was just that night I knew something was wrong."

Jane put her card down on the coffee table and Defino did the same.

"I'm sorry we dragged you into the city for this interview," Jane said.

"I'm glad you're still trying. Someday someone will crack this case, probably by accident. I hope it's in my lifetime."

Jane stood and went to the window. The view was everything she had expected, the river, the southern tip of Roosevelt Island, and beyond it, Queens. Turning left and right, she saw the view extended grandly. To the south she could just see the Williamsburg Bridge in a New York haze. The other two bridges over the East River were invisible around the bulge of southern Manhattan that had become known as Alphabet City.

She followed Mrs. Appleby to the door, past a narrow galley kitchen that would have fit in her own kitchen twice. They shook hands and Mrs. Appleby thanked them for looking into Micah's murder.

"Well, at least I get to see real estate I can't afford on this job," Defino said when they hit the street. "Toni'd go nuts in a kitchen that small. For what those apartments cost, you'd think they'd make it bigger than a closet."

"With that much money you don't cook. You have it catered."

"I'll remember that."

"Gordon, let's get a cup of coffee somewhere and talk."

"You're about to make me unhappy, aren't you?"

"I'm about to make everyone unhappy."

They walked quickly to Lex and found a coffee shop. Defino called in for both of them and returned to the table.

"I don't want to canvass the neighborhood where they found him," she began.

"OK," he said warily.

"And I don't want to reinterview the first cops on the scene and the detectives and the crime scene guys."

"Where is this going?"

"None of that stuff has worked for ten years. I suppose it could work this time, but I'd like to try something different."

"I'm listening."

"If nobody does anything, the gun'll turn up someday or someone'll try to buy himself a short sentence by ratting out the killer—if anybody out there knows who it was. Or one of the two hundred twenty-seven missing guns will turn up. I want to get inside what Micah Anthony was doing."

"You got some brilliant idea how?"

"Just a sketchy beginning. I want to get hold of the transcript of the trial of the three guys Anthony was doing business with."

"It could take six months to get through that transcript. It's probably ten thousand pages long."

"MacHovec can do it. He'll know what we're looking for and he'll find it. Maybe one of those guys is back in prison and we can talk to him, make him an offer."

"Graves won't like it." Defino signaled for a refill. "He goes by the book."

"He'll give us some rope. He knows we get results. If we come up with one new thing, he'll settle down."

Defino contemplated his coffee. "Let me say I agree with you. If this case wasn't a dead end, someone would have broken it years ago. The best hope now, except for what you're talking about, is a lucky break. That could happen today or not for ten more years. How do you want to proceed?"

"Tell McElroy what we want to do. If he goes along, we avoid Graves, at least for a while."

"McElroy won't OK anything without the whip."

Jane knew he was right. Lieutenant McElroy, the second whip, was a good guy, but when important decisions had to be made, he passed them along. He had not benefited personally from the general promotions around the office; the only way to get to captain was to take the exam. After captain, promotions came from One PP or City Hall.

"Let's write up a little proposal," Jane said, "and run it by him. Nothing long. And then let's get the transcript or have MacHovec go over to the court and sit and take notes on it. And before he gets started, he can check out those three guys, see where they are, what kind of trouble they've been in."

"OK, I'm with you. We should get back and start writing."

THEY HUDDLED WITH MacHovec, writing brief nonsentences that would become a proposal. MacHovec bailed after half an hour, his patience worn thin. He was itching to get back to what he was good at. The computer they figuratively shared was on his desk, and no one besides him had touched it since last fall. He wanted to find out where the three guys in the West Fifty-second Street crib were.

Jane and Defino kept at it. They wanted the names of witnesses at the trial as well as defendants, lawyers, the assistant district attorneys who had prepared the case and prosecuted it, and the names of cellmates of the one man who had served time, Carl Randolph.

"One's dead," MacHovec said, staring at his screen.

"You sure?" Jane asked.

"As sure as a death certificate is. Curtis Morgan. Died three years ago." He laughed. "Lung cancer. Works better than bullets. He was arrested for a B and E and they took him to a hospital. Died before he said anything."

"Try Carl Randolph. He's the one who served time for

possession of stolen weapons." She went back to the proposal. "Somebody working at the armory had to be in on the theft of the guns," she said to Defino.

"I bet they kept that quiet as long as they could. The Feds never want city cops nosing around."

"But Bowman knew the number, so it became a matter of record."

"It became a matter of record when they raided the crib and found the three weapons. When the guns took a walk, those jokers conducted an internal investigation and came up with nothing, so they kept quiet. Trust me." He was right on that. "And if they ever locate the guns, they'll make a big public splash as if they'd been working on the case every day for ten years."

"They won't locate them. They're waiting for a miracle. Let's see if we can make it happen."

"Randolph," MacHovec said, "Carl J. You know what, girls and boys? He just got himself arrested a couple of weeks ago."

"What for?" Defino asked.

MacHovec pressed keys. "Possession of pot. They still smoke that stuff? I thought it went out of style."

Jane smiled. "Where is he?"

"He couldn't make bail." MacHovec whistled. "I guess they've got his number. Judge set half a million. He's in Rikers. Looks like he's in the Bing. Strong stuff for possession."

"My favorite place on earth," Jane said under her breath. "We can do that, huh, Gordon?"

"I'll drive in tomorrow, pick you up."

"I'll be downstairs at eight. I like this."

Defino picked up his phone and called his wife. From the sound of the conversation, she could do without the car.

Jane went back to the list of half sentences, pulled over another piece of paper, and started to shape them into readable English. Then she thought of something. "Sean? There was a third guy. What happened to him?"

"You're not gonna believe this." He was looking at his screen, shaking his head and grinning.

"What?"

"Sal 'Lucky Dog' Manelli, forty-seven, nice little rap sheet. Looks like he's settled down in a love nest on Minetta Street. I make it about two blocks from Waverly Place."

Defino was out of his chair as fast as if he'd gotten word of a 10-13, the code for an officer in trouble. "Let's go," he said. "Anything's better than paperwork."

Jane stopped at Annie's office and told her where they were going. They they dashed down the stairs. A couple of subways got them to West Fourth Street, Jane's usual station. From there they walked to Minetta Street, a short, narrow, tree-lined street of residential buildings that angled northeast from Sixth Avenue and Bleecker. Hidden from the traffic and chaos of those streets, it was a secret oasis. They found the brownstone Manelli used as his address halfway down the block. Upstairs they rang several times and listened at the door; no sound was audible.

"Go down a flight," Jane said softly to Defino. "I want to ring a bell."

Defino went down and she rang the bell across the hall from Manelli.

An eye peered through the peephole; then the door opened. An old man on a single crutch stared at her.

"Hi," she said cordially, not showing her shield. "I'm looking for Mr. Manelli. Sal?"

"Over there? I haven't seen him for weeks."

"He move out?"

"Couldn't tell you. She's there, though. She's been there since World War Two, or her mother has. Maybe her grandmother. They all look the same."

"You know her name?" The name at the bell downstairs had been JF/SM.

"Franklin. Judith, I think. I run into her sometimes. Dark-haired woman, kind of nice-looking. What she wants with a leech like him, I've never been able to figure out."

"Isn't Sal working?"

"Who knows? He moves in, he moves out. He shouts at her, she cries. What kind of a life is that? She should find herself a nice man and get married. It's not so bad. I did it for forty-three years."

"Well, thanks for your time." She nodded and went to the stairs, hearing the door close and lock before she was down one step.

"I heard it," Defino said when she joined him on the lower floor. "We better see if he has a parole officer, find out where he spends his time when he's not here."

"I'll come back tonight and talk to Judith. MacHovec can get me a phone number."

"I'd like to know how long this mutt's been living here. It's far enough away from where Anthony was found that they wouldn't have canvassed this block."

They went back to Centre Street, and Defino typed up the proposal, a twenty-minute job. They made copies and went over to McElroy's office.

The second whip was on the phone, but waved them in. He said, "Yeah," a lot of times, then hung up. "I see you're on the Micah Anthony case."

Jane led off. "Lieutenant, we've got some ideas. Got time to listen?"

"Sure."

She gave him a copy of their miniproposal and started her spiel.

Built like a rectangular chunk of stone, McElroy listened, barely nodding. Then he glanced down at the sheet of paper. He didn't look happy, but didn't look ready to explode either. "Randolph's in Rikers?" he said finally.

"Yeah," Defino said. "Just got collared a week or two ago. They're holding him in the Bing, so they know who he is."

"Sure, go see him. I'll run this by Inspector Graves. I don't know what he'll say but it's worth a try."

"There's something else," Jane said. She told him about Manelli and Minetta Street.

"Minetta. Wasn't Anthony found on Waverly?" It was the kind of information anyone who'd been on the job for ten years would know automatically.

"Yeah," they both said.

"Ten years of investigators couldn't have slipped up on something like that."

"He may not have been there ten years ago, or even five," Jane said. "The man across the hall said the woman had been there forever, not Manelli. MacHovec's getting her number. I'll call and go over tonight."

"OK, do that. We better talk about this in the morning."

"We're going to Rikers in the morning, Loot," Defino said.

"OK, go see Randolph. We'll talk when you get back."

Jane called the number for Judith Franklin six times that night and got nothing, not even an answering machine. From the tone of her conversation with the neighbor, she was pretty sure he hadn't waylaid Franklin when she came home and told her a woman had been looking for Sal. Jane hadn't shown her shield, so he had no way of knowing who she was.

4

RIKERS WAS AN island. Special buses ran to and from the jail, some carrying visitors and some prisoners who had just been freed, dropping them in Queens, where they could buy a doughnut and pick up a city bus. Visitors were cautioned when they arrived at Rikers to leave narcotics and weapons on their seats before exiting. A large number of them did so. Defino arrived at just about eight and they drove to the parking lot at the bridge to Rikers. No unauthorized vehicles were allowed on the island, and no one was allowed to walk from building to building. Anyone seen walking was presumed to be an escaped inmate. They hopped on a bus for the short trip across the bridge.

Rikers Island consisted of ten separate prisons, most of them for men. They ranged from the military-style boot camp for young men of high school age to buildings housing men who had committed crimes less serious than homicide and other felonies using weapons. The toughest prison was nicknamed the Bing, presumably for the sound the gate made when it closed behind you, although no such sound could be heard. The officers who worked in these separate prisons were unarmed. The joke was that the only weapons at Rikers were in the possession of the prisoners. Jane and Defino checked their guns before they passed through the gate and had their hands stamped to show they had entered legally. MacHovec had set up the meeting with Carl Randolph the day before, and they followed Officer Ben Clark down a long hall.

About a minute into their walk an alarm sounded, and they flattened against the wall. Seconds later, a group of helmeted officers in protective black clothing, armed with clubs and shields, dashed down the hall to the scene of the trouble.

"Second one this morning," Clark said. "Something's on for tonight; we don't know what. They want to tire us out before they spring the big one."

The alarm over, they resumed their walk, and the special team returned at a slower pace from whence they had come. There were worse jobs than directing traffic at Forty-second Street.

The long walk continued. Jane recognized the ever-present competing smells of disinfectant and sweat, and the low-level din that emanated from areas off the main corridor. Finally, Officer Clark opened a door and led them inside a room with a table bolted to the floor and four chairs. Clark took one of them. A black inmate about forty years old sat on the far side of the table and watched them enter, a scowl on his face.

"Mr. Randolph," Defino said, "I'm Detective Defino; this is Detective Bauer. We'd like to talk to you."

" 'Bout what?"

"What did you do to get yourself in the Bing again?"

"Nothin'. Just had a little pot to sell so I'd have some money for food. Wha' kinda crazy judge puts you in the Bing for that?"

"Maybe you've got a reputation."

"Yeah. I'm a husband and father. That the reputation you mean?"

"I was thinking of the other one."

Randolph looked at them blankly.

"Something to do with guns, Mr. Randolph," Jane said.

"That's a long time ago."

"We're still looking for them."

"Yeah." The stern face broke into a smile. "You keep lookin'."

"I hear your friend Curtis Morgan died," Defino said.

"Yeah. Curtis smoked too much. Getcha every time."

"So there's just you and Sal Manelli left. Sal smoke?"

"I don't remember." He frowned.

"You got an address for Sal?"

"Where he live? I ain't seen Sal for years. He used to have a girlfriend in the Village, street with an Eye-talian name. But he could have a new one now. Sal always have a girlfriend."

"That's convenient."

"Yeah." Randolph pushed his chair away from the table a few inches, and Officer Clark took notice. Even sitting down, Randolph looked big. "You come all this way to ask me 'bout Sal's girlfriend?"

"We're looking for him," Jane said. "And we're looking for the guns. We think you know where they are."

"I tell you, miss, I didn't know ten years ago and I don't know now."

"Somebody knew."

"Wasn't me."

"Who was it?" Defino asked.

Randolph shrugged. "Maybe Sal, maybe Curtis. Oh, Curtis don't know nothin' no more, do he? He dead. Well, they call Sal 'Lucky Dog.' Maybe Lucky Dog can tell you. I'm just a guy does what he's told."

"Really?" Jane said. "They put you away for doing what you were told?"

"Sometime justice don't work."

"Sometimes people know more than they let on."

"Not me, Detective." He smiled.

"We need to find those guns," Defino said. "I would guess you'd like to make this marijuana charge go away."

"Yeah, I would. Like to get back to my family. I'm a real family man. I don't need Attica no more."

Defino stood. "We'll get back to you, Mr. Randolph. Think about what we said."

"You wanna gimme your names?" For the first time, he seemed worried.

Defino threw his card on the table and turned to leave. Jane and Officer Clark followed him.

"I know this prisoner," Clark said as they walked. "He's got two personalities. The one he showed you is the dumb guy who doesn't know where he's at. That's a put-on. If he has a mind to, he can talk to you like a guy fresh out of Harvard. When that happens, you know you're getting somewhere."

"I want a record of every phone call he makes for the next week," Jane said.

Clark took out a notebook and wrote something. When they got to the gate, Clark had it opened for them. As it closed behind them, Jane listened for the *bing*.

Before meeting with Inspector Graves, they huddled. MacHovec had reached Manelli's parole officer that morning. His address for Manelli was Minetta Street, and he was unhappy to hear that Manelli hadn't been seen there for a while. Manelli had checked in on schedule and had claimed to have a part-time job selling shoes. He was due to check in again a week from Thursday.

"So maybe he'll check in," Defino said, "and we can pick him up. But that's more than a week away."

"Randolph's got your number," Jane said. "After he calls Sal or his lawyer or someone else, maybe he'll get back to you. Meanwhile, I'll try this Judith Franklin again. Unless she's off with Manelli, she should come home eventually. She's the paycheck in that relationship."

"Inspector Graves will see you now," Annie said, standing in their doorway.

"I see you spent some time at Riker's this morning," the whip said when they had sat down in his office. Ellis McElroy was there too, but Annie was absent, so no notes would be taken.

"Carl Randolph is in the Bing," MacHovec said. "Waiting to be tried for possession of pot. The car he was in was stopped for a traffic violation and they found the stuff."

"Seems like small potatoes for him. He say anything useful?"

They went over it, adding what Officer Clark had said about Randolph's two personalities. "Seems like he uses the dumb one to start off with. If he gets serious about helping us, he may start to sound like the smart guy he probably is," Jane said.

"They thought he was the top guy ten years ago," Graves said. "He's the only one that served time. One of those three guys is dead. We wait much longer, they'll all be gone, one way or another. What is your plan?"

"It's not a plan yet, Inspector. We thought we'd start by rattling cages. I asked the Rikers officer to give us a list of all the calls Randolph makes in the next week. He should try his lawyer pretty quick, and maybe someone else."

"With his record, he could be looking at a lot of time, even for small stuff," Defino said. "That could be a factor."

"Let's hope he makes some calls." Graves pulled over the Defino-Bauer proposal. "That's a surprise that Manelli lives so near where they found Micah Anthony. Follow up on that. I'm going to give you folks some latitude on this one. Rattle your cages, put out your feelers. If anything comes up, check with me before you go out on a limb. That's an order. If Randolph shot Anthony and got away with a short sentence, he's pretty damn smart. I don't want to scrape the two of you up off a sidewalk."

"Thanks, Inspector," Jane said.

Defino said, "Ditto," and the three of them got up. McElroy, who hadn't wanted to give permission, hadn't said a word.

5

AFTER LUNCH JANE and Defino went back to the Village. The shoe store Manelli worked in was on West Eighth, once a vibrant street with jewelers, bookstores, and class. Only one customer sat in a chair trying on shoes: a lean, dark-haired man surrounded by a dozen open boxes.

"Can I help you?" The graying proprietor got off his low stool.

Defino flashed his shield so the customer could not see it.

"I'll be right with you." He had a conversation with the customer, who either wasn't able to make up his mind or had come in for fifteen minutes of human contact. He stuck his feet into the shoes he already owned and left the store.

"You from the probation department?" the owner asked. "Looking for Sal?"

"We're looking for Sal. We're not probation."

"I haven't seen him for a couple of weeks. One Tuesday morning he just didn't come in. I did my best, Officers. I have a brother who spent time in prison, and I try to help out if I can, but this one didn't work out."

"You have an address for him?"

He went in the back and returned with the Minetta Street address on a slip of paper. "I hand him his checks, so I haven't used the address for mail. I can't tell you if he still lives there—or if he ever did, for that matter. But that's the address he gave me."

"He cash his checks?" Jane asked.

"Yes. They all came back from the bank. You want to see them?"

"I'd like to see where they were cashed."

Another trip to the back, this one a little longer. He had two checks with him when he returned. Manelli had signed both of them with a squiggle beginning with *M* and had cashed them at a bank on Sixth Avenue. Jane wrote down the name and thanked the owner.

Defino handed him his card. "You ever hear from him, please give me a call."

"Sure thing."

"May as well try the bank," Jane said when they were outside. "It's only a couple of blocks."

The bank manager balked at giving out information but finally read to them from his screen. Manelli had only a checking account. None of his paychecks going back two months had been deposited. At the moment the account had a balance of fifty-seven dollars.

"When was the last activity?" Jane asked.

"He wrote a check to a pharmacy that cleared six days ago. My screen doesn't tell me the date the check was written. Probably a day or two before that. It's local." He wrote down the name and address.

"If he never deposited his check," Defino said, "where'd the money in the account come from?"

The bank manager frowned, scrolled his screen, and looked at it intently. "Here's a cash deposit for a hundred dollars." He scrolled again. "Here's another for a hundred fifty. It's possible he cashed his check and then deposited part of it. Of course, in order to cash it he would have to have at least that amount in his account."

"Does Judith Franklin have an account here?" Jane asked.

"You know I'm not allowed—"

"OK, we'll do it officially. Thanks."

"Just a moment." He worked the screen. "You have an address for her?"

She gave the Minetta Street building.

"Yes. She has an account."

"Thank you," Jane said. They left.

Back at Centre Street, MacHovec had come up with a current address and phone number for Carl Randolph. It was in the section of Brooklyn called Bedford Stuyvesant—Bed-Stuy to most New Yorkers. Jane dialed the number but no one answered.

As she hung up, her phone rang. It was Officer Ben Clark at Rikers. "Randolph hasn't been near a phone all day. He's been sitting in his cell reading a book, playing the part of a pussycat."

She muttered a four-letter word under her breath and asked him to stay on it. "We said the right things, Gordon," she said to Defino after the call. "I can't believe he didn't call his lawyer. Something's screwy."

"Give it another day."

She got up and went to Annie's office. "Sorry to bother you," she began.

"No problem, Detective. What can I do for you?"

"My partner and I have been in and out all day." She knew Annie would know she meant Defino. "Did anyone leave a message for either of us today?"

Annie's face showed instant consternation. "I would have . . ." She shuffled through some papers. "I don't remember any."

"OK. Guess we jumped the gun. Thanks, Annie." Back in the office she said, "No messages for us from Annie. That means Randolph didn't call you and didn't call anyone else. And he's playing the part of a very good boy, according to Ben Clark."

"So he had someone else make the call."

"That's what I think. But we'll never find out who. Randolph probably slipped someone a phone number with a message and a pack of cigarettes."

"You'll find out who," MacHovec said. "Watch your back. If Randolph made a call, something's gonna happen."

"You're right," Jane said. "I hope this Franklin woman isn't in trouble."

"Time to go home, boys and girls. Anything I can get you on the computer before I leave?"

"Maybe tomorrow. I hate to think that I have to stake out that apartment. I need my sleep." It was worrisome. She had visited someone for information in the winter and a killer had been on her heels. It was hard to forget something like that. "I'll keep calling."

MacHovec waved as he left. Jane tried the Franklin number again, with no success. Maybe Franklin had taken off with Manelli when he quit his job. Another day and Jane would ask the super to open the apartment. Meanwhile, it was time to go home.

When the phone rang at nine in the morning, Jane suspected trouble. The squad worked eight forty-five to four forty-five in a 9×5 tour, unusual for NYPD, but this was an unusual squad. The voice on the other end was Officer Ben Clark.

"An inmate was murdered overnight," he said.

"Randolph?"

"No."

"Is that the trouble you were expecting?"

"I don't think so. Some other stuff was brewing, and this may have been timed to coincide with that. The victim was stabbed with a shank made from a plastic toothbrush that wouldn't show up in the metal detectors they walk through. It was as pointy as an ice pick and sharp as a steel knife."

"Did you find it?"

"The killer dropped it. He knew there'd be a close inspection and a cell shakeout after the body was found. I'm telling you this because it happened, not because I think Randolph was behind it, but he could have been. He and the victim had cells near each other. They may have mixed in the food line."

"Thanks for the call. If you learn anything else—"

"You'll hear about it."

"What trouble?" Defino asked when she hung up.

She told him, MacHovec turning away from his screen to listen. "A little early, but we may have stirred things up," she said at the end. "This guy could've made a call or calls for Randolph, and Randolph got rid of him before he could use it for his own good."

"Didn't take long to rattle the cage," Defino said. "Here come the bulletproof vests just as it's getting warm out."

"He couldn't have called Randolph's lawyer. A call to a lawyer isn't suspicious. Everyone makes that call. He called someone else."

"Those guys are on the phone all the time," MacHovec said. "They call their lawyers, their families, their girl-friends. Even if we got a record of all the calls the inmates made from ten o'clock on yesterday, it would be hell to figure out which call connected with Randolph."

"Morning." It was McElroy, passing their doorway.

They called him in and briefed him.

"That didn't take long. You know if Randolph had any visitors yesterday besides you?"

MacHovec picked up his phone.

"It's possible this isn't what it looks like." McElroy waited while a short conversation ensued.

MacHovec hung up. "Randolph had two visitors, Detectives Defino and Bauer. I can give you the times they arrived and left. That was it."

"So he didn't pass any messages out that way. You know the identity of the victim?"

"Clark didn't say," Jane said.

"I'll let the inspector know."

"What happened with the Franklin woman?" Defino asked when McElroy had left.

"I called till midnight. No answer. Her whereabouts have nothing to do with this investigation. We just got on this case on Monday and we looked for her on Tuesday. Let's see if her landlord knows where she works." She wrote down the building address and handed it to MacHovec, who started working the phone.

It took him half an hour to get the name of the building

owner and then another fifteen before he could speak to him. Two minutes more and he hung up. "She works at Macy's; how do you like that?"

"I love it," Defino said, ripping a Five out of his typewriter. Defino was master of the typewriter as MacHovec was master of the computer. "Let's visit Macy's. They tell you what department she works in?"

"Handbags. Maybe they're having a sale."

"I can't afford sales." He looked at Jane. "You ready?"

MACY'S WAS AT Herald Square: Thirty-fourth Street, which ran east–west, and both Broadway and Sixth Avenue, which were north–south streets. Broadway meandered from southeast Manhattan toward the northwest, crossing major avenues, continuing into New York State when it left the city. The triangle formed by the intersection of the two north–south avenues at Thirty-fourth formed the "square." Crossing the street at the point where they met was not for the faint of heart, although thousands of people did it daily. Macy's covered the square block from Sixth to Seventh and from Thirty-fourth to Thirty-fifth.

Inside, they located the business office. Displaying their shields put them up front in the line, sparing them a wait.

A thin, tight-lipped woman with hair dyed as black as coal

checked their IDs and then went to her computer. "Judith Franklin has been working here for seventeen years. She's on her annual vacation now. She'll be back on Monday."

"How far in advance did she book her vacation?" Defino asked.

The woman looked as though the question had come from another planet. "I have no idea. I'm sure it was well in advance. We can't have several people in one department going away at the same time."

"How's her work record?" Jane asked. "She have many absences, latenesses?"

"Her work record is excellent," the stony-faced woman replied. "She's rarely out and almost never late."

They went downstairs and found an unoccupied saleswoman at the handbag counter.

"Judy's on vacation," she said in answer to their first question. "Is something wrong?"

"Nothing," Jane said. "We just wanted to talk to her."

"Is her boyfriend in trouble again?"

"What do you know about him?"

"Just that he can't seem to hold a job. Judy doesn't talk about him unless things are terrible, and then I'm one of the people who gets an earful. She's a really nice person. I don't know what she sees in that guy. But it's been going on for years, on and off. Sometimes . . ."

"Yes?"

"I've seen her come in with a bruise here and there. She's never said he did it to her, but she never has a good explanation for what happened. If my husband hit me, there'd be no second time, I can tell you."

"Have you ever seen the boyfriend?" Defino asked.

"Never. Judy leaves here when she's done and goes home by herself. He doesn't stop by. But neither does my husband."

"We're told she's coming home this weekend."

"I would think so. She's scheduled to work Monday morning."

"Do you know if they went away together?"

"She said they were. They may be renting a cabin or

something in the Catskills. Like a little togetherness could
help the relationship. If I were her, I'd try a little apartness
for a change."

With that homey philosophy echoing, they left Macy's.

At 137 Centre Street a message from Officer Ben Clark
lay on Jane's desk.

"We don't have a clue who did the killing," he told her
when she returned the call. "But if proximity means anything, the victim, Tommy Swift, occupied a cell two down
from Randolph and was scheduled for a shower right after
Randolph, so that could have been a point of contact. They
ate meals at the same time, but I don't think they sat at the
same table."

"I assume you've questioned the other inmates on the
block."

"And got nothing. That's what we usually get. And the
shank was so clean it was shining like a diamond."

"I appreciate the call, Ben." She hung up. "Nothing new
on the Rikers killing, but he thinks Randolph could be a
suspect. I'm expecting another shoe to fall."

"Me too," Defino said, his phone ringing.

The subsequent conversation made no sense to Jane, but
Defino took notes as he spoke, saying little. Finally, he hung
up. "I think we've got our second shoe," he said, turning to
his partners. "That was Captain Bowman. He just got a call
from one of the original detectives on the Anthony case.
This is really nuts. A dog walker in Riverside Park early this
morning found a shiny new gun lying on the grass where it
couldn't be missed. He had a cell phone on him and called
nine-one-one. The guy in ballistics who got the gun recognized it as the kind of Beretta he used when he was in the
army, and instead of putting it aside for a couple of weeks,
he researched it right away. It's been identified as one of the
two hundred twenty-seven."

"Shit," MacHovec said.

"They're taunting us," Jane said. "Randolph got the word
out that we're on the case. That cocky son of a bitch. Whoever's hiding those guns took a walk in the park last night and
dropped it, just to let us know. It didn't take much, did it?"

Defino tapped a pencil on his desk. "One visit to Randolph. This better go straight to the whip. MacHovec, what can you find out about this guy Randolph killed?"

"Tommy Swift," Jane said, "last known address Rikers Island." She and Defino left the office to find Inspector Graves.

"Riverside Park?" Graves's usual reserve had evaporated. He was stunned.

Defino went over it. "I wonder what would have happened if the dog walker hadn't made the call, or if he'd taken the gun home with him."

"He wouldn't have gotten that far," Jane said. "Randolph's contact was probably hiding in the trees, maybe walking a dog of his own."

"You have Captain Bowman's number?" Graves asked.

Jane wrote it down for him.

"Looks like that visit to Rikers was more than productive. Give me what else you have."

They told him about Judith Franklin and their trip to Macy's.

"If you look for her over the weekend, don't forget to put in for overtime." Graves looked at his watch. "I hope they can keep that gun out of the news."

"If the guy was watching, he saw the police come. He knows that gun'll be traced. That was damned fast. So it looks like Manelli had no part in this."

"Looks that way," Jane said. "He's up in the mountains beating up his girlfriend. It's called a vacation. And they've been away—or at least she has—since Tuesday at the latest."

"Watch yourselves," Graves said.

The warning sounded familiar and carried no comfort with it.

Tommy Swift, who had half a page of aliases and a much longer rap sheet, had been arrested one day after Randolph and was awaiting trial on robbery and several related charges. He had earned the title of career criminal, having done little else in his thirty-two years. His record went back to adolescence, and part of that was sealed, as though it might provide further damning insight into his character. On the surface, nothing linked him to Randolph before their current stay at Rikers Island. Swift was white, born in the Bronx, and lived at too many addresses to count, but never anywhere near Bedford-Stuyvesant, where Randolph lived.

At Jane's request, MacHovec called the Two-Six Precinct and asked for the exact location where the gun was found.

"About a hundred feet uphill, that's east, of the Henry Hudson Parkway between a Hundred Sixteenth and a Hundred Fifteenth. Plenty of early-morning joggers and dog walkers. It was spotted about seven, before the park got crowded."

Riverside Park was a sloped strip of green that ran from Riverside Drive down to the highway starting at Seventy-second Street and going north to Grant's Tomb in the One-twenties. During the day people walked there with slight caution. In summer sunbathers indulged themselves on blankets on the grass, visible to passing cars. At night the park was little used, for obvious reasons.

"Maybe I'll take a walk there tonight," Jane said.

"You tempting fate?" Defino asked.

"No one'll be there. The guy probably lives miles away."

"Have fun."

"So what's next?"

"Keep a low profile while we wait for shoe number three. These guys are for real. I hope they put Randolph away for a good long stretch."

"Doesn't matter. The guns and their keepers are out there."

7

HACK CALLED WHILE she was eating a dinner of warmed-up leftovers and fresh salad.

"How's the case?" he asked.

"Hot." She told him about the killing at Rikers overnight and the discovery of the missing gun that morning.

"I think I'll stay away from you."

"Don't even try it, Hackett."

"Well, it sounds like this is what you wanted. You got things going."

"I think I'll go up to Riverside Drive this evening and walk around the area where the gun was found."

"I'll meet you there. I haven't had a walk in the park with the girl of my dreams for a long time."

"More like the black widow."

"Suppose I meet you at a Hundred Sixteenth and Riverside. If I can't park, I'll think of something original."

"Remember what you told me about original thinkers on the job. What time?"

"Can you make it by seven?"

"Just barely."

She got off the Number One train on Broadway and One Hundred Sixteenth Street at seven sharp, mounting the stairs to the Columbia University side of the street. She was at the back of the train and exited at One Hundred Fifteenth, then crossed Broadway and walked one block sharply downhill to Riverside Drive. Hack, also in jeans, walked the short distance between them. They kissed and crossed the street to the park. It was a fine evening and still light, the river calm, high-rise apartments along the Palisades forming the New Jersey skyline. In a little while the sun would set just across the river.

"What did you want to see?"

"If someone could have been hiding in the brush nearby."

"Looks possible. You think he was waiting for a guy to call nine-one-one?"

"I'm sure of it. If the dog walker had picked up the gun and put it in his pocket, he wouldn't have gotten very far."

"Sounds about right."

They walked downhill to the highway and stood in the evening breeze, looking out over the quiet river. Several miles off to the right the George Washington Bridge glistened in the late sunlight, a tanker sliding under it.

"Did you see what you wanted to see?"

"Uh-huh. You have time to wait for the sunset?"

"Sure."

"Good. I like sunsets."

He drove her home afterward, although it was out of his way. "I can't come up," he said. "Parking is impossible. And I thought about what you said, that lovers don't always get together for sex. Sometimes it's for a sunset."

"I like that."

"So do I."

She awoke wondering what new disaster had happened overnight. She had tried Judith Franklin twice more but with no response. Franklin would probably return this weekend.

The morning news had nothing related to the case, and no desperate messages lay on her desk as she slipped into her chair. By this morning the partners had all finished or nearly finished the three sections of the Micah Anthony file. Even after a cup of coffee, no one had any ideas gleaned from the file that hadn't been worked over and found to yield nothing.

"Randolph was the leader," Defino said, almost as though he was talking to himself.

"So we should start with him," Jane said.

MacHovec had just turned on the computer and it was making musical sounds. "You want a life history." It was a statement. "A lot of it's in the file, but I'll dig up the last ten years and print it out. You're a glutton for punishment. You see he's a Brooklyn boy? Didn't grow up anywhere near Anthony."

In New York, living in different boroughs could be like living in different countries. People attended distant schools, played pickup ball with their immediate neighbors, shopped in local stores, went to their own clubs, and married spouses doing all of the above. They might as well have spoken different languages.

"That's why the gun deal worked."

"I'll get on it."

The idea of canvassing streets in Bedford-Stuyvesant was more than unappealing. Two white cops walking through a poor all-black neighborhood, where trouble sprouted intermittently, was almost an invitation to trouble. And no one would say anything useful to them. They would display hard faces and pretend not to recognize the name. Unless they had been personally harmed by Randolph and bore a grudge against him, the people in Bed-Stuy would simply not be forthcoming. The only hope was that some connection might be drawn on the basis of an address or a workplace, if he had ever held a real job.

"Let's pay a visit to Manelli's PO," Jane said.

MacHovec turned away from the computer and picked up the phone as his partners sat back and waited. Hanging up, he said, "He can see you this morning. He didn't sound happy when I mentioned Manelli's name, but who would be?"

Jane took her bag out of her drawer as Defino pushed away from the typewriter. The parole officer's name was Alan Williams, and his office was on Thirty-first Street between Sixth and Seventh. Williams was black and had the tired look of a man who had come to realize that even the best he could give would not only not change the world, it wouldn't change one small actor in it.

"Sit down, Detectives," he said after shaking hands. "I take it you've been to the shoe store Sal has been working in."

"Probably not working," Jane said. "We talked to the owner."

Williams raised his eyebrows. "He quit?" He pulled over a file and opened the folder, shaking his head. "I went over there a few weeks ago"—he looked at something in the folder—"maybe a month ago. He was still working there. And last time I saw him here he said he was still selling shoes."

"He hasn't been there for a month. Right now he's supposed to be on vacation in the Catskills with his girlfriend."

"Franklin?"

"Yeah," Defino said.

"Some women just don't get it. He brought her in once to show me what a nice woman he's hooked up with. Even that day you could see a little green and purple on her face where a bruise hadn't finished healing. She must be a glutton for punishment. Here's this guy never did a nice thing for anybody in his life and this good-looking woman with a good job lets him live with her. Probably gives him money when he needs it, too."

"You know how long they've been together?" Jane asked.

"More than five years that I know of. I would guess longer."

"We're looking into the murder of Micah Anthony," Defino said.

"The big moment in Sal's life. And he got away with it. He's done time for lesser crimes but nothing I know about recently. We don't talk about the Anthony killing."

"His apartment is a couple of blocks from where they found Anthony's body," Jane said.

Williams's eyebrows went up. He rummaged through the file. "He listed his mother's apartment as his address till a couple of years ago. He must have changed it when she died.

He could even have been living there on and off. I don't think the Franklin woman can take him as a steady diet, not that his mother could."

"She's not in the Anthony file at all. The only addresses for him are the place on West Fifty-second where the three of them were picked up and another address in Brooklyn."

"That's his mother."

"So he could have kept Franklin a secret for ten years," Defino said. "Maybe they were driving Anthony to her apartment and he broke out of the car on Waverly Place, and they shot him so they wouldn't lose him."

Jane nodded. "Or they'd already talked to him in her apartment and they were on their way somewhere else. Either way, the location makes sense if Manelli was involved with Franklin at the time."

"I'd bet on it," Williams said. "There could have been other girlfriends, but she's been in his life awhile. She's the one who always takes him back. Like I said, she's a glutton for punishment."

They talked another few minutes and then left.

"He learned more from us than we got from him," Defino said when they hit the street. "I bet Sal's gonna miss his next appointment while he thinks up a good story about why he's not working."

"Maybe he'll duck out on her and find another girlfriend to sponge off. Williams is right: They never learn. Think that old guy across the hall from Franklin would remember a night ten years ago when there could've been a lot of noise?"

"Frankly, no. He said he always heard screaming from the apartment. What would've been different that night?"

"Men's voices."

"Let's give it a try."

The man remembered Jane, and this time they showed their ID. "You're the one asked me about the woman across the hall, aren't you?"

"That's right. Now we want to ask you about a night ten years ago when you might have heard a man shouting or a bunch of men shouting."

He shrugged. "When her father was alive—that was a long time ago—he was always yelling at her. 'Why don't you find yourself a nice guy and settle down? Why don't you get a job that pays more? You think your mother and me are gonna leave you a million bucks?' But I don't think he hit her."

"We don't mean the father," Defino said.

"How long was that? Ten years? You think I remember a noisy night ten years ago?"

"This was men's voices," Jane said.

"What men? What are you talking about?"

"A crime may have been committed."

"And you come back ten years later to ask about it? Where were you ten years ago?" He looked as annoyed as he sounded.

"Don't lecture us," Jane said, reflecting his annoyance with her own. "We're reinvestigating the murder of a New York City police officer and we need your cooperation."

"I'm cooperating the best I can. If I heard anything, I don't remember. OK?"

Jane handed him her card. "What's your name, sir?"

"Sklar, Phillip Sklar."

"If you think of anything, Mr. Sklar, if you remember that night when the officer was killed, please give me a call."

"I'll do that." He sounded as though he would burn the card the minute the door closed.

She said "Thank you" and turned away, glad to see the last of him.

"We've pushed that as far as we can," Defino said in the street. "We should be able to talk to Franklin on Monday."

"I'll keep calling over the weekend. Maybe I can find Sal at home, but we need to talk to them separately. She'll say what he wants her to say."

They had lunch and went back to Centre Street. Mac-Hovec had printed out two copies of a long history of Randolph's last ten years, half of which had been spent in prison. He had served most of his sentence but not all. He knew how to make nice when it counted.

They each read a copy, Defino holding a highlighter, Jane with a red pen. She looked for Manelli's name or even Curtis Morgan's, but neither appeared. The three men had severed their relationship after Anthony's death or had kept it so secret that no one uncovered it. Now Randolph was dealing pot and Manelli was living off a Macy's handbag saleswoman.

The rap sheet was a depressing story of how a man with brains enough to switch from educated English to neighborhood lingo could apply his talents in ways that alternately made him money and gave him power, but put him away for years on end. Even after reading dozens of similar life stories, she wanted to ask the obvious questions.

"The three of them split up," Defino said, looking up from his copy.

"I noticed. I wonder if Randolph talked to his cellmate in Attica."

"He's too smart."

"You want some names?" MacHovec asked.

"Can't hurt. Just in case Manelli and his girlfriend don't pan out."

MacHovec got on the phone. Jane hoped the cellmate was back on the streets of New York. She didn't need a trip to Attica after her visit to Rikers.

She picked up her phone and dialed Judith Franklin's number, which by now she knew by heart. On the second ring, a woman answered, "Hello?"

Jane hung up. "Franklin's back, Gordon. She just answered her phone."

Defino looked at his watch. "Want to go?"

"You could be late getting home."

"They know how to eat without me. Come on. Reading about Randolph is turning my stomach."

MacHovec hung up. "They'll check for me. If they come up with a name today, I'll leave it on your voice mail."

"Thanks, Sean. Have a good weekend." She stopped in at Annie's and said they wouldn't be back.

*　　*　　*

Jane knocked on Franklin's door. They had decided on the way over that if Manelli were home too, Defino would stay in the apartment with him and Jane would take Franklin out to a coffee shop to talk.

"Who's there?" a woman called from just inside the door.

"Jane Bauer," Jane called back, holding her shield where it was not visible.

A bolt turned and the door opened. "Yes?"

"Ms. Franklin?" Jane held her shield up.

"Oh, Christ."

"We'd like to talk to you and Mr. Manelli."

"What's he done now? He hasn't even been in New York all week."

Defino was already in the apartment, striding through it to find Manelli.

"Who is it?" a man called, and Defino picked up speed.

Franklin didn't answer. A loud obscenity emanated from somewhere in the apartment, then a flood, and Defino returned, one hand firmly on Manelli's arm, the other holding Defino's ID.

"Why don't you come with me, Ms. Franklin?" Jane said.

"Where are you taking me? I can't leave my husband."

"Husband?" Jane said.

"Well—"

"Let's go downstairs and talk."

Franklin looked back at Manelli, who shook an index finger at her meaningfully as she turned to leave.

8

DOWNSTAIRS, JANE STEERED her to a small restaurant that in a couple of hours would be serving dinner to Village regulars and tourists. "Just coffee," Jane said as they entered. The maître d' looked unhappy, but led them to a table near the kitchen.

"What do you want from me?" Franklin said. "I just got home. I haven't even unpacked yet. The refrigerator is empty and Sal's hungry. He's a guy that can't wait when he's hungry." She looked as though she was afraid he might eat her if she didn't come up with a satisfactory meal.

"Ms. Franklin—may I call you Judith?"

"Judy. Just try to make it fast so I don't come back to a fight."

"Judy, I want to ask you about the night Det. Micah Anthony was shot."

"That thing? It happened ten years ago. They tried to pin that on Sal and he was acquitted. You can't get him for that. He was just in the wrong apartment at the wrong time."

"I'm not trying to 'get him.' I'm trying to figure out what happened that night. The detective was shot a few blocks from here. Sal is the only one of the three men who had a connection to the Village."

"He didn't have a connection. He lived with his mother. He visited me sometimes but he didn't live with me."

"But you lived here and he had a relationship with you."

"A relationship," she repeated, as though she wished it were more of one. "Yes, we had a relationship."

"Did he come to you that night?"

"You expect me to remember ten years later?"

"That was a big night in your life, Judy. Your boyfriend, whom you now refer to as your husband, got himself involved in the killing of a cop."

"I told you, Sal didn't do it, they never proved he did, and they can't try him again for it. And I don't remember if he came over that night. I think he didn't. I think he called me the next day and told me he was in trouble."

"Was he driving a car in those days?" Jane asked. None of the three men had had cars registered to them.

"I don't think he's ever owned a car."

"I didn't ask you if he owned one. I asked you if he was driving one."

Franklin's nervousness was increasing with each question. She was a thin woman with dark hair, wearing a light blue blouse and black pants, her traveling clothes. Silver hoop earrings pierced her ears, and her fingernails looked freshly polished. She kept herself looking good for Sal.

"If he was driving a car, I don't know about it," she said. "I've never had a car. You have to be crazy to have one if you live in the Village. You know what parking's like down here?"

"I have a good idea. What about his mother? Did she own a car? His brothers or sisters? His friends?"

"His mother never learned to drive. Look, I can't answer questions that I don't know anything about. Can we finish this?"

"Soon."

Coffee had been served, and Franklin put sweetener and milk in hers and sipped it. "Good coffee," she said.

"I only take people to nice places," Jane said with a smile.

Franklin smiled back. "What else can I tell you besides about the car?"

"Did you ever meet Curtis Morgan or Carl Randolph?"

"You mean the men who . . . ?"

"Yes, the men who were arrested with Sal."

"I never laid eyes on them till the trial. Sal never mentioned their names. I only went to the courthouse one day. Sal said I should keep a low profile; he didn't want anyone to know I existed. So I went on my day off and sat in the back, and I left at lunchtime. It was boring. The lawyers kept arguing and nothing happened. That's the only time I saw those men. That Randolph, he was a big guy. Curtis coughed a lot. That's all I can tell you."

"What did Sal do when the trial was over?"

"He got a job. I can't remember what. He's had a lot of jobs. Most of them don't interest him, so he doesn't stick with them long. And it's not easy to find work when you've got a record." She looked pained, as though the world had slighted Manelli when he deserved a fair shake.

"He got out of jail recently," Jane said.

"That was so unfair. He was meeting someone in a bar, a guy who owed him money. The guy didn't have it and they started arguing. Sal got so mad, he threw a punch, and the bartender called the police and had Sal arrested for assault. It was a trumped-up charge, believe me."

"You've been on vacation the last week or so. Where did you go?"

"We got a little cabin in the Catskills. It's so nice up there, cool at night. You can do a lot of walking, even fishing if that's your thing."

"Were you together all the time?"

"You mean like did we stick together like glue? No. Sal likes to walk early in the morning and I'm not a morning person. I'd rather go after breakfast. I need my coffee first thing." She had finished her cup and Jane signaled for refills.

"He get any calls while he was there?"

"Phone calls? I don't know. He has a cell. I don't remember if he used it. The cabin didn't have a phone. If you wanted to make a call you had to hike a mile to a grocery store."

"Did he meet anyone while you were up there?"

"You mean like a friend? I didn't see anyone. Why are you asking? This was a vacation. We didn't do any entertaining. We just wanted a rest and some peace and quiet."

"Did you know that Sal quit his job at the shoe store?"

Franklin's face became fearful. "That's not true. He just

took unpaid vacation. He didn't work there long enough to get time off. He's going back to work on Monday."

Jane said nothing. Sal would keep up the hoax as long as he got away with it. It was the way he lived. She looked at her watch. They had been at the table for half an hour. If Defino had been as successful talking to Sal, together they wouldn't have one untainted piece of information.

"All right, let's get back. It's after four."

"I hope I've been helpful," Franklin said.

"I hope you've been truthful."

"Why should I lie to you?" She used the voice of an innocent.

Jane dropped some bills on the table and said, "Let's go."

$$\boxed{9}$$

JUDITH FRANKLIN RANG the doorbell to alert Sal, and put the key in the lock. Inside, she called, "We're back," in a lilting girlish voice. When no answer came she cooed, "Hello?"

Jane moved past her to the empty living room, where, she saw, a floor lamp had been knocked over. She unholstered the Glock, feeling a chill. Hurrying, she checked the kitchen—empty—and the bedrooms in the rear of the apartment, also empty. "Gordon?" she called. The apartment was silent.

"They must've gone out," Franklin said.

In the larger bedroom the window that opened onto a fire

escape was closed and locked, and dust had accumulated on the horizontal surface. A smaller bedroom was made up as a guest room, and no one was there. Jane opened the closet door but found nothing but clothes. She passed the bathroom on her way to the kitchen, feeling adrenaline moving through her and hoping it would outweigh the beginnings of panic. Except for the two women, the apartment was empty.

"Any note from them?" she asked Franklin.

"I don't see any. Maybe they went out for a beer."

Jane pulled her cell phone out and dialed Defino's number. He didn't answer. She called McElroy's number at 137 but he was apparently gone for the day. She tried Annie, then MacHovec, which was a joke. Finally she keyed the number for Graves.

Everyone was gone. She called McElroy's cell number. He was probably on his way home, somewhere between 137 and a train, or already on a train.

He answered quickly.

"Lieutenant, Jane Bauer. We may have a situation here." She gave him the details quickly.

"A lamp overturned?"

"Yes."

"Anything else?"

"Not that I've seen. I've only looked quickly. But that lamp is his message to me. He didn't leave voluntarily."

"Give the Six a call. He could be interrogating Manelli in the house. And keep me informed."

"Yes, sir." She dialed the Six and gave her name and shield number to the sergeant, and then on his request, her tax registry number, which he could use to confirm her identity. Finally, she asked if Defino was at the precinct with a suspect. As she waited for an answer, she watched Franklin, who had become pale and tense during the phone calls.

"Sorry, Detective," the sergeant's voice came back at her. "No outside commands in the interview rooms."

She left a message for Defino, in case he showed up, then turned to Franklin. "All right, Judy. My partner is missing and Sal is with him somewhere. You are now going to talk to me truthfully. You lie and my partner is hurt, you are an accessory to a violent crime."

"How could I know anything? I was with you."

"Were you or Sal expecting anyone this afternoon?"

She shook her head. "I wasn't, and he didn't say anything."

"During your vacation, did he meet anyone? Did you see him talking to anyone?"

"Um . . ."

"Judy, a police officer is missing and I have to find him before something terrible happens. If you know something, you tell me now."

"One day, maybe yesterday, maybe two days ago, I thought I saw someone through the trees talking to Sal."

"Was there a car?"

"I'm not sure."

"Did you recognize this person?"

"I couldn't even see them clearly. It was a man, I'm sure of that. That's all I can tell you. They were standing and talking. I thought maybe Sal met someone from one of the other cabins and they were just being neighborly."

"What did he look like?"

"A man, I don't know."

"Was he black or white?"

"White, thinner than Sal, not much hair."

"You ever see him before?"

"I don't *know*. He was just a man through the trees."

"Stay here. I'm going downstairs. Don't touch that lamp." She went down to the street and wrote down the plate numbers of the cars parked on both sides. Then she went into the dry cleaner across the street and asked if they'd noticed two or three men getting into a car or van in the last half hour.

"There was a blue van parked illegally across the street for a while," the woman said. "I noticed it because a car was honking at it to move. They should know better but they never do. Then I looked over and it was gone."

"Any lettering on the side?" Jane asked.

"Nothing. Just blue. Could've used a paint job."

"Thanks." She dashed back, went upstairs, and rang the bell to Philip Sklar's apartment.

"You," he said. "Didn't I just talk to you a little while ago?"

"Mr. Sklar, did you see anyone go in or out of the Franklin apartment this afternoon?"

"I didn't see but I heard. Remember you asked about men's voices ten years ago? I don't know about ten years ago but this afternoon, just a little while ago, I heard them, men's voices. How do you like that?"

"How many voices did you hear?"

"Two anyway. And people going downstairs. But I didn't look out so I can't tell you who it was."

"Thanks."

She banged on Franklin's door and, once inside, made a careful search of the apartment, checking her watch as she moved. Time was passing too quickly and she had accomplished little. Aside from the lamp, nothing else seemed awry. She asked Franklin several times if things were correctly placed and she said yes each time.

"You're sure nothing's missing? Sal's suitcase is here?"

"I'll look again." Franklin went to the master bedroom. "It's here," she called. "It's in the closet. Mine's on the bed where I left it."

A blue van parked illegally. That meant another person in addition to Sal. He knocks on the door, Defino stands back and lets Sal answer while Defino watches. The other man—or two men—come in, enough to overpower Defino, who might not have had his weapon out, as he wasn't expecting trouble.

How did they get him to go downstairs without making the kind of racket that would motivate Phillip Sklar to call 911?

"His raincoat's gone."

"What?"

"Sal's raincoat. He walked in the apartment with his suitcase and went into the bedroom to take off his raincoat. It was on the bed the last I saw it, and now it's gone. Maybe he put it on when he left with the other detective."

Or maybe they threw it over Defino while they took him down the stairs, and told him they'd kill him if he made a sound. Jane looked at her watch again. They could be in any of the five boroughs by now, in New Jersey through the tunnel, or on their way to Long Island. She pulled out her cell phone to call McElroy when the phone rang.

"Lieutenant McElroy. What's going on?"

"He hasn't been seen in the station house. The store across the street saw a blue van parked in front of this building about the time Gordon disappeared. No ID on it. A man's black raincoat is missing from this apartment."

"I see. Describe the building."

She told him it was a brownstone, two apartments on a floor, Franklin's on three. She described her search of the premises, and the lack of any message except the lamp lying across the sofa.

"OK. I think it's time to call in the Borough Detective Task Force. Let them get started canvassing. I'll get back to Centre Street as soon as I can. I'll leave a message for Inspector Graves. I don't like the look of this. We've got a murder in Rikers Island, a weapon missing from an armory for over ten years found in Riverside Park, and now a detective missing along with one of the original suspects in the Anthony case."

"Right on all three."

"Get yourself back to Centre Street as soon as the borough detectives arrive. Don't hesitate to call."

"Yes, sir." She hung up and called the task force, going through the identification process once again and explaining the situation. She spoke to a lieutenant who promised two detectives ASAP and as many as might be needed later. Off the phone, she called back the Six and asked to be connected to the sector car that covered Minetta Street.

The car was only a block away, and they drove over rather than talk on a staticky line. Officers Piedmont and Glover pounded up the stairs, something exciting finally happening on their watch.

"A blue van?" Piedmont said. He looked at Glover for confirmation. "Yeah, we saw it."

"Yeah," Glover agreed. "It was pulling out when we came up Minetta."

"You remember anything about it?" Jane asked.

"A Ford maybe. Double doors in the back."

"Can you give me a time?" Jane asked.

"Right near the beginning of our tour. Could've been four thirty."

"Shit, we just missed them. You didn't see anyone get into it?"

"They were moving when I saw it," Piedmont said.

"OK. Thanks, guys."

"Anything we can do?" Glover asked.

Jane shook her head. All she could do now was wait for the borough detectives to show up, then go back to Centre Street and put in a hellish weekend.

When the sector cops had gone, she made the call she had left for last. They needed MacHovec on this. MacHovec was the best researcher she had ever known, even if he rarely got off his ass or put in a second of overtime.

He answered on a cell phone she knew he carried but that never rang in the office, not that hers or Defino's did during the workday.

"Sean, it's Jane. We've got a problem."

She had anticipated trouble from him, excuses for not working at night or over the weekend. The brief pause between her explanation and his answer was the only hesitation.

"I'm almost home. I'll take a shower and come back. It sounds like a long night."

"A long weekend."

"Yeah. See you later."

After the detectives came, she did the same thing.

[10]

McElroy was already back at 137 when she arrived. One team of detectives had been requisitioned and another might be called. Inspector Graves had been informed and would show up if needed.

The two detectives arrived first and sat with Jane and McElroy to be briefed. They would try to track down every known business and personal associate of Sal Manelli, talk to as many as they could reach, and attempt to find the missing suspect. The detectives set up an office in the conference room and carried in computers not in use and telephones. By the time they got started, MacHovec arrived.

"Anything?" he said.

"Nothing." She told him what was going on in the conference room.

"Why don't we try Randolph? They've got Manelli covered."

"OK."

MacHovec flicked on the computer and began to work. "Tell me what happened," he said. "I probably have enough of a brain left to key and hear at the same time."

She ran through the visit to Franklin's apartment, the interview in the coffee shop, the return to the empty apartment.

"Just one lamp?"

"Just one. I think Gordon kicked it over to send me a message."

"Could be."

"The rest of the apartment was untouched. The man across the hall heard at least two men's voices and footsteps going downstairs."

"Gotta be more than two. Defino didn't let that creep get his gun all by himself."

"Right." She told him about the van. He nodded and hit the print key and paper started flowing out of the printer.

"There's enough here for both of us for a while." He handed her one sheet, put the other down on his desk, and picked up the phone.

Names, addresses, and phone numbers filled her page. She began with a man named James Randolph Jr., a brother. A woman answered. She had never met James's brother Carl and didn't know where he lived. It was news to her that he was in jail. What had he done? Her voice turned up like a child's. No, she said, James wasn't home just now but maybe later. Try back about eight.

Jane hung up and listened to MacHovec's call for a moment. It sounded no more enlightening than hers had been. Either Randolph had trained his family well, or he kept his life so separate from theirs that they honestly knew nothing.

MacHovec put his phone down. "You try the wife," he said, switching sheets.

"I'm out of charm, but I'll give it a try."

Randolph had spoken fondly of his family when they saw him at Rikers. Maybe there was a relationship there, a wife who might believe she could help him.

"I hear he's in jail," the woman at the other end said in answer to Jane's first question.

"Does he live at your address, ma'am?"

"Well, he drops in now and then, when he needs a good meal, you know?"

"Mrs. Randolph, do you know who his friends are?"

"You askin' me about girlfriends?" The voice turned cool.

"No, ma'am. I'm trying to locate someone who might have done business with your husband."

"He got a brother James and he got another one, Raymond. I could give you their numbers."

She took them, although they were already on Mac-Hovec's sheet. "Do you have children?" she asked.

"I got a son and a daughter."

"Are they at home with you?"

"They're grown-up now. They got apartments of their own."

Nothing Randolph had said was true. "Do you know where your husband stays when he's not with you?"

A breathy silence. "My daughter knows. I'll give you her number." She gave numbers for both of them and ended the conversation.

"I hope they put him away for a thousand years," she said when she hung up.

"Randolph?"

"Yeah. What a shit. Here, you take the son; I'll take the daughter."

They developed some new contacts, but no new information. No one knew anything; no one was talking. Most of them swore they hadn't seen Randolph in a long time. But they were Randolph's friends and relatives; they would swear to anything.

At eight Jane got back to James Jr. He was actually there and they had what passed for a conversation. He sounded high on something, slurring words, answering questions that hadn't been asked, gliding past those she needed answers to, humming a tune. She was glad to get off the phone.

The phone rang almost immediately.

"Jane?" It was a frightened female voice. "It's Toni Defino."

"Toni. We're all working to find him."

"What happened? Lieutenant McElroy called. I was going crazy. Gordon's always on time or he calls."

Jane sketched it out, omitting details. "We're going to find him, Toni. It's just a matter of time."

"This seemed like such a safe job. I kidded him about taking his gun to work."

"I promise you, I'll call the minute we know something."

"I'm scared."

"I know. I am too. But Gordon's smart, and we're smart, and we'll find him."

She got off the phone and let out a breath.

"You lie as well as Randolph's family," MacHovec said.

"I didn't know what to say. Jesus, where did they take him?"

"You want a list?"

"No, I want one place. Randolph's got so many connections in Bed-Stuy we could spend a week looking."

"Let's see what the Manelli crowd is doing."

A second team of detectives had moved into the conference room. Sitting in shirtsleeves and T-shirts, they could have been a boiler-room operation for selling penny stocks.

"What's up?" MacHovec asked.

"They're sweatin' the girlfriend at the Six right now," a guy named Finster said. "Nothing yet."

"She's a dead end," Jane said, knowing they were doing what they had to. "What else?"

"Warren and me are going to Brooklyn. Manelli's mother lived there most of her life and he lived with her. We'll do a little canvassing. There may be some boyhood friends there." He stood as he spoke, grabbed his jacket, and headed for the door.

That might yield something, Jane thought.

"You Bauer and MacHovec?" another detective asked.

They said, "Yeah."

"Chris Collins." He stood and shook their hands. "George Clemente." He nodded to the fourth detective, who was copying something off the screen. "We're trying to find his cellmate from the last time he was inside. George found a wife but not the guy. What else is new?"

"So you've got Manelli pretty well covered," MacHovec said.

"As good as we can," Collins said with a shrug. "Manelli didn't go far from home. His friends and relatives are all right here, almost walking distance. Same with the guys he did business with. If they wanted to hide Defino somewhere, there's a dozen places they could've gone in a mile radius, waited for dark, and taken him out of the van. What are you up to?"

"Looking into Randolph's contacts. No one's talking."

"This isn't a Randolph operation," Collins said. "Manelli's behind it."

"I'm not so sure," Jane said. "Manelli didn't have time to call for help after I left his place with the girlfriend this afternoon. I think all of this comes from the visit Defino and I made to see Randolph at Rikers on Wednesday. He got someone to make a phone call and that started the ball rolling. The girlfriend saw Manelli talking to someone at their vacation place yesterday or the day before, and that's what put the blue van in front of their building at four o'clock today."

"Just when Defino was there alone with Manelli."

"Right. Someone dropped by to tell Manelli what was going on, that new people were looking into the Micah Anthony homicide."

"Well, we'll do our best."

"Thanks," Jane said.

They ran into McElroy on the way back to their office, but he had nothing new either.

"You want to keep after Randolph's friends?" MacHovec asked.

"I really don't. Unless we find one of them at Rikers and we can make a deal with him, these people aren't going to help."

"OK," MacHovec said, waiting for another idea.

"When did Curtis Morgan die?"

He opened a file folder and turned some pages. "Three years ago. Lung cancer. About a week after a B and E."

"How old was he?"

"Fifty-one. These guys never give up."

"Address?"

"Brooklyn. But he was white. He didn't live in Bed-Stuy."

"See what you can find out about him, Sean."

He began his search, said, "Shit," under his breath, and kept at it. He shook his head, kept keying, then gave up and picked up the phone and dialed. "Yeah, Det. Sean Mac-

Hovec." He went through the ID procedure and asked about the file for Curtis Morgan, giving the date of his last alleged crime. "I really can't wait, Sarge. We've got a missing detective, possible kidnap, and we—Thanks."

"What's going on?" Jane asked.

"My computer's not doing its thing. I'm calling the Eight-eight in Brooklyn, where he was last arrested. The son of a bitch had the good grace not to pull a job in his own precinct. They should have something on file. Yeah, I'm here," he said into the phone. He listened for a full minute without comment, then said, "Can I have the name and phone number of the detective who caught the case?"

Jane watched him write, listening to his murmurs.

"And that's it?" he asked finally. "OK. No, I appreciate it." He hung up and turned to Jane. "This is gonna blow your mind. My computer tells me there's nothing on Morgan besides information on his death, and they just looked at the paper file at the Eight-eight and it's empty."

"What?"

"Got his name, the detective's name, and a notation that Morgan died at Kings County Hospital. That's it."

"This guy had history."

"Yeah. And someone wants to keep it a deep, dark secret."

11

JANE TOOK A few seconds to consider it. "You're right. It does blow my mind. I think the whip has to hear about this. I'll find McElroy."

He was in his office, a day's growth of stubble darkening his face. He looked up and motioned her in. "What?" he said.

She told him.

"Shit."

"Right."

"You got the name of the catching detective?"

"Sean does."

"This better go to the inspector. Keep at it." He picked up the phone as she left the office.

MacHovec was on the phone with the detective when she returned. "Hold on," he said. "I want to conference my partner, Jane Bauer."

She got on the phone and wrote down the detective's name, Greg Turner.

"Sean's just telling me about the Morgan file. It's a couple of years ago and I didn't do much on it—the guy died—but it's coming back to me. I think we arrested him and he started coughing up blood and we bussed him over to Kings County. He never came out and that was the end of the case. He had a partner, I think, and we made a case against him. Morgan didn't live long after the arrest, a week at the most.

I don't know why the file would be empty. I typed up some Fives, did some follow-up." His voice petered out.

"Anyone talk to you about the case?" Jane asked.

"Not that I remember. Morgan and his partner had broken into an auto parts store at night, cleaned out the cash that was left, and picked up a lotta stuff they could sell. Looked like they were working for a chop shop about a mile away. It wasn't their first, I can tell you that. Morgan was too old and too sick to be doing that kind of work. His partner was younger but I can't remember his name."

"Any reason you can think of why Morgan's file would be missing?" MacHovec asked.

"Not offhand. This wasn't big stuff."

Jane nodded to MacHovec, and he thanked Turner and finished the conversation.

"This feels bad to me," MacHovec said. What no one had said out loud, including McElroy, was that the empty paper file and the missing computer information indicated a high-level police intervention.

"Me too." She looked at her watch. It was after nine. "I'm calling Kings County."

Like Bellevue Hospital in Manhattan, Kings County Hospital in Brooklyn had the reputation of working their tails off to save police lives. Cops were known to stuff a wounded comrade in a radio car and take him to Kings County rather than call an ambulance from a nearer hospital that might not try as hard. The hospital itself was a collection of many buildings, old and new, on a large campus. At this hour Jane had little hope of getting a quick response to a question that required searching a three-year-old file. As expected, she was shunted from the first human voice to another and another. Each time she introduced herself, she talked about the urgency of her request.

Finally, a woman said she would personally see to it that the file on Curtis Morgan was retrieved in the morning.

"If I come over tonight, can someone direct me to the files and let me search myself?"

Silence. "I don't know if we can."

"Ma'am, a police detective has been kidnapped and we fear for his life. Mr. Morgan's file may help us in our search."

"All right." The woman sounded beat. "I'll take you there myself." She gave Jane her name and an easy location to find. Then Jane could call on an internal phone.

"I'm going," Jane said, gathering her notes.

"I'll look in on the Manelli crowd."

She checked in with McElroy, who had spoken to Graves. "You got money on you for cabs?"

"Plenty."

Downstairs the evening had turned cool and pleasant, an unaccustomed freshness in the air. She saw a cab coming toward her, its roof light on, signaling that it was empty, and she hailed it.

She got in and said, "Kings County Hospital."

The cabbie, a Pakistani, turned and gave her a skeptical look. "The one in Brooklyn?"

"Right, Brooklyn."

"I don't know if I can find it."

Jane took out her shield and stuck it in his face. "I'll help you get there."

"Yes, ma'am." He flipped the meter and headed for Brooklyn.

The nurse's name was Melissa George. She was young and cute, but looked as though she needed a night's sleep. "I'll unlock the door for you. When you leave, it'll lock automatically. There's a phone in there if you need help." She asked about the year the patient was at the hospital. When they got to the records room, she went inside and pointed Jane in the right direction.

Curtis Morgan had died in June, nearly three years before. When she finally found the file, the death certificate was on top. She copied down the name of the doctor, the cause of death—mesothelioma—and Morgan's address. Then she called Melissa George.

The phone rang several times before an older woman answered. Melissa was on break; she'd be back in ten minutes.

"This is Det. Jane Bauer, ma'am. I'm researching a death at Kings County Hospital. Can you tell me what mesothelioma is?"

"It's a kind of lung cancer."

"And do you know a Dr. Darshna Patel?"

"No, I'm afraid I don't. What department is he in?"

"I guess lung cancer."

"I'm sorry. I can't help you. Wait a minute. I have a directory here." She put the phone down and flipped pages. "Yes, he's listed here. You can probably reach him in the morning."

"Does he have a home phone listed?"

"I couldn't give that out."

She went through her story.

"Give me your shield number and I'll call and check it. Wait a minute. Here's Melissa."

Jane went through it again and Melissa gave her the number. It was 516, a Long Island area code.

"Thanks. I really appreciate it."

"I hope it works out."

Not as much as I do, Jane thought. She found a place to sit down and dialed the number for the doctor.

He answered on the second ring. She went through her story again.

"Three years ago? I'd have to refresh my memory."

"He was a prisoner when he was brought in. He'd been arrested for breaking into an auto parts store and when he started coughing up blood, the police brought him to the emergency room."

"Yes, I do remember. What is it I can tell you?"

"According to the death certificate in the file, he died of mesothelioma. What exactly is that?"

"It's a kind of lung cancer, not the kind you get from smoking, although he may have been a smoker, too. I can't remember a detail like that without looking at the record."

"What causes that kind of cancer?"

"It was probably work related. He may have inhaled steel dust or asbestos. Again, I would have to check to be sure."

"Thank you, Doctor. I'm sorry to have disturbed you at home."

Something was starting to play in her mind. She found the address for Morgan and called the operator for the phone number, identifying herself once again. The operator came back with a number and Jane dialed it. It was near midnight now, and no one was going to be happy to get a phone call. A woman answered, sounding wide-awake.

"Is this Mrs. Morgan?"

"Yes. Who's this?"

Jane went through it again.

"What do you want?"

"I need information on Curtis Morgan."

"He's dead."

"I'm aware of that, ma'am. I'd like to know what kind of work he did."

"He wasn't working the last few years of his life. He was too sick to work. He was on disability."

"Before that. What did he do?"

"He was a track walker for the Transit Authority, you know, an inspector on the rail system. It's what killed him in the end, all that dust. It got into his lungs. He was only fifty-one."

"Yes, ma'am. I'm sorry about that. Did he work on one particular area of the subway?"

"The Lexington line for a lotta years."

"Thank you, ma'am. Are you at this number during the day?"

"I work. Can't live on his pension, can I?"

Jane got the daytime phone number from her and thanked her again. Then she called MacHovec.

"Yeah," he said after several rings.

"It's Jane. I've got something."

"Thank God. Nothing's turning up for Manelli."

She gave it to him.

"OK. I'll get into the TA system and see what I can dig up on Morgan. Sounds promising."

"Let's hope. I'm on my way back."

Inspector Graves had arrived at 137 by the time Jane got there. She and MacHovec went into his office and sat down.

"What've you got?" the whip asked curtly.

She told him.

"So you think they've got Defino hidden away in the Lex."

"I think it's possible. I think we have to try it. Morgan may just be the key to this whole thing. He worked the tracks and he knew every in and out of the Lex. There have to be alcoves there where you could tie a guy up and leave him. When Morgan was working with Randolph and Manelli, he could have taken them down there and taught them the ropes."

"Do we have a prayer of getting something out of Randolph?"

"No, sir."

"Inspector," MacHovec put in. "Jane called me from Kings County and I've been playing around the TA computer system."

"Got anything?"

"I found what we've been finding. Most of the information on Morgan has been expunged. There's no record of where he worked or in what capacity. They've left the stuff they need for his pension, length of service, cause of death. Someone went in there and sanitized the file."

Graves said, "Shit," under his breath. "I like this less and less. We're all gonna be wearing bulletproof vests pretty soon and looking over our shoulders." He rubbed his eyes. "All right. Where was I? Jane, where would you start to look? There has to be twenty miles of track on that line."

She had thought about that on the taxi ride back from Kings County. "They got Defino in the Village. If they drove east and a little north, they'd hit the Astor Place station."

"You yourself said they'd wait till dark to transfer him out of the van. They could have been cruising around for hours."

"Right. But they don't want a brightly lit area, and Astor Place is on the dark side. Look, I could be wrong, but we have to do something and we have to start somewhere. The teams in the conference room are searching for Manelli. We should look somewhere else. Randolph is a dead end. The girlfriend doesn't know anything. This could be a lead."

"I don't see it," Graves said. "Morgan's been dead three

years. You're telling me he showed Manelli and Randolph how to get down into the subway ten years ago. Why? What does it buy them? You have to love rats to walk around down there."

MacHovec turned to her. "You think they planned to take Micah Anthony down to the tracks?"

"No. I think they made him, and they wanted to know what he knew before they killed him. He was a dead man when they picked him up. But they may have had another use for the subway. They may have stashed two hundred twenty-seven stolen guns there."

Graves said, "Hm."

"I like it," MacHovec said.

"All right. We'll give it a try. This will take a while to set up. I'll have to get the Transit Authority in on this. They'll have to slow down the trains and maybe cut the power to the third rail. This is a big operation."

"Then we should do it at night," Jane said.

"Right." He shook his head. "I hope this isn't a wild-goose chase. I'll let you both know what's going on when I know."

"I'm part of it," Jane said, aware that she should have asked, not announced.

"I think you're better off here."

"Sir, he's my partner."

After an indecisive moment, Graves said, "You'll need the right shoes and your bulletproof vest."

"I've got both here."

"Give me half an hour."

12

"DEFINO LEAVE ANY clothing here?" It was Graves, standing at the door, jacket gone, shirtsleeves rolled, stubble visible. "They're bringing in the canine unit."

That was welcome news. "Maybe a pair of shoes." Jane slid over to Defino's desk and looked underneath. "Yes. He kept them here in case of snow." She pulled them up and set them on the desk. They were old and worn, the leather cracking, but they would do the job.

"Perfect. You can take them over to Astor Place. We've set entry time at two A.M. Gives you an hour and a half. Go home, clean yourself up, and go over there. Take your cell phone with you. I'm going to meet you over at Astor Place at two, see who's there, give them a pep talk." No one could do that better than Frank Graves.

Jane got up. "See you then. Sean, what are you doing?"

"Going home for a few hours of sleep. I'll talk to you in the morning."

In the apartment, Jane plugged in the cell phone, which she rarely used, hoping for an adequate charge. Then she showered, changed into jeans and a sweatshirt, and put her shield on a cord around her neck. She emptied her bag, holstering the Glock and distributing the necessities of her life in pockets. Then she slipped a small, high-intensity flashlight into a nylon scabbard, checked the batteries, and slipped her belt through the loop. She checked her magazines and put the extra pouches on the belt. A pair of tight leather gloves went into her back pocket. On her feet she wore the sturdy boots that she reserved for such infrequent occasions.

She arrived at Astor Place ten minutes before two, a chill in the air. Graves, who was running the operation, was already there, along with a group of more than ten people plus a dog. When introductions were made, she learned that the group consisted of the dog handler, a young woman with startling red hair; and NYPD Emergency Service cops, including several bosses of various ranks up to a Patrol Borough Manhattan South one-star, a deputy chief. The ESD were specialists in tough situations like rescuing hostages, taking out barricaded bad guys, and talking down bridge jumpers. Their motto was, "When you are in trouble, you call a cop. When a cop is in trouble, he calls ESD."

Also in the search party were civilian workers from the Transit System Signal Department, Maintenance of Way, Electrical Department, and the local tower master.

On the street an NYPD Temporary Headquarters van was coordinating all communications and department personnel. Also at the curb were two ambulances, "buses" to cops, with a full staff of EMTs in case of injury, and a fire department unit. A missing cop was a big deal.

A young captain from DCPI, the Deputy Commissioner of Public Information, was on hand to control press releases and information to media outlets and reporters, who were getting nothing but stock statements. No one in the search party would go near them. This was a life-and-death situation involving a missing MOS, a member of the service. "Fuck you very much" was the attitude toward the news media.

Rousted from their beds in the last two hours, the assembled cops and transit workers moved around, talking, getting to know one another. Jane introduced herself to all of them, barely remembering names, but it didn't matter; everyone wore ID. A can of bug spray was passed around with the instructions to spray shoes, pants, and jackets.

"Just to keep the bugs away," one of the bosses said lightly. "You don't want to take any of the wildlife home with you."

On the tiled wall of the station Jane saw the image of a beaver, a relic of John Jacob Astor, who had made his fortune selling their skins. The group went down to the platform and walked to one end, where stairs led down to the tracks.

A Transit man went down and tested the third rail. "It's OK," he called up. "It's been deenergized. We're safe to go."

The group descended to the track level and formed a skirmish line, spreading across the tracks and walking north. Even though the third rail was deenergized, it was always safest to stay away from it. It was near the outer track of each pair and the group was instructed to walk between the tracks to avoid contact.

The dog, a beautiful black Lab named J. J., after John Jay College of Criminal Justice, led the way north. Jane had been allowed to walk near the dog because of her almost sacred status as partner of the missing detective, and after a little while, she felt herself in danger of falling in love with it. But she knew she would have to fight his handler, Detective Specialist Jennifer Quinn, to the death for him, and she liked Quinn.

Walking the tracks anywhere in the system bordered on the disgusting. Although homeless people found places to live in safe alcoves, rats lived wherever even a small pool of water collected, and they were covered with fleas. The water also bred roaches and water bugs, some of the latter as big as tarantulas.

Jane had walked the tracks earlier in her career when she had to chase a perp down into the subway system. She had hated it then and she knew she would hate it now. That said, she fell in line as they moved uptown.

Spaced periodically along the walls of the tunnels were indentations called manholes, where one subway worker could flatten himself to avoid oncoming trains. Besides the deenergizing of the tracks, the track signals had been programmed to alert train crews to the emergency, slowing them down or stopping them as required. Few trains ran at this time of night even in normal circumstances, and tonight the number had been cut to prevent accidents.

Besides the collected water, garbage was dropped along the floor, meals and snacks discarded by riders. Filthy slobs, Jane thought, not for the first time. As they walked, she called Defino's name, hearing the echo, hearing Graves's words at 137: "I hope this isn't a wild-goose chase." She was so tired, it was a struggle to keep going. She gave up counting rats after the fifth one. The temptation was to shoot them, for which she might lose her shield.

They pressed northward, inspecting alcoves, climbing up to station platforms and waiting for trains to pass before returning to the track level. Jane's voice became hoarse, and fatigue threatened to take her down. Their goal was the Fifty-ninth Street station. That would take them through huge stations like Fourteenth Street and Forty-second Street, where several lines converged and tracks branched, leaving spaces where someone might be stashed. But exhaustive searches turned up nothing.

By the time they left Forty-second Street, Jane was starting to feel that nothing would come of the search. Graves would be furious and Defino would still be missing. She stumbled and caught herself before she fell.

"You OK?" Jennifer Quinn asked.

"I'll make it. Thanks."

"How much sleep did you get?"

"None."

"You shouldn't be here."

"He's my partner."

They kept going. At the Fifty-first Street station they agreed to stop for a rest. Jane sat against a pillar and fell asleep. The cop who roused her was gentle and concerned.

"You should go home. You look beat."

"We'll be done soon. Then I'll sleep."

He pulled her up and they went down to the tracks and picked up the search.

She wasn't sure what was worse: the smells of the subway or the stink of the bug spray. They combined to keep her from feeling hungry. She couldn't remember when she had last eaten or what it was. She just knew she had to keep going. Gordon was in this fucking tunnel, and she had to find him before Manelli's gang decided to get rid of him. He would have dropped something to guide them if he were able, but she was sure they had used his handcuffs to keep him disabled.

It was six in the morning when they left Fifty-first Street. They had spent an hour at the Forty-second Street station. It was Saturday morning, a low traffic day, but more trains were scheduled from six on than during the night.

At Fifty-ninth Street the deputy chief stopped them, went out in front of the line, and addressed them. "This is as far as we go. I'm sorry. I wish we'd found him. Let's get up on the platform." He got a signal on his walkie-talkie and said they were on their way. When everyone was accounted for on the platform, he gave the order to reenergize the third rail. The operation was over.

Jane thanked each of the participants. If she looked anything like the way they did, she would need a scouring brush to get clean. The sympathy of the party cheered her, but it didn't make up for their failure to find Defino. She started thinking of walking the tracks south of Astor Place. Graves would flop her back to the bag—her uniform.

The deputy chief thanked them all and they scattered, some of them going back down into the subway to ride back to Astor Place for their cars. Jane took a taxi home.

She slept for two hours, having set her alarm, and woke up feeling worse than when she lay down. She wanted to speak to Mrs. Morgan again, to find out where else besides the Lex her husband had worked. She showered first, and then put some bread in the toaster and coffee and water in the coffeemaker. Her mouth was parched. A large glass of orange juice helped a little.

While she ate, she called McElroy's number at 137. She left a message on his voice mail and hung up. Then she found Mrs. Morgan's number. It was Saturday and probably not a workday, so Jane called the home number.

"Hello?"

"Mrs. Morgan, this is Detective Bauer."

"Who?"

"I talked to you last night about where your late husband worked."

"I don't know what you're talking about."

"Mrs. Morgan—"

"I don't know who you are. Good-bye." A click ended the conversation.

Jane put the phone down, a chill passing through her. Someone had gotten to her. Someone had called and told her to keep quiet about her husband.

Jane checked the address for Morgan. It was in the Eight-four precinct on Gold Street in Brooklyn, not far from where the wife worked. She called their number and identified herself. "I need to have a witness picked up ASAP and brought down to the house. I'll be there as soon as I can to question her."

"OK, Detective. You got a cell phone we can call you at if we need to?"

She gave the number, stuffed the rest of her toast in her mouth, finished the coffee in a gulp, and left everything where it was. Fuck the roaches. Then she went downstairs and hailed a cab.

Mrs. Morgan, a smartly dressed graying woman, sat in an interview room looking frightened. She turned as Jane opened the door and entered.

"I'm Detective Bauer, Mrs. Morgan."

"Am I being arrested?"

"You're here so I can talk to you."

"You had to send cops so my neighbors would see?"

"I had to be sure we reached you before you left your apartment. I have some questions to ask you."

"I told you, I don't know anything."

"Who called you, Mrs. Morgan? Who told you not to talk to the police?"

"Nobody called." She fidgeted, pressed her lips together, and looked worried.

"That's not going to cut it. You talked to me last night, and this morning you don't know who I am."

"Well, maybe I remember now. You called late last night."

"Right. And I need to know more about where your husband worked."

"I told you, the Lexington line."

"Before that."

"I don't remember."

"Who told you not to talk to me?"

"Nobody. I just don't remember."

"Well, start remembering. A man's life is at stake."

"Please. I just don't know. Leave me alone."

"I don't want to threaten you. I just want to find my partner alive." She waited.

The woman sat looking at her hands. She took a tissue out of her handbag and blew her nose. "I don't know who called," she said in a low voice. "But he scared me. He said bad things would happen if I talked about Curtis, if I said anything at all to the police."

"Did you tell him you'd spoken to me?"

"You think I'm crazy?"

"Where did your husband work before he was a track man on the Lex?"

"What if they come and kill me?"

"We'll see to it that they don't." Her cell phone rang. Jane took it out and said a curt, "Bauer."

"Jane." It was Hack. He had probably been trying to reach her since the night before.

"I'm all right. I can't talk now. I'm at the Eight-four."

"I'll call in an hour."

She turned back to Mrs. Morgan. "Answer my question."

"When I first knew him—it was a long time ago—he was working on the Second Avenue subway."

"What did he tell you about it?"

"He talked about the men he worked with, how much progress they were making on the section they were working on."

"What section is that?"

"He started at Sixty-third Street. They were going to connect up the Lex and the Second Avenue with lines that went east and west. They worked on that tunnel for years and then the money ran out, and that was it."

"And after that?"

"After that he worked on the Lex."

"Thank you, Mrs. Morgan. I appreciate your honesty."

She arranged with the detective squad to have Mrs. Morgan taken home to pack, and then to be delivered to her sister. That accomplished, Jane went home by subway. She had a lot of hard work to do on her two hours' sleep.

13

THE GREAT UNDERGROUND fiasco in New York, the Second Avenue line was the subway the city couldn't live without and never managed to complete, the subway they threw billions of dollars into over many years and then abandoned. It was a New York legend, a project of several beginnings and an equal number of endings. On and off for many years— off during the Second World War—it was finally back on again with a projected opening date in the early fifties.

In the mid fifties, however, the ancient Third Avenue El began to be dismantled, leaving the city with no north–south subway east of Lexington Avenue, and the idea of the Second Avenue subway began to be tossed around again. Jane's father remembered the El, the dark street below it that eventually saw sunlight with the removal of the structure, and then the amazing transfiguration. Old tenements were replaced with luxury high-rises, and dinky antique shops with expensive stores, later called boutiques. John Bauer often shook his head as he thought of the transformation he had never believed would take place. But once again the Second Avenue subway didn't get off the ground. Money appropriated for it was spent on other projects, not unusual in a city with many needs.

Finally, in October 1972, on the anniversary of the opening of the old IRT line, and with adequate funds and plenty of optimism, ground was broken at East One Hundred Third Street and Second Avenue. This was the subway Curtis Morgan worked on until it was once again abandoned several years later.

What Jane's father recalled was the years of barricaded streets in Midtown, endless traffic detours, and the difficulty walking in the area. Recently, new rumblings had surfaced about building the subway. The cost had gone from millions to hundreds of millions to more than sixteen billion, but if it had been necessary in the twenties, the forties, and the seventies, it was crucial now. Surface traffic was a nightmare; underground was the fast way to go.

So, Jane reflected as she rode home underground, Curtis Morgan had intimate knowledge of the Second Avenue subway tunnel in the East Sixties. The tunnel was still there. If plans to complete the line were reactivated, the existing tunnel would be used, completed sections linked, tracks would be laid, and lighting provided. What she had to do was get over to the portion of the tunnel Morgan knew and make a search—and to do that, she needed assistance.

In the elevator in her building, her cell phone rang. It was Hack.

"You take part in that Lexington search party?"

"I got Graves to authorize it. I got a lead and thought Defino might be hidden there. We didn't find anything. But I've got another lead, the Second Avenue subway." She explained as she walked down the hall, put the key in her door, and went inside.

"Graves'll be apoplectic."

"I have to do this, Hack. They're holding Gordon some-where, and I've got to find him before they kill him."

"It may be too late."

"I know that, but I have to try. My God, what if they didn't do it for me?"

"I would take care of that."

"I know you would, and I have to do it for him. I'm ex-hausted. I wish we were back in Paris."

"So do I. We'll do it again, baby. I'm just concerned about you right now. Have you slept?"

"A couple of hours this morning." She sat on the sofa. Her body ached and she was parched again.

"Watch yourself. Keep in touch. You have plenty of phone cards?"

"Yes." They used phone cards whenever they could to dis-guise the origin of the calls.

"Call me anytime. If you luck out on the search, I can come over tomorrow."

She drank some ice water and carried a fresh glass with her to her desk. She needed a phone number and had little hope of reaching the contact on Saturday, but it was worth a try.

In a career with NYPD, a cop made many friends and even a few enemies. The friends could be called on for fa-vors, and right now she needed one badly. Back when she was still in the bag, and then later when she got her gold shield, Jane had needed assistance in the subway and had met an older transit police detective named Ron Delancey. He was one of those knowledgeable men who remembered everything, and whose hobby was the history of the subway system. He collected old maps and had picked up souvenirs of the system: old lights, bits of track, an occasional sign that was being replaced. Jane had never seen the collection, but Ron had told her of his wife's threats to move out if he didn't stop adding to it.

In an irreplaceable file in her desk, she found a work num-ber for Ron and dialed it.

A man answered. "Peterson."

"This is Det. Jane Bauer. I'm looking for Ron Delancey."

"You're a few years too late, Detective. Ron retired."

"Do you have a home phone for him? It's very important."

"Sorry. Try the DEA hotline."

The DEA was the Detectives Endowment Association, the best detectives on earth. Since the Transit Police and the NYPD had merged in 1995, the DEA represented both branches. The union offices were closed Saturday, but the hotline would respond. Cops got in trouble on weekends as well as weekdays, and might need advice or a lawyer.

She left a message on the machine and waited. A few minutes later the phone rang.

"This is Detective Gorman at the DEA."

"Thanks. This is an emergency. I need to find a retired TA detective."

He checked her shield number, then left the phone. How old could Ron be? she wondered. Fifties or sixties, not more. She had been—

"I got a Yonkers number for him, Detective."

"Great." She wrote it down, thanked Gorman, and dialed the number.

A woman answered and called Ron to the phone.

"It's Det. Jane Bauer, Ron. I hope you remem—"

"Of course I remember you. We did a terrific chase on the Number One line back when my knees were better. How's things?"

"Very good and very bad. Ron, my partner's been kidnapped and I think they may be holding him in the Second Avenue subway tunnel near Sixty-third Street."

"You part of that search party last night?"

"Yes. We came up with nothing, but I have new information."

"Who's authorizing this Second Avenue search?"

"No one yet. I have to talk to the whip in my office. He's more likely to say no than yes. Does that make a difference to you?"

"You want me to go down there with you?"

"Please."

"Makes no difference at all. What'll they do to me, dock my pension?"

"Thanks, Ron."

"I need a couple of hours to prepare and get down there. I'm living in Yonkers now."

"I can use a little time, too. I have to ask for permission—"

"Which you won't get."

"Which I won't get. And I could use a little sleep. I've only slept two hours in the last two days."

"OK. I'll pick up some industrial-strength bug spray and a few other goodies. Where can I reach you? We should do this at night."

She gave him her home, office, and cell numbers, then called Graves's number.

"Where are you?" he asked.

"I'm home. I have a new lead."

"It better not take you down to the subway."

"In fact, it does, sir."

"Get over here right away. We have some talking to do." He hung up.

She called Hack on the way over.

"Find your guy?"

"Yes. He'll help me. We'll do it tonight."

"And Graves?"

"I'm on my way over to 137 now. He's in a foul mood."

"He won't let you do this."

"I know."

"But you'll do it anyway."

"You want deniability?"

"I don't know you, Detective. I don't need to deny anything."

"I love you, Hackett."

"Whoever you are."

Her assessment of Graves's response was on target. For a man who had made his reputation as a calm, moderating individual, his demeanor was shocking. He was fuming.

"You have any idea what that tramp through the Lex cost this city?"

"Yes, sir."

"How many man-hours, how much equipment was used?"

"Yes, sir."

"And you want to try another subway line?"

"A piece of the Second Avenue tunnel. I don't need an army to go with me."

"You listen to me, Detective. You stay the hell out of the subway unless you're riding a train. You got that?"

"Yes, sir."

"That's an order. Go home and get some sleep—you look like hell—and show up here when you're rested."

"Yes, sir." She stood and started out of the office.

"An order, Detective. You know what an order is?"

MacHovec raised his eyebrows as she walked into their office. "Guess you got the word."

"Guess I did."

"So what're you doing now?"

"You want deniability?" she asked for the second time in an hour.

"Wouldn't hurt."

"I'm going home and getting a few hours' sleep. And that's the truth."

"Good luck."

"Thanks. Anything doing here?"

"Carl Randolph's former cellmate is dead. Otherwise squat."

"Shit."

"Yeah."

"I'll talk to you, Sean. I just don't know from where."

She called Hack and let him know. "I'm afraid I'll lose my badge," she said.

"If it doesn't work out, he won't know you did it. And we'll get you a good lawyer."

She laughed. "I'm glad you're thinking ahead. I'm going to sleep if I'm not too keyed up. Ron'll call to let me know he's ready. He's out buying bug spray."

"Who is this guy?"

She told him. He approved. She went to sleep.

When Ron Delancey called in the afternoon, she was sleeping so deeply, she awoke disoriented. He had everything they would need, and he was looking forward to his first trip down into the tunnels since his retirement.

"You have the keys we need?" Jane asked.

"I have everything. I'll call you before I leave."

The keys were important. They were unusual in shape and could not be duplicated outside the TA. That he had them at all meant he had taken them with him. And Curtis Morgan had probably taken his with him to retain access to the tunnel.

She showered and put on a pair of jeans, then opened a can of tuna. Sitting at the kitchen table she ran her hand over the smaller of the two holes left by two bullets in the winter, bullets that had been meant for her. One had almost passed through the table, and the second had gone only partly through, leaving the smaller hole. If either one had gone all the way through, Jane would be dead. The holes were a daily reminder.

The phone rang. It was Toni Defino.

"There's nothing yet, Toni."

"Were you in the Lex last night?"

"I was. I had a lead. I thought he might be stuffed in an alcove there, but we didn't find him."

"Oh, God." Toni started crying.

"Toni, no one's given up, and no one will. I'm chasing down another lead in a little while."

"Where?"

"I can't tell you. Just believe me when I say we are all working to find him."

Toni needed more reassuring and Jane did her best, then finished the light lunch that would have to hold her till later tonight.

Then Flora called. Flora Hamburg was an aging inspector who ruffled many feathers on the job, Hack's included, but was well loved by the group she cared most about, career women.

"That's your partner, right?" she said with no introduction.

"Yes."

"You folks ever learn how to keep out of trouble?"

"When we find him, I'll take a refresher course."

"Jane, what's happening?"

Jane gave her a rundown.

"Graves must want your ass."

"He does."

"So what now?"

"I'm following up a lead. If it works, you'll hear about it."

"Watch yourself. You want to be around for Medal Day."

Medal Day was in June. Jane had earned a medal for her first case at 137, the case that promoted her from third grade to first grade. Her father was counting the days. As she cleaned up the dishes, she wondered if they would still give it to her if she'd been fired. It would break her father's heart.

Finally, Ron Delancey called. He would meet her on the northeast corner of Sixty-third and Second Avenue and they would go on from there. He questioned her about her clothes and her sleep, sounding relieved that she had managed a few more hours.

She called Hack and told him when and where. Then she traveled uptown.

14

"WELL, YOU'RE LOOKIN' good. That your picture I saw on the front of the *Daily News* a while ago?"

"That was it. Got myself in a little trouble and everyone thought I did something special."

"If this works, it'll be special."

"It has to work, Ron. I have to find him. Two guys, maybe three, stuffed him in an old blue van, and no one's seen him since. I'm really worried."

"We'll give it our best."

This time they descended to the tunnel by lifting a grate on the busy sidewalk, the kind that Marilyn Monroe had stood on to have her skirt blown up. Ron had brought a backpack with flashlights for both of them, as well as night-vision goggles they would wear below.

He went down first, showing her how to replace the grate after her and lighting the ladder they would use, rungs embedded in a vertical concrete wall. Concerned, he kept the rungs above him lit for her and descended slowly.

They went down at least sixty feet, possibly eighty, the longest vertical descent on foot of her life. She felt relief to reach the bottom, a line that carried trains to Roosevelt Island in the East River and from there to Queens. Ron had it timed so they could get to the Second Avenue branch before a train came by. At that point, the lighting stopped and they turned onto a trackless bed.

They stopped there, and Ron dug in his backpack for two pairs of goggles, which they donned before continuing. Then he led her into an unreal underworld.

"This is it," he said. "The famous Second Avenue subway. There's lots of places to hide someone around here. I can show you side passages used for storage. We've got bypass tunnels the guys use for working around utility lines. It wouldn't be smart to hide something there; it could be found."

"What do they store?"

"Machinery, steel girders, track and signal equipment, lots and lots of cable reels, including empty ones."

"Shit, we'll never find him."

"Let's get our bearings." He leaned against a ten-foot-high chain-link fence and took some papers out of his backpack. "These are maps and they're fairly up-to-date. I've penciled in what's stored where, and that should give us some help deciding where to look."

"Fantastic."

"Only if it works. Look. We don't want to go here or here

or this area over here. They're stacked high with machinery. But these areas"—he ran his index finger over them—"these are places you could open the gate, stuff something in, and be on your way."

"Then let's look there."

Although there was no danger of trains, the rats were plentiful and the water bugs more so. She called Gordon's name several times and they stopped to listen for an answer, although none came.

"Let me do the calling," Ron said as they walked. "Your voice sounds like you were shouting all night."

"I was."

"Gordon," he shouted, his voice much louder than Jane's. "Gordon Denno. Rattle a fence if you hear me."

They stood still, Jane not breathing. Nothing stirred. Toni would call her again that night or the next morning, hoping for news. They had to find him.

They checked out one of Ron's storage areas, going inside and inspecting the contents, but it was just what it was supposed to be. They went on to a second one with the same results. They stepped into an alcove but found only pipes and tubes without marking, colors so faded they could not be identified.

They came close to sewer pipes and water mains. This was what it took to run a city of eight million people. When a water main broke, as they did from time to time, flooding building basements and well-trafficked streets, this was where the fixers came, down to the netherworld beneath the streets.

"Steam lines, over there," Ron said, pointing. "Hot as hell." Then he called Gordon again.

Jane flashed her light on her watch. It was two hours since they had descended at Second Avenue. They were outside another storage area and Ron had his key out.

"Something's covered up in there," Jane said. "Looks like burlap. Nothing else has been covered."

"Let's take a look."

He fumbled with the key and dropped it. "Oh, shit."

"We'll find it." She sounded more certain than she felt as she dropped to a squat. He had said he had knee trouble, and she didn't want him getting hurt. "Just shine your light over here, Ron. I'll do the crawling."

She had put on a pair of gloves and she leaned on the ground as he moved the light slowly from side to side. Where was the fucking key? He had been standing exactly in front of the lock, and she was sure the key had not dropped inside the fence, although she had heard it tinkle as it fell.

He moved and looked at the ground where he had stood while Jane gently fluffed the earth or dirt or whatever it was. She was afraid of burying it deeper if she weren't careful.

"I'm sure it's on the outside," he said.

"So am I."

She moved her finger carefully along the ground where the fence met it, but found nothing. He ran the light inside the fence, just to be sure, but there was no sign of the key.

"I can get another key, but it'll take a day or two."

"Ron, that key is here. We'll find it."

He got down on the ground himself and started searching. He moved back a few paces and then forward, slowly. "What's that?"

"What? Where?"

"Under your right foot."

She retreated carefully. A tiny piece of silver metal showed through the dirt. She ripped her right glove off and used her fingernails to coax it up. In half a minute she had the key. She couldn't help smiling.

"I knew I shouldn't've taken it off my big key ring," Ron said, putting it back where it belonged and then inserting it in the lock. He pushed open the gate and they went in.

Jane pulled the burlap off whatever it was covering. Underneath was a stack of olive-drab metal boxes with yellow markings.

"Jesus, Mary, and Joseph," Ron said.

"What is it?"

"Guns. Look at the yellow stencil on this one. Berettas, .40-caliber. I bet these were owned by the federal government."

"Are you sure?"

"Yeah. That's how they were packed when I was in the

army." He flipped open the top box and pulled out a dull handgun, dust on its oiled surface. "A Beretta," he said. ".40-caliber. They don't use 'em anymore, but they were standard army-issue."

"Two hundred twenty-seven missing guns," Jane said. "They were stolen over ten years ago from the armory at West A Hundred Sixty-eighth Street and Columbus Avenue. They were involved in the killing of Micah Anthony."

"I remember that. Is it ten years already?"

"Yeah. That's what my team's been working on. Let's look around this area for Defino. If he's not here, he's not in the subway. I think they would keep him near the guns. They all knew where the guns were."

They spent fifteen minutes and came up with nothing. Then they covered the boxes again. Jane took one Beretta with her to prove her story in case the guns were gone when they sent a recovery team for them. Then they reversed direction and went back to the city above their heads.

On the street level, her legs shaking from the climb, she found a pay phone and called McElroy. He was gone for the night. So was MacHovec. Reluctantly, she keyed Graves's number.

"Graves."

"This is Jane Bauer."

"Where are you?"

"Second Avenue and Sixty-second."

"I want you here. Five minutes ago."

"I found the missing two hundred twenty-seven guns, Inspector, and I'm holding hard evidence in my hand."

"Are you on a cell phone?"

"No, sir, a landline." Cell phones were easier to pick up by eavesdroppers.

"Say that again."

"I'm on my way."

Ron drove her downtown, although home was in the other direction.

"How do I look?" she asked him.

"Not too clean."

"He'll have to take me as I am. This may be the last time we meet on the job."

"He won't fire you, Jane. You just made a big find."

"Thanks to you. If I were cleaner, I'd give you a hug."

"Let me know how it turns out."

She got out and called Hack from a pay phone.

"The guns from the Anthony case?"

"Right there in their original boxes stenciled in yellow and covered with burlap. Some grenade launchers too. I hadn't heard they were missing."

"You talk to Graves yet?"

"I'm on my way up."

"You're good, Bauer."

"It was Delancey. He knows every nook and cranny down there."

She took the elevator up, too tired to try the stairs. She stopped in the ladies' room, looked sorrowfully at her reflection, then washed her hands and face. The smell of the spray was still there, or perhaps it was stuck in her nostrils, where she would smell it for the next week.

Inspector Graves looked up as she reached his doorway. "Sit down."

She took a chair, dropped her jacket on the floor, and waited.

"You disobeyed a direct order."

"Yes, sir."

"Who the hell do you think you are?" Anyone else would have used an obscenity. Through all his anger, he still maintained a surface polish.

"I'm a detective's partner."

"That doesn't override an order."

"I'm sorry." She stood, removed the Beretta from her pocket, and laid it on his desk.

He stared at it, faced with a dilemma. His detective had disobeyed a direct order but had made the biggest find in ten years. "Where did you find them?"

"In a storage area in the Second Avenue subway tunnel near Sixty-third Street. I have a map." She pulled it out of her jacket pocket and held it.

"How did you get there?"

"With someone I know. He's not on the job."

"You and I have a rip coming."

"Yes, sir."

"Meanwhile, we'll have to pick up those guns."

"Inspector, if I can say something. If Gordon is still alive and his kidnappers find out that we know about the guns, that could be a signal for retaliation."

"True." He looked at her and then away. "We'll have to post people at the site in case they check it. Stay where you are in case I have questions." He dialed a number from memory. "This is Insp. Frank Graves. I have an urgent notification for the chief of detectives. . . . Thanks, I'll wait for his call."

They sat in silence for a few minutes while Graves waited for the phone to ring. It was Saturday night. The chief of D's might be spending time with a fabled lady friend whose number was known only to the person Graves had spoken to. When the phone rang, Graves wrote down a number and then dialed it.

"Insp. Frank Graves here, sir. I have an urgent notification for you. I'd like to know where to deliver it. . . . That's fine. I'll be there within half an hour."

He hung up and started writing. When he finished, he passed the sheet of paper across the desk. It was a brief description of the events of the night. Jane corrected a detail and passed it back.

"I'll need the map," he said.

"I'll make a copy. It doesn't belong to me."

"Who knows about this find?"

"You, me, and the man who took me underground. He understands the importance of secrecy."

"You tell a boyfriend where you were going? A girlfriend? Your mother and father?"

"No, sir."

"Then it's three people. We keep it at three. I'm delivering this letter to the Major Case Squad in a sealed envelope. They'll get some detectives to go down and guard the stash. Get me a copy of that map. Make it two."

"Yes, sir."

When she returned to his office, he was writing the letter on a UF49, uniform force, in longhand, as Annie was not there to type it. He took the maps from her and set them aside.

"Anyone turn anything up?" she asked.

"Nothing. Manelli's girlfriend got herself a lawyer, but I don't think she has any idea where Manelli is. She's home now, and we've put a bug on her phone."

"That's good."

"That scumbag won't call her. She's a convenience in his life even if he's more than that to her."

"Right."

"Anything else you want to tell me?"

"I wish there were."

"Go home and sleep. You think all the missing guns are there?"

"I didn't count. But there are some grenade launchers, too."

"I'll have to find out if they were listed as missing. If you get any cute ideas this weekend, you check with the lieutenant before you do anything."

"I will."

"I'll see you Monday."

She picked up her jacket and dragged herself home.

"You still got your shield?" Hack's voice said in her ear.

"For the moment."

"I could use a few grenade launchers. Maybe we'll make a trip down there together."

"Hack, I've had my fill of rats and water bugs for the rest of my life. It's late, I'm tired, and after my tenth shower, I'm going to bed."

"I'll join you. We'll have a good brunch together."

"Don't wake me."

She didn't hear him enter the apartment, but she woke briefly when he slid in beside her. "If it's not Chief Hackett," she mumbled, "I'm too tired to get my gun."

"I'll give you mine."

She scrambled across the bed to press her bare back against the warm, hard, naked front of his body. He kissed her shoulder and dropped his arm over her side, letting it rest there. Comforted, she fell asleep.

[15]

IN THE MORNING he went out to pick up the Sunday papers and the fixings for a New York–style Sunday breakfast: smoked sturgeon, whitefish salad, a couple of other cold salads, cream cheese, and onion-covered rolls that whetted the appetites of true New Yorkers everywhere. Waiting for him, she set the table, took out the frying pan, and remembered Paris.

After the case they had cleared in Alphabet City, she and Hack flew to Paris. A planned long weekend grew to a week, which they took in March. Neither had ever been there. They stayed in a small, elegant hotel on a residential street on the Left Bank, half a block from the Seine, with a view of the Eiffel Tower almost directly across the river. They walked miles and took the Metro, the trains so quiet on their rubber tires that their arrival in stations surprised them. They ate sandwiches of French ham and cheese on baguettes, sometimes in cafés, sometimes on the move, and dined fabulously and expensively at night. It was the longest period of time they had stayed together, and Jane could not deny how much she loved it. After ten years of an evening here, an afternoon there, a precious weekend away from New York, she sensed their staying power, their ability to talk about anything, to make each other laugh, to disagree and move on. Until the last night.

The key in the lock brought her back to her West Village apartment. Hack tossed the papers on the sofa and brought the bags into the kitchen.

"I forgot to ask you if you needed eggs."

"I've got them."

"Put the papers away for later." He unpacked the groceries, and Jane set the fish and salads on the table, covering the bullet holes. When they had eaten, they moved to the living room, each taking a different paper to read. Eventually, they sat on the floor, tossing finished sections recklessly aside on the rug, making intermittent conversation, reading small items to each other, laughing. Hack picked up the *Times* crossword puzzle and started working on it, asking her for input until she worked her way over to where he was sitting to look at the clues herself.

It was two when they got off the floor and made their way to the bedroom, stripping each other as they went, leaving behind a trail of clothing, a living room that looked as though the heavens had opened and rained down newsprint, dirty dishes on the table in the kitchen, the puzzle and its clues on the sofa. In Paris they had made love in the afternoon and felt renewed. Anything you could do in a Paris hotel room, you could do in a New York apartment. They hadn't been together for a while; sleeping and eating and reading and puzzle solving had made them hungry. But they were always hungry.

He kept her close as one pleasure subsided and another took its place. "Jane?" The voice near her ear.

"Hmm?"

"Fuck sunsets."

Later they talked about the case. "Graves said they've bugged Manelli's apartment," she told him. "But he's such a creep, he won't even think to call his girlfriend."

"So they've got Defino somewhere, and you've looked in some likely places and he's not there."

"And now I'm stuck. I'm terrified that they've killed him. What do they need him for?"

"Maybe to bargain, although I don't see for what at this point. The kidnapping was almost an accident: A cop was there; they couldn't let him go because they thought he knew something he probably didn't know. They didn't think; they just followed their instincts."

"I suppose we can try to chase down every blue van, starting with Fords, in the five boroughs. And then find it came from New Jersey."

"Get your friend MacHovec on it. He shouldn't be spending a single second doing nothing."

"I'll talk to Curtis Morgan's wife," Jane said. "We've got her staying with a sister somewhere; I think I have the address. Morgan's friends may also be Manelli's friends. Maybe the bargain they want is for Randolph."

"The guy in Rikers?"

"Yeah. The one who set all this in motion. That swine."

"Don't get personal. Just do your job."

"Where did they put Defino?" It was a question to herself.

"Where the neighbors won't be aware of a body. I need my ice cream."

She grinned. "I picked up some chocolate syrup."

"You are one good woman, Bauer."

"Come and scoop it out of the container."

After he left, she checked her notes. Mrs. Morgan's sister also lived in Brooklyn, out near Kings Highway. That was far but not inconvenient to reach; the D train ran from West Fourth all the way out there. Jane took some unread parts of the paper with her and left the apartment.

The train ride was long and she finished the paper before she arrived. She walked up East Seventeenth Street to Quentin Road and found the apartment house for Mary Ann Gibbons. On the second floor she pressed the bell for 2C, and Emma Morgan herself opened the door.

"You're the detective."

"Detective Bauer, Mrs. Morgan. I'd like to talk to you."

"Where are you taking me?" She looked fearful.

"We can talk right here."

Emma Morgan backed up, letting Jane inside. They sat in the living room, a homey place with pictures of weddings and babies. The sister looked in, asked if they wanted coffee, and left them alone.

"Mrs. Morgan," Jane began, "we have a very serious situation. A police officer, a detective, has been kidnapped. We haven't received any word from his kidnappers. All we're sure of is that it ties in to the murder of Det. Micah Anthony ten years ago."

"I don't understand. My husband had nothing to do with that and I don't know anything."

"Your husband may not have known who killed Micah Anthony, but he knew the people involved in stealing the guns—guns that have never been recovered."

"He told me he didn't." She was starting to look uncomfortable. "He said he was in the wrong place at the wrong time and he got arrested with those men. He stood trial and he was acquitted."

"I know that. And I'm not here to besmirch your husband's name. I know he died a long, painful death, and I'm sorry for that. What I need to know from you is who his friends were that worked with him on the subway."

"You mean from the Lex?"

"I mean the Second Avenue subway. You said he was involved in the building of the tunnels."

She shrugged as though to dismiss the question. "It's so many years since he worked there. I haven't seen any of those people—it could be twenty years."

"What was the name of his supervisor?"

"Who, Collins?"

"Do you have a first name?"

"Larry, maybe, Larry Collins. No. Maybe it was Barry. It's hard to remember. I never knew him. Curt would come home and bitch about him. 'We took too long a break. We didn't clean up right.' Things like that."

"How about someone he liked, someone he maybe had a beer with after work?"

"That would be Holy Joe Riso," she said quickly.

"Holy Joe Riso?"

"That's what the men called him. He was a charmer. I met him a couple of times. He had me in stitches. His wife was this little woman who giggled a lot. They were made for each other, I used to tell Curt. He told the jokes; she laughed at anything he said."

"You remember where he lived?"

Emma Morgan shook her head. "I was never there. We met in the city once or twice for a drink or dinner. Curt liked him. I could see why. The union'll have his address."

"Anyone else, Mrs. Morgan?"

She closed her eyes. "Someone named Willie. I don't remember the last name. Oh, yes, there was also a Ronnie or Donnie something. Let me think. Parnell? Parelli? I think it was Parnell. They were friends for years, him and my husband. They even went fishing a few times, no women allowed."

"That sounds good." Jane looked up from her notes. "I'll take all the names you can give me."

Emma Morgan shook her head. "I'm surprised I remember that many. It's been so long. What are you looking for, Detective Bauer? What can these men tell you?"

"I don't know, but maybe one of them knows something that will help." She waited a moment, hoping for another name or two, but Emma Morgan was finished. Jane shook her hand, thanking her for her trouble. "If anything comes to you . . ." she said.

"I have your card. I'll call. But don't hold your breath."

Ten minutes later Jane was back on an almost empty D train heading for Manhattan.

On Monday morning she told MacHovec that she would keep quiet till Graves allowed her to talk. She knew Sean had figured out where she had gone, although he could not know about the find. By late the night before she was sure a detail of a boss plus a couple of detectives from the Major Case Squad had been dispatched to the site in the Second Avenue tunnel, where they would guard the boxes of guns and take into custody anyone coming near the storage area.

"I talked to Curtis Morgan's wife again last night," she told MacHovec. "She gave me some names of friends of his who worked on the subway. Also his supervisor, but it sounded like there wasn't any love lost between them." She passed the names across to him.

"Holy Joe?"

"That's what Morgan called him. A jokester, according to Mrs. Morgan. She met him a couple of times."

"I'll give it a try. These guys may have retired by now."

"Or died."

"Or been done away with," MacHovec said, meaning, she assumed, by the people around Carl Randolph.

Annie came by and said the whip wanted both of them in his office right away. She didn't accompany them, but McElroy was there, and he closed the door behind them.

"What I'm about to say is top-secret," Graves said without introduction. "Detective Bauer knows most of it." He had become formal in addressing them, and his face reflected the seriousness of the situation. "On Saturday night Detective Bauer and an unknown person went into the Second Avenue subway tunnel and found the cache of weapons stolen from the armory over ten years ago, the weapons that figured in the death of Det. Micah Anthony."

MacHovec gave Jane a look of surprise that was noticed by Graves. "I am told all two hundred twenty-six weapons are accounted for. In addition, several grenade launchers are packed away, ammunition, and some other assets. A lieutenant and three detectives from the Major Case Squad are guarding the find until we determine what the next move is. Defino's life is in the jackpot here, and we don't want to jeopardize it by removing the weapons. On that score, we are no closer to finding him than we were Friday night, although the team in the conference room has been looking into Manelli's life with a fine-tooth comb. We have a tap on Manelli's phone at the Franklin address on Minetta Street, but so far he hasn't called her. And her lawyer has ordered her to keep quiet.

"What I have told you doesn't leave this room. You don't talk to your wife and kids about it"—he looked at

MacHovec—"or your parents or your lover or your girl-friends." His eyes flicked over to Jane. "If you talk in your sleep, you'd better cover your mouth with duct tape. The chief of D's is personally involved at this moment." He stopped. "Any questions?"

Jane said nothing.

"The conference room is working on Manelli," Mac-Hovec said. "That leaves Morgan for us."

"Sorry. I meant to say that. Where are you right now?"

Jane briefed them on the previous night's interview with Mrs. Morgan. "Sean's about to look up the names she gave me."

"That sounds like a good move. See if you can get more out of her, high school friends, neighborhood friends. Find out what school he went to. How old was he when he died?"

"About fifty."

"And he worked on the subway in his twenties."

"That's the way it sounded."

"You have her work address?"

"She's a secretary at the Brooklyn Academy of Music. I'll give her a call."

"Get over there fast. Morgan's got to be the key, now that we know about the subway connection."

"Yes, sir."

"This unknown person who accompanied you in the tunnel. How sure are you that he's not involved?"

"I met him years ago, Inspector. I'd have to check records to find a date. He wouldn't have led me to the stash if he'd been involved."

Graves looked at his watch. "Get to work."

It was what Jane wanted to do most.

[16]

BAM, THE UNIVERSALLY used acronym for the Brooklyn Academy of Music, was on Lafayette Street in Brooklyn, not a long trip on the subway. Jane decided not to call first, in case Mrs. Morgan decided to take some time off. It was midmorning when she arrived, and she found Emma Morgan at her desk in an office with several other workers. As Jane entered, Morgan's eyes flitted uneasily from Jane to her coworkers, and she rose from her desk before Jane reached her.

"What is it?" she asked.

"I have to ask you more questions. It's urgent."

"I'll talk to my supervisor."

Jane watched as Morgan bent over a desk, then returned to the door. "Come with me," she said. She led the way to a grouping of comfortable chairs and they sat. "I've told you everything I know," she said. "I thought about it after you left last night, but nothing else came to me."

"I need to go deeper into your husband's past," Jane said. "I want names of friends of his from high school, from the old neighborhood, people he went to kindergarten with. Brothers, sisters, cousins."

"One brother is dead. His sister moved out to Los Angeles a long time ago. I haven't seen her in years. She didn't even make it in for Curt's funeral. One brother . . ." She faltered. "His brother Tim is in jail."

"What were the charges?"

"Armed robbery."

Nice family, Jane thought. "Where did he work?"

"A company out on Long Island that makes tools."

"He have a wife?"

"She divorced him after he was convicted. Not the kind that stands by her man."

"Where's he serving time?"

"Upstate in Attica."

"Let's go back to friends."

They sat for another half hour while Emma Morgan searched her memory for names, addresses, and phone numbers. Jane took several pages of notes. Finally, the voice stopped.

"Your husband was arrested shortly before he died," Jane said. "The man he was arrested with—how did your husband know him?"

"He never told me. When Curt left his job because he was sick, he just about went crazy. He was a man that needed something to do. He couldn't sit around and watch TV. He wasn't a cardplayer. He didn't have friends he could hang with. Everyone he knew was working. He met this guy somewhere—Sommers I think his name is—and Sommers was looking for someone to . . . you know, what they got caught doing. Curt would go out at night sometimes; I didn't know where, I thought maybe a bar. I didn't ask him. Even if he came home late, I just kept quiet. Then one night he didn't come home, and I got a call from him at two in the morning from the police station, telling me that I should get him a lawyer. That was the first I knew of what was going on."

"That's when he ended up in the hospital?"

She nodded. "He never came home again."

"I'm sorry."

"I can't give you anything else, Detective. I've given you his brothers, his sister, all the friends I can think of. I'm sorry that detective has been kidnapped, but my husband didn't do it."

"Thanks for your help." Jane got up and left Mrs. Morgan still sitting on her chair.

*   *   *

"That should be easy," MacHovec said, looking at the name of Curtis Morgan's brother. "I'll call Attica after I check him out. You up for a trip upstate?"

"Whatever it takes. How do I get there?"

"Fly to Buffalo and thumb a ride."

"Thanks."

"Where's the old Jane Bauer enthusiasm?"

"I lost it in a subway tunnel. You ever been down there?"

"Not in this life. Rats with four feet give me the willies."

"What've you got?" It was McElroy, standing in the doorway.

"Morgan's brother is doing a bit in Attica for armed robbery. Sean's checking it out."

McElroy closed the door. "Any connection to the TA?"

"Not from what Mrs. Morgan told me." She flipped open her notebook and gave him what she had.

"What about those TA people you mentioned this morning?"

"We haven't even had a chance to talk about it. I just got back from BAM, Loot."

"Maybe we should pull in a couple of detectives from the conference room."

"We may have to. And I may be on my way to Attica when Sean gets off the phone."

When McElroy left, Jane called for a sandwich to be delivered. This was not a day to take time off to eat. MacHovec's brown bag was on the floor as usual.

"Timothy Morgan's been transferred to Sing-Sing," MacHovec said as he hung up. "Or to be politically correct, Ossining Correctional Facility, which means he must've found God or turned his life around. He's a model prisoner. You can talk to him any time you want."

"Good. I can drive up tomorrow morning and do it all in half a day. What do you have on Holy Joe?"

"Joe's alive and well, living across the river in New Jersey. He took early retirement a couple of years ago. You can take a ferry and then a cab, you can rent a car, you can even have the fun of a bus from Port Authority. And a cab after that."

"New Jersey. It'll take all afternoon."

"It's not that far."

"Riso know I'm coming?"

"He said he'll be home all day."

Just as her sandwich came, Graves asked for them in his office.

"You going to see Morgan's brother?"

"Yes, sir." She explained where he was.

"You can do it tomorrow. Rent a car. Use your credit card. We'll square things and take care of the paperwork later. We're being careful not to alert anyone."

"Sounds good."

"What else've you got?"

She told him about Joe Riso and said she would leave for New Jersey in half an hour.

"Do that. Maybe you should go with one of the conference room detectives."

"Sure."

Graves told McElroy to pick one.

MacHovec then read off the results of his other queries, the names of old fellow workers of Curtis Morgan. He had located Barry Collins, Morgan's supervisor. "Sounds like a hard-ass." Collins would be working tonight and could be reached at the Forty-second Street station. MacHovec had the details. He had also located William Parnell, one of the friends Emma Morgan had mentioned the previous night. Parnell had a desk job now and would be at work Tuesday and Wednesday.

"I'll see him Wednesday," Jane said.

"You can't handle all these interviews yourself, Jane," Graves said, using her first name for the first time in several days.

"I know that, but I'd like to choose the ones I talk to."

"Fair enough. All right, reserve your car for tomorrow, get up to Ossining and back. Let's hope Curtis Morgan and his brother had heart-to-hearts."

When a doctor says, "Let's hope," you know he's run out of science. When a detective says it, he's run out of leads. Jane nodded and got to her feet. She had little time and much to accomplish.

"Make your rings," Graves said as she opened the door.

MacHovec offered to reserve the car, and she handed him her credit card as she ate. By the time he hung up, she had finished lunch and McElroy was at the door with a guy about her age.

"This is Det. Warren Smithson," McElroy said.

"Jane Bauer." She stood and leaned over her desk to shake Smithson's hand.

"Nice to meet you. We leaving soon?"

"Right now. We can take the ferry."

"I've got a car."

She smiled. "I like you already."

McElroy nodded. "Jane's the senior detective on the case," he said, then departed.

"If you don't come back today," MacHovec said, "here's the confirmation number on the car."

17

THEY DROVE THROUGH the Lincoln Tunnel and got to Joe Riso's house before two. The area was half high-rises and half little houses from another era. They talked on the way, Detective Smithson asking about Defino. It was obvious his group had exhausted every possible lead in trying to find Manelli.

Jane heard the dejection in her own voice, which had still not healed completely from shouting Defino's name in the Lex early Saturday morning.

"You guys close?" Smithson asked.

"We're partners." Her voice had a frosty edge.

They got out of the car and went to the door of Riso's house. A tall, lanky, muscular man, he opened it himself and gave them both a welcoming handshake. "Come in. We can sit in the garden. Lizzie made some lemonade."

They followed him through the living room to the backyard, and they sat at an umbrellaed table on comfortable outdoor chairs. The house was situated high up, and the breeze was so refreshing it was a pleasure just to inhale.

"I hear you want to talk about Curtis Morgan. Nice guy, Curtis. Got himself in some stupid trouble way back and ruined his life. But at least he stayed out of jail."

"Mr. Riso," Jane began, "that stupid trouble you mentioned. We think Curtis Morgan had someone in the TA he was working with or reporting to."

"Hey, don't ask me." He rolled up the sleeve of his left forearm, baring a large tattoo of a crucifix. "I worked with Curt, I drank with Curt, I think we even went out with our wives once or twice, but I didn't know nothin' about what he was involved in."

"When did you find out about his involvement?"

"When he was arrested. It was in the papers the next day."

"Did you talk to him about it?"

"After the trial I did. You know, they gave him back his job after he was acquitted. He said he was in the wrong place at the wrong time."

She was getting tired of hearing the phrase. "Curtis Morgan was involved in the theft of guns that he was going to sell for a lot of money."

"Curt? You got the wrong guy."

"Mr. Riso," Smithson said, "we already know we've got the right guy. What we're looking for is who he was working with."

"How would I know?" Holy Joe looked insulted. "I didn't have no part in that."

Mrs. Riso came out of the house at that moment with a tray of tall glasses of lemonade. As Emma Morgan had described, she was a little woman with a giggle. She left the tray, told them to enjoy it, and went back inside.

They each took a glass and a napkin. When Joe reached for his, Jane saw a simple cross tattooed on the back of his hand. She flicked her eyes upward to the vee of skin at his open collar. A chain around his neck with a cross hanging from it was tattooed on the visible skin. Holy Joe.

"A detective was murdered over those guns," Jane said.

"Curt was acquitted. That's good enough for me."

"It isn't good enough for us."

"You think I was involved in that murder? In that gun deal?"

"We think you may know something about it, and you may have an idea who else in the Transit Authority was involved with Curtis Morgan."

"You got the wrong guy." Joe pulled a pack of cigarettes out of his shirt pocket and tapped one out. He lit it from a book of matches and left the matches on the table. "Curt was a friend. If he was involved in something like that, he kept it to himself."

"Tell us about Barry Collins," Jane said.

"The supervisor? What a shit. Nothin' was good enough for him. Didn't matter how much you worked, how hard you worked, he was always on your back to do more, do better. If Curt was gonna kill anybody, it would've been him."

"I'm told he's still alive," Jane said.

"Only the good die young." He took a long pull on the lemonade and drew on the cigarette, flicking the ash on the patio. The loose, friendly demeanor had vanished. Holy Joe was under siege.

"If you know something, Mr. Riso," Warren Smithson said, "now's the time to come clean. We're sitting here talking to you. You know what that means."

"You done a lot of digging."

"Right."

"And you're gonna keep digging till everybody's in the shit."

"So tell us," Jane said.

Mrs. Riso poked her head out the door. "Joe, honey, you shouldn't be smoking."

"Give it a rest, Lizzie." He was angry and agitated. His wife retreated. He finished the cigarette down to the last quarter inch, dropped it on the brick patio, and stepped on it. "Look, I heard a few words once. I wasn't part of it. Curt had a friend, a piece of trash named Sal something. Guy was always looking for an angle, never held a real job. They hooked up with a third guy, the one that took the fall in the cop's murder. I don't remember his name. Black guy. I don't know how Curt knew him, maybe through Sal. He was the one stole the guns."

"Where did he steal them from?" Jane asked.

"Beats me. I just know there were guns and the black guy stole them. He was making a deal to sell them when they got busted."

"What happened to the guns?" Smithson asked.

"How should I know? Maybe they're in Sal's house. Anyone look there?"

"We looked there."

"So they're somewheres else." He moved his shoulder. "Look in the black guy's place. He's the one made the deal."

"How do you know all this?" Jane asked.

"I heard Curt on the phone once. He was talking too loud, and what he said didn't make sense. When he got off, I asked him what was going on. He said he was doing a little deal that would get him some tax-free cash, a onetime thing, he said. I asked him how much cash and he gave me a number, maybe ten thousand, maybe twenty, I don't remember."

"He talked about this on the phone?"

"He was in an empty office. I saw him inside and went in and got an earful."

"Who was he talking to?" Smithson asked.

"Damned if I know. He never said a name." He looked up at the house. "Lizzie, this is a private conversation, you mind?"

"OK, honey." She smiled brightly and backed away from the screen door.

"And he talked about the guns over the phone?" Smithson said.

"He said something that made me think guns. Look, this conversation was about ten years ago. I don't remember every word."

"Did he say where the guns were hidden?"

"I already answered that question. I didn't hear and he didn't tell me."

"If you're holding back, Joe—"

"I'm not holding back," Riso said, raising his voice. "I'm telling you what I never told anyone. I don't see what difference it makes. Curt's dead. He didn't kill the cop."

"How do you know?" Jane asked.

"All those guys were picked up at that place the black guy had somewhere over on the West Side. You think they would've killed a cop and gone right back to where they'd been? Where the cops knew they had a place? Those guys weren't crazy. They didn't know the cop was dead or they'd've scattered. Doesn't take a lot of brains to see that."

"You're a smart guy," Smithson said. "You got it all figured out."

Holy Joe gave Smithson a withering look. "I'm smart enough," he said in a low voice. "I keep out of trouble. And that's all I know, folks, so I think it's time for you to go." He pushed his chair away from the table and walked to the garden, hands in his pockets, looking at the shrubs that surrounded the yard. He bent and pulled a weed at the farthest point, the domestic gardener at home.

"Let's go," Jane said under her breath.

"He knows more."

"He's done talking today." Jane faced Riso's back. "So long, Joe. Thanks for everything."

Joe didn't answer. Jane and Smithson walked through the house to the front door.

Jane got back in time to brief Graves. Smithson joined her, but let her do most of the talking.

"You said you think Riso knows more," Graves summarized. "Are you telling me he was involved?"

"I don't know," Jane said. She looked at Smithson, who shrugged. "He was getting pretty agitated at the end. I think maybe Morgan told him more. He could know who else was involved, but it was in his best interests to keep quiet ten years ago—"

"Because of his job?"

"Yes. And if he talks now, well, he's been withholding evidence. He doesn't know where Defino is, and that's our priority now. We need to find out who the big guy in the TA is, the one who ordered the hit on Micah Anthony, the guy who's behind leaving the Beretta in Riverside Park and kidnapping Gordon. I'm seeing Collins, the supervisor, this evening, and then I'll talk to Morgan's brother, Timothy, at Sing-Sing tomorrow, see if either of them can take me a step higher."

"The guy in Sing-Sing may want to deal."

"I'll call you if I think he has something."

Graves considered this. "I'll be at my phone till I hear that you're leaving."

"Thank you."

Smithson left at five. Jane stayed in her office. Rather than go home and then walk back to the subway to go up to Times Square, she would have a bite nearby and then go uptown.

She called her father and had a leisurely talk with him. Then, on a lark, she called her daughter's number at the dorm in Kansas.

"Hello?"

"Lisa, it's Jane."

"Oh, hi. Sorry, I'm half-asleep. I'm studying for exams."

"Shall I call another time?"

"Oh, no. It's good to hear from you. I put a couple of pictures in an envelope for you last week but I haven't mailed it yet."

"That's OK." Jane was smiling. "When they come, they'll cheer me up."

"Is something wrong?" The young voice sounded concerned.

"I'm on a tough case. It's driving a lot of us crazy. How're you doing?"

"Not bad. It's just the biology that's killing me. I stayed up most of last night to study and now I can't keep my eyes open."

"When's the exam?"

"Tomorrow morning. Then I'm done till the next day. You know what? I got a job for the summer, right here on campus."

"That's great. Won't your parents miss you if you're not home?"

"Oh, they'll get to see me. We're practicing independence this summer."

Jane laughed. "I've been practicing it for twenty years and I still haven't got it down."

"I'll give you some tips if I learn any."

"I have to go, honey. I just had a few minutes and thought I'd like to hear your voice."

"I'm glad you called."

Strange feeling, she thought, being a mother twenty years after giving birth, strange and rewarding. She looked at her watch. Time for a quick supper.

Barry Collins's office was buried in the Times Square station. Without assistance, Jane could never have found it, but when she arrived Collins was there, sitting at his desk, his face contorted over a long printout. She knocked; he looked up, waved her in, and set aside the printout as though he were glad for an excuse not to contend with it.

"Yes?"

She held up her ID. "Det. Jane Bauer. I'd like to have a word with you about a man who reported to you some years ago."

"Sit down if you can find a place. What man?"

"Curtis Morgan."

"Morgan. Yeah. I remember Morgan. You may have to refresh my memory on details."

"He got caught up in the murder of an NYPD detective."

"Right. Tried and acquitted. I remember that."

"I understand he was given his job back after the acquittal."

"Not the same job. I never saw him again. He was reassigned. I think he died."

"He did."

"Got arrested again, too."

"Right on that also. You keep up with your former employees."

"It made the papers and the rumor mill. What do you want to know?" Suddenly he seemed anxious to return to the boring work he was glad to leave five minutes before.

"Besides the murder of the cop, that group was involved in stealing guns. You ever hear anything about that?"

"Me? You kidding? All I know about Morgan and his pals is what I heard on the news. I had a lot of people working for me at that time. We weren't friends, you understand? You go to dinner with your captain? You sit around and gab with him? It's all business down on the tracks. You get too friendly with the men, they don't respect you."

"You know who Morgan was friendly with?"

A small smile crept over his lips. "Yeah. I remember. A jerk named Joe something, Holy Joe. I can't remember his last name, but he covered himself with religious tattoos. Fucking idiot. He and Morgan were bosom buddies. If anyone knows what Morgan was up to, Joe does. Sorry I can't think of his last name."

"You think he was involved?"

"I didn't say that," Collins said quickly. "I said he knew Morgan, and if Morgan was up to something, Joe would know. Rizzo, his name was. No, that's not right."

"We think Morgan was connected to someone higher up in the TA who was giving the orders."

"I wouldn't know who. I used to get pretty dirty doing my job, but I lived a clean life."

"Who did you report to in those days?"

"Why are you doing this?" Collins said with annoyance. "Morgan's dead and they didn't convict anyone of the cop's murder. Why don't you leave it alone?"

"Because it's my job. Because a cop got killed. Because I

don't want firearms in the hands of the people on the street."

He shot her a look intended to shrivel her. She met it without blinking. Then he said, "I reported to Orville Chambers at that time. Is that it?"

"That's it for tonight, Mr. Collins." She made her way through the corridors and tunnels till she reached her subway line. In less than half an hour she was home.

[18]

SHE PICKED UP the car after breakfast and got on the West Side Highway going north, away from the bulk of the traffic. Beyond the northern tip of Manhattan it became the Saw Mill River Parkway. She took that to Hawthorne, picked up the Taconic Parkway, and continued to Ossining.

The prison stood at the top of the hill, where she left her car at the outer perimeter fence. Inside, she checked in, had her paperwork authenticated—Graves had taken care of that—and surrendered her weapon and her handbag. After the metal detector, she was escorted by a corrections officer to a secure conference room.

She had made good time and was seated with Timothy Morgan before ten a.m. He had the sallow look of a man who had spent time inside, but his arms were muscular, the skin taut.

"Mr. Morgan, I'm Det. Jane Bauer of NYPD. I'm here because your brother's name has come up in an old case."

"Who? Curt?"

"Yes. He was arrested about ten years ago in a case that involved the murder of a police detective."

"He was acquitted. And he's dead."

"We want to know who his contact was in the Transit Authority, the person who was running the operation."

"You came up from New York to ask me that?"

"It's important."

"Suppose I don't know."

"Then maybe you know something else that will give us a lead."

"A lead on what?"

"Stolen guns were found in the apartment where your brother was arrested."

"They belonged to the guy that rented the apartment. Curt didn't know nothin' about them."

"How long are you in Sing-Sing for?"

He paused, considering the implication of the question. "I got three more years."

"Long time."

"Yeah."

"Did Curt talk to you about the gun deal?"

"He didn't say anything that would help you."

"He talk about the killing?"

"He said he didn't know the black guy was a cop and he didn't know who killed him. *I* sure as hell don't know who killed him."

"And you don't know who stole the guns."

He didn't answer. He looked like a man who needed a smoke or a long walk, time to be by himself and think about alternatives to sitting in Sing-Sing for three more years.

"I know something," he said finally. "I didn't know before the trial. I stayed away from Curt till it was over. I've had my own problems." He looked around at the secure room they sat in. "I didn't want any more than I already had. But when he was acquitted, it was OK for me to talk to him; he wasn't a known convict."

Jane waited. She hadn't asked him for the location of the stolen guns because they already knew that, and if he gave them that, it would show cooperation but they wouldn't be any farther ahead than they were now. What she wanted was names. Why recommend a shorter sentence for old information?

"Curt knew the black guy from somewhere, the guy who was convicted. If he told me where, I forgot it. The black guy stole the guns from an armory in New York."

"Randolph," Jane said. "His name is Carl Randolph."

"Right." Morgan nodded. "Randolph. He stole the guns. Curt told him there was a safe place to hide them; they'd never be found. Problem is, Curt never told me exactly, and what I know isn't going to reduce my sentence a week."

"Let's leave that for a moment, Mr. Morgan. Do you know anything about the third man in the group?"

"Guy with an Italian name? Yeah, a little. Always seemed to me he was the loser in the pack. Never married, lived with his mother, for chrissakes. I think he was the guy who said he could sell the guns. That was his job."

"So Randolph stole them, your brother hid them, and Manelli was going to sell them."

"Right. But it didn't work out is what I remember. Manelli had a buyer who backed out. Then Randolph met this guy, the one who turned out to be a cop, and made a deal with him. It looked solid. He had cash, he had buyers, he didn't fuck around."

"Tell me what you know about the shooting."

He shrugged. "The buyer was there in the place in the Fifties. They were talkin' about when and how and how much and then he left. Next thing happens, the cops're breaking down the door."

"Anyone leave with the cop?"

"If he did, my brother didn't tell me. I wasn't interested in details. I wanted to know if my brother was involved. He wasn't."

"Did the cop know where the guns were hidden?"

"I couldn't tell you, Detective. We didn't talk about that."

"So you don't know if the cop left alone or if someone went with him."

He shook his head. "Curt just said when the cops came to the door—that was a few hours later—it was a surprise to him. That's all I know."

"You in touch with Randolph and Manelli?"

"Me? I never met them. I don't talk to no one. Even my lawyer don't always take my calls. I call Emma sometimes, my brother's wife. She's a nice woman, nicer'n the bitch I was married to. Soon as I got locked up, she filed for divorce. At least she don't get alimony from me."

"Let's get back to Manelli for a minute. If the deal Manelli made to sell the guns fell through, what did they keep him for?"

"Beats me. Maybe he told good jokes. Maybe they thought he'd rat them out if they cut him out of the deal."

"You're sure your brother never said that Manelli left that apartment with the cop?"

"Never said a word."

Which didn't mean he hadn't. She was running out of questions, and he had few answers that added to what they already knew. "OK, Mr. Morgan. What do you know that you think could help us out?"

"Two things. I can't give you names and places because I don't know them, but Curt told me the guns were hidden in the subway. Curt was a track man. He worked down there all his life. In the end, that was what killed him, the steel dust. He said they had a perfect place where no one would find them. That's all I can tell you. Those guns are somewhere down there. Curt never told me where, and I don't think he ever told anyone else."

That, at least, was the truth. "And the second thing?"

"I wanna know what it's worth."

"I'll be back." She signaled the officer outside the door and had herself escorted to an office with a telephone. Graves had said he would wait for her call, and he was as good as his word.

They talked for about five minutes, Jane emphasizing that

whatever Morgan had would not be a specific name and that
what he had told her about the location of the guns was true.

"Tell him we'll cut his bit in half. I'm pretty sure we can
get an ADA interested if we mention the guns and Micah
Anthony in the same sentence. The DA's office loves good
publicity."

"Thanks, Inspector."

"So that leaves me eighteen months," Morgan said when
she gave him the news.

"And leaves us with something but not as much as we
need."

He turned his face away from her and looked at the insti-
tutional walls and ceilings, as though they could measure
the depth of his misery, the difference eighteen months less
of it would make in his life. "You asked me who his contact
was in the TA. I don't know the name and I don't know if
Curt knew it. But I know one thing. The guy wasn't in the
TA. He was a cop, a transit cop."

"Thank you, Mr. Morgan." Ideas were flooding her
mind. "You'll be out in eighteen months."

[19]

ON THE DRIVE back to New York, Jane thought about
what she had learned. It explained a few things. Mrs. Appleby had said whoever was driving the car that picked up
Micah Anthony had to be someone he trusted. He would

trust a cop; he would recognize the car. If the cop was wearing a uniform, he would get in with little hesitation. That this cop was on the other side might not occur to him till it was too late. Morgan might have known who the cop was; Randolph definitely knew. That was ultimately the person Randolph had called from Rikers, the one who had seen to it that the Beretta was left in Riverside Park, because his call from Rikers had almost certainly gone to an intermediary point, one with no suspicion attached to it. From that point a call had gone to the transit cop.

The Transit Police and NYPD had merged in 1995, uniting them in a single department with almost identical benefits. Even so, they didn't pal around with each other and they tended to work on different kinds of cases. Jane had met Ron Delancey while she was chasing a perp into the subway. Other than him, she couldn't think of a single Transit cop whom she knew personally.

This new piece of information would give MacHovec a ton of work. He would have to identify all the transit cops who were active ten years before and see if some connection existed between one of them and Randolph or Morgan, a monumental task. Perhaps, she thought, a cop lived down in the Village at that time and had driven Micah Anthony there in the hope of getting him to talk before killing him. She made a written note to have MacHovec check addresses. This indefinite piece of information might evolve into a solid lead.

"Keep me busy till Christmas," MacHovec said when she told him and Graves what she had learned.

"You think this Transit cop drove Anthony down to the Village to his apartment?" Graves said.

"Maybe to find out what he knew. I'm sure they intended to kill him, but they wanted to see what they could learn first. Just happens, Anthony saw a chance to get out of the car and run when the car slowed down, but whoever was sitting next to him shot him as he hit the street."

"It's a theory," Graves said noncommittally.

"And maybe Defino's in that apartment now. Maybe when Manelli and his pals grabbed Gordon, they called this cop—if he's still a cop—said they were in the Village, asked what should they do with this cop who was investigating the Micah Anthony death, and the cop said, 'Take him to my apartment.'"

"It's a long shot." Graves was still smarting over the failed search in the Lex. "But if it works, we find Defino and the guy responsible for Anthony's killing at the same time."

"Right."

"Get to work on it," Graves said, looking at MacHovec.

Back in their office, they spread out a map of Manhattan on Defino's desk and drew a rough circle with the location of Anthony's body at the center. The car could have slowed when they neared their destination, or someone could have pulled a car away from the curb ahead of them, causing them to slow blocks from their destination. That area had been canvassed thoroughly several times and no one suspicious had turned up. The original team that investigated the shooting had returned to the block many times. That was in the file. No one had vacated an apartment precipitously after Anthony's death; no one had disappeared.

"You know," she said as MacHovec peered at his screen, "Manelli's never coming back."

"Right. He surfaces, we nab him for the kidnapping, assault, God knows what else."

"I wonder if the girlfriend's aware of that."

"Whatever she tells us, it won't make any difference to him. He's looking forward to the rest of his life underground unless he gets out of the country."

"Sean, there's been no body. I've got to believe—"

"I know."

She got up and went to Graves's office.

"Got something?" He was reading some department forms.

"I'd like to grab Smithson before he leaves and canvass the block they found Micah Anthony on. Tonight. When everyone's home."

"Can't hurt."

"I was just thinking that a Transit cop could have taken Anthony to a friend's apartment, an accomplice's apartment, a married sister's apartment. It's worth a try if Defino's in the same place."

"Catch him before he leaves."

It was quitting time, not that people were sticking to a schedule anymore. She went into the conference room. It stank of cigarette butts, coffee, and sweat. Smithson looked up, eyebrows raised, sensing that Jane was about to ruin his evening. She went over and explained what she wanted. To his credit, he said, "Sure. Let me make a phone call," and he called his wife and told her not to hold dinner.

Parking was allowed on most Village streets overnight, and as in Jane's neighborhood farther west, cars parked within inches of each other. Assuming that the car carrying Micah Anthony slowed for whatever reason, he would have had to skip between bumpers to reach the sidewalk, probably with someone carrying a gun at his heels. The original plan could not have been to shoot him on Waverly Place. Hundreds of people lived in the apartments that lined the street. Although it was late at night, the chance of someone hearing a gunshot or shouts was good, and they would want to avoid that. So it had to be that Anthony was taking advantage of an opportunity to run.

Jane and Smithson had eaten dinner before driving up to the Village in his car. They began their canvass at one corner at seven o'clock and worked their way down the street to the far corner. Jane kept a record of which apartments didn't answer the bell; she could come back the next night. On the assumption that Defino might be held in one of these apartments, they attempted to enter each one that answered and look around. No warrant was needed to eyeball what was visible.

The residents were a representative sample of the population of the Village. There were singles, male and female, couples, families, roommates both heterosexual and homosexual. Many of the younger people had not lived there ten years before; most of the older ones had and remembered the incident.

"I didn't hear the shot," an old woman said, "but my husband did. It woke him up and then I got up. He thought it was a car backfiring. We never dreamed it was a gunshot or we would have called the police."

Others told similar stories. One man thought he heard the car gunning its engine as it drove away. No one actually saw the car, but several apartments with windows facing the street had changed hands. That didn't matter to the canvass. If those tenants were gone, they weren't holding Defino on that block.

When they finished the first side, they stopped for coffee. It was a depressing job.

"Think it's still early enough to do the other side?" Smithson asked.

"Let's give it a try."

They were no more successful across the street, and it was close to ten when they finished. Smithson dropped her off at her building and went home. Upstairs, there was a brief message from Hack. She played it twice, enjoying the low rumble of his voice even more than the sense of the words. She would not call him back. It had been a long day and she didn't want to take any chances.

[20]

"JANE, TELL ME what's happening." It was Toni, Defino's wife. Jane had talked to her daily since Gordon's disappearance on Friday. It was nine o'clock Wednesday morning.

"We have dozens of people working on it, Toni. New ideas pop up all the time and we're acting on all of them."

"What you're saying is you're no closer to finding him than when he was kidnapped."

"Not exactly." Jane was becoming an artful hedger. She couldn't say what Toni wanted to hear, but she couldn't lie. Cops' wives were hard to deceive, and she owed Toni honesty. "We've come up with some good leads, and MacHovec is working night and day to follow up on them."

"I know I'm bothering you."

"You're not. I should have called you but I drove up to Sing-Sing to talk to a prisoner yesterday, and when I got back we canvassed a street in the Village."

"You're working so hard. I feel so guilty."

"Toni, you're number one on my list. When I know anything, you're the first one who'll hear after the inspector."

"Thanks, Jane." The voice was almost a whisper.

"Hang in there."

"I will." Now it was a whisper.

Jane hung up and took a moment to calm herself. It was always right there, the possibility that Gordon was dead, that the kidnappers had gotten nothing from him because he knew nothing, and they couldn't let him go because he could identify them.

"His wife?" MacHovec asked.

"Yeah. It gets harder every time."

"I'm going through blue vans registered in the five boroughs, starting with ten years old."

"Old ones first."

"Right. There aren't as many so it goes faster. When I get bored with that, I'm looking at Transit cops' addresses for ten years ago. I actually found one, but he was a rookie and lived with his parents at the outside of the perimeter."

"He still on the job?"

"Yeah. Lives in Queens."

So not a suspect. "I actually made a list last night of women on Waverly Place who might have been somebody's lover ten years ago."

"What'd you use, bra size?"

She smiled. "Partly. Also age. One woman said she had lived there alone ten years ago and when she got married, her husband moved in with her. She had the better apartment. So she's a possible."

"Not likely she's hiding Defino there."

"Not likely."

"Maybe we should just get the guys in the conference room to start canvassing from that point outward. It's too much for two people."

It was. She went to talk to McElroy.

"I'll OK it," he said, standing up. As Jane returned to her office, he went to the conference room.

Ten years before, when the first canvass had been performed, the purpose was to find witnesses to the killing, people who might have seen or heard the shots, glimpsed the car or any of its occupants. Even a partial license plate number might have helped to locate the car. Nothing had surfaced.

Because it had been assumed at the time that the location of the shooting was accidental, as Jane thought originally, the canvassers were seeking witnesses. Under the new theory, the killers were on their way to a specific apartment in the Village, an apartment connected to the killers. If they had reached their destination when Micah Anthony flew out of the car, then the connection was on that block. If the destination was around the corner or in the next block, a wider canvass might turn up the link. And Defino. They had to find Defino. Five days would have elapsed by that afternoon.

As she contemplated her next move, MacHovec tossed some papers onto the desk. "Blue vans," he said.

"Thanks."

She started reading the information written in MacHovec's clear, almost schoolboy print. All three vans were registered in Manhattan, two of them to what appeared to be small businesses, one to a man in his sixties.

"Probably not the one owned by the old guy," MacHovec said, reflecting her thoughts.

"But worth checking out. He might have a son or a nephew or a younger brother."

"I like the one registered to the video place. Anything could be going on in the back room."

"And probably is." She took her bag out of her drawer.

"You got your cell phone in case I come up with something else?"

"Thanks for reminding me. I plugged it in somewhere. There it is."

"And do me a favor, Jane. Don't go alone."

This new, gentler MacHovec still surprised her. She smiled. "Good idea. I'll grab someone in the conference room, if anyone's left."

Warren Smithson was left. They stopped at McElroy's office on their way out, McElroy happy that someone had something new to look at.

The video store was north of Fourteenth Street, the unofficial boundary between the Village and Chelsea. They took the subway to Twenty-third Street and walked from there. Smithson seemed happy to be out in the fresh air.

"So we're looking for the van that picked up your partner."

"The sector cops remembered an old blue van, nothing else. They could be holding him in the back room."

"Then you've given up on finding him in the subway."

"For now."

They turned a corner and found it. It was a good-size store, twice the width of most of the stores on the street. They walked in like a couple, Jane's hand through Smithson's arm. Several customers were at the counter and searching the shelves. A clerk was just coming out of the back room, carrying a couple of videotapes, perhaps porn, she thought. She nudged Smithson, who grunted, "Yeah," under his breath. He walked to the break in the long counter where clerks could pass through. Jane followed, holding her shield high.

"Hey," one of the young men behind the counter shouted.

"Hey, yourself," Smithson said, turning the knob on the door to the back room.

"You can't go in there." The voice was anxious.

"Sure I can."

Jane followed him into a room with a number of machines making copies of tapes.

"Where's your van?" Smithson asked the man who raced in behind them.

"What van?"

"The one registered to the store. You want me to read off the plate number?"

"I don't know where it is."

Jane turned to face him. "Take us to the guy who does know."

"He's not here."

She pulled out her notebook and a pen. "Looks like a Title Seventeen violation here. There's a U.S. code against copyright law violation. Big fines involved. Put your boss out of business."

"Gimme a break. There's a First Amendment."

"Not for reproducing and selling copyrighted material."

Smithson was pushing open the back door. "Not here," he said.

"The owner takes it home with him," the clerk said. He was young, possibly into his thirties, with thick, dark hair that moved as he tossed his head.

"Give me an address."

"I don't have it."

"Well, *find* it," Smithson ordered.

They followed him back to the store, where he had a frantic conversation with an older man. Thick Hair came back with an address on a slip of paper.

"I don't know if he's there, but that's where he lives."

"Thanks," Smithson said in a surly tone, and Thick Hair backed away from him.

The address was in the West Village, which was good news, Jane thought.

"That's in the perimeter," Smithson said. "I can't believe we could've gotten the right one the first time out. It'd be a first for me."

"Let's go."

On the sidewalk, Smithson put up his hand to hail a cab that was driving south. They hustled inside and he gave the address, pulling out bills a few minutes later as the cab slowed.

The building was on Bank Street, a structure ripe for gentrification. A cursory look around the block turned up no blue van. The name of the owner of the video store was Peter Montana, and next to one of the bells in the entry were the initials PM, an apartment on the second floor.

They pressed bells till someone buzzed them in. Then they ran up the stairs, found the door, and listened. A voice inside might have been someone talking on the phone or an afternoon TV show. Smithson pushed the bell.

"Yeah?" A man's voice.

"Mr. Montana, please open the door," Smithson said in a polite, calm voice.

The door opened. "Who're you?"

"Police detectives," Smithson said. Both of them had their shields visible.

"What the fuck?"

"Watch your language. Let's go inside and talk."

"What for? What do you want?" Montana, a husky man in his fifties, backed into the living room, a good-size room furnished with leather and fabric, pictures on the walls, and what might have been an Oriental carpet on the floor.

"You own a blue van?" Smithson read off the plate number.

"My business owns it. What about it?"

"We're looking for it. Where is it?"

"I parked it a coupla blocks from here. You can't get a spot nearby."

"Come with us and show us."

"What's this about?"

"Get your keys," Jane said. "We're in a hurry."

Montana looked from one to the other. Then he said, "I forgot. I don't have it today. I lent it to a friend."

"You forgot you lent it to a friend?"

"I'm sorry. You pushed in here and shook me up."

"Who's the friend?" Smithson asked.

"Just a guy. He needed to haul some stuff; he asked me for the van."

"When did you give it to him?"

"Uh, let's see. What day is today? Wednesday?"

"Wednesday," Jane said, wondering if he were playing for time.

"Could've been last Friday he took it. He came in the store for the keys and that's the last I saw of him. Or the van."

"What's his name?" Jane said, her notebook in her hand.

"Jack Spiegel."

"Address?"

"Gee, I'm not sure."

"You'd better get sure, Mr. Montana. What's his phone number?"

"I gotta look for it." He started for a back room, and Smithson and Jane followed.

The room was a home office, a cluttered counterpart to the neat living room. A computer with all its accompaniments sat on a table. Stacks of videos, boxes, papers, and files lay on the floor. A file cabinet was open, one folder standing vertically to mark a place.

Montana sat in front of the computer and pulled over a Rolodex, flipped through it, and removed a card. He passed it to Jane.

She copied the information and gave the card back. "Come with us, Mr. Montana."

"What for? I'm cooperating. What do you need me for?"

"To make sure you don't tell your friend Jack we're on our way." She called the Six and asked for a car to pick up Montana on Bank Street and hold him at the house for a couple of hours.

He was fuming when the car arrived.

"No calls till we get there," Jane said. "Check him for a cell phone." Then she and Smithson took a cab to the garage where his car was parked. They ran up the steps and slid into their respective seats in seconds. Her heartbeat was up and her spirits along with it. They drove south to an area of old buildings being converted into new, expensive lofts in the typical cycle of the city: When it gets too delapidated to be of use, renovate it and charge a fortune.

As they drove, Jane said, "We need backup, Warren."

"Call for it." When they got there, he parked in a no-parking zone and stuck his plate in the front window.

Two sector cars arrived seconds after they did. They

briefed the uniforms, one of whom went around the back of the building.

"There's an easy way out back there, also fire escapes. I'll watch the rear," he said when he came back.

Inside, real elevators had replaced the old ones that had been used to haul whatever product had been made in the building's former life. They grabbed the super, who came upstairs with them with a key to the Spiegel loft.

"I'm not supposed to do this," he said.

"But we're cops," Jane said, "and we'll cover your ass."

They moved quietly from the elevator to the door of Spiegel's loft. The uniform rang the bell and a tune played in chimes. No response came from inside. A second ring elicited nothing.

The super looked at Smithson, who nodded. Two keys were needed to open the door. Inside they stepped onto a beautiful hardwood floor into a huge living room with contemporary furniture, murals painted on the walls, and a complex set of switches that probably dimmed and raised the lights besides turning them on and off.

Smithson and the uniform disappeared down a hall to check out the entire apartment while Jane surveyed the living room for signs of life. A TV monitor as big as her fireplace hung on the wall, and a couple of pornographic magazines lay on a sofa. Otherwise, the room was empty. She moved into a huge kitchen filled with stainless-steel appliances, an island in the center. This is what a hundred-thousand-dollar kitchen looks like, she thought, opening drawers and cabinets, not sure what she was looking for—anything to tie Spiegel or his loft to Defino's disappearance.

She knew if she found something not in plain sight it could be challenged in court, but locating Defino was life-and-death, so she decided to chance it. From the other end of the loft she could hear Smithson and the uniform talking intermittently, nothing they said intelligible. Then, as she was opening a drawer, she heard a sound at the front door. Shit. Spiegel was coming back.

She took out her Glock and walked back to the foyer, watching the doorknob turn. Holding the gun at approximately the height of a man's chest, she waited.

The door opened and a woman screamed.

"Keep quiet," Jane ordered. "Get inside and close the door." She held her shield up in her left hand. "I'm Det. Jane Bauer, NYPD."

The woman was about Jane's age, well dressed and carrying a shopping bag from Bergdorf Goodman. She followed Jane's instructions, backing against the door to close it.

"Put the bag down."

The woman obeyed, clearly terrified.

"Who are you?"

"Renée Spiegel."

"Jack Spiegel's wife?"

"Yes. What are you doing here? Where's my husband?"

"We're here on business. Walk away from the door."

The woman came a few steps closer.

"What's up?" Smithson said. Then, "Oh. We have company."

"Mrs. Spiegel," Jane said. "She wants to know where her husband is."

"Funny, so do we."

"He left after breakfast. I haven't seen him since. What is this about?"

"How do we reach him?" Smithson asked.

She gave a cell phone number.

"Is he usually at work?" Jane asked.

The woman nodded.

"What's his business?"

"He's a furrier. Spiegel Furs."

"Address?"

She gave a downtown location. Jane had been to one of those places years ago—on police business—and she knew what it would be like: a showroom in the front and workrooms in the rear. The one she had visited had had something more than workrooms in the back, and she had made an arrest.

She turned to the uniform. "Stay with her till we call you.

No calls in or out. You got a number where we can reach you?"

He wrote it down, and Jane and Smithson left, stopping to tell the second cop to go upstairs and keep his partner company.

21

WHEN THEY ARRIVED at Spiegel's address, they circled the block, pushing the perimeter search to three blocks on each side, looking for the blue van. It wasn't there. Then they went into the building. The furrier was just what Jane expected. In the showroom, a young, good-looking woman sat beside a handsome, much older man while a model pirouetted in front of them, wearing a fabulous fur that probably cost half of Jane's annual income. The three were startled by the intrusion, but Jane and Smithson moved quickly to the back of the business, a woman chasing them, calling for them to stop.

Before reaching the work area, they came to a tiny, cluttered office where a man sat at a desk, talking on the phone.

"Jack Spiegel?" Smithson said.

He dropped the phone. "What is this?"

"Detectives Smithson and Bauer. Stand up and let me see your hands."

"What the—" But he pushed his chair back and stood, showing his empty hands.

Jane walked around the desk and patted him down. "Where do you keep your gun?"

"What gun?"

"The gun you use for protection. Don't move your hands."

"It's in the bottom drawer on the right side." He nodded in that direction.

Jane had her gun out. "Move out from behind the desk. Slowly." Satisfied that Smithson had Spiegel under control, she opened the drawer and removed the pistol. Using her cell phone, she called MacHovec and asked him to check for a license.

"It's registered, for Christ's sake," Spiegel said. "You think I keep an illegal weapon here?"

No one answered him. "Where's the van you borrowed from Peter Montana?"

"I'd like to know that myself."

"Don't give us a runaround," Smithson said. "Montana says he gave it to you last week. Where the fuck is it?"

"Look, I'm telling you the truth. I needed a van for a delivery. I called Pete and he said I could have his. I've borrowed it before; it's no big deal. We're old friends and we do favors for each other. I sent one of my men to pick it up Friday morning. He made the delivery and never returned the van. I don't know where in hell it is, and if you find it, I want it back."

"You report it stolen?"

"Not yet."

"This employee of yours, he do this as a regular thing?"

"He never did it before."

"You call and ask him what's going on?"

"I haven't been able to reach him. Not for lack of trying." Jane's phone rang. "Bauer."

"It's legal," MacHovec's voice said. "He has a permit to carry."

"Thanks, Sean." She snapped the phone shut. "The gun's legal."

"What did I tell you? I'm not a criminal. I'm an honest businessman."

"Whose employee steals vans. What's the guy's name?"

"Gregory Testa. He's worked for me for years. He wouldn't do something like this on his own."

"We need an address and phone number."

Spiegel looked at them. "May I check my Rolodex?"

"Just keep your hands where we can see them," Smithson said.

Spiegel leaned over the desk and flipped through the cards. He read off an address, also in Manhattan, and a phone number. "He doesn't have a cell. If he's not home, I don't know where to reach him."

"And he hasn't shown up for work since last Friday?"

"I saw him Friday morning. That's when I told him where to pick up the van. That's all I can tell you. You find him, you tell him he's fired."

"We find him, we'll do more than that." Smithson looked at Jane.

"I'll call the uniforms."

They let the sector cops go, and Jane told the uniforms at the Spiegel loft that they could leave. As they drove, she called MacHovec and asked him to put the van in the alarms as a possible vehicle in an armed robbery. This would put the uniforms on guard without broadcasting the real reason for the stop. If the van was spotted, it would be taken in for examination. Then she called the Fifth Precinct for backup. Smithson zigged and zagged toward the Mercer Street address, a block west of Broadway between Broome and Grand Streets, an area where gentrification had made its mark. But many buildings were still almost uninhabitable, just waiting for an enterprising builder with bucks to move in and do the kind of job that had been done on Spiegel's residence. Eventually, Jane feared, all but landmarks would succumb to the real estate industry, gutting the rich historic past out of the city, enriching the rich and pushing the poor into ever poorer circumstances.

Smithson came to a hard stop, jolting both of them. He shoved the plate back in the window and jumped out of the car.

Testa's address was an old law tenement, a building that dated to the turn of the century or earlier. As Jane reached

the curb, a radio car squealed to a stop and double-parked
on the far side of the hydrant in front of Smithson's car.
Two uniforms leaped out and Smithson quickly advised
them of the situation. One uniform took off for the rear of
the building and the three of them went inside, finding the
name Testa on the fourth floor. They got someone to buzz
them into the lobby. A knock on the super's door produced
only silence. They went up the stairs quietly and rang the
bell, which sounded loudly inside.

"Yeah?"

"Hey, Mr. Testa?" Jane said, using her girlish voice. "It's
Jane from downstairs. Can I talk to you?"

"Who?"

"From downstairs. The super said I should come up."

Two locks opened, then the door. Smithson and the uniform charged inside, grabbing Testa, who spewed a series of
obscenities as Jane dashed past them to search the apartment.

It was empty. "Shit," she said both aloud and to herself.
Where did they have him? She went into the main bedroom
and looked around. It was messy but showed no evidence of
another person. She opened the closet, found nothing but
clothes and shoes, then went into the other bedroom.

Something there was different. She took out one of the
two pairs of rubber gloves she always carried in a plastic
bag and put them on before entering. A single bed, little
more than a spring with an old mattress on it, sat in the center of the room. A cursory glance along the wall, where a
window led to a fire escape, showed accumulated dirt and
dustballs. They had moved the bed so it would not be near
the window.

The bed was unmade. Food garbage dotted the floor, paper cups, pizza boxes, plastic utensils, used and unused. Her
heart racing, she opened the closet door, took out her flashlight, and swept the interior. Some men's clothes hung on
wire hangers, and a pair of shoes were on the floor. She
picked them up. Could they be Defino's? She didn't know.
They were black leather, lace-ups, very plain. The clothes
were not his. She remembered what he was wearing on Friday, and besides, they were too large for the wiry Defino.

She pushed the shoes aside. Something black lay on the closet floor. She bent and picked it up. With her rubber gloves, she could not feel the texture of the item, but the size and shape were recognizable. She flipped it open.

"Holy Mother of God," she whispered. Inside were Defino's shield and photo ID.

[22]

SHE RAN BACK to the living room, where Smithson and the uniform were keeping watch on Testa. "Cuff him," she said to the uniform, whose name she had already forgotten. She opened the ID wallet and showed it to Smithson.

"What the . . ." Testa looked nervous.

"You son of a bitch," she said. "Where is this man?"

"What man?"

"*This man,* you—" She shut her mouth, trying to control her rage.

Testa looked at the ID photo. "Where'd you find that?"

"I'm asking the questions, Testa. You're answering them. Where is this man?"

"I don't know. I don't know what's going on."

"Tell me everything you know, and make it quick. If this man dies, you're an accessory to murder. Unless you killed him yourself."

"I didn't kill nobody. I picked up a van on Friday morning to make a delivery for my boss."

"What's his name?"

"Mr. Spiegel."

"And who gave you the van?"

"Guy named Montana, owns a video store. I went over, I picked up the van, I did what Mr. Spiegel asked me to do. Mr. Spiegel said, 'Bring it back to Mr. Montana when you're done.' I got done early, so I called a friend."

"What's his name?" Smithson asked.

"Charley Farrar. And I says, 'Charley, I got a van for the afternoon. You wanna take a ride?' and Charley says, 'Sure. Pick me up.' So I pick him up and he says, 'You know what? A friend of mine over on Minetta Street, he just came back from vacation. Let's drive over and say hello.'

"So I drive over to Minetta Street and I leave the van like I'm making a delivery, and we go upstairs and Charley rings the bell. His friend opens the door and then everything goes crazy."

"What happened?" Jane asked.

"His friend is inside, Sal something. And another guy. Sal says something quick to Charley, we go inside, and him and his friend, they take this guy down." He snapped his fingers. "Just like that. They just fall on top of him and Sal cuffs him. Charley calls me over; I should make sure the guy doesn't get up. So I sit on him." Testa probably weighed one-ninety. "Then this guy Sal, he goes in the back, comes back with a raincoat, a black one, throws it over the guy, and we take him down the stairs, careful-like, so no one sees us. Do I know he's a cop?"

"So it's three of you and the cop."

"Yeah, Charley, his friend Sal, and me. I run out the front door and unlock the back of the van, open the doors, and go back into the building. This cop, he's like a wild animal. He's kicking and elbowing and trying to get away. But he doesn't make any noise because it turns out this guy Sal, he taped his mouth shut with duct tape."

"Then what?"

"Then we get back in the van, I'm behind the wheel, the other two are in the back trying to tie up the cop, who's still fighting them."

"Where did you go?"

"We didn't know where to go. Charley, he's got a wife, we can't go to his place. This guy Sal says there's another cop out with his girlfriend, so I say, 'OK, bring him to my place.' And we come here."

"How long was he here?"

"Too long. I thought this was, like, for an hour or so. Those guys, they don't know what to do. You can't kill him; he's a cop. I don't know what's going on. They won't let me get the van back to Mr. Montana. I can't go to work. I got this cop in the bedroom."

"Answer my question," Jane said. "How long was he here?"

"Till last night. They gave him something to knock him out and we got him down to the van and they drove away."

"Was he alive?"

"Yeah, he was alive. We fed him. We took care of him. But I'm gonna lose my job over this."

"You already lost it," Smithson said.

"Does Charley Farrar work?" Jane asked.

"Yeah. He's got a good job, works for the TA."

OK, Jane thought. We've got the connection. "Did he go to work this week?"

"He called in for time off."

Charley could go back to work as long as Gregory Testa kept quiet, but Manelli couldn't go back to his apartment ever again.

"Where did they go?"

"For a ride."

"A ride *where?*"

"Charley said something about his sister had a place in the Rockaways, a summer place. She wouldn't be there for a couple of weeks. Maybe that's where they went."

"Tell us where the house is."

"I don't know where the house is. How the fuck should I know? I don't know Charley's sister."

"He call her?" Smithson asked.

Testa thought about it. "Yeah, I think he did."

"From your phone?"

"Yeah. From this phone here."

Jane flipped her cell phone open and called MacHovec. Quickly she outlined what they had and what they needed, a list of numbers called from Testa's phone in the last forty-eight hours.

"You got it," MacHovec said. "I'll get McElroy in on this. Where can I find you?"

"Use my cell. We'll take this guy in now and head out to the Rockaways in Smithson's car. You get something, you give me a call before you tell McElroy."

"Done."

Testa had listened to the conversation with obvious distress. "Where you takin' me?" he asked when Jane got off the phone.

"To the precinct."

"I didn't do nothin'. I'm an innocent man. All I want is to get that van back and go back to work."

"You should have thought of that when you were kidnapping a cop."

The two uniforms took charge of Testa, and Jane and Smithson started driving toward Long Island. Smithson knew his way and he leaned on the pedal, putting his flashing light on the roof and using his PD plate at tolls. As they drove, MacHovec called back and said, "I've got the address. There were only a few calls from that number yesterday. One of them was to a number assigned to a Richard Porter, who also has a phone in the Rockaways. The phone company confirmed it's the same Richard Porter." He gave her the address and she took it down, juggling the phone and the pen. "I'm taking it to McElroy now."

"Good work. Tell him we're on our way."

The Rockaways were as far as you could go in Queens, to the shore of the Atlantic Ocean and to the edge of Long Island. They lay at the end of a peninsula jutting into the Atlantic Ocean with the bay on the other side. Part of the borough of Queens, it ran from Rockaway Point on the west to the Nassau County line on the east, the line marking the end of the city and the beginning of Long Island. The house owned by Richard Porter was in the One Hundredth Precinct.

They passed from Manhattan through the Brooklyn Battery Tunnel, once the longest tunnel in the world. They exited onto the Brooklyn-Queens Expressway, familiarly known as the BQE. This took them around the curve of Brooklyn with its view of the Statue of Liberty and the Verrazzano Narrows Bridge. Smithson got off at Flatbush Avenue and grabbed his PD plate to avoid the toll on the Marine Parkway Bridge. On the far side, they were finally on the Rockaway Peninsula, traveling east on Rockaway Beach Boulevard.

As they drove, their phones rang several times and Jane answered. Four detectives, two from the One Hundredth Detective Squad and two from the Precinct AntiCrime Unit, would meet them in two unmarked cars a block away from Thursby Avenue in Arverne, where the Porter house was located, between Beach 72 Street and the bulkhead above Vernam Basin. It was an area of houses built before World War Two as summer homes, most of them long ago converted to year-round residences with the addition of heating systems and storm windows.

Smithson stopped behind the second unmarked car, and they got out and introduced themselves. One car had driven down Thursby Avenue and noticed no unusual activity. The house itself was quiet, with no cars visible. The missing van was also nowhere on the street and probably too large for the old garage at the end of the narrow driveway.

They moved in a convoy around the corner and stopped before reaching the Porter house, a two-story wood frame on a stone and concrete foundation. The house was covered with siding over the original clapboard, painted a drab white and needing a fresh coat to perk it up. The shingle roof sloped on both sides, and a wooden porch ran the width of the house and along the left side.

Two detectives went to watch other doors, and the remaining four mounted the porch steps and walked across the gray peeling deck to the door. One of the precinct squad detectives rang the bell. No answer.

He knocked hard and called, "Anyone home?"

A neighbor opened a door and stood outside, watching.

"We go in?" the detective said.

"Now," Jane said.

The door broke open easily, no match for the shoulders of the two detectives. Made of wood and fastened with a simple lock, it was old and painted many times. In New York City apartments, fire doors were reinforced with steel, and only on television could a man's shoulder do the trick.

They walked in, the silence thick. Then there was a sound, something falling upstairs. They all took off.

Two bedroom doors were open and the rooms empty. The third door was shut and locked. This one took only one shoulder, the wood splintering before the lock gave way. They stepped through the hole and found Gordon Defino.

The bus from Peninsula General Hospital came so quickly, Jane thought it might have been camped around the corner. She rode with Defino while Smithson followed in his car; she needed a ride back to the city. Defino had been barely awake when they burst into the room, lying on a bed made for a child. Stuffed animals and rag dolls were strewn on the floor, as though thrust from the bed. He was filthy, dried blood on his face, either drugged or dying, and both possibilities scared the hell out of her. The only word he said was, "Toni." There was something to be said for marriage.

She assured him that Toni would be her second call, but he had lapsed into unconsciousness and probably hadn't heard. In the ambulance she called McElroy, who let out a cheer at the news; then she called Toni, who was too distraught to speak. Jane put one of the paramedics on the phone to tell her where they were going. When they were done, she held Defino's hand and kept talking to him. His eyes flickered once or twice, giving her hope that some of what she was saying had gotten through.

A medical triage team was waiting for him at the ambulance bay, and moved so quickly she felt cheered. Smithson joined her, her new, temporary partner, and she realized how much had happened since Friday afternoon, when she sat drinking coffee with Judy Franklin, leaving Defino in the apartment with Manelli.

They sat in chairs near the emergency room, not talking much. Jane was afraid her cell phone would lose power, and she pulled out a plug for a lamp no one was using and plugged it in.

"Don't let me forget it," she told Smithson.

"Use mine," he offered. "You've been using yours all day."

She did, calling McElroy, who put Graves on. Their voices had changed since that morning; the tension was gone, their man had been saved, and by the most rudimentary of police work. Graves said "good job," a little grudgingly, she thought. He hadn't gotten over her disobedience on Saturday night. He would not forget to exact penance from her, but she didn't care. They had found Gordon alive.

She gave Smithson the phone, found a pay phone, and used a phone card to call Hack.

"You OK?" he asked.

"We found him, Hack. He's alive."

"Good job. Tell me."

She did it quickly, leaving out most of it.

"You don't sound good."

"I'm OK. It's just—it was so close, Hack. He looked so awful."

"I'll bring dinner tonight and we can talk."

She smiled. "OK. I can use some good talk."

Toni arrived just as the doctor came out with a report. Defino was dehydrated and under the influence of a sedative that would wear off in the next couple of hours. He had been kicked around and might have a fractured rib or two. They would give him tests and monitor him for a few days before they let him go home. The doctor took Toni in to see him briefly. She came out with a smile and a tearstained face.

"He wants to see you," she said to Jane.

Jane looked at the doctor, who said, "Two minutes. No more," and she followed him to the room. Defino lay on two pillows with his eyes closed, IVs in his hands, monitors near the bed.

"Gordon?"

He opened his eyes and raised a hand, reaching for her. "Jane, c'mere." His voice was raspy and he looked like hell. "Sit down."

"You're going to be OK."

"I know. Just out for a while."

"I heard."

"How . . . ?" He cleared his throat. "How'd you find me?"

She told him, racing through the search for the van as though she were reliving it. "It was the first van we looked for, just a stroke of luck. We've learned a lot, Gordon. I'll tell you all about it when you're home and feeling bored."

"I still don't get—"

"Detective," the doctor's voice sounded sharply. "That's a long two minutes."

She grinned at Defino and squeezed his hand. "Get back soon. I miss you."

A weak smile fluttered over his lips and his eyes closed.

Entering 137, they had to dodge TV cameras. McElroy and Graves were waiting for them upstairs, along with several of the conference room detectives and a few others from the squad. Applause greeted them. The rescue of a cop was a big deal.

After a lot of handshakes, Graves asked them if they wanted to be interviewed for the evening news.

"Let Warren take it. I want to get home."

"Not without you," Smithson said.

Nice, she thought. She would remember that.

McElroy let the cameras up and they stood before the microphones in the briefing area, saying little because they were still looking for the van and the two missing men.

"Just a lot of rudimentary police work," Jane said.

"And rubber and shoe leather. And cooperation from plenty of good people," Smithson said.

Graves took over, his good looks and smooth patter bringing smiles from the interviewers. Jane ducked to her office, checked her messages, made a quick call to her father to watch the news, and went home.

23

HACK ARRIVED SOON after Jane did, carrying a bag with a dinner of hot Japanese food, a bottle of sake, and chopsticks. While Jane warmed the sake, he set the table, covering the two bullet holes with dishes. The holes bothered him. He had wanted to fill them in with wood putty but she wouldn't let him. All she allowed was for him to sand the rough edges.

They ate and talked, she more than he. The tension of the day dissipated with the food, wine, and talk, and with the easy feeling of being with him.

"I cost the department a lot of money," she said when they were clearing the table. "That foray into the Lex must have cost a bundle."

"You went with your intuition. It's never a hundred percent, but yours is on the high side. Graves'll make you give up some pay, but you've probably got as much lost time as I have and it won't cost you anything." Lost time was hours worked without pay and banked at time and a half. She could use it at her discretion, and she could trade it in to pay for Graves's punishment.

They sat down in the living room and the phone rang almost immediately. It was Flora Hamburg.

"So you found him alive and got your face on the news," she said when Jane answered.

"Flora. Yes, we found him. It all worked out. He'll be home in a few days and he'll be fine." She glanced over at

Hack, who was grinning at her. Flora wasn't one of his favorite people. "I could have done without the TV, but you
know Frank Graves: The more the better."

"And your father will love it."

"He called already. He thinks I'll get a Hollywood con-
tract."

"What, and leave me in the lurch?"

"Not a chance."

Hack came over and put his arm around her.

"I gotta go, Flora. I'm exhausted and tomorrow's a
workday."

"Glad you're OK and it worked out."

"So what's on Flora's mind tonight?" Hack said when she
hung up.

"Just checking on me. What's with the two of you? You
never talk about it, but whenever she mentions your name,
she says 'that son of a bitch Hackett.'"

He laughed as they walked back to the living room. "An
unforgiving woman. Like most, I'd guess."

"So what happened?"

"It was a long time ago; I couldn't give you a year. I think
I was a captain at the time. No, maybe still a lieutenant, and
maybe she was a captain, too—so ten, eleven years ago. I
knew of her but I don't think we'd ever met. I got word of an
opening for a sergeant and I had a great one working for me,
smart as a whip. The grapevine said the guy who got the job
would serve a short period to learn the ropes and get a
non–civil service bump-up in salary, almost to the lieutenant's level."

"SDS," Jane said, referring to a Supervisory Designation
Salary. "Suds money." That referred to the beer the guy
would lavish on the cops and detectives who had made him
look so good.

"Right. Flora had a candidate too, a woman—"

"Of course," Jane interjected. Flora's life mission was
moving women up in the job.

"Of course. And she got pretty nasty about it. My candidate was much better qualified than hers and I said so, and
she didn't take it well. My candidate got it."

"And she never forgave you."

"As I said, she's not the forgiving type."

"So who was the guy? Did he work out?"

"Ah." He was enjoying this. "Interesting question. Yes, my candidate worked out and went on to lots of good things. But there's something you missed, something that ticked Flora, and that's what she'll never forgive me for."

"I'm not following you."

"My candidate was a woman."

"That's a good punch line, Chief. You're right; she'll never forgive you. It took away her best argument."

"Exactly."

"You're very up tonight, Hack. Something doing? You turning the Bronx around single-handedly?"

"Do I look like the Messiah?"

She laughed. "So tell me."

"All in good time. Let's have our ice cream. It's getting late."

After he left, she thought about his mood. He was a man who could switch from dark to light. His work was the greatest influence on his temperament, and she could often discern just from the tone of his voice on the phone whether something had gone wrong or less frequently, if he had heard good news. In the ten years they had been together, she had learned to read the moods, to sense when to try to change them and when to leave him alone to work through them himself.

It had taken a while. Ten years ago, when they first started to see each other, they were on their best behavior. They met for a furtive cup of coffee or a drink at a bar, often with other cops around. Then a day came when he wanted to see her alone. He would drive into the city to pick her up instead of taking the train, and they would sit and talk, eat Chinese in the car, and talk some more. A New Yorker and a cop with a law degree, his bag was city politics and deparment politics, but his interests extended well beyond that. He was a family man, too, and he spoke often of his daughters and his parents, but never mentioned his wife.

He had described his marriage once as having drifted away or off course; she couldn't remember the exact words, but it was not a subject of further conversation.

Her mother was still alive at that time, and she told him one cold evening that she was adopted, that she felt lucky beyond anything she could explain to have ended up with her parents. He touched her hand while she spoke, sending heat through her body, but that was the extent of their intimacy, talking and touching hands. The tension drove her nuts. She had made up her mind, even if he hadn't.

She could not recall clearly how long the courtship took. It was more than days and less than months, probably several weeks, maybe a bit more. One night he drove her home—she lived in the West Eighties at that time—and a car pulled out of a space as he turned onto her block. He slid into it and she swallowed and said, "You want to come up?"

"You know I want to come up."

"Then let's do it."

It had come out sounding flip, which she hadn't intended, but he didn't seem to notice. Inside the apartment, their relationship changed forever. He paused only long enough to put his gun on top of the refrigerator—hers was in her bag—and then nothing stopped until they lay resting beside each other on her bed, the faint taste and scent of sweat and tobacco and satisfaction wafting between them.

It was what she always thought of as the moment of truth, the time when someone said, "See you tomorrow," or "Jeez, is it that late?" or "Shit, I'll miss my train if I don't run." She listened to the silence that night, waiting for his truth to be spoken.

"We're a good fit," he said finally. He reached out to the night table and she realized she had not thought to give him an ashtray. He was a smoker at that time; he smoked until she severed their relationship the previous year and then couldn't live with her decision.

She sensed he had measured his words carefully, and she measured hers with just as much precision. "You're a good lover."

"I hope," he said, his right hand barely skimming her left arm, "that I can be more than that and better than that for you."

"And me for you."

"Good enough." He sat up and she touched the smooth line of his back. "You mind if I smoke?"

"I'll get you an ashtray."

"Stay there; I'll get it myself."

It was the quietest time they had spent together, a warm, intimate quiet, two decisions made, one cigarette smoked, a silence they had earned after the weeks of spicy chicken and unending talk. When he started to dress, she told him to shower.

"I'll shower when I get home."

"Do it now, Hack. She'll know. I'm all over you."

He gave her an odd look and took her with him, and they somehow managed to get clean under the clogged showerhead—he installed a good one the next time he came—and then he left. She had broken her rule about married men, but she knew she was in love with him, and for the first time in a long time, she refused to consider consequences. She just wanted to see him again. And again.

When the phone rang about an hour later, she knew it was Hack, and she answered with, "Hi."

"You a mind reader?"

"Not exactly."

"I just found a pay phone and I thought . . . How's Thursday?"

"Thursday's fine."

"No more Chinese, OK?"

"I'll pick something up."

"I'll get there when I get there."

"Sounds good to me."

"Jane?"

"Yes?"

The phone clicked and the coin dropped.

"I'll see you Thursday."

[24]

THE MOOD AT 137 the next morning was expectedly up. Graves was a happy man, and McElroy wore a smile that never faded. To add to the good feelings, the van had been found overnight, parked on the street near Peter Montana's video store. It was already in custody, to be worked over by the crime scene unit.

Jane called Defino at nine, elated to hear a clearer voice and the intelligibility that came with the sedative wearing off. He wanted to know the whole story, and she gave him as much as she could in a few minutes.

"You looked *where?*" he said when she mentioned the foray into the Lex. "The whip must've been ready to kill you."

"He was. He still is, but he's keeping it to himself till this is over."

"Shit, where'd you get the Lex from?"

She told him about Curtis Morgan and said there was more. She didn't want to mention the Second Avenue subway over the phone. He would get a charge out of that when she finally let him in on it.

McElroy came by and said that Graves wanted to see them in his office. Smithson was already there.

"The three of you did real good," the whip said. "Detective Smithson, you'll get a recommendation from me, through channels, to the chief of detectives. You deserve it. Glad you and Detective Bauer worked well together."

Smithson thanked him. A letter like that from a man like Graves would go a long way to giving him an upgrade, not to mention another bar for his medal board, and maybe an eighth of a point on the next sergeants' promotion list.

"I'm releasing the detectives in the conference room to return to their commands effective sixteen hundred tomorrow. That should allow for a wrap-up of the paperwork and an extended lunch. Until Detective Defino is allowed to return to work, you can stay on as Detective Bauer's temporary partner, if you'd like to."

"Sure," Smithson said. "Thank you, sir."

"OK with you?" Graves looked at Jane.

"Fine. Very good."

"Then that's settled. I'll square it with your lieutenant. I'd like to remind you all that our case is the murder of Micah Anthony, just in case anyone's forgotten. What you two dug up yesterday about the TA worker Charley Farrar is the best lead we've had since what Jane and Sean developed about Curtis Morgan. Let's find out where Farrar works, where he lives, who his friends are. You've got his sister's name and address if you need it. The Rockaway cops are keeping a watch on that house where Defino was found in case those two mutts turn up there. And we'll find out from the crime scene folks what they dig up." He looked around. "Any questions?"

Jane wanted to know what was happening with the cache of guns in the subway, but that was a secret, even from the detectives in the conference room, so she kept quiet.

"OK. Let's get some work done around here for a change." Graves offered a small smile to indicate he was being humorous.

Smithson moved into the office and sat down at Defino's desk. He brought little with him, just a jacket he hung on the pole. He was a shirtsleeves man.

"Here's what I've got," MacHovec said, assembling papers. He handed two copies off to them and started reading. "This guy Farrar's been with the TA since he was twenty. I can't check his career against Morgan's—you know about that, Warren?"

"Not yet."

"Jane'll brief you. Anyway, he's done the same kind of work Morgan did, so we can assume they met somewhere earlier in their careers. You've got Farrar's address there, his wife's name, all the stuff I could get on his sister. Looks like he pulled his sister's house out of a hat to hide Defino in."

"That was my impression," Jane said. "Testa didn't want him in his place. Manelli couldn't use the apartment he lives in with Judy Franklin, and Farrar's married. Not sure his wife would've approved of a kidnapped cop in her guest room."

"I gave you everything I could get on his career. Don't know if it'll help," MacHovec said.

"Did he ever work for that guy Barry Collins, Morgan's supervisor?"

MacHovec riffled paper. "I'm not sure." He made a note.

"Or if he knew Holy Joe Riso."

MacHovec was scribbling. "I'll see what I can do. But it's sure starting to look like this guy Farrar was a player in the Micah Anthony case. I'll look for a family member that could be a Transit cop."

"Good idea. Meanwhile, let's get started looking for him."

"He could've gone to work today," Smithson said. "Even if he knows that Defino's been found, he doesn't know Testa gave him up. He and Manelli dropped Defino off and returned the van, maybe put the keys through the mail slot at the video store."

"Farrar must have been the person who drove to the Catskills last week to talk to Manelli," Jane said, remembering what Judy Franklin told her. "And Farrar could be the guy Randolph called from Rikers after Gordon and I visited him."

"Nice when it falls into place," Smithson said.

"Nicer if we can find Farrar."

"Let's get on it."

They started by checking the TA to see if Charley Farrar had reported for work that day. He was expected at four, Jane was told. That was still many hours away and he might call in sick again. In the meantime, he could be at home, if they were lucky. His home address was in Brooklyn, which was also the home of his sister. They lived about two stations apart on the subway.

Jane took Smithson to the coffee room, where she filled him in on what they had so far, except for the guns.

"The way it looks now," she said, "is that Charley Farrar was an unknown participant in the Micah Anthony killing. He may have been the connection between the three guys who were found in the crib in the West Fifties and the unknown Transit cop we think was running the show. Defino and I talked to Carl Randolph at Rikers a week ago yesterday. We didn't get anything out of him, but that night an inmate was murdered, someone Randolph knew. We think Randolph paid this guy, Tommy Swift, to make a phone call to say we'd been there and then killed him so he wouldn't talk."

"How do you know about the phone call?"

"Something happened, Warren. I can't talk about it unless Graves gives the OK. But we know Randolph got a message out of Rikers, and they were watching him, so we know he didn't make the call himself. Now that we have Charley Farrar's phone number, MacHovec can find out if Farrar's number was called that day from Rikers. We won't be able to find out who made the call, but it would confirm our theory."

"And on Friday Defino got snatched, which looks like a crime of opportunity if what this guy Testa said is true."

"But Charley's the link," Jane said. "Charley knew Manelli. Manelli and his girlfriend were up in the Catskills for a week on vacation, and the girlfriend saw Manelli talking to someone through the trees. I have to believe that was Charley Farrar because he's the guy who got the call from Randolph."

"So Farrar has wheels of his own. He didn't need that van."

"It was his friend Testa who had the van, and they used it to drive over to Manelli's. It works, Warren. And you're right, the kidnapping was a crime of opportunity. Farrar didn't expect to find a cop in Manelli's apartment. Testa was there because he's Charley's friend. They rang Manelli's bell, Defino told him to answer and waited a few feet behind him, Manelli signaled these two guys to overpower Defino, and the rest is history."

"Why did you look for Defino in the subway?" Smithson asked.

"Because we couldn't get anything out of Randolph, and he's in Rikers. You guys dug into Manelli's background from when he was in the womb—"

"And found nothing."

"But there was a third guy who was in the crib the night Micah Anthony was murdered, a TA trackman named Curtis Morgan. He died of natural causes a few years ago, so I chased down his wife and found out he worked on the Lex. I figured he might know a place in the tunnels where he could hide a person or a body."

"Why did you need his wife?" Smithson was making notes, trying to put the pieces together. "He's got a file at the TA."

"It's been expunged," Jane said.

Smithson's eyebrows went up. "Shit. The whole file?"

"His work experience. Where he worked, what he did. His name's there, his Social Security stuff, insurance, pension, just nothing about where he worked."

"You think Charley Farrar got rid of it?"

"Could be. Or the Transit cop who was running the show."

Smithson looked at his notes. "I've got the picture. Now we find Farrar and get him to talk."

"Sounds simple," Jane said. "Got your car?"

"Right downstairs."

25

CHARLEY FARRAR WAS expected at work at four. It was a good bet he was at home sleeping, preparing for a shift that would end at midnight. They picked up Smithson's car and drove to Brooklyn, using the tunnel. Smithson seemed to know his way around the borough.

"You ever work in Brooklyn?" he asked as they approached Prospect Park.

"Never. I've spent my career in Manhattan."

"And glad of it."

"You bet. I worked the Six for ten years. Now I live there."

"And you work the city."

"That's how it's turned out. The Six is in my blood. I see faces sometimes when I'm out walking and they look familiar. I just can't remember whether they're the good guys or the bad guys."

Smithson laughed. "Probably not much difference."

She had thought that herself, how slight the difference could be. "It was a lot of fun," she said. "I had a great partner and we never stopped running."

"You still friends?"

"Oh, yeah. We went up to Rodman's Neck together a couple of months ago." Rodman's Neck was the range where cops learned to shoot and then continued their annual firearms qualification and tactics training.

"Reminds me." He stopped for a light at a busy intersection. Women pushed strollers, old people hobbled on canes, building heights were low, store followed store followed store. "Should be around the corner." The light changed and he turned right, moving slowly to check numbers on buildings. Everything here was old, prewar at the newest. Apartment houses alternated with groups of single- and two-family homes. Between them were narrow driveways that tested the skills of any driver who backed a late-twentieth-century car out of an early-twentieth-century driveway, built when cars were shorter and narrower.

"Must be in the next block," he said. "These are all sixteen hundreds." He crossed Quentin Road and parked in a space just vacated by a van.

They got out and walked half a block to a redbrick six-story building. An elderly tenant was leaving, and they got in without ringing the Farrars' bell. The elevator was new, indicating that the old one had died a permanent death. No landlord of a rent-controlled building would spring for a new elevator if not pressed to the wall.

A smell of cooking permeated the fifth-floor hallway, which was dark in spite of several bare ceiling lights.

"Pee-yew," Smithson said, stressing the second syllable. "Glad I'm not married to her."

Jane smiled. They stopped at 5D and Smithson pressed the bell. A sharp ring sounded inside.

"Who's there?" a woman called.

"We need to talk to Charley," Jane called.

The door opened. A woman of about fifty looked at them. She was dressed in jeans and a gray shirt, no jewelry except for a gold ring on her left hand. "Who are you?"

They showed their shields. "Detectives Smithson and Bauer, Mrs. Farrar. May we come in?"

She backed up. "What's wrong? Is Charley hurt?"

"No, ma'am," Jane said quickly. "We need to talk to him."

"He left. I don't know where he is. You sure nothing's wrong?"

They walked into the living room, where a vacuum cleaner stood in front of the sofa. Mrs. Farrar moved it and sat.

"He's fine," Smithson said. "We're just looking for him. When did he leave?"

"I don't remember. He got up, had breakfast, and said he had to go somewheres before he goes to work. He's working this afternoon at four."

"Does he have a car?"

"Not anymore. We got rid of it a couple of years ago. If he has to drive somewhere, he borrows one from a friend."

"What friend?"

"There's a gas station the other side of Kings Highway. Charley knows the owner—what's his name?" She closed her eyes and rubbed her forehead. "Dante something. The place is called Dante's."

"Did your husband borrow the car last week?" Jane asked.

She thought about it. "He didn't mention it, but he had a couple of days off, Thursday and Friday, I think. I didn't see him all day Thursday, and then on Friday he got a call and he went out with a friend. I don't think Charley had the car that day."

"You know the friend's name?" Smithson asked.

"Charley has a lot of friends. He knows them from the TA. They're always going somewhere on a day off, having a beer. I couldn't tell you who it was. Why are you asking me?"

"We have some information we need to confirm," Jane said. "You think Charley may have borrowed Dante's car on Thursday?"

"I think it was Thursday."

That would fit. Jane and Defino had seen Carl Randolph on Wednesday morning, meaning that Charley Farrar had gotten the message from Rikers the night before or possibly even Wednesday afternoon, giving him time to get into the Second Avenue subway tunnel and retrieve the Beretta. After leaving the gun in Riverside Park and making certain it was found, Charley could then have borrowed the car and driven to the Catskills to tell Manelli what was happening. Manelli would have told Farrar as a matter of course where he would be that week. They kept in touch.

"Did Charley get a phone call Wednesday afternoon or night?"

"A phone call? Charley gets phone calls all the time. I told you. He has a lot of friends."

"After the phone call, he would have left the house."

"I'm not sure," Mrs. Farrar said, her voice less certain. "He works odd hours and he could have been going to work."

"Does your husband have a cell phone?" Smithson asked.

"He hates them. He had one once for a month and he got rid of it. This is his only phone."

That squared with what Testa had said.

Jane glanced at Smithson, then said, "Thank you, Mrs. Farrar."

"What should I tell Charley?"

"I wouldn't tell him anything if I were you."

"Why?"

"You want him to come home tonight? Keep quiet about our visit."

They went down to the car. The next chance to find Farrar would be when he showed up for work, several hours later.

"So what's next?" Smithson said.

"Let's go back to Manhattan. Maybe we can find Manelli's girlfriend and have a heart-to-heart. She has to know that she's never seeing Manelli again outside of prison. If she knows something, she can help herself."

"Your call. Where do we go?"

"Let me try Macy's and see when she's working." She managed to get the information without talking to anyone in the handbag department who might tip Judy Franklin off. Judy was working all day today.

"We'll have to get rid of the car," Jane said as Smithson took off. "I wouldn't try to park near Macy's if you want to see your car in one piece again."

"I know a place."

She smiled. There were cops who always knew a place.

Back in Manhattan, Smithson drove up the West Side on the highway that wasn't, the old West Side Highway having almost fallen down when Jane was a child. The elevated structure had been removed from the Battery Tunnel up to Fifty-ninth Street and replaced with a street-level low-speed substitute with traffic lights. He turned right in the Thirties and parked in a garage where he got a hearty welcome, probably, Jane thought, because of favors he had given in the past. From there they walked to the western end of Macy's and worked their way to the handbag department.

Jane let him go ahead, as Judy Franklin had never seen him and would not be anticipating trouble. From a distance, Jane watched as he smiled and talked his way over to her, then let her know who he was. Jane could see her face collapse as she realized she'd been had.

Smithson walked her over to Jane.

"What do you want from me?" Judy said. "My lawyer doesn't want me to talk to you. I haven't seen Sal. I don't know where he is. I'm working and I can't take time off."

"We want to tell you something," Jane said quietly.

"Not here where people can see. I'll lose my job if they find out about you."

"We can go outside."

They made their way to the Herald Square exit, stood in front of a display window, and Smithson lit up. Judy said nothing.

"Your boyfriend's in big trouble," Jane said.

"I told you. I haven't heard from him."

"Really big trouble. Kidnapping a cop is not the way to go when you report to a parole officer."

Judy remained silent but her eyes misted.

"You are never going to see Sal again outside of prison."

"He didn't do anything," Judy wailed.

"He kidnapped a cop."

"They found him, right? The cop? I watched the news last night."

"No thanks to Sal. If you know where Sal is and you tell us, things'll go a lot better for you."

"I didn't *do* anything. You know I didn't. I was with you, for God's sake. You know that. They were gone when we got back to the apartment."

"Judy, when we find him, we are going to prosecute him

for the kidnapping and assault of a policeman. That's not eighteen months like his last bit."

"I don't know where he is," Judy said in a low voice. "You have to believe me. Sal hasn't called since that day. Nobody's called. If I knew where he was . . ." She looked distraught, but she didn't finish the sentence.

"I want names and addresses of his friends."

Judy shook her head. "I don't know them. He talks on the phone to people, but I don't know who they are. Sal's a real family man. He likes to have a hot meal and sit with his feet up. We go to a movie sometimes. We don't go out with his friends."

"We heard he had a friend named Charley," Smithson interjected.

"Charley. Maybe I've heard him on the phone with a Charley, but I've never met him."

"Who comes to the apartment?" Jane asked.

"Now and then some guy."

"What guy?" Smithson said, sounding annoyed.

Judy shrugged. "They come to the door, Sal goes out with them. They don't hang around the apartment. It's not a cocktails-and-snacks visit."

"Sal know anybody who works for the Transit Authority?" Jane said, her final question.

"I wouldn't know."

"Think about it. Think hard." Jane handed her her card.

"I have one of those."

"Here's another one. Put it where you'll see it. It may remind you of what you have to do." Jane turned and walked away, Smithson just behind her.

"What do you think? She holding back?"

"I don't know. I hope we can break Charley Farrar."

They went back and got the car—"No charge, Detective. Come back and see us soon."—and drove to Centre Street for lunch and a few hours of waiting before going down to where Charley worked.

"Preliminary report from the crime scene guys," MacHovec said when they got back after lunch. "They got nothing. That is, they got a lot but it doesn't mean much. That van's been used to transport so many things, the list's half a mile long. Fur—"

"The furrier Testa worked for borrowed it last Friday. He may have had some coats moved," Jane said.

"Sounds like good stuff, mink and maybe sable. But no blood. Van looked like it had been washed down before it was left on the street. But they're still looking. Something may turn up, you know, Locard's Exchange Principle." He was referring to the French criminologist Émile Locard, who said that any person passing through a space will unknowingly leave something there and take something away, essentially the basis of crime scene work.

"We've got Defino. He knows he was in the van."

"I guess you didn't bump into Farrar."

"His wife said he went out this morning," Smithson said. "We'll head over to the TA this afternoon, see if he shows up for his shift."

"Not if his wife tells him we were there," Jane said.

"He doesn't sound like the kind of guy that rings his wife every time he's got a free minute."

"Let's hope."

Defino had called in the morning and Jane called him back. He was itching to leave the hospital—no surprise there. The broken rib hurt him and affected his ability to walk. But he was feeling much better and wanted to hear about the case. Jane briefed him.

"This guy we're hoping to get hold of this afternoon works for the TA," she told Defino.

"So you could close this soon," Defino said with a hint of regret.

"Nothing goes smoothly, Gordon."

"They find anything in that van?"

"Fur and a lot of other things, but nothing important so far. Hold on." She turned to MacHovec, who was butting in. "What's up?"

"We got it, the phone call from Rikers. Look at this." He underlined something in red and passed the paper over.

"Is that Farrar's number?"

"You bet."

"Gordon, listen to this."

It was good news, even though they couldn't prove that Randolph was involved in the phone call. Charley Farrar had received a call from Rikers the day Jane and Defino had talked to Randolph. She let Defino know, feeling good. Their theory was right. Farrar had been a key person in the Micah Anthony killing and had avoided being in the crib that night, by plan or by lucky accident. This time they would get him. This time they would make him talk.

[26]

THEY ARRIVED AT Farrar's station, Canal Street on the A line, at three. Smithson hung around the area where the workers punched in. Jane made herself scarce, not wanting to stand out as a woman in a crowd of men. They had no photos of Farrar, but they snagged a TA supervisor to identify him when he walked in. He would change his clothes before beginning his tour and change them back afterward. After Jane's two hikes into the underworld, she understood why. Remembering those walks on the tracks gave her a chill.

At four she got nervous. At four fifteen she called Farrar's wife.

"I haven't heard from Charley since you were here."

"If you're holding back, Mrs. Farrar, you'll—"

"I told you the truth. He left this morning before you came and I haven't seen him since. Or heard from him. And now you've got me scared."

They could check the calls to her phone, but that might not yield anything besides a pay phone number if she were lying. Jane made her way to where Smithson and the supervisor were observing incoming workers. She didn't have to ask.

"Looks like he got the word," Smithson said.

"He's got a good record for punctuality," the supervisor said. "And I checked. He didn't call in. He's called in for the last few days. Today he was supposed to come back."

"You know who his friends are?" Jane asked.

"I don't get involved in personal lives. Farrar's a good worker, a maintainer. He walks the tracks looking for problems. Got a lot of years and a good record. I can't help you any more than that."

"Let's give it more time," Jane said.

They stayed till five. Jane called McElroy and said they were giving up.

"You think it was the wife?" he asked.

"Could be. Randolph doesn't know what we're doing. Manelli's out of the loop now. I believe Judy Franklin doesn't know Manelli's friends. He would keep her out of it. Farrar's never seen us, so he couldn't have made Smithson, and I kept out of sight."

"OK. You did what you had to. It's after five. I'll have Annie sign you out. Go home."

"Thanks, boss."

She sent Smithson on his way and took the subway home, since she was already in a station. In the Village, she picked up dinner at a takeout, not in the mood to cook and clean up. After she had eaten, Flora Hamburg called.

"How's your partner?"

"He's doing fine. They won't let him back for a while. That rib has to heal, and he'll have to go through all the crap I went through in December. But he's in good spirits."

"You did good, Jane."

"You know the drill, Flora. We all did good."

"You sound tired."

"Not tired, discouraged. We had a guy in our sights and we lost him. Someone tipped him off, probably his wife. We'll never find him now. He's the second guy we've lost, and this one was key. He knows something we have to know, and there's no one else."

"What about the guy in Rikers?"

"I don't think he knows. I think this guy today was the crucial link. He may even be the one who shot Micah Anthony."

"No fooling." The wily inspector sounded genuinely impressed.

"But he reported to someone else, and without him, there's no link."

"Listen, I'm close by. You up for company?"

Why not? "Sure. I've already eaten and I'm just lying around thinking about how we could've avoided screwing up."

"I'll be there in five. Make coffee."

Jane went to the bathroom and removed Hack's toothbrush, then pushed the hangers with his jeans and shirts to the back of the closet. Not that Flora would conduct a search; she had visited before and looked the apartment over, but just to make sure.

It was more like ten minutes till the bell rang. Jane flicked on the coffeemaker, buzzed her in, and opened the door to the hallway, listening for the elevator. Flora wouldn't walk. Hack walked unless the lobby was clear. Flora was of indeterminate age, but not young, overweight, and carried her belongings in a shopping bag. After years of wondering, Jane had finally decided she did it to annoy her colleagues, not because she disliked handbags. Her gun flapped on her hip and never moved from that position.

The elevator door opened, and Flora stepped into the hall and waved. "Good to see you," she called, a slight echo preceding her. At the door, she gave Jane a motherly hug and they went inside. "I stopped at a bakery."

"You'll be my downfall."

"Well, I was instrumental in your rise; now we'll even things out."

"What are you doing in the Village?" They went into the kitchen and Jane poured.

"Having dinner with an up-and-coming young sergeant."

Jane smiled. "She gonna be commissioner someday?"

"Maybe. I think she's got what it takes. Except that male appendage that counts for more than brains. Good coffee."

"And dessert. How did you know I loved cannoli?"

"You must have told me. I love them too. Can we talk?"

"I thought that's what we were doing."

"Seriously. I'm thinking of retiring."

The word hit Jane like a blow. "Flora."

"I'm not young anymore."

"What's that got to do with it?"

"My knee hurts when I walk. I don't talk about it but I feel it."

"It'll hurt just as much if you're home."

"Probably more. You mind if I smoke?"

"I'll get you an ashtray."

"Thanks, Jane." Flora lit a cigarette and took a couple of drags before continuing. "I didn't say I was retiring. I just said I was thinking about it."

"Your health OK besides the knee?"

"Pretty good. These things'll get me someday." She held up the cigarette before flicking off the ash. "I'm glad you never started."

"Flora, when you think about retiring, give a thought to the people on the job who will vote against it. Like the young sergeant you just had dinner with."

"I know. You women are my pride and my burden. Well, I didn't come here to talk about myself."

Jane refilled both their cups. "What can I do for you?"

"You have twenty years and you're a first grade. It's time you took the sergeant's exam."

"We've talked about this. I don't want to study. I'm not an administrator. I want to work. It's what I do best."

"And you don't want to be chief of D's."

"Never. Besides, I'm too old to go through the ranks."

"I think it would be good for you to study, keep that brain of yours working."

"I read, Flora. That keeps my brain going."

"With me, every test I passed boosted my ego. I loved moving up. I loved the power, if you want to know the truth. With rank I could accomplish more. I could get in more people's faces."

It was an old story. Flora was forever pressuring her women to do more, achieve more, rise in the ranks. Jane suspected Hack would be pleased if she took the sergeant's exam, but Hack's career and hers had diverged near their starts, reflecting their different goals—Hack's closer to Flora's.

"You know I'm not interested in rank. I get my highs figuring things out, not doing paperwork."

Flora exhaled, clouding the air between them. "It's not all pushing paper."

"I know that. Look, I'm first grade. I know that's the end of the line, but I never thought I'd make it. And this cold case stuff has turned out to be much more challenging than I thought it would. Making sergeant would mean a pay cut."

"I withdraw."

"You're annoyed."

"I just think you could do more. Let's change the subject." She looked down at the table. "You didn't fill in those bullet holes."

"I'm not going to."

"They're not a happy reminder."

"They remind me I'm alive. There are nights I need a little prodding."

Flora laughed. "I know the feeling. Make me a fire and when I'm nice and warm, I'll leave you to your bullet holes and your case."

They moved to the living room. Jane had already laid a fire. Now she lit it, hoping it would not embarrass her. Fires were undependable, sort of like most of the men who had been in her life. You went through the process each time and sometimes it worked and sometimes it didn't.

This time it worked. The flame flared, the starter caught, and the logs began to burn. She sat back with pleasure, watching.

"You're a real master at that," Flora said approvingly. "I've never learned the trick. Not that I've tried many times."

"It's your rank, Flora. When you're an inspector, you're expected to have a sergeant light your fires for you."

"Touché. I won't mention it again."

Jane gave her a disbelieving glance. "That'll be the day." Flora raised her eyebrows. "Enough chitchat. Tell me about the Anthony case."

"It's in big trouble. We lost our best suspect today. His wife probably warned him off. He wasn't where he should have been this afternoon, and we don't have a clue where to look."

"Today you don't have a clue. Tomorrow you'll have seven. Who is this guy?"

"A TA worker, a track maintenance man. He's the guy that wasn't in the crib when they arrested the three that stood trial."

"There was a fourth man involved?"

"And a fifth, the brains. This guy knew him, maybe the only one of the four who did."

"You've come a long way, Jane."

"Not far enough. Shit, we were this close." She held her thumb and index finger an eighth of an inch apart. "We were waiting for him and he didn't show up for work at four. He'd been taking days off, one at a time, when they were trying to figure out what to do with my partner. Today he was going back to work."

"I would guess you had the place in Rockaway covered."

"Solid." She got up and nudged the fire, renewing the flames.

"You do that like a pro," Flora said.

"My next career, lighting fires."

"You've been doing that for twenty years."

"This is a big case, Flora." She put the poker back on its stand and returned to her chair.

"And you can't discuss it. Well, Medal Day's coming up. I bet your father can't wait."

"He's buying a new summer suit for the occasion."

"A suit! Who wears a suit in New York in the summer anymore?" Her voice rose and fell in an old New York cadence.

"John Bauer."

"Well, God bless him." Flora shook her head in disbelief and perhaps some admiration. As she began to add another comment, the phone rang.

It was McElroy. "Hi, Loot."

"Got some bad news."

"Farrar?"

"One and the same. His body was found near a siding about an hour ago. He'd been dead for a while, maybe since this morning. Whoever did it made sure his body was away from the track."

"A transit cop," Jane said miserably.

"Could be."

"And he was the link. We were just one day too late."

"Not your fault. I'll give Smithson a call. You can tell Defino. Have you told him about the guns?"

"Nobody."

"Keep it that way."

"Lost your guy?" Flora said.

"Yeah, our missing link, the only one who could lead us to the top guy. They just found his body." She sat down in the living room, trying to think where to go next.

"Sleep on it, Jane." Flora raised herself from the sofa and retrieved her shopping bag.

Jane got her coat out of the closet and helped her on with it.

"Don't agitate yourself."

"This guy has lived ten years too long. I want him."

"We all want him."

When Flora had left, Jane called Defino and gave him the news. Smithson called a little while later.

"I need some inspiration," Jane told him.

"That makes two of us."

"I'll see you in the morning. I'm all talked out."

She washed the dishes and poked the fire. That was depressing news, their one lead gone. Whoever the TA cop was, he was free as a bird now, safe and secure. Neither Randolph nor Manelli could finger him. She wondered what Graves would do about the guns in the Second Avenue subway.

* * *

They had traded war stories, she and Hack, after the relationship became firm. They were, after all, cops, and they had lots of stories. But their careers had been so different, they could have worked at different jobs. He had made detective much earlier than she, and then with his law degree and his appointment as sergeant, his life on the job became largely political. He worked with cops. Jane worked with crime, with criminals. His tales were of cops in trouble, cops trying to move up in a system that was often hostile, cops dying; hers were of collars cleverly orchestrated, of close calls and near misses, of panic and fear and, occasionally, laughter. And of cops dying.

He didn't use the *L* word for weeks, maybe more than a month; she couldn't remember now. It happened the first night he brought ice cream, as though a connection existed between love and sweet food, and maybe it did. What it meant for Jane was that she would always think of love when she ate ice cream, not a stretch, really, as almost all the ice cream in her life was eaten with Hack.

About a year into the relationship, he told her he wanted to leave his wife and marry her. He had alluded in the past to their being together on a permanent basis, but that night he laid it out. He would give his wife the house and he would put his daughters through college. He was a captain now and he could manage it.

"I just want to be with you," he said when the plan was on the table.

She was sitting next to him on the sofa, nestled against him, his left arm around her. Feelings of comfort, love, and security enveloped them. They had eaten, left the dishes, and moved to the living room because he wanted to talk. Listening to him she felt a conflict so sharp, so severe, that for a moment she could not find her voice.

"Something wrong?" he asked easily.

"Your daughters need you. You shouldn't leave them, Hack. They're early teens. It's so important for them to grow up with a father in the house." She had told him that she was adopted but hadn't said anything about the child she had given up. Even a dozen years later, it was hard to talk about.

"They'll have me. I'm not going to the end of the world. I love you, Jane. It's hell waking up without you every day."

"I know. But their lives are important too, maybe more important than ours."

"Do we have a problem?"

"*No!*"

"You sure?"

"I'm sure. You know I'm sure." She hadn't looked at another man since the first time they'd had a drink together. She started unbuttoning his shirt.

"We'll talk about it again."

"OK."

He stayed longer that night, and he smoked more. She found herself feeling terrible. She had disappointed him. And she had disappointed and confused herself. Her reaction to his proposal had been double-sided: profound happiness that he loved her so much, and absolute certainty that she did not want to marry.

She wasn't sure why. His relationship with his daughters was certainly part of it, but the stuff that made her who she was was at least half of it. It wasn't fear of commitment; she was committed to him. It was something about a togetherness that went on without break. What he wanted, to wake up next to her each morning, scared her. She had a need to spend time alone, to talk out loud to herself if she had something to say, to take off down a street if the mood struck her, to eat when she felt hungry and sleep when fatigue hit her, even in the middle of the day. All of that said, or reflected, she wanted him forever. It crossed her mind that if she maintained this stance, however, she might lose him.

Perversely, she found she could understand him better than she could understand herself. Her parents would love to see her married, and they would somehow get over the fact that he had had to leave a wife to become their daughter's husband. She wished she could explain what made her the way she was. Was it knowing she was adopted? Was it giving up that baby girl she had seen only once?

Whatever, she thought, pushing away shadows, moving a large log out of the center of the dying fire. Charley Farrar was dead and the man who had killed him was on the loose, maybe for the rest of his life. The man, she thought, who had ordered the death of Micah Anthony.

[27]

IT WAS NOT a happy Friday morning. MacHovec, who didn't like to think about work after he left Centre Street, got the word when he sat down with his coffee. He had hardly uttered his four-letter comment when Annie placed herself in their doorway.

"The inspector's office, Detectives. *Now.*"

"She taking over for McElroy?" MacHovec growled in a low voice as she left.

"Save it," Jane said.

"You've all heard the news," Graves said before they had finished sitting down. "This puts us in a tight spot. I think we go back to Randolph now and squeeze him. Offer him a better deal, get him sprung, whatever it takes to get him talking."

Jane shook her head absently. "You have a better idea, Detective Bauer?"

"Randolph doesn't know Farrar's contact. They worked it so only Farrar knew him. The other three may have known there was a cop at the top—Curtis Morgan knew it—but that's all they knew."

"But they knew Farrar."

"We've established that. Manelli knew him. Curtis Morgan had to know him because Morgan told his brother there was a cop at the top. Randolph had Farrar's phone number, but I'll bet he rarely used it."

"Till you and Defino went to visit him," Smithson said.

"Detective Smithson, your group looked into Manelli's life from birth to last week. You come up with anything we can run with?"

"Sorry, sir. Manelli's friends were a bunch of dirtbags, but there's no indication they were in on the Anthony hit. And he kept them separate from the woman he lived with."

"Has anyone talked to her recently?" Graves's eyes swept the room.

"We did, yesterday morning," Jane said.

"Do I have a Five on that?" Graves was sounding more like an irritable boss than a smooth-talking TV head.

"On my desk." Defino had taken care of typing the Fives. She had done that one while they were watching the clock before going after Farrar.

"I want it on *my desk.*"

"Yes, sir."

"What did she say?"

"Manelli had friends. They called, they came over and picked him up, but they never stayed. Or he went out to meet them. She didn't know them. She thought maybe he had a friend named Charley."

"Joe Riso," Graves said, pulling out the last name Jane could think of. "Is it worth going back with some tough questions? Or bringing him in?"

"I think he told us all he's going to, maybe all he knows," Smithson said.

"That leaves us with no one." Graves looked at Mac-Hovec. "You got any ideas?"

"Manelli's a dead end, Morgan's a dead end. I've been looking into Charley Farrar's work record."

"OK," Graves said with a note of hope.

"It doesn't appear to have been tampered with. He looks to have a pretty clean record. I've got names of supervisors going back twenty years."

"He ever work on the Second Avenue subway?"

"I haven't gotten back that far. And he could've met Morgan somewhere else in the system. It's hard to pinpoint it, since Morgan's got no history."

"OK, Detectives, that's where you pick up the case." Graves put down the pen he had been holding. "Any questions?" It was clear he didn't want any. "Then get cracking."

They got up and Jane hung behind as the men left. When they were gone, she closed Graves's door. "Smithson doesn't know about the guns."

"Right. That slipped my mind. I mentioned the Second Avenue subway, didn't I? Tell you what, brief him. We can't have him working on a case he isn't fully informed about."

"Thanks, Inspector. Are you leaving the guard there?"

"With Farrar gone, I think we'll pull them. I'm talking to the chief of D in half an hour. We'll work something out."

In the office, with the door closed, she and MacHovec told Smithson the story.

He whistled at the revelation of the guns in the subway. "How'd you find them?"

"That's my secret."

"*You* found them?"

"With someone I know who has access. We knew roughly where Curtis Morgan had worked and we looked in likely places. I wasn't looking for them; I was looking for my partner."

"Some find."

Jane took the Fives she had completed yesterday and dropped them in Graves's in box while MacHovec dug up Farrar's work history. He pulled the names of supervisors going back to the beginning of Farrar's career. The work assignments were similar, just in different locations. He had worked Manhattan, Brooklyn, and Queens, and he had lived in Brooklyn for over thirty years at the address Jane and Smithson had visited the day before.

"OK, here's the connection," MacHovec said. "Farrar worked on the Second Avenue subway at least part of the time Curtis Morgan did." He had two sheets side by side on his desk, the one on the left a printout, the one on the right handwritten notes, which had to be information Jane had gotten on Morgan. "Doesn't look like he worked there a long time, but you only need a day to meet a guy."

"That was about twenty years before the Micah Anthony killing," Jane said. "They could have met and stayed friends, or they could have been assigned the same location again later."

"Hard to tell without Morgan's record. I would guess these guys run into each other from time to time. Cops do. You think his wife remembers where he worked?"

"She gave me the Lex and the Second Avenue subway. I'll give her a call." Jane dialed the number.

"Detective, I don't have the time, and I'm sitting with all of these people around," Emma Morgan said.

"A couple of quick questions, Mrs. Morgan." She asked about locations and took notes as the woman spoke.

"Did your husband know a track maintenance man named Charley Farrar?"

A phone rang in the background and a distant voice answered. "I think he knew a Charley," Mrs. Morgan said. "I don't know if I ever met him. He wasn't a good friend like some of the others I told you about."

"Did he ever know a Transit cop?"

"A cop? Never."

"You're sure."

"I'd swear to it."

"Thanks for your help." Jane hung up. "She remembers the Broadway line in Manhattan before 'the incident with the cop,' and Morgan never knew a Transit cop. We're not going to get much more out of her."

"Farrar worked the Number One line," MacHovec said. "About two years before Anthony was killed. So we've got two overlaps. Give me a minute and I'll have it all together."

Smithson took the supervisors during the first half of Farrar's career and Jane took the rest. One of Smithson's was dead; one of Jane's was off today. As she was about to make another call, McElroy appeared at the door.

"We've got a preliminary report on Farrar's body. My office."

They trooped over. What he had was handwritten notes, obviously taken from a telephone conversation.

"One shot to the back of the head," McElroy said when they were seated.

"Gun?" The word came from Jane and Smithson at the same moment.

"Small-caliber. Probably a throwaway. Body looked like it had been dragged, but not far. The shooter wanted him off to the side, not on the tracks, not where he'd be seen readily. He was probably dead six to eight hours when he was spotted."

"Who found him?" Smithson asked.

"A homeless guy who sleeps down there. He walked to the nearest station and told a clerk."

"A Good Samaritan."

"Probably thought he'd get a reward," MacHovec said glumly.

"He available for questioning?" Jane asked.

"I've got a fax of the Five, the names of the cops who responded, and the detectives who caught the case." He pushed papers across his desk.

Jane grabbed the Five and read it, Smithson looking over her shoulder. The man, who gave his name as Catty Fellows, had been questioned and released by the time McElroy got the news the night before. By now he could be sleeping in the Bronx.

"They didn't get much out of him," she said.

"I don't think there was much to get. The guy stumbled over a body. We should thank him for reporting it before the rats got to him."

"So Farrar was shot with a small-caliber gun," Smithson said, "and Fellows says he didn't see anything."

"He reported it several hours after the shooting."

"Doesn't mean he didn't see it and wait."

Smithson was right, Jane thought. Fellows could have been around, hunched up in the shadows. He could have heard the shot even if he didn't see anything, and then waited, maybe trying to decide whether to report it or forget about it.

"We should look for him," she said without enthusiasm. The prospect of another hike in the tunnels left her cold.

"You get your kicks down there?" Smithson asked.

She gave him a look and said nothing.

"You're right, Jane," McElroy said. "That's your next step. You may want a change of clothes, and we'll get you a guide from the TA." He turned to MacHovec. "You dig up anything?"

"Two overlaps between Farrar and Curtis Morgan."

"Good work. Take the paperwork and get busy."

"Why don't you let me call Farrar's supervisors while you folks enjoy yourselves in the tunnels?" MacHovec said when they were at their desks.

Jane pulled out an old pair of sneakers and socks that she kept in a drawer for emergencies and left the office. Next case, she thought, maybe I'll get to take a trip on a cruise ship. Back in the office, Smithson was pulling a T-shirt over his head. He, too, came prepared. His shirt and jacket hung over the back of his chair, the tie neatly folded on his desk. He looked down at his pants as though wishing them a fond farewell.

Annie came by with the name of a TA worker and where they could find him. "What's it like down there?" she asked.

"Hell with rats," Jane said.

Annie shivered. "Sorry I asked."

"We may as well take the subway," Smithson said grimly. His mood had changed. The case had turned sour. Maybe rats weren't his thing.

28

"YEAH, CATTY FELLOWS," Carl Hidalgo, their TA contact, said when they arrived. "He gets rousted a lot. Nice guy except that he stinks. Don't seem to be crazy. Don't fight you, kinda docile. You wanna see where he found the body?"

They said they did, and followed Hidalgo to the front of the platform and descended the stairs. It was a fairly long walk, and they did it without saying much. When they got to the crime scene, it was taped off, an unlighted triangular area a few feet from the tracks. Hidalgo flashed his light around the ground. Rusty bloodstains were still visible, though hard to see. The area was clean of debris, possibly not the way it had been found.

"I heard they found a coffee cup around here," Hidalgo said. "Maybe they got some DNA off of it."

And maybe it came from some other homeless guy, Jane thought. Whoever the killer was, he wasn't stupid.

"Yeah," Smithson said, and Jane knew he was thinking what she was.

"How far is the next station?" Jane asked.

"This is, like, halfway," Hidalgo said. "Catty coulda gone either way. Maybe he went back, because that's where his friends are."

A train approached and they moved toward the wall, although they were safely away from the tracks. There was no conversation until it roared past.

"What friends?" Smithson asked. "Where do they hang out?"

"There's, like, four or five of 'em. Sometimes they're on the street, sometimes down here, 'specially in the winter. It's getting warm out now so they stay aboveground more."

"Show us where they stay," Smithson said.

"We gotta go back." He said it as though it might be negotiable.

"Let's go."

The place where they often found Catty Fellows was between the crime scene and the station they had come from. It was another small alcove that could accommodate one man, maybe two if they were small. No full-size human being could stretch out; he would have to sit with his knees up, his back against the wall. But the area was dry, unlike some others they had passed.

"You show the cops this place?" Smithson asked.

"I didn't, but someone else did. I know they came here. See how clean it is? They musta taken all his junk."

"What kinda junk?"

"He coulda left garbage, like that cup I told you about. Maybe some rags. No food, though. Catty wouldn't leave food."

It would be eaten by the rats if he did. "You know where we can find him on the street?" Jane asked as they started back to the station.

"Just up the stairs and down the block. You won't find 'em all together when it's daylight. They scatter like roaches."

Thanks for the graphic description, she thought.

They walked in silence, mounted the stairs to the platform, and thanked Hidalgo for his help. Then, brushing off their clothes, they went up to the street.

The sunlight was blinding. Jane pulled sunglasses out of her bag and put them on as she fought off a sneeze. "I see a guy down the block on this side," she said to Smithson, who was facing her. "He's sitting against a building. Looks pretty gross."

"Can't be any worse than what we've just been through."

"That your first time?"

"And my last. I think I'd rather freeze my ass on the streets than spend the night down there."

They walked slowly down the street. The man propped against the building had long filthy hair, a straggly beard, and the expected layers of disintegrating clothes. On either side of him stood a couple of fat shopping bags that probably held his worldly possessions, most of them worthless except to him. His head hung over as though he were half-asleep. One hand grasped a Styrofoam cup that stood on the sidewalk. As Jane and Smithson approached, the man lifted the cup for a donation. Smithson dropped a couple of quarters in it.

"Thank you, sir. Thank you, ma'am. God bless you."

"You the guy they call Catty?" Jane asked.

"Nah. Catty's gone."

"Where'd he go?"

"I couldn't tell you. I saw him yesterday. Maybe it wasn't yesterday, maybe the day before. Said he was going to Brooklyn. He's got a place there."

"You know where?"

"Just over the river. Stanley can tell you."

"Where's Stanley?"

The man leaned forward, and for a moment Jane was afraid he might topple over. He pointed his glazed eyes farther down the block. "He's usually down there, other side of the street. Tell him Rocky sent you."

"Thanks, Rocky." Jane put a dollar in the cup and they walked away to Rocky's blessings.

"You see anyone?" Smithson asked.

"No. Let's keep walking. He could be taking his constitutional."

"What's constitutional about sitting on the sidewalk?"

"I'm not in the mood for politics. Keep your eyes open."

They walked two blocks, turned around, and came back on the other side of the street. Smithson said he was hungry, so they found a coffee shop and had lunch. That killed half an hour. Jane called McElroy and kept him posted.

"Keep at it."

That was the name of the game.

They resumed their walk but found no Stanley. They started looking inside places where he might be picking up food. Still no luck.

"What's that?" Smithson said, shading his eyes. "Down there?"

A man who might be their guy or might just be a sloppy dresser had just emerged from a store. He stood on the sidewalk as though deciding which way to go. Finally, he turned away from them and started walking.

"Let's get him," Jane said, and they started to run.

Traffic at the corner was heavy and they had to wait for it to go by.

"We're gonna lose him," Smithson said, edging forward.

The light changed and the usual three cars went through the red before the fourth one stopped. They pushed through the pedestrians and down the street. Their target was still visible, walking slowly, eating something, Jane thought. As they caught up with him, they slowed, still behind him, Smithson walking to the man's left, Jane to the right. The man had a backpack that looked new and stuffed to capacity, torn faded jeans, two or three shirts, disintegrating sneakers, filthy hair, and a smell.

Jane moved forward to the man's side. "Stanley?"

He stopped cold. "Who wants to know?"

"I do. Rocky sent me to find you."

"Yeah?"

"I'm looking for Catty Fellows. Rocky said you'd know where he is."

"What'd he do?"

"He didn't do anything. I have to find him."

"You wanna buy me lunch?"

"Sure."

Stanley suddenly became aware that Smithson was standing to his left. His eyes showed his fear. "Who're you?"

"I'm with her. We need to talk to Catty."

"You're cops, right?"

"We're cops," Jane said, "but we're not after Catty. We just need some information from him."

"About the body he found?"

"Right."

"Who was the dead guy?"

"We're trying to find out. You want lunch, Stanley? You can have a great lunch. Just tell us where to find Catty."

He considered his options. He wasn't as thin as the last guy they had talked to, but he could use some calories, not to mention a bath. "First station over the East River on the A train. Catty likes the A train. That'll put you in downtown Brooklyn, near Borough Hall. High Street I think is the station."

"Where do we find him when we get off the train?"

Stanley looked around, up at the sky, down at the street, as though taking a measure. "It's nice weather. He'll be on the street near the station. Catty likes to stay near stations. Makes him feel less stressed."

I should try that myself, Jane thought. "You're sure about this, Stanley?"

"Yeah, I'm sure."

"You send us on a wild goose chase, we'll find you, man," Smithson said.

Stanley turned away from him. "You taking me to lunch?"

"Will a ten buy you a good one?"

"Ten dollars?"

"You heard me."

"Yeah, a real good one."

Jane took a ten out of her wallet and handed it over.

Stanley stared at it. "Thanks," he said. "I'll remember you." He stuffed the ten in his jeans pocket and walked away.

[29]

THEY FOUND CATTY Fellows walking around near the High Street–Brooklyn Bridge station, holding a Styrofoam cup that jingled when he shook it. When Smithson said his name, Catty tried to run, but Smithson had a good grip on his arm.

"What you want?" Catty said. "I didn't do nothin'."

"You found a body yesterday."

"I already talked to the police."

"We're police too," Smithson said, showing his shield. "We have a few questions."

"Shit."

"Let's go somewhere and sit down," Jane said.

"I'm not going to no station house."

"All right. Let's stay here." She didn't want to take him into a restaurant and she didn't want him sitting in a radio car. He was probably crawling with lice. "When did you find the body, Catty?"

"I don't wear no watch."

"Was it morning? Afternoon?"

"I was gettin' hungry. It must've been, like, late afternoon. Time to eat something."

"You see the guy who shot him?"

"No, ma'am."

"Was he still alive when you saw him?"

"He was deader'n dead. I looked at him and I knew. And there was blood all around."

"What were doing over there, Catty?" Smithson said. "That's not where you usually sleep."

"I was . . ."

Smithson waited. Then, "You were what?"

"Takin' a walk."

"That where you do your walking? Along the tracks?"

"Sometimes."

"Catty," Jane said, "we're just trying to find out when this murder happened and who did it."

"*I* didn't do it." His voice rose. "I'm no killer."

"We know that. But maybe you saw a little more than you told us about."

"I didn't see anything," he said glumly.

"Maybe you saw two men walk by the place where you sleep."

Catty said nothing.

"Maybe you heard a shot fired."

"You can't hear a shot when a train goes by."

"That's right. I forgot about that. If you wait for a train, you can shoot and no one would hear you."

"You got it."

"So maybe you saw a guy with a gun but you didn't hear anything except a train."

"I didn't see it. I found the body later."

"Detective Smithson and I just can't figure out why you walked over to the place where the body was. It's way down the tracks from the station where you and Rocky and Stanley hang out."

They had talked about it on the way over. Catty had his favorite sleeping place, which they had seen, but the crime scene was farther down the line from the station where he and his pals congregated. What had motivated him to walk toward a station he wasn't known to use? Maybe he had seen something and kept it to himself. The cops who had interviewed him yesterday saw him merely as the person who reported finding a body, and they had little reason to think he was the killer, especially when they learned that an alarm was out for Charley Farrar. But the geography of the situation indicated a different scenario to Jane and Smithson.

"I told you," Catty said impatiently, "I was takin' a walk."

"You know what, Catty?" Jane said. "I think you saw a guy with a gun. I think maybe you saw him use it."

"I didn't see him shoot. I didn't."

"But you saw the man with the gun, didn't you?"

Catty thought about it. "Maybe I did."

"There's no maybe. You saw him, right?"

"Yeah, I saw him."

"OK. How 'bout you tell us exactly what you saw? Everything."

"What if I tell you something a little different than what I told the other cops?"

"You weren't under oath, Catty," Smithson said in a cajoling tone. "Maybe when you talked to them, you forgot to mention a few things."

"Yeah. That could be."

"From the beginning," Jane said.

"Let's see. I'm resting in my usual spot, OK?"

"Fine."

" 'Cause I had, like, a bad night, you know?"

"OK," Jane said.

"And the way I sit, they come from behind me so they don't see me but I see them go by."

"I got it."

"And there's two white guys, not young guys, older, and big." He raised his right hand to indicate a six-footer. "And the guy in the back, he's holdin' a gun in the back of the other one."

"What were they wearing?"

"Shit, it was dark down there. I don't check out their clothes, and I couldn't see them anyway. It was just pants and shirts, maybe one had a jacket."

She had wondered if one was wearing a uniform. "What else do you remember?"

"The guy behind, he got one hand on the arm of the guy in front, like he's makin' sure he don't run away. And the other hand got the gun."

"Did they say anything?"

"Nothin'."

"They just walked by?"

"Yeah. I watched 'em go, but it's dark down there. I couldn't see much."

"Did you hear the shot, Catty?"

"I don't know."

"What does that mean?"

"A train come by. Then another. Maybe I heard something when the second one come by."

"What did you hear?"

"Maybe like a bang."

"I thought you said you couldn't hear a gunshot when a train was going by."

"Yeah, I said that, didn't I?" He screwed up his face. "But I think maybe I heard a bang, even with the train."

"So what did you do?"

"Nothin'!" He seemed shocked at the question. "I ain't goin' after no dude with a gun. You think I'm crazy?"

"I think you're very sane, Catty, and I want to hear your whole story, so keep going. What did you do after the train went by and you heard a bang?"

"I froze. I just sat there. I was scared."

"Did you go to see what happened?"

"No, ma'am. I said to myself, 'You get yourself outta here or you could be next.' He could be comin' back and he'd see me for sure. So I got up and I went back to my station."

"Did you hang around to see if the man with the gun would come back?"

Catty smiled. "Yeah, I did. But he didn't show up. I waited a long while, maybe an hour, but no one came up outta the tracks. So I figured he just kept walkin' to the next station. See, then if somebody saw him comin' in at my station, they'd never see him again. They wouldn't see him once with the other guy and then once by himself."

"Good thinking," Smithson said. "You're a smart guy."

"Yeah." He said it with no pleasure. He knew the game Smithson was playing.

"So then what?" Jane asked.

"So then I went back down there to see what happened."

"Tell me about it."

"I just kept walkin' till I came to the body. I gotta tell you, it was pretty bad to look at. Half his head was blown away. There was lotsa blood."

"Did you touch him?"

"Who, me?"

"You're the guy that found him," Smithson said. "You move him at all? Put your hands in his pockets? Take something?"

"No, sir. I just looked at him and went back to my station."

"Then what?" Jane said.

"I was pretty shook, you know. I had to rest awhile before I figured out what to do. After I rested, I knew it was my duty to report what I found. So I went to the token booth and said what I'd seen."

"You hang around for the police or did they have to find you?" Smithson asked.

"I waited for them, Detective. I know my duty as a citizen."

"Yeah, right." Smithson looked at Jane.

"OK, Catty. Thanks for your help."

As they started to leave, Smithson turned back. "Where'd you get the name Catty?"

Catty gave them a smile, reached into his shirt, and pulled out a small gray kitten. "I just love cats," he said. "That OK with you?"

Smithson didn't answer.

[30]

"So FELLOWS SAW them walk by," McElroy said. "Two men he can't identify."

"Or won't," Jane said.

"Same difference. But what he said makes sense. If he'd been facing them as they approached, they would have seen him. This way, they just appeared and kept going and all he saw was their backs. After the shooting, the killer kept walking to the next station, went up on the platform and out to the street, just another anonymous straphanger."

"And if he's smart," Smithson said, "he got rid of the gun last night. Not that it matters. He's gone."

"What do we know about him?" McElroy asked.

"Catty Fellows said both men were white, older, or at least not young," Jane said. "That's no surprise. Micah Anthony was murdered ten years ago. This guy probably wasn't a rookie at the time. Look, I've got two ideas."

"Let me hear them." It sounded as though McElroy had none of his own.

"When I went up to Sing-Sing, I didn't ask Curtis Morgan's brother if he knew what rank the Transit cop was."

"Good thought. We could get a list of names from the year Anthony was killed."

"And I could call Anthony's wife and ask if they knew a Transit cop. It's possible a friend set him up."

"Wouldn't be the first time." McElroy looked at his watch. "OK. Go to it."

They stopped for coffee on the way back. The pot was full and it smelled good.

Sitting down at his desk, Smithson said, "Am I missing something or is McElroy as out of ideas as we are?"

"McElroy's not an idea man. But he recognizes good ones when he hears them."

"Graves has the brains."

"And the sweetness and charm," MacHovec chimed in. "Not always for us."

"Warren," Jane said, "how 'bout we split up the Fives?"

"I'll do them. I took the notes."

Jane dialed Mrs. Appleby's number to the uneven tune of the typewriter. Her machine picked up and Jane left a message. Then she called Sing-Sing and made an appointment to talk to Timothy Morgan at five o'clock that evening. She stressed that Morgan had to be in a private setting. No one was to know he was cooperating with the police.

When she hung up, Mrs. Appleby called. "Are you making any progress?" she asked.

"Quite a bit. We've had some lucky breaks."

"Your partner, Detective Defino. I heard about him on the news. Is that connected with my husband's case?"

"It is."

"I'm so sorry. How is he?"

"He's doing fine. He's very anxious to come back, but they won't let him for a while."

"So you've shaken things up."

"We have."

"That sounds good to me, especially after so many years. What can I do for you?"

"I have some questions, and I'd like to ask that you keep them strictly to yourself."

"I understand."

"Did your husband have any friends among the Transit cops?"

"Yes, he did, someone he went to high school with. We didn't see them often, maybe once a year, but Micah always talked fondly of him."

Jane grabbed her pencil. "What's his name, Mrs. Appleby?"

"John Beasely. His wife's name is Cynthia."

"Are you still friendly with them?"

A breath found its way across the distance. "I haven't heard from them for a couple of years. A few. Widows don't get the same social consideration that married women do."

"I understand. When was the last time you saw them, or him?"

"Probably five years ago. They took me to dinner. I invited them out to the house after that, but they couldn't make it. I tried a few times and then I gave up."

"Do you recall what rank he was when you last saw him?"

"I think he had just passed the lieutenant's exam but he hadn't been promoted yet."

"What was his rank when your husband died?"

"I think he was a sergeant. He was a smart fellow—both of them were—and he took the sergeant's exam as soon as he could. I seem to remember he passed it the first time."

"Did he and your husband go on the job about the same time?"

"Micah joined just after he graduated from John Jay College. I don't think John was ready then. He went to City and then took some time off. He probably lost a year, so he would have gone to the Academy about a year or so later. May I ask why you're interested in him?"

"I can't answer that. I'm sorry. How did he react when your husband died?"

This time there was a distinct pause. "Detective Bauer, John Beasely may have stopped calling me, but he wasn't involved in Micah's death." Her voice was strained, the impact of the questions having hit their mark.

"I have to ask."

"Yes. Yes, I know you do. And I will answer because I have no choice and because you and Detective Defino have obviously made more progress than ten years of other detectives' work. And Detective Defino almost gave his life for this investigation. You wanted to know how John reacted when Micah died. He heard about Micah while he was at work and he found me at the hospital where they had taken me. He had thrown a coat over his jeans but he had no shirt on over his T-shirt. He was in tears. He hugged me and we cried together." She sounded near tears herself. "That's how he reacted. He was my husband's friend, one of the oldest friends Micah had."

"Thank you. I have another question."

"Go on."

"You told us last week that you thought your husband would get into a car with someone he trusted."

"Yes. I still think so."

"If it was someone in uniform, or someone who had a shield, even if he didn't know the person, do you think he would get into that car?"

"That's very difficult to answer. Since he started working that case, he was always on guard. He didn't want me answering the phone. I remember that. He was talking about putting in a second line, unlisted, just so his parents and a few close friends could call us. He became preoccupied with security, especially since I was visibly pregnant. Would he get into a car with a stranger who had the right ID?" The silence that followed the echoed question answered it. She couldn't be sure. "I don't know, Detective Bauer. Would I have gone with an unknown cop who showed up at my door with a badge and told me he had to take me to safety? Maybe I would. But Micah . . . I don't know. You think someone in the car that picked him up showed him a shield?"

"I think many things are possible," Jane said.

"He'd be alive if he hadn't gotten into that car."

"He may not have had a choice, Mrs. Appleby. There may have been several men with guns. We just don't know yet."

"But you're coming closer. Your partner—"

"Yes, we're closer, just not close enough."

"Was there anything else?"

"Not today. I'm sorry I disrupted your afternoon."

"Just get them. I'm not made of steel but I won't collapse. I want those people in custody."

"We'll do our best."

MacHovec's hand was reaching across to her desk for the sheet on which she had written the name. "You got something."

"Anthony had a childhood friend who became a Transit cop a little after Anthony came on the job."

"Beasely. Let's see where it takes us."

He went to work at the computer, making small sounds as he flipped from screen to screen. At least this man's work history hadn't been expunged. When he finally began to print it all out, Jane realized the typewriter had grown quiet. Either Smithson had finished the Fives or he had sensed a possible lead and was waiting to leap at it.

"Looks like a good career," MacHovec said. "There may be issues in the personnel file, but from what I see here, he's OK." Personnel files were off-limits to them. McElroy or Graves could access them with the OK of the chief of personnel via a request from the chief of D's office if they became necessary. He handed Jane some papers and started printing another set. "What I'll do now is cross-reference this with Charley Farrar, see if they overlap anywhere. It won't be obvious. One's a cop; one's a maintenance man. Maybe Beasely made a collar at a station where Farrar was working. Kinda thin, but what else do we have?"

"Not much," Jane said. "They belong to different unions, different organizations."

"And these guys wouldn't socialize. A black cop and a white track man."

"Sean, maybe Farrar had a brother or cousin who was a cop."

"I'll look into it later." He tossed a second set of the printout on Jane's desk for Smithson and started one going for himself.

Jane turned to Smithson. "Let's look at the year before Micah Anthony was murdered. Think guns. Think armory. He ever cross paths with Carl Randolph or Sal Manelli or Curtis Morgan?" She found the page she had directed him to and started reading.

[31]

SMITHSON AND MACHOVEC were out of the office at four forty-five, and Jane pushed back from the desk and closed her eyes. It was Friday afternoon and she was exhausted. Considering that they had found Defino alive, it had been a good week.

The phone rang and Hack's voice said, "When did I see you last?"

"Sunday?"

"Feels like a month ago. You OK for tonight?"

"Oh, yeah. I just have to talk to a guy at Sing-Sing at five."

"I missed lunch today. I'll bring something nourishing."

She smiled. "I'll be home by six."

"I'll be there when I get there."

It was almost five when she hung up. She placed the call to Ossining and reached the officer she had spoken to earlier. Timothy Morgan was in a private room, awaiting her call.

"Mr. Morgan," she said when he answered, "are you alone?"

"Yes, ma'am."

"I have a question about something we discussed the other day."

"OK."

"Your brother told you there was a Transit cop involved in the gun deal."

"That's what he said."

"Do you know what rank the cop was?"

"Jeez," he muttered. "Yeah, he did say. Gimme a minute. I think . . . He used to say, 'The sarge says.' Yeah. I think it was a sergeant."

"Did he know him well? Were they friends or just partners in the deal?"

"I couldn't tell you. But I don't think they were friends. I don't know if they ever met."

"Did he mention if the cop was black or white?"

"Nah. He just said 'the sarge.' "

"Would he have mentioned it if the sarge was black?"

"He might've. He might not've. Those things didn't make a lot of difference to Curt. He had his gripes against this one and that one, but it wasn't a big deal with him. Like I said, I don't know if they met."

"Do you know anything else about this cop? His age. Where he lived. What district he worked out of."

"I wish I could help you." The tone of his voice told her he believed more information would yield greater benefits to him. "It was just some talk between us. The sarge said this, the sarge said that."

"Did your brother ever mention a Charley Farrar?" She had learned about Farrar the day after her trip to the prison.

"Farrar." He was silent. "Charley. Charley Farrar. Yeah, maybe. But I'm not sure, Detective. Charley's a pretty common name. I've known a few myself."

So had Jane. "Think about it. I could call you back."

"I don't think so. It's so long ago, I don't think I can dig it up."

She decided to give up. If she pushed him, he would start to believe his brother had mentioned the name. If he wasn't sure, he wouldn't be able to tell her anything useful about Farrar anyway.

It was the end of the day, the end of the week. The man she loved was coming over with stuff to nourish her body and her soul, to give her what she needed to keep going on a case that was teetering between hopelessness and a strand of hope. For a while, she would stop thinking and give it some rest.

*   *   *

She showered and changed into clean clothes, touched her skin with cologne he had bought her in Paris, a delicious scent she used only when she was with him. Hurrying, she neatened the apartment, which usually got cleaned only between cases or when she was so dizzy with facts and theories that she needed to do something mindless. As she gathered up papers and magazines, and ran a cloth over the coffee table and a wet rag over the kitchen table, she thought about Warren Smithson and Gordon Defino. The partner relationship was key to good police work, but it was often uneasy, sometimes failing completely. Jane had never partnered with another woman. In the last twenty years, there had been several men, the best of them Marty Hoagland, her longtime partner in the Six. Over the years she had become friends with Marty, and also with his wife, which pleased Jane. Marty had briefly had a female partner who was so sexually aggressive, he eventually asked for a new one.

Defino, with whom she had worked since the previous fall when the cold case squad was organized, was a good detective and a good family man. She liked and respected him, and they got along well. She sensed she would never feel about Smithson the way she felt about Gordon. Smithson was more guarded, less a partner than someone working on the same case. MacHovec was another matter. Badly dressed, unwilling to leave the office except for an occasional trip to an inanimate source of information, he was largely an unknown. He occasionally drank during work hours and had made the worst possible impression on Defino. Their relationship had eased somewhat since MacHovec's involvement in a shooting in the winter, when they were all working on a homicide that had taken place in Alphabet City a number of years earlier. Jane could see that Smithson couldn't quite make out what kind of a man MacHovec was, and she had not discussed either man with the other. She knew she would feel more comfortable when Defino returned, but she assumed that it would not happen until the Micah Anthony case was cleared or abandoned.

Hack arrived at seven, carrying with him two enormous steaks and some accompaniments.

"Haven't had any red meat for days," he said. "Mind sticking these under the broiler for a few seconds on each side?"

She laughed and set the timer for five minutes. She came from a family where food was cooked to death—so did Hack, he had told her—and it had been a long metamorphosis to enjoying meat that was not dark brown and dry in the middle, and vegetables that were not falling apart, most of their taste left in the water they had cooked in. Hack's turnaround had been rapid, initiated when he moved out of his parents' home and sampled a world that was not Irish and insulated from the devils outside.

"The body in the subway," Hack said when they were eating, "that's your guy, right?"

"Right. We put out an alarm after he didn't show up for work yesterday, and by the time it got to the detectives who questioned the homeless guy who found the body, they'd released him. We found him in Brooklyn. He changed his story for us. He saw two guys walk past where he sleeps in a little alcove off the tracks. Their backs were to him but he saw the guy in back holding a gun on the guy in front. And he probably heard the shot."

"But the shooter never came back."

"He must've gone on to the next station. The meat is great."

"Don't leave any over."

She would hand over a piece of hers in a few minutes. For a man with a flat stomach, he had an enormous appetite. "It's a great meal."

"So you think the Transit cop who ordered the killing of Micah Anthony killed this guy Farrar."

"I'm sure of it. He got rid of the only link between himself and the three guys who were tried ten years ago."

"And now he's home free."

"And we're out in the cold. I got one scrap of information from the guy in Sing-Sing. His brother referred to the cop as 'the sarge.' On Monday I'll tell MacHovec to start looking at all the Transit cops who were sergeants at the time Anthony was shot."

"Some job."

"That's what he does, Hack, sits at the computer and phone and pulls out facts. He's also good at charming the women at Motor Vehicles."

"They're uncharmable."

"Guess you just don't have what it takes, buddy." She grinned at him across the table. "And he's good at Social Services—at least better than I would be—and all those other hellholes. We'll check Farrar's incoming phone calls, but this sarge guy is too smart to call from his desk."

"Or from a phone booth in his district. Maybe he uses phone cards, the way we do."

"There is one more thing." She told him about Micah Anthony's old friend John Beasely. "Mrs. Anthony—uh, Appleby—thinks he was a sergeant when Anthony was killed."

"I like that."

"But the homeless guy said it was two white guys who passed him. Beasely's black."

"It's dark down there."

"True." She passed a third of her steak over to his plate.

"Ah. You're a generous woman."

She smiled, happy, comfortable, and well fed, dessert still to come.

She awoke after one, half the bed empty. Tying her terry-cloth robe, she went out to the living room. "Hack?"

"I'm here. Don't turn the light on."

She could see his silhouette on the sofa. He was wearing the terry robe he left in her apartment. "You OK?"

"Just couldn't sleep. I fell off right away, but I woke up an hour later and couldn't get back. Too much going on in my head. Sit down, baby."

She sat beside him. "What's going on?"

"Just a lot of things. We'll talk about it, but not tonight. You smell good."

"It's Paris."

"Does it bother you that I call you baby?"

"Why should it? I like it."

"I heard a woman with attitude on the radio complain that her husband called her that, and she told him not to. I thought maybe I'd missed something important in human relations."

She smiled. "There's not much you miss."

"Jane."

"What, baby?"

He chuckled. "I'm going to be busy for the next week or a few weeks. I may not be able to see you."

"Should I worry?"

"Nothing to worry about. That's why I'm telling you. And I'll see you in June on Medal Day, if not before. I'm giving out the medals, remember?"

He had arranged that early in the year when he was still working for the chief of D's at One PP, before his promotion to deputy chief.

"I remember. My father's coming."

"Armed with a camera, I bet. I've got someone to take pictures for me. I want one of the two of us I can hang in my office."

"Make me a copy." It would be her first picture of him. "Hack."

"Hmm?" He sounded tired.

"This problem of yours that's going to keep you busy for a couple of weeks. If there's another woman in your life, I'll find her and kill her."

The startled look on his face softened a second later, changing to an almost smile. "Is that a promise?"

She didn't answer. She put her arm around him and drew him down to rest against her, encircling him with the other arm. It was a sweet reversal of what had happened several times over the last ten years, nights when she was too upset or keyed up to sleep and he had come over to be with her and comfort her.

He nestled himself against her body. In two minutes, he was asleep.

32

SHE TOOK THE weekend off. From the stillness of her phone, she knew everyone else had done the same. Only Defino called. He was going stir-crazy and was driving Toni out of her mind.

"I'll come and visit you," Jane said.

"The trip'll kill you," Defino said glumly.

"It hasn't killed *you* yet. There have been developments we could talk about."

"If you have the time, you know I'd like to see you and talk."

"I'll give you a heads-up."

Hack stayed through Sunday breakfast, then drove her partway to Defino's house in a distant part of Queens. Toni wrapped her arms around Jane and cried while Defino paced.

"Have you had lunch?" Toni asked. "I could make you—"

"I've had plenty to eat. I just want to talk to Gordon for a while."

"I'll leave you alone. If there's anything—"

"Honey, we're fine. Don't hover."

"You're looking good," Jane said when Toni had left them.

"I feel fine. Just this damned ache in my chest. One rib's fractured; a couple are bruised. The doc said it could take six weeks till the fracture heals. I'm working on five."

"You'll make it. Let me tell you where we are."

She gave him the whole story. McElroy had said it was OK to tell him about the guns. He was impressed, not just with the find but that Jane had disobeyed the whip.

"You've got guts," he said.

"I was desperate to find you. You give anyone a statement yet?"

"Yeah, but it happened so fast in Manelli's apartment, I hardly saw the faces of the two guys at the door. They drove me around for a while arguing about what to do with me. They never used a name I could hear, and I was covered up in the back of the van, so I couldn't tell where we were going. With all the turning and braking, I started feeling sick to my stomach. I figure if you found me, you followed a trail and you know more than I do."

"We do. Let's start talking and see if we can come up with something."

"You said Anthony had a friend in the Transit Police."

"John Beasely. He was a sergeant ten years ago. Mac-Hovec's going to find every Transit Police sergeant and check him out. One of them could have lived in the Village."

"Or had a friend there," Defino said. "That's a dead end. You think Randolph knows who this cop is?"

"No. Farrar was the link between Randolph's group and the sergeant, and Farrar's dead. Beasely's the only name we've got and it's a long shot. The homeless guy said the shooter and the victim were both white men."

"Tell MacHovec to check out Anthony's class at the academy. See how many of those guys made sergeant by the time Anthony was killed."

"Good idea." She smiled. "Your brain's working, Gordon. Better than mine is."

"Some cop could have intervened in Randolph's cases. Maybe MacHovec can come up with a name."

"OK." She was making notes.

"The night of the killing: When the cops got to Randolph's crib, all three of those guys were there, right?"

"Right."

"That's gotta mean none of them shot Anthony. They couldn't have been that stupid, to kill him and go back."

"Maybe Charley Farrar picked up Anthony and—"

"Does Anthony know him? Why does Anthony go with him?"

She thought about it. "He has some ID with him. He's driving with a Transit cop."

"OK. It could even be an official car."

"Right. With or without Farrar. Gordon, did those guys talk about the Anthony killing?"

"Not once. At least, not that I could hear. When I was in that apartment—"

"Testa's apartment."

"Whoever. They kept the door shut. They talked so all I could hear was a mumble. Their problem was what to do with me."

"None of those three guys owned a car, Gordon. I'm talking about ten years ago."

"So it's unlikely any of them did the killing. Randolph must have left the apartment and called Farrar or the Transit cop from a pay phone."

"Wait a minute. Maybe Farrar was in the crib the whole time, hiding in a bedroom. He stays hidden from Anthony because he's the link to the cop. He could be the one who followed Anthony out of the apartment. He motions to the cop who's parked down the block and they follow Anthony."

"This is sounding good," Defino said. "Farrar briefs the cop and they pick up Anthony when he's done making his calls. Randolph and the others don't know what's going on. That's why they're not in a hurry to leave. When Anthony's killed, the crib is the only address anyone has for them. You know, they ran this like a communist cell from the old days. Only one person in a cell is connected to one person in another cell."

"Gordon, this is the most investigated case in the last decade. Why didn't anyone see this before?"

"Because those three mutts were well trained. They knew one thing: Keep quiet and stick to your story. As long as they maintained that they were three guys doing business with Anthony, whose real name they didn't know, nobody could break them."

"But they had three guns that were traced to an armory."

"What I remember from that trial is that Randolph said that Anthony was trying to sell them guns. Those were samples he dropped off. Manelli and Morgan played dumb. They didn't know anything. Randolph said the guns were Anthony's. They put Randolph away for possession. None of them were ever charged with the murder. There wasn't enough evidence."

"So Farrar was the only one who knew who the cop was. And he stayed the only one up until his murder. That's why Randolph called Farrar after our visit."

"And Farrar called the cop, who told him to go down to the stash and dig out a Beretta, and drop it where it would be seen in Riverside Park. And now Farrar's dead, and we have no trail to the cop."

"MacHovec'll dig something up," Jane said. "That cop thinks he's home free now. Nobody alive knows who he is. What a sweet operation."

"If I thought Randolph knew more than he let on . . ."

"You said it yourself, Gordon. He's well trained. Those guys, including Farrar, kept everything to themselves for ten years. They went through a trial and nobody broke them. That prosecutor did his damnedest and didn't get anywhere."

"So even if we got Manelli back, he doesn't know anything."

"And all Randolph has is a phone number to a dead man's apartment."

Defino got up and walked around, as though he needed to stretch his legs.

"It's a good scenario, Gordon, the car waiting a block away, Farrar going to meet them to report. You think Anthony said something that night that got him killed?"

"Anthony was too smart to say anything. Bottom line, someone followed him to the pay phone and saw him make his call. Anthony didn't see him. They may not even have heard what he said, just that he made a call, which meant he had a connection he hadn't told them about."

"So they may not even have made him."

"Yeah."

"And the cop in the car was watching."

Sometimes the inevitability of the tragedy became too much to bear. Had Anthony walked a few blocks to another pay phone, he might have survived the night. Had he hailed a cab as he hung up from calling his wife, he might still be alive.

"Gets to you, doesn't it?" Defino said.

Jane nodded. "Maybe we can get him out in the open with the guns."

"You thinking of going undercover?"

She could hear that he wasn't serious. She smiled. "I'm forty-one and white."

"Hey, the squad's equal opportunity, or hadn't you heard?"

"Thanks, partner." It was time to go. "Maybe we can use the guns for bait. This Transit cop doesn't know we know where they are. Farrar didn't know I was there. Nobody's been there since Graves put that detail at the site."

"Talk to Graves. You leaving?"

"It's time."

"We'll drive you to the subway. I don't want you waiting for that bus on a Sunday."

"How's your daughter?"

"She's doing fine. She thinks the world of you, Jane."

It was something that had happened in the winter months, a frightening experience none of them would ever forget. "Tell her I feel the same way about her."

She thought about the case on the subway home, a long ride back to Manhattan, and then sitting across from the dark fireplace in her living room, the reason she had taken the apartment in spite of its cost. It was warm enough that she opened a window and let the fresh air in.

Farrar and the sarge hadn't needed a phone call; they were right there. Maybe they were there every time Anthony visited the crib. Something had happened that night to evoke a flicker of distrust in the sarge, making him feel that the gun deal was a set-up or had become dangerous for some other reason. They would never find out what it was.

Defino was right: The men had been trained well. Only Curtis Morgan had broken ranks by talking to his brother, and that was after he had been tried and acquitted. Morgan had not killed anyone. Manelli had not killed anyone. Timothy Morgan had been right: The group had retained Manelli after his deal fell through to keep him from talking, even though the proceeds would be smaller. They had the rigor of a military group and it had kept most of them out of jail, two of them unidentified until this week. Randolph had taken the fall, but not for as long as accessory to murder would have given him.

The one breach that Jane could detect was that Morgan knew about the sergeant. Farrar must have talked about the sarge, which meant that the breach was Farrar's fault, not Morgan's.

Now that Farrar was dead, Jane wondered whether Randolph had been given a new contact number. It wouldn't be easy to get it to him while he was in Rikers; the Transit cop would be crazy to chance a visit. So what would Randolph do if he got another visit from the police? Probably nothing, she thought. For him, the Anthony case was finally over. He didn't know who had killed Anthony and he didn't care. He hadn't, and no one could prove that he had. He didn't know where the guns were stashed and probably didn't know that one of them had been left in Riverside Park. And there was no proof that he had made a phone call to Charley Farrar a couple of Wednesdays before. Except for the current charge that had put him in Rikers, Carl Randolph was a free man.

As Jane ran the known and presumed facts through her mind, something leaped out at her. Why had Morgan, Manelli, and Randolph kept quiet during their questioning and the trial that followed? At least one of them, and probably all of them, knew Farrar, yet his name never surfaced. At least one of them knew there was a Transit cop involved, yet he remained a secret.

How had the cop managed to keep them quiet? Money was the only viable answer. Where would the sarge get enough money to pay off the four men in the crib?

It struck her that those questions were key, that no one

had asked them ten years before because it was assumed that only the three men caught in the crib were involved in the sale of the guns. Had they been the only people involved, there would be no money if they failed. But if they reported to a superior, that person could be pressured for money to keep them quiet. After all, if they turned in Farrar, that information could be used to cut a deal.

OK, she thought, these three mutts get arrested and the sarge is scared. At least one of them can rat out Farrar. The sarge has to pay them to keep quiet, or promise to pay them as soon as he comes up with the money. But how does a police sergeant put his hands on enough money to pay off three men—four, actually—so they won't tell what they know?

Jane could feel her adrenaline pumping. She was onto something. The gun deal was either not the first or not the last operation that the sarge was involved in. He had done something before or after the murder of Micah Anthony that had given him enough money to pay off the men in the crib. Were there other stolen assets he had managed to sell in deals unknown to the FBI and the NYPD? Maybe he had retired a wealthy man and moved out of the city, even out of the country.

At eight, Jane called Ron Delancey.

"Hi, there," he said buoyantly. "I see you found your guy. Good work. You inviting me on another trip down below?"

"Hardly. I've had my fill of rats and roaches, and my boss wants a piece of me for disobeying a direct order."

"He'll get over it. It may cost you some lost time."

"That's what I think. Ron, are you aware of any large losses in the TA through theft in the last ten years?"

"Pilferage is always a problem on work sites."

"I mean something bigger than what you'd call pilferage. Maybe a cash haul or a theft of equipment worth tens of thousand of dollars."

"That has happened."

"You find out who did it?"

"In one case they practically left their calling card for us and they're doing time upstate."

"And the other cases?"

"One is still open. A big one. I can check on it for you."

"When did it happen and what was the value of the loot?"

"Five to ten years ago. I was still on the job. The street value was probably close to a million dollars."

"That's what I'm looking for. Any suspects?"

"There are always suspects, but in that case they led nowhere. The TA was able to keep it out of the news but it was common knowledge."

"It didn't happen to be in the Second Avenue subway, did it?"

Delancey laughed. "You're hooked on that, aren't you? No, I don't think so. It was four other work sites in the system. I'll look into it tomorrow and get back to you. Can I call you at work?"

"Yes, but don't leave a name or number if I'm not there. I've kept you a secret from everyone."

"Always wanted to be a man of mystery. OK, Jane. I'll call you."

Once she had the details, MacHovec might be able to tap into the file. Then she would have the suspects, the location, and the value of the theft. In the meantime, they had to decide how to interview John Beasely. The thought of it made her unhappy. By now he had surely gotten his lieutenant's bars. Because of his rank, Graves or McElroy might talk to him. The last thing she wanted was to act accusatory toward Micah Anthony's oldest friend.

[33]

THE FIVE OF them huddled on Monday morning. Graves had chosen the conference room over his office, sitting at the head of the table with McElroy and Jane on his left, the others on his right. Annie was absent, but Graves had sheets of paper on which Jane could see handwritten notes. It was a planning session.

Graves had a little speech to start things off. Across from Jane, MacHovec looked as though he might fall asleep. She hoped he would restrain yawns.

At the end of the short pep talk, Jane proposed the new theory she and Defino had devised about what had happened the night of Anthony's murder: four men instead of three men in the crib, Charley Farrar meeting the sarge.

"You're saying those original three guys didn't do it?" Smithson said.

"Right. Which explains why they were still at the crib when the cops arrived. They didn't know what was going down. All they knew was that Anthony had left, that one of them, probably Farrar, followed him out. And later that night the cops showed up."

"And Farrar, with or without the cop, killed Anthony," Graves said.

"That's it."

"They were well disciplined. Detective MacHovec, maybe you can find a Transit sergeant with a military background."

"I'll give it a shot."

"Anything else, Detective Bauer?"

She suggested trying to draw the sergeant out by offering the guns for sale.

"We could do that," McElroy said. "Get a phone and have it monitored twenty-fours hours a day. We can trick it out with a recorder and backtrace capability."

"We'll need someone to monitor it," Graves said.

"Gordon can do it," Jane said. "He's home. He's not going anywhere. It'll put him back in the game."

"Good idea." McElroy was almost glowing.

"Take care of this, Ellis," Graves said.

"You bet."

"I don't think anything will come of it, but it's worth a try. If this cop is as smart as he seems to be, he's not going to fall for something like this."

"It's got to shake him up," Jane said.

"Any other ideas?" Graves looked at her.

She had told them she had discussed this with Defino, that he had contributed much of the new scenario. "One thing that came up in our conversation is how those three guys got paid."

"For what?" MacHovec said. "For getting collared with three stolen guns?"

"For keeping quiet about Farrar and the sarge. For going as far as they did with Anthony."

"Are you suggesting," Graves said, "that the gun deal was only one operation the sarge was involved in?"

"Yes, sir," Jane said.

"Then he could have had the proceeds of other operations to pay them with."

"It's possible." She didn't want to give Delancey away.

"You have something to back this up?"

"Not right now. I have to look into it."

"Then do it."

"Yes, sir."

They bounced a few ideas around and then Graves said, "Lieutenant McElroy will interview Lt. John Beasely. From what you've told me, he's a long shot as the sergeant we're looking for, and I want this handled delicately. OK, get to work."

As they left the conference room, Graves stopped Jane. "Detective Defino looking good?"

"Very good. The rib hurts but he's anxious to come back. That's an understatement."

"I can imagine. Thanks for going there. Sounds like his mind is in high gear. Get MacHovec working on your theory."

"I will."

In the office, she closed the door. MacHovec and Smithson had refilled their cups.

"Looks like you're the only one with ideas," Smithson said.

"It was mostly Defino's. Sean, hold off on that stuff about heists in the TA."

"You got an anonymous friend working on it?"

She nodded. "I should hear something later today or tomorrow. Work on finding the sergeant. I'm glad we're off the hook on Beasely."

"You're right," Smithson said. "Those guys got paid for keeping quiet."

"And the money had to come from somewhere. They didn't sell any of the guns, and sergeants don't make enough to grease four palms. Not those palms. I'm told there was a major case of theft at some TA work sites that's never been cleared. There would have been enough for the four guys with plenty left for the sarge."

"This case has tentacles. It keeps creeping wider."

"That son of a bitch could still be in business," Jane said. "I want to put an end to him." She pulled out notes and asked Smithson if she could use the typewriter. She wanted to keep Graves up-to-date.

Ron Delancey called back after lunch. "I think I've got what you want," he said. "It's not the Second Avenue subway but it's big, happened about eight years ago, half in Queens, half in the Bronx. In all instances, they were widening a tunnel, laying new track, updating stations. In Queens, two pieces of heavy equipment, cable trucks, disappeared from the site. In the Bronx, one truck disappeared from each of two sites. These are huge things, cost the TA about a quarter of a mil each, which is what they paid to replace them. Fully loaded with new cable and equipment, street value is anywhere from half a mil to whatever they could get for them. The thefts all occurred on the same night."

"How do you steal them?" Jane asked.

"You move them somewhere away from the work site, store them temporarily, dismantle them, or sell them in one piece. The buyer ships them out of the country and resells them. Big bucks to be made all around. And the copper cable is a bonus, new, unused stuff for resale. The copper could also wind up as mungo, you know, scrap, to a wholesale metal dealer."

"If the stuff is in parts, they get trucked away."

"In the middle of the night."

"That's not a one-man operation."

"Not a chance. Whoever did it had a gang, probably experienced TA workers. They didn't leave a trace. We put out feelers everywhere to find where they went, but we never found them. I suspect they had a buyer before they removed the trucks and they changed hands right away, maybe the same night. Then the guys went home, took a shower, and turned up at work to find the trucks missing."

"Who did you like for it?"

"I'll give you some names. I can fax some stuff to you. Give me a number."

"Any Transit cop among the names?"

"As a perp? No. That what you're looking for?"

"Could be."

"OK. We'll do the looking."

"Talk about cost overruns," Jane said after she had read the faxes. "Replacement value a million bucks."

"So they could have realized half of that," Smithson said.

"Nice little deal." Jane passed the list of names to Mac-Hovec. "I was hoping to see Farrar here, but he's not. If the sarge was involved in this, he kept it separate."

MacHovec studied the names, then started working the computer.

34

DEFINO LIKED THE idea of monitoring the phone. He would be able to turn Toni down when she tried to drag him out to go shopping and breathe some fresh air. And maybe it would work.

McElroy said the phone company would install the equipment the next day, and they would run the ad from Wednesday through the weekend. If nothing happened by then, they would give it up. He was scheduled to talk to John Beasely at four at another location.

MacHovec worked on the names from Ron Delancey for the rest of the afternoon. From his mutterings, Jane could tell he was coming up with nothing useful. Still, if that operation was run like the Anthony one, only one person in the gang knew the man at the next higher level.

"There's nothing here that makes one guy a standout," MacHovec said. "It could be any of them or all of them. It could even be none of them, and there aren't any cops on this list."

"I know that."

"But I like your idea that the sarge needed to pay hush money. And there was plenty from this heist. Any way we can trace the stolen goods?"

"The Transit detectives would have done it, Sean. The stuff was probably on a freighter to Saudi Arabia the next morning."

"With my tax dollars," he grumbled. He turned back to

the screen, hit some keys, shook his head, hit some more. "If I had to pick one of these 'possible suspects,' I'd take this one." He hit a key and his printer started churning out paper. He tossed the first copy on Jane's desk and the second on Smithson's.

The man's name was Terence Garland. He had been working on the site since the construction began. A detective who interviewed him had noted that Garland had been warned about pilfering. Nothing he took was of great value: a few tools and some other things he could use to improve his house. It amused Jane because MacHovec did similar things. He loaded up on pencils and paper, pens, paper clips, rubber bands, and notebooks. It was more a matter of convenience, Jane thought, than of saving money, although MacHovec spent almost nothing—brown-bagging his lunch and drinking free coffee, not unusual in this squad.

"You pick him because of the pilfering?"

"Yeah. It's a small step from taking a hammer and nails to moving on to something bigger."

"I think you're wrong." She pushed her chair back from the desk. "It's a big step. If this sergeant was as smart as we think he was, he would pick people with clean records. Someone who's got comments like this in his file is a likely suspect. I want to see the guys who were clean as virgin snow."

MacHovec gave her a look, then printed out another file. "Try this." When he had slapped a second copy on Smithson's desk, he got up and left the office.

"Touchy," Smithson said. "But I agree with you."

"Let's talk to this guy."

"Let's talk to all of them. It's been years since this happened. Maybe they'll be off guard."

The printout showed that the first man, Mickey Crawford, was still working. Jane called the TA and was told he would report for work the next day at eight A.M. She and Smithson agreed to meet at his station at nine and have him paged. Let their arrival be a surprise.

MacHovec returned and began to print out the rest of the suspects' files. When he had finished, it was time to leave. He and Smithson walked out together. Jane sat in the quiet office and read the histories and the cops' comments about each man. Sean was right: Nothing in any file made you sit up and take notice. The detective who interviewed Crawford remarked that he was polite and straightforward, didn't fidget or seem nervous, answered all questions, and was cooperative when asked to appear for a second interview.

The detective had put him on the list of suspects because Crawford could not account adequately for his time on the night of the robbery. The interviewer added that Crawford seemed too good to be true.

That, of course, was the way an innocent person might come off. As for not being able to account for his time, how many people who have slept through the night could account for theirs?

Jane read through the files of the other suspects.

"Why are you always the last one out?"

She looked up. McElroy was standing at her open door. She glanced at her watch. It was six. "Just reading the files of suspects in a big TA theft eight years ago. Did you talk to Lieutenant Beasely?"

"Just came back." McElroy came in, pulled Sean's chair out, and sat down. "I don't have an answer for you," he said, addressing the question she had not asked. "Was he the sarge? He could have been. Is there any evidence? None. If he did it, he got away with it. This is one smart guy. He's believable. Listen to him and you know he loved Anthony like a brother. On the other hand . . ." He shrugged. "If he did it, we'll never pin it on him unless Randolph or Manelli saw him and can ID him."

"Randolph won't, and we'll never find Manelli alive." Jane tapped the papers in front of her. "Smithson and I'll be talking to the suspects in the theft starting tomorrow."

McElroy didn't move. From the look on his face, he might not have heard her. "I think you hit on it, Jane," he said finally, "that somebody paid those three mutts to keep quiet. When the Anthony killing happened, everyone thought it was a closed circle, three guys who were selling stolen guns and had to kill the buyer because he found out something he shouldn't have. But if they were the ground floor reporting to the sarge, it was the promise of money that kept them quiet. At least one of them could have ratted out Farrar and maybe the sarge.

"Look, I don't think it's Beasely. Your homeless guy said they were two white men, right?"

"Right."

"No way in hell could Beasely be taken for a white man, even in low light. Unless he's a damn good actor, he wasn't involved."

"I'm glad to hear it, Loot."

McElroy stood and walked to the door. "Doesn't mean he wasn't. Go home. We'll talk in the morning."

She walked home, turning it over. In her apartment, she called Defino. They had hooked up a phone with all the accompanying paraphernalia in his living room. Annie had managed to get an ad in the next day's *News* and *Post*. He was looking forward to hearing the phone ring.

"It may not happen," Jane warned.

"Anything's better than being pampered."

She followed her intuition and checked out the least likely suspects, and got nowhere. She found some pleasing music on the radio and turned it on to play softly, sipping some Stoli on the rocks. In Paris they had drunk wine, Hack swirling it in his glass before inhaling it and tasting it. He made good choices. In the few days they were there, Jane developed an appreciation for red wine.

"You're making my life more expensive," she teased.

"Keep you working hard."

The vacation was more than she had hoped for, more than she had expected, and her expectations had been high. She had never spent that many days with a man, that many hours of concentrated togetherness. They laughed and talked, walked miles, visited museums. One afternoon they rode the funicular up to Montmartre, where she sat for a

portrait in pastels done by a long-haired, dark-eyed fellow
in his thirties who leaned over his easel intently, one foot
bare and one stuffed into a ratty sneaker.

Hack thought the portrait was a perfect rendering of her
face; she wasn't so sure. She remembered seeing drawings of
people she knew and finding in them images of their parents
and siblings, records of relationships she had not noticed in
real life. Looking at the picture of her face, she wondered if
it harked back to a natural mother or father she would never
know.

"Don't you like it?"

"I'm not sure it's me."

"I'm sure."

He wanted to keep it, but knew he couldn't. "That's your
birthday present," he said. "I'll have it framed and give it
back to you."

Then they visited Sacré-Coeur, Hack carrying the rolled
portrait as they strolled into the church, neither of them dip-
ping into the font or genuflecting.

The next day was their last, and Hack had saved the best
restaurant for that night. They dressed and took the
Metro to the Right Bank, then walked a short distance
from the Arc de Triomphe to the restaurant, where only
cheese and dishes made with cheese were served. They
were seated against the wall at a table for two. Hack ordered a fine wine and they both enjoyed a choice of the
more than one hundred cheeses offered on one round
thick wooden board after another.

They began to talk. Before her first sip of the wine, Jane
felt high, excited. She had turned forty-one and they had
completed ten years of loving each other. Then Hack
touched her hand and said something, and everything they
were celebrating began to disintegrate.

[35]

SMITHSON WAS ALREADY at the station when Jane arrived at nine on Tuesday. Mickey Crawford's supervisor listened to their request without comment and called Crawford to the station.

"Take a while," the supervisor said, "maybe fifteen minutes."

It was an accurate estimate. At twenty after nine, Crawford appeared at the supervisor's door. Smithson and Jane took him to an empty office and Jane closed the door. Crawford was a good-looking man in his late thirties. He was unperturbed and asked no questions, sat where Smithson directed him, and waited quietly.

"There was a major theft of equipment about eight years ago," Jane began. "You remember being questioned about it?"

"Yes, ma'am."

"You were unable to account for your time that night."

Crawford said nothing.

"You remember what you were doing?" Smithson asked.

"It's a long time ago. Whatever I told the detectives then is what happened."

"Were you married at the time?"

"Married but separated."

"You sleep alone that night?"

Crawford shrugged. "Probably. I don't remember."

"You married now?"

"Yes, sir."

"I would think you would remember," Jane said, "whether you were sleeping alone that night. You don't get questioned by the police very often."

"No, ma'am. I think that was the problem back then, whether anyone could vouch for me that night."

"Problem?" Smithson asked.

"When you sleep alone, no one knows if you're gone. If I'd had a girlfriend over, she could have told the police I was there all night."

"You have any friends in the Transit Police at that time?" Jane asked.

"I run into them sometimes, but I can't say I've ever had a friend."

"Did you know a Sergeant Beasely back then?"

"Doesn't ring a bell."

"Maybe someone who joined a few guys for a beer after work?" Jane said.

"Not that I remember."

"You know anyone named Charley Farrar?" she asked.

"I don't know any Farrars."

"You ever hear the name mentioned?"

"No, ma'am."

Smithson picked up the questioning. "What about Curtis Morgan?"

"I don't think so." He hadn't blinked at either name.

"A track man. You could have worked with him once."

"I've worked with a lot of men and I don't remember all their names. I don't think I ever knew him."

"You have kids?" Jane asked.

The question startled him. "Yeah, a son and daughter. Why?"

"Who had custody when you separated?"

"During the separation, my wife did. We worked out something else for the divorce. I get them alternate weekends and some holidays."

"Where were your kids the night of the theft?"

"I was separated," Crawford said. "They would have been with my wife."

"You have a girlfriend at that time?" Smithson asked.

"Yeah, maybe. I'm not sure. But no one was in the apartment with me that night."

"You're pretty sure of that."

"Yes, sir." He was as calm as he had been when they sat down. The questions rolled off him, leaving him dry as a bone.

They went at him for another ten minutes and he answered as he already had, remaining unconcerned, never displaying anger or even discomfort. Finally, they let him go.

They went up to the street level and found a place to sit and talk over coffee.

"I don't like him," Smithson said. "He's too sure of himself, maybe too rehearsed."

"I agree. And if he was going to be involved in that heist, he wouldn't have a girlfriend over."

"So we keep him on the list. Who's next?"

Jane pulled a sheet of paper out of her bag. "That was Crawford. The one MacHovec liked for this was Terence Garland. He's working out of the Seventy-second Street station on the West Side."

"He in today?"

"Looks like it."

Smithson finished his coffee, dropped some bills on the table, and picked up the check.

"I'll call him, but I don't know how fast he can get here. He's working down the track. What do you need him for?" The TA supervisor's reaction to the two shields was an instant lack of cooperation.

"We want to talk to him," Smithson said.

"About what?"

"About the weather down there. You his private secretary?"

The supervisor scowled and picked up a phone. The message had to be relayed, and the supervisor's temper grew shorter with each exchange of words. Finally, he hung up with a bang. "He'll be here when he gets here. You want a place to sit, you'll have to stay put. We're short of space."

Jane walked out of the office and called Annie, letting her know where they were. There were no messages. "We'll be back after lunch. This may take some time."

Terence Garland showed up in his work clothes, having surfaced from the rat-infested tracks. "You wanted to see me?" He eyed the detectives as though they were the enemy.

"You want privacy?" the supervisor said, standing. "You can talk to him here. I'm leaving." He shut the door behind him.

"What's this about?" Garland asked, looking for a place to sit.

Smithson sat behind the desk, leaving his chair free. Garland took it.

"We want to talk to you about a theft that occurred about eight years ago, while you were working on a renovation."

"They talked to me about it. I didn't steal anything."

"You know anyone who did?"

"No." He fidgeted. "I thought that case was over."

"It isn't," Jane said. "It's just beginning."

"What do you mean?"

"I mean we're starting from scratch. We want the guys who stole that equipment."

"Don't look at *me*."

"Where were you that night?"

"I told the cops the first time around. I was home with my family. I never left my house."

"Your wife vouch for you?" Smithson asked.

"Yeah, my wife vouched for me. I was there the whole time. I watched TV, I ate some fruit, I drank a beer, and I went to bed early."

"What are you so nervous about, Terry?" Jane asked.

"I'm not nervous. I got a job to do. I don't know why you're asking me these questions. I wasn't involved in that and I don't know anyone who was."

"You have a friend named Charley Farrar?"

Garland looked her in the eye. "Never heard of the guy. Should I of?"

"Not if you don't know him."

"You know any Transit cops?" Smithson asked.

Garland shrugged. "I seen 'em. I don't know 'em. This some kind of guessing game?"

"Yeah," Smithson said. "Get the right answer and we let you go."

Garland said nothing. He glanced over at Jane, who avoided his gaze, then looked down at the desk in front of him. "What is it you want to know?" he asked Smithson.

"We want to know who was involved in the theft."

"Not me."

"Then who? You got a name? A couple of names?"

"Look, Detective, I wasn't there, I didn't do it, nobody told me who did. I came to work the next morning, the place was crazy. There was cops all over the place. They hauled us in and talked to us for hours."

"Transit cops?" Jane asked.

"Yeah. Detectives like you. That's all I can tell you."

"Nobody called you and told you what was going down?"

"Nobody called me. Nobody told me nothin'." He took a deep breath and sat back in the chair. Then he said, "Who's this Charley guy you asked about?"

"We're asking the questions, Terry. You remember him?"

"I told you, I never heard of him."

"How 'bout Curtis Morgan?"

"Who's he?"

"You tell me."

"Curtis Morgan." He said it softly. "I could've heard the name."

Smithson jumped on him. "Where? What's the connection?"

"Just a name. You hear a name sometimes, it sticks with you. He work for the TA?"

"He's a track man," Smithson said. "Just like you."

Garland considered it. "If I ever met him, it wasn't in the last couple of years."

Smithson handed him a card. "If you remember anything about him, you call that number."

"Sure."

"You ever know a Transit cop named Beasely?"

"I never knew no Transit cops. I told you that already. And I don't know no city cops neither."

"Just asking, in case it comes back to you."

"I told you what I know."

Smithson glanced at Jane. She turned to Garland. "You ever work on the Second Avenue subway?"

"Nah. I hear they're gonna give that another try. Throw another billion bucks down the drain."

"OK, Terry. Go back to work."

They went back to Centre Street and had lunch. In the office, Annie had left each of them a note to see McElroy. MacHovec joined them. McElroy began by talking about his interview of Lieutenant Beasely. Then he asked Jane and Smithson to report.

"Zip," Jane said. "One guy's smooth and relaxed and the other's a bundle of nerves; thought maybe he'd heard of Curtis Morgan but backed off. Which probably means he's never heard of him. If you asked me to pick one of them, I'd flip a coin."

"You got more names?" McElroy asked.

"I gave them all the suspects the Transit detectives picked," MacHovec said. "These two were the most likely and the least likely."

"You working on Transit sergeants from ten years ago, Detective?"

"As much as I can." MacHovec sounded put-upon.

"Keep at it." McElroy waved them away.

"What's biting his ass?" Smithson said as they walked back to the office.

"Lack of results," Jane said.

"You want some sergeants?" MacHovec asked.

"Yeah, give us some sergeants," Smithson said. "These track guys smell of bug spray. Maybe the sergeants'll smell better."

MacHovec printed out a sheet. "I've only checked down to here." He underlined a name. "This one's dead, these two retired. This one's a lieutenant."

"That's Beasely," Jane said.

"Oh, yeah. And he's been cleared. I was thinking. You ask these guys if they knew Farrar or Morgan?"

"Yeah," Smithson said.

"One of them might try to call them if he doesn't know they're dead. Farrar's murder didn't get a lot of coverage."

"They kept his ID out of the news," Jane said. "The funeral's probably today or tomorrow. We'd better get that telephone tapped ASAP. One of the guys from this morning could call. I'll talk to McElroy."

McElroy took care of it. Jane regretted involving Mrs. Farrar at this time of crisis, but if one of their suspects made a call, they had to know about it. She walked back to the office slowly, thinking about Farrar's phone. Randolph had gotten a message to Farrar from Rikers Island. If Randolph knew Farrar was dead, he had no one to call now, unless he had the sarge's number, and he probably didn't. But Farrar knew Manelli. Farrar had gone to the Catskills to brief Manelli, and Farrar had gone to Manelli's apartment. Manelli might have Farrar's phone number.

Jane dialed the number. A young woman answered.

"Mrs. Farrar?"

"This is her daughter. Can I help you?"

"This is Detective Bauer. I'm sorry to bother you but I need to talk to your mother."

"Just a moment."

Jane could hear voices in the background.

"Hello?"

"Mrs. Farrar, this is—"

"I know who this is. You got my husband killed. I never heard from him after you came here."

"I'm very sorry about your husband, ma'am. We never saw him. I'm sorry to bother you but I need to know if you've gotten any phone calls from your husband's friends, men friends."

"A lot of people have called."

"Did someone named Sal call?"

"Sal, yes, he did. He called after you left last week. He

said he was Charley's friend and he had to talk to him. He said it was urgent."

"Did you give the message to Charley?"

"I never talked to Charley after you left. The man left a number. I was going to give it to Charley when I saw him that night but . . ." She sobbed.

"I understand." Jane waited till the woman calmed herself. "Do you have the number?"

"Here it is." She read off a 718 number, Brooklyn or Queens.

"Did he call back?"

"I don't think so. If he did, I didn't answer the phone. Wait a minute. Let me see if there's a message I didn't read." She went through paper, then came back to the phone. "No, it doesn't look like it. That must have been the only time."

"When is the funeral, Mrs. Farrar?"

"Tomorrow morning."

"Thank you." Jane hung up. "Manelli called Farrar last Thursday, just after we were there. Here's the number." She handed it to MacHovec, who grabbed it and started working the keyboard. He would check Cole's Directory online and get the address.

"She call you?" Smithson asked, coming in with coffee.

"I called her. The funeral's tomorrow. Manelli called after we left last Thursday, said it was urgent, left a number. She never gave it to Charley because she never talked to him again."

"Got it," MacHovec said. He wrote an address on Jane's slip of paper. "It's an auto repair place. Looks like Long Island City."

"Think it's a pay phone?"

"It's not. I'll check my map, but I think it's near Queens Plaza. Lot of industry. Maybe he's sleeping on the floor with a lot of boxes."

"And running out of money, and he can't call Judy."

MacHovec pulled a map out of a drawer and opened it on his desk. "Here it is." He showed it to Jane.

Smithson came over for a look. "You're right. Queens Plaza, just over the bridge. We can get there in half an hour or so. Forget the sergeants. We get Manelli, we've got something."

They ran it by McElroy, whose spirits rose visibly as he heard the story. "You need backup. I'll call the One-oh-eight. Hang on till they tell us where to meet them." He reached for the phone.

[36]

SMITHSON GOT ON the FDR and drove north. They exited and took the Fifty-ninth Street Bridge over the East River to Queens. Just off Queens Boulevard, they found an unmarked vehicle and a sector car waiting for them a block away from the auto repair shop on Van Dam Street. The sector cops explained that the repair shop had a chunk of land behind the structure, typically inhabited by four dogs and broken-down cars and trucks awaiting repair or destruction. It was bounded by a chain-link fence that was so rusted and loose in the overlapping sections that a man could easily squeeze through. The grease-soaked earth held the skirt and bottom rail of the fence secure enough, but any athletic person could easily vault over the top rail, although he might sacrifice a shirt in the venture.

The sector cops moved to cover the back, and Smithson, Jane, and the two Queens detectives drove to the shop and went to the front door. The Queens detectives remained outside while Jane and Smithson went in, shields raised.

An unhappy man with the name Roger embroidered on his pocket looked at them with distress. "How can I help you?" he asked, his face almost contorted.

"We're looking for a man who may be staying here, Salvatore Manelli. Ring a bell?"

Roger made sounds under his breath. "He was here, yeah. I don't know where he is now."

"How long was he here?"

"In and out for maybe a week. He needed a place to stay, and I like having a guy sleep on the premises. Keeps trouble away."

"Where is he now?" Jane asked.

"He left this morning. I don't know where he is."

"You got a number to reach him?"

"He used to live in the Village. I don't know where he lives now."

"He say where he was going?"

"He just said, 'So long,' and walked out. He usually comes back at night."

"He friends with anyone here?"

"He talks to everybody, brings us lunch, plays with the dogs."

"You pay him to stay here?"

"Pay him? I give him a cot to lie on, a TV in my office, a bathroom. I should pay him too?"

"Just asking," Jane said.

"You gonna tell me what he did?"

"We just want to talk to him."

"Hang around. He should be back tonight. You know what? Lemme look at the cot, see if he left his stuff."

They followed Roger to a storeroom at the back of the building. An unmade cot was pushed against the wall and a few pieces of dirty laundry were stuffed in a corner on the floor.

"Looks like he's coming back," Roger said.

"We'll stick around," Smithson said. "He get phone calls here?"

"Sometimes. I need to get back to work."

Jane and Smithson talked to the detectives out front. They agreed to let the sector cops go. One detective would stay near the front, one near the back. In the meantime, Jane and Smithson would interview the men working inside.

Automotive establishments like this one were often casual in their hiring practices, taking on men with records, men who had served time. Jane and Smithson made a list of the names to phone in to MacHovec for checking. One mechanic spoke freely of his background, which included a bit at the military camp at Rikers when he was a teenager. Now twenty-seven, he assured the detectives he was straight, and grateful that Roger had hired him when he needed a job.

All the men had talked to Sal but none knew anything important about him. He had told them he'd had a fight with his girlfriend and had to find a place to stay till he could patch things up. He hadn't mentioned her name or where he lived, and he didn't seem to have a job.

Jane called MacHovec and gave him the list of names, although it was too late in the day for all of them to be checked out. Then she gave him the pay phone number, telling him everyone used it along with the phone on the wall.

"I'll get the list of calls but I won't look at it till I've done these other things. I take it Manelli's not there."

She told him the story.

"Let's hope he comes back tonight."

"Light a candle."

The men left at five, and Jane and Smithson sat down with Roger. He had nothing new to contribute about Manelli.

"You have any idea where he spends his days when he's not here?" Smithson asked.

"He walks out the door and that's the last I see of him. Could be he hangs around Queens Plaza, but I don't think so. I think he takes the subway. Maybe he's trying to make peace with the girlfriend."

After Roger left, they went into the room with the cot and the dirty laundry, put on rubber gloves, and looked carefully at the bed. They lifted the mattress, which disclosed nothing except a spring, and started going through some boxes that shared the space. The boxes had auto equipment that matched the outside markings.

Out back, the dogs were on leashes that gave them each about twenty feet of running space. The cop watching the back door remained inside. Roger had said that lights went on at nightfall, both front and back, and inside several lights were left on overnight. If Manelli returned, they would see him approach.

"Heads up," the cop at the front door called. "This could be him. Guy coming down the street."

Jane and Smithson backed into the work area, out of sight of the front windows. The street was entirely commercial, not a place where a couple would stroll on a spring evening. Jane had her right hand on her open holster.

"Looks like he's coming to the building." A concrete driveway three or four cars wide ran from the sidewalk to the garage doors at the front of the building. To their left was the customer door.

There was no sound. Jane strained to hear a key in the lock. Nothing. Come on, Sal, she implored silently. She looked over at Smithson, who shrugged. Neither of them had any view of the front windows.

"How old a guy is he?" Jane asked.

"Thirty? Thirty-five?"

"It's not Sal. Sal's gotta be fifty or near that."

"He's feeding the dogs," the staticky voice said from the nearer detective's shoulder. "Looks like a wacko, long hair—ah, jeez, he's feeding the dogs bread. He must think they're pigeons."

"Tell him to stay where he is," Jane cautioned. "The dogs'll survive."

The man stayed almost fifteen minutes, talking to the dogs and feeding them. When the bread was gone, he tossed the bag over the fence and wandered off.

"Litterbug," the detective growled.

They went back to their posts.

Like many a stakeout, it was long and boring. No one had thought to go out for food and everyone was hungry. Finally the detective named Wally called the station house and asked for someone to go out and get dinner for four.

It took forty-five minutes and a check of the street before two pizzas and four Cokes arrived. One Queens detective went out a side door and picked it up while the cop who delivered it, wearing plain clothes, walked back to his car in a circuitous route.

As they ate, the sun went down. Lights went on behind the building and streetlights went on in the front. Stray cats walked by. From a distance two dogs barked and the four in the back joined in the chorus.

Then the phone rang. Jane dashed to the office, Smithson at her heels. It rang four times, and Roger's voice picked up and gave a canned speech. After the beep, a man's voice said, "Roger, it's Sal. I'm down in the Village. Something came up and I may not make it back tonight. If I don't get there, I'll see you in the morning."

Smithson opened his cell phone and called the telephone company. While he was making his inquiry, Jane called McElroy.

"He called from a pay phone on Sixth Avenue in the Village," Smithson said, hanging up. "You think he's crazy enough to go to the apartment?"

Jane relayed the message to McElroy.

"Leave the Queens detectives at the automotive place and get yourselves down to the Village. You know what this guy looks like?"

"I saw him the day Defino was kidnapped."

"Well, if he tries to see the girlfriend, you pick him up. He may go up the fire escape. Call for backup while you're driving into the city."

They took off. It was past rush hour and they got down to the Village in good time. Smithson parked, putting the plate in the window, and they headed for Judy Franklin's apartment. They spotted the car from the Six and went through the introductions. The detectives from the Six split up, one taking the back of the building. Manelli had seen Jane but not Smithson. They stood at the corner and looked down the dark street. There was some pedestrian traffic but no one was lingering in front of Judy Franklin's stairs. Jane and Smithson went to the building with one of the detectives from the Six, and up to the apartment.

Judy Franklin opened the door and then, angrily, tried to slam it shut. The detective from the Six stopped her easily, pushed the door open, and the three of them went in, Jane and Smithson running through the apartment looking for Manelli.

"He's not here!" Judy screamed, fury pouring out of her.

"When did he leave?" Jane asked, returning to the living room. "Where did he go?"

"He wasn't here. I haven't seen him since that day. Why don't you believe me? I'm not lying to you. Sal's gone. He's just gone." She began to cry bitterly, berating Jane, the police department, anything she could think of.

"He was in the Village half an hour ago," Jane said.

"How do you know?" Judy sniffed and wiped her face with a tissue.

"He was here."

"He wasn't *here*. I haven't seen him since—"

"OK, I got it." She turned to Smithson. "You think he knew where we were? You think he was trying to lure us down here?"

"Or lure us away from the place. Maybe the guy's got more brains than we gave him credit for."

Jane took out her cell phone and called the automotive shop. When the beep sounded, she said, "Hey, Wally, Bill, this is Jane Bauer. Pick up."

No one answered. Jane kept talking to keep the connection, but there was no response. She waited until she got beeped out, then closed her phone.

"Not there?" Smithson said.

She shook her head. "I didn't get their cell numbers, if they have them. They must have gone outside. Something's up, Warren."

"Sal couldn't have ambushed two armed detectives."

"We've got to get back there. I'll call the One-oh-eight and have them check out the shop."

The sergeant who answered said he would send a sector

car out immediately, and Smithson told the men from the Six to stay in case Manelli showed up.

Judy Franklin watched them as they spoke. "What will you do if you find him?" she asked softly.

"Turn him over to the DA," Jane said.

"Oh, my God."

Jane ignored her. "Let's get going." They ran to the car.

37

"SHIT, I HOPE one of those cops doesn't shoot Manelli. He's all we've got." Smithson had put the light on the roof and was tearing uptown on the FDR, using his horn liberally.

"That son of a bitch," Jane said. "He really set us up."

"But he was calling from the Village. He didn't just say it on the message."

"And then he turned around and went back. What's he doing up there?"

"Call the One-oh-eight and see what's going on."

They learned that the detectives had called in to report that Manelli—or someone who they thought was Manelli—had shown up and they had gone after him. So far, they had failed to make contact.

Smithson zipped across the Fifty-ninth Street Bridge, turned off the roof light and the headlights, and stopped the car before making the turn onto the street of their destination. They got out and turned the corner. Down the block they could see the flashing lights of two radio cars. They went back to Smithson's car and drove over, getting out of the car with their shields raised.

"Hey, Detectives. I'm Officer Dwayne Carlson. This place is empty and we can't raise the detectives who were here."

"You call the owner?" Jane asked.

"He's on his way over. The patrol supervisor and the duty captain from the borough are also on their way over. This place is gonna be top-heavy with bosses in a few minutes."

"Anything on the answering machine?"

"You Detective Bauer?"

"Yes."

"Just a message from you."

"Their car here?"

"Around the corner."

"Then they're on foot. We have to find them. Manelli could be armed."

Jane reported to McElroy. She had lost track of time. It was night, and there were many empty streets and dark lots behind businesses closed till morning.

"Call the Borough Detective Task Force office and request help," McElroy ordered. "I'll get the boss to call and clear it. Then get a search party going. Keep me informed."

"Yes, sir."

Cops arrived in minutes and they started combing the area, through weedy fields and garbage-filled alleys between buildings. About a quarter of an hour later, one of the men around a corner called. "Hey, this way. I think we've got them."

Jane and Smithson broke into a run. Bill and Wally, their hands cuffed behind their backs, were surrounded by cops from the precinct. One of them was about to use a key to uncuff Wally.

"Wait!" Jane shouted. "Don't touch those cuffs." She pushed her way forward. "You guys OK?"

They said they were. She put a pair of gloves on and unlocked each cuff carefully in case a print had been left on it.

"Was it Manelli?" she asked when they were shaking their hands to get the circulation going.

"Manelli and another guy."

"What other guy?"

"Could have been a cop," Wally said. "Manelli asked him if he was the sarge."

They had begun walking back to the shop. "You up to talking?"

"Sure. It was crazy, but I remember almost everything."

"OK. Take your time. We can do this sitting down."

On the way she called McElroy and told him what she knew. "I'll get back to you, Loot. The men are all right. Warren and I'll talk to them at the shop. I want everything they remember before they lose any of it."

A lieutenant from the One-oh-eight was waiting at the shop, and Roger arrived at the same time the search party did. Amid the bedlam, Jane and Smithson took the two detectives into Roger's office, closed the door, and sat down with them.

"From the top," Jane said.

"I saw him approach," Bill said. "He didn't try to come inside. He was just looking to see if anyone was there. He walked around the front, the side, talked to the dogs in the back. I thought he might be like that first guy who fed the dogs, but this one fit the description. While he was out back, we walked out the front way, but he must have circled the building because he came up behind us, said he had a gun, and told us to keep walking."

"How far did you go?"

"Quarter of a mile maybe, behind a big industrial building a few blocks from where we met up with you. Looked like he knew where he was going. You agree?" He looked at Wally, who nodded.

"That's when the other guy showed up."

"What did he look like?" Smithson asked.

"We never saw him. He told us to stop, put our hands on our heads, and if we turned around we'd get a bullet. Where we were, he could've shot us and no one would've heard it. We stopped."

"You said Manelli called him 'sarge'?"

"Didn't call him that," Wally said. "He asked him: 'Are you the sarge?' like he'd never seen him before but he'd heard of him."

"And the guy said?"

" 'Yeah. Do what I tell you.' "

"Was he white?" Jane asked.

"We didn't see him," Wally said. "He told us to lie face-down on the ground, hands behind our head, and then he told Manelli to cuff us and take our weapons." Wally turned to his partner. "Did you get a look at him?"

"Not me."

"Then what happened?" Jane asked.

"I heard them walking away. The guy who did the talking told us to stay where we were or he'd shoot us. I could hear them talking but I couldn't get anything. We stayed there, I don't know, maybe five minutes, and we heard what could've been a gunshot."

Jane and Smithson exchanged glances. Then Smithson said, "We gotta look for a body."

"Take it easy, guys," Jane said. "Thanks. I'm sorry we got you into this." She called McElroy, who was on his way. Then she and Smithson took two uniforms and went out in the direction Bill and Wally had come from.

They checked out alleys and areas behind buildings, much as they had done a little while earlier, walking around cars and trucks, crates stacked high in rows, and through weeds littered with discarded objects.

"What do you know about the guy we're looking for?" Officer Samson asked.

"He was involved in something ten years ago and he's one of the guys who kidnapped my partner a week ago Friday."

"The detective working on a cold case?"

"That's the one."

"How's he doing?"

"Going stir-crazy, but he's feeling much better. This son of a bitch Manelli and his pals were close to killing him when we found him. What's around the corner here?"

"More of the same. We should go behind this warehouse. There's a lot of open space."

They shone their flashlights through the chain-link fencing, but saw nothing that looked like a body.

"There's a gate down here," Smithson said. "Let me see if

it's open." He sprinted along the fence and called them to come.

The gate was open. Inside were several trailer trucks, two unattached cabs, and two smaller trucks. They walked between the vehicles, squatting and shining their lights under them.

"Over here," Officer Samson called.

They joined him at the cab of one of the large trucks. He pointed his light out onto the empty concrete, weeds sprouting between the rectangles, at something that looked like a man's body lying on its stomach in the moonlight, a pool of blood seeping around it. All four of them ran toward it.

"That your guy?" the second cop asked, stopping a few feet away.

"That's him, Salvatore Manelli, dead with all his secrets." Jane approached the body. After a good look, she opened her cell phone and started making calls.

38

THE CRIME SCENE unit arrived faster than ever before in Jane's experience. Something positive to say about the borough of Queens. She left the two uniforms to guard the body and she and Smithson went back to the auto shop to wait for McElroy, who arrived quickly and kept in contact with Graves.

They all drove to the crime scene and searched the area

carefully for the detectives' missing guns, but found no trace of them or anything else useful. The sarge had probably shot Manelli with one gun and then took both of them with him.

McElroy phoned in a description of the body and the detectives' story to Graves. Manelli had a wallet with ID and cash in his pants pocket, but no weapon, which didn't mean he hadn't been carrying one. The sarge had been thorough in leaving no weapons and no clues to his identity at the scene. Manelli had been shot once in the back, the force of the bullet pushing him forward. Judging from the abrasions on his face, he had slid along the concrete a few inches.

When the ME arrived, he said Manelli had lived only about five minutes after the shot. By the time the two detectives had managed to rise from their prone position, not an easy feat with hands cuffed behind their backs, Manelli was, in all likelihood, dead, and the sarge putting distance between himself and the crime scene. An expert at keeping his identity a secret for ten years, he had managed yet again.

"According to what those detectives told you," McElroy said, "Manelli didn't recognize the sarge."

"Looks that way," Smithson said.

"So all we know is that he's alive and well. And now he's cut the last cord between himself and the guys in the crib. Randolph didn't call him, did he?"

"He called Farrar," Jane said. "I wonder if the sarge found Manelli through Farrar's number."

McElroy looked at her with a frown. "You think after he killed Farrar he called Farrar's wife and asked if Manelli had called?"

"Why not? That's how we found Manelli. The sarge may have asked Farrar where Manelli was holing up, but Farrar didn't know. Those guys split up after they left Defino in Rockaway. The sarge would have Farrar's phone number and Manelli's. He's too smart to call Manelli's apartment in the Village. He's a cop. He'd guess we'd put a trace on that phone. But we just discovered Farrar after the kidnapping."

"And we didn't monitor his phone." McElroy sounded as though he just realized he'd missed something.

"I'll call Mrs. Farrar," Jane said, looking at her watch with a flashlight. "It's too late tonight. She's burying her husband tomorrow. Another few hours won't change anything."

"Do that." McElroy went over and talked to the crime scene detectives. When he came back, he said, "I don't think they're gonna find anything useful. It's a clean shot, up close, no footprints on concrete, no car tracks. This guy is smooth, knows what he's doing."

"There's still Randolph," Smithson said.

"Randolph doesn't know the sarge," the lieutenant said. "He knew Farrar. Randolph's a waste of time."

"Let's ask MacHovec tomorrow to check the incoming calls to Farrar's phone from the day he died," Jane said. "See if anything interesting turns up. And I'll call Mrs. Farrar after the funeral."

McElroy sent them home, telling them to sleep in the next day. Smithson drove Jane home over her objections. She was too tired to make it an issue. They talked sporadically. When Smithson stopped in front of her building, she thanked him and said good night, although it was closer to morning.

Upstairs there were messages from her father, from Hack, from Defino, and from an old friend who wondered if she were still alive. "I'm wondering myself," she murmured, stumbling to the bedroom.

"Just check out calls from pay phones, if there are any," she told MacHovec at ten thirty when she arrived at Centre Street. Smithson was still out.

"You look like death warmed over."

"I feel like it. After forty you shouldn't have to pull all-nighters. Or almost all-nighters."

"Don't tell me you're forty. I'll crawl into a hole." He got on the phone to his contact at the telephone company and gave Farrar's number and some dates, asking for a quick response. MacHovec knew someone everywhere: the post office, the board of education, the telephone company, almost every part of city government, and some useful contacts in D.C. as well.

While he was on the phone, Jane returned her father's call

and left a message for the old friend. Then she returned Defino's call.

"Where the hell have you been?" Defino said when he recognized her voice. "I've got something."

"Tell me."

"I got a call last night from the ad in the *Post*."

"About the guns?" She saw MacHovec look her way.

"An inquiry, kind of cagey, never used the word 'gun.' Said he'd call back. I can't tell you much more but it's on tape. I left a message for McElroy too. You all out on the town last night?"

"Oh, Gordon, do I have a story for you." She gave him the highlights, finishing the conversation when McElroy appeared at the door.

"Our ad in the *Post* backfired," he said with a grim smile.

"Backfired how? I just heard from Defino. He said—"

"I know what he said." McElroy yawned. He was over forty too and he had been at Centre Street when Jane walked in. "Inspector Graves got a call from someone who works for Captain Bowman. They spotted the ad and called Defino to find out what was going on."

"Shit."

"Right. The only people looking for ads are our people. I told Detective Defino to stay on it, but I'm not expecting much. By the way, we're still the only ones who know we have the guns, and I want to keep it that way."

"No problem," Jane said. Defino would be disappointed, but that was three-quarters of their job.

Smithson walked in and she told him about the call to Defino.

"Anyone got any *good* news?" he said.

"You'll be the first to know."

"MacHovec." He picked up the phone, said "Yeah," and grabbed a pen. "That's it." He wrote. "You got an address? . . . Say that again? . . . Shit. Yeah. Thanks. I owe you a big one." He hung up, swiveled toward Jane and Smithson. "That was the guy at the phone company. A call came in to Farrar's phone from a pay phone, I make it a cou-

ple of hours after Farrar was shot. Short call, couple minutes. The phone's on Broadway in the One-fifties; he'll get
me an exact address. Know where that is?"

Jane ran the map of Manhattan through her mind.
"Hamilton Heights, Sugar Hill."

"Sugar Hill it is. The Three-oh."

Sugar Hill was an area north of Harlem whose residents
were middle-class blacks. Many of the homes there were
fine old town houses. The crime of Harlem did not extend to
this community, nor did the poverty. But that was not what
struck Jane.

"Sugar Hill," she said again. "That's where——"

"Right. Where Lt. John Beasely lives."

[39]

"THERE'S A SUBWAY station at a Hundred Forty-fifth on
both the Number One line and the A and D," McElroy said
when they were all together in Graves's office. "One's on
Broadway; the other's on St. Nicholas Avenue. He gets off
the subway, makes his call, and walks home. I don't know. I
thought Beasely was clean."

"Let's slow down," the inspector said. "He may be.
Could Manelli have made this call? Could Manelli have shot
Farrar?"

"Manelli could have shot Farrar," MacHovec said, "but I
don't see what he gets out of it. And I don't see Manelli tak-

ing the train up to the One-forties just to make a phone call so we can trace it later. Why did he call Farrar's number and leave his Queens number if he just killed him?"

"Then we have to look at Beasely again," Graves said.

"The homeless guy who saw the shooting of Farrar said it was a white man who did it," Jane said. "His description is general enough to include Manelli. But I agree with Sean; I don't see a motive."

"Let's think. Suppose the sarge tells Manelli to kill Farrar."

"How does the sarge find Manelli?" MacHovec said.

"Through Farrar. Farrar is the conduit. Farrar has always been the conduit."

MacHovec looked ready to explode. "You're saying the sarge calls Farrar, tells Farrar to call Manelli and have him get back to the sarge? The sarge wouldn't do that. He has to keep the discipline. No one can contact him except Farrar."

"Calm down, Detective," McElroy said.

"Yes, sir." MacHovec muttered.

Jane restrained a laugh. Whatever else you could say about MacHovec, he didn't beat around the bush.

"It works if the sarge is planning to kill Farrar anyway," Graves said, sticking to his theory. "There are two possibilities here. One is that the sarge locates Manelli by calling Farrar's number. Whether he talks to Farrar or the wife doesn't matter, as long as Manelli has called first and left his new number in Long Island City."

"According to the phone company, Manelli called Farrar's number after Farrar was dead, or maybe during the day that Farrar was killed," McElroy said in a peacemaking voice.

"The second possibility," Graves said, ignoring McElroy, "is that the sarge killed Farrar and then called Farrar's number to see if Manelli had reported in to Farrar. He has no other way to find Manelli. Randolph doesn't know where he is. We couldn't find him. So he gets lucky. Manelli has called in and left a phone number. The sarge calls Manelli and says to meet him in the Village or go down to the Village and make the phone call to the auto shop, leave a message, and then come back. He makes a trail we can follow, but the sarge is waiting for Manelli over in Queens and that's it for Manelli."

"Why does Manelli do it?" MacHovec asked. "It's a wild-goose chase."

"Because Manelli still believes the sarge is in charge and that there's a big score for him at the end of the job." Graves turned to Jane. "You working on that TA heist, Detective?"

"Yes, sir. We interviewed two suspects, got nothing promising."

"Keep at it. Where was I? Manelli. If Manelli shot Farrar, the sarge could be black. If the sarge shot Farrar, either our information is wrong or your homeless man didn't see straight, or Beasely's not the sergeant. These phone calls to Farrar's number: Did you check back before Farrar died?"

"No, sir," MacHovec said, on good behavior again. "I just checked from the day he died forward."

"Go back to the day before you found Defino. Manelli may have called in more than once, telling Farrar where he was staying. And maybe the sarge called in, too. I'd like to see what pay phones he used. The sarge may have told Manelli to call Farrar and leave the Queens phone number even after one of them killed Farrar just to lure our detectives up there. This is a smart guy."

"Beasely's smart," McElroy said sadly.

"A Hundred Forty-fifth Street," Graves said reflectively. "How many white men get off a train up there?"

"Some," Jane said. "They walk up toward Washington Heights."

"True."

"You want us to do anything about Lieutenant Beasely?" McElroy asked.

"Not at the moment. Get back to work. Get a list of every call to and from Farrar's phone from the day before Defino was found. Check out every sergeant in the TA and start talking to them. We are going to clear this case."

"He's right," MacHovec said in their office. "We need to go back further in time, see who Farrar called."

"Farrar didn't use his phone for outgoing calls," Jane said, "certainly not after Randolph made that last call. The sarge wouldn't allow it. After that gun in Riverside Park, he had to know we were on his trail, that we might find Farrar and check his phone."

"Why the fuck did he leave that gun there?" MacHovec asked.

"Because he's a cocky bastard and he was playing with us. I'd like to get him just for that. Unless . . ." She considered. "Maybe Farrar acted on his own, decided to leave the gun in the park and the sarge offed him for it."

"So the mistake was Farrar's," MacHovec said. He put in a call to the phone company, enlarging the scope of his request. Jane and Smithson went out for a late lunch. She really hated getting up late. It threw her day into chaos. They talked about the case. Graves had proved to be inventive. The idea that Manelli could have shot Farrar had occurred to neither of them.

"Graves has a brain," Smithson said.

"And ambition."

"Good combination. When he said Manelli could have shot Farrar, that hit me like a thunderbolt. It gives us Beasely as a possible for the sarge and makes Catty Fellows sound like a goddamn oracle. We just have to figure out the phone calls."

"MacHovec'll have that soon. These guys really come through for him. We have to start looking at Transit sergeants, Warren. Graves doesn't want this to be Beasely. I don't either. Mrs. Appleby is sure he's OK. If it turns out he isn't, she'll be destroyed. This was her husband's closest friend all his life."

"Those are the breaks," Smithson said breezily.

When they got back, Jane made the call to Mrs. Farrar, working her way through protective relatives.

"Detective Bauer?" Mrs. Farrar said finally.

"Yes. Mrs. Farrar, I know this is a difficult day for you, but I need to know if anyone besides me called to find out Sal's phone number."

"Someone may have called Charley and talked to him. I wouldn't know about that."

"If you find any written messages, would you get back to me?"

"Of course." The weariness in the woman's voice was a reminder of the ordeal this day had been for her. "Detective, if my husband got a call and I left a message for him, that message wouldn't be around anymore. Charley was very good about cleaning off the answering machine tape and throwing away little pieces of paper. I'll look, but don't expect me to find anything."

"Thanks, Mrs. Farrar." Jane hung up. "I've pushed her as far as I can. She doesn't remember anyone calling for Sal before the day of Charley's death, and the message chits don't go back that far. We'll have to wait for the phone company to come through."

"Tomorrow," MacHovec promised. "What are you thinking?"

"That the call from Manelli on the day Farrar was shot was for show. It was to lead us up to the auto shop. I'm betting the sarge already knew where Manelli was. He found out from Farrar. He was checking to see what we knew, figuring eventually we'd think to check Farrar's phone."

"So what's the point? Why get us up there?"

"Maybe to arrest Manelli. Get him out of the sarge's hair. Maybe to see what we know and when we found out."

"So you think this guy, the sarge, is staking out the auto shop to see if we show?"

"He could be retired by now. He could—" Her phone rang and she picked it up.

"Detective Bauer, this is Mrs. Farrar. My sister-in-law tells me that a man called, she doesn't know when but probably over the weekend, to ask if anyone had called to get Sal's phone number. And someone called here yesterday—I talked to him. It was after you called and he asked the same thing. I said the police had called."

"Thank you, Mrs. Farrar. I appreciate your calling." She turned to MacHovec. "The sarge has been calling her number to find out if anyone else was looking for Manelli. He called yesterday after I talked to her. She told him the police had called."

"OK, how'd he get hold of Manelli to make that call from the Village?"

"Manelli carries a cell phone. Farrar could have given the sarge the address in Queens. Or they had a time and place to call each other every day."

"Just keeping you on your toes," MacHovec said. "So the sarge knows we know where Manelli is. Maybe he calls Roger's place and one of the guys tells him Manelli's gone for the day. The sarge knows we're gonna have people at the auto shop waiting for Manelli to come back. He tells Manelli to make that call from the Village and leave that message, then get a taxi or whatever and go back up to Queens. You won't be there because you heard the message, checked with the phone company, and verified where the call came from. Maybe he doesn't count on the local cops being there. But he's sure he can get to Manelli before you get back to Queens."

"It could work," Smithson said. "He makes sure we won't interrupt him while he takes care of Manelli. Except there are two detectives looking for Manelli when the sarge gets there."

"And Manelli takes care of them. Don't those guys look over their shoulders?" He looked at his watch and started printing out a file. "Here's what I got on your sergeants. This is how you're spending the rest of your life."

The list was pages long, with retired people starred and dead ones starred twice. Jane passed a copy to Smithson and looked down the list to see if any names looked familiar. "How many sergeants do we have to check out?" she asked.

"Four hundred, give or take. There were about four thousand Transit cops at that time. About ten percent were sergeants."

"Any women?"

"I noticed a few names. Probably not more than a dozen."

"You hit it right, Sean. This is how we're spending the rest of our lives. We'll divide the list up tomorrow. Better cancel your vacations. Nobody's going anywhere."

"Start with the retired guys and the dead ones," MacHovec said. "There's less of them."

"That wasn't any dead man over in Queens last night," Jane said.

"It'll give you some Fives to fill the file. Graves likes thick files."

"I want a living killer, not a lot of paper."

"Hey, everybody wants something. Me, I want to go home." MacHovec turned off his computer. "I'll bet you he's retired."

"You're on," Smithson said. "He's on the job."

Jane was tempted to bet that the sarge was dead, but decided to keep her mouth shut. "See you tomorrow," she said to MacHovec, who was locking his desk drawer. He waved as he flew out the door.

Jane took the list of sergeants home with her. MacHovec had included a history for each name so she could see what district each had worked out of ten years before and at the time of the cable truck thefts. She began with the names at the district closest to one of the thefts, although any Transit cop had access to any area of the subway system. Beasely was not among those names. Several were retired and a few were dead. After dinner she called the first retired cop on the list. He answered and she asked him what he remembered about the theft. Plenty, he said, although he had not worked the case.

He went on to tell her what she already knew and little else. She threw out a few names—Farrar, Morgan, Riso, Garland, and Crawford—but he claimed not to know who they were. Like many retired cops, he was eager to talk to her, to bring back the good old days, and she let him ramble, hoping something new would emerge, but it didn't. She ended the conversation with thanks and went on to the next name.

It was more of the same, and so was the one after that. When she hung up, her phone rang. It was Hack.

"You talking to suspects?" he asked.

"I wish they were. They're Transit sergeants who've retired. If they're telling the truth, they know nothing, and I have no reason to doubt them, at least at this point."

"Tell me what's going on."

She told him what had developed, the shooting of Manelli, the appearance of the sarge, whom no one except Manelli had eyeballed.

"You're really moving," he said.

"I thought so last night, but today we're checking out four hundred sergeants, dead or alive, and this guy is smart enough to know how to answer questions. I started with the retired ones and all they want to do is reminisce."

"Sounds familiar. Try the dead ones."

She laughed. "That was my first idea, but this guy over in Queens last night was very much alive."

"If he's smart, he knows how to fake his death."

"Then he loses his pension. And Social Security."

"His wife'll collect, and he probably put away enough to live on for a long time."

"I'll give it a try."

They talked about other things till his phone card ran out. OK, she thought as she hung up. In the morning I'll check out the dead guys.

40

BEFORE SHE HAD a chance to make her first call on Thursday morning, her phone rang.

"You got him killed, you miserable—" The woman broke into tears.

"Judy," Jane said, recognizing the voice, "your friend Mr.

Manelli was in a dangerous business. I'm sorry for your loss, but I'm not surprised at what happened."

"He didn't *do* anything," Judith Franklin screamed into the phone. "He was in the wrong place that day when you were here. He's dead now. My life is over. Who's going to give me back my life?"

"I'm sorry. I can't help you. Perhaps your family—"

"Thanks a lot." The phone was slammed, and Jane felt relieved.

"Franklin?" Smithson asked.

"Yeah. Now I have to repair her broken life. How does a nice woman get involved with a creep like Manelli?" She dialed the number for the first dead cop on the list. The phone rang several times and then a machine answered with a man's voice: "You have reached Garrett and Rosemary Fitzhugh. Leave a message and we'll get back to you."

She looked down at the list after hanging up. Garrett Fitzhugh was the name of the "dead" sergeant. According to MacHovec's record, he had died more than three years before. She wrote a question mark next to the name and dialed the next dead man on the list. She talked to the dead man's daughter, then his wife. The sergeant had talked about the big theft "because it was so spectacular." But they had nothing to contribute.

To Jane's left and right Smithson and MacHovec were also on the phone, talking to living cops or their families. She tried another dead cop and then another one. She was working her way down her share of the list. Each of them had over a hundred names, but Jane had reserved the dead and retired cops for herself.

By noon they had covered many of the names, although a third of them had to be called back. After lunch she tried the number for the dead cop, Garrett Fitzhugh. The same message came on and she hung up once again. Was he alive or dead? Had his wife kept the message out of sentiment? Or perhaps he was alive, unbeknownst to the Transit cops.

Defino called and said no one else except jokesters and creeps had called about the ad in the paper. He was bored and disappointed, and thought maybe he would take the subway in and they could have lunch and talk.

The call from the phone company came halfway through the afternoon. "The answer is yes," MacHovec said. "Farrar got phone calls before the day of his death from pay phones and phone cards. I have to believe the pay phones were set-ups. The phone cards were used when the sarge didn't have time to call from the right pay phone."

"You're saying it's not Beasely?" Smithson asked.

"I'm just saying this guy is covering his tracks when he wants to. There's one call from that phone in Sugar Hill and two calls from phone cards."

Annie appeared at the door with the fax of the calls. She dropped it on MacHovec's desk and left.

"OK," he said, "now we know that the sarge could have known where Manelli was before Manelli left his own message."

By late afternoon they were all making callbacks to numbers that had not answered. At four fifteen they hung up and exchanged information. Each of them had several favorites that rated face-to-face interviews.

"Let's do this solo," Smithson said. "I've got a Fourth of July vacation bought and paid for and I don't want to be sitting here talking to Transit cops all summer."

"Defino'll be back by then," MacHovec said. "He gets his OK from the doc, you're outta here."

"Thanks," Smithson returned. "I'll remember that."

"How'd it go today?" the lieutenant asked from the door when the two men had left the office.

She gave him the gist of it, the calls, and the information from the phone company.

"Tell me, how are Smithson and MacHovec getting along?"

"We're all working together, Loot. No problems."

"Because MacHovec's behavior yesterday with the inspector was almost over the line."

"You know MacHovec," Jane said. "He says what he thinks. It's nothing personal."

"We'll talk tomorrow."

She got her lists together and went home, stopping for a take-out dinner. When she had eaten, she began making calls, getting nothing useful. Finally, at eight, she called the Fitzhugh number with the dead cop's voice on the answering machine. The phone was answered by a woman.

"Mrs. Fitzhugh, this is Det. Jane Bauer, NYPD. May I speak with your husband?"

"My husband died, Detective. What is this about?"

"I'm sorry for your loss, ma'am. We're investigating a theft in the subway system, a large theft that took place several years ago." She added a few identifying details.

"I know nothing about it."

"Was your husband involved in the investigation?"

"I'm sure I don't know." Nothing in the tone of her voice hinted at cooperation.

"May I ask why your husband's voice and name are on your machine?"

"For my protection. I don't like strangers to know that I live alone."

"Well, thanks for your help."

"No bother." The woman hung up.

Jane looked at her watch. It was too late for Mrs. Fitzhugh to be leaving for the evening. Jane could be at the Queens address in forty minutes or less. She put her Glock in her bag, slipped into a jacket, and went to the subway.

The door was opened by a good-looking woman in black pants and a pink silk shirt. Her left hand had a diamond engagement ring next to a band of diamonds. A pendant of diamonds in the shape of a heart lay exactly at her throat. Gold bracelets jingled sweetly on her right forearm.

"I'm Detective Bauer, Mrs. Fitzhugh. We spoke earlier this evening."

"I told you all I know. What are you doing here?"

"I had a few more questions." And a desire to see how the widow looked and where she lived.

"Come in."

The apartment was on a high floor of a building housing

middle-class New Yorkers. From the outside, there was nothing special about it. But inside this apartment, the name of the game was luxury.

Mrs. Fitzhugh led the way to the living room and sat in a chair upholstered in a fine silk print. Jane took a firm side chair and pulled her notebook and pen from her bag. Her feet rested on a large Oriental carpet, and when she looked up she faced windows at the far end of the room. The apartment cleared other buildings by several floors and was too high to allow sounds from the vehicles below. The sky outside was cloudless.

"Can you tell me how your husband died?" Jane asked.

"Colon cancer. He was sick about a year."

"What hospital did he die in?"

"Long Island Jewish Medical Center here in Queens."

Jane wrote it down. That was easy enough to check. "I have some names I'd like to read to you. If you recognize any, please tell me." She went through them all, her eyes on the attractive woman, her legs crossed, her left hand rubbing a ring on her right hand that Jane had not noticed. "Nothing?" Jane asked.

"Nothing. I don't understand why you're asking me. Whoever they are, they certainly weren't friends of ours. If my husband knew them from work, there's no reason why he would have mentioned their names to me."

"You seem to live quite well, Mrs. Fitzhugh. I wonder how you've managed that on a sergeant's salary."

A faint, condescending smile crossed the red lips. "We invested well. I inherited a little money from my parents when my mother died, and Garry did too from his. When I worked, we put away every cent I made."

In a little tin box, Jane thought, remembering the lyrics of an old Broadway show song. "May I use your bathroom?"

"Of course." Mrs. Fitzhugh pointed to a door and Jane took her bag and went.

The bathroom was fitted with a marble pedestal sink and a matching marble toilet. The faucets were gold. The floor and walls were also marble. She opened the mirrored cabinet and looked at the bottles to see if Fitzhugh's name was on any labels. It wasn't. She flushed the toilet, then ran the water in the sink, wetting her hands and using a guest towel.

When she returned to the living room, Mrs. Fitzhugh was standing at the window. "It's a clear night," she said. "You can see the stars and the lights in Manhattan. We don't get many nights like this in the city."

"You're right. You're lucky to see it without obstruction."

"It's the main reason we picked this apartment."

"Thank you for your help."

Mrs. Fitzhugh opened the door for her and said good night.

[41]

FITZHUGH HAD BEEN dirty. The story of inherited wealth and nimble investing didn't wash. That didn't mean he was the sarge, just that there was enough there to pursue the investigation.

Feeling restless, Jane took out a box of gun-cleaning equipment and took apart her S&W. It hardly needed attention, but it was the kind of mindless activity she turned to to avoid cleaning the apartment. She and Hack had left their guns in New York when they flew to Paris. One of the joys of walking along the Rue de Rivoli or the Champs-Elysées was not being weighed down with all the metal that cops routinely carried. It had made her feel light—in spirit as well.

They had been so happy for so many days, and then, that last night, sitting at the small table in the restaurant near the Arc de Triomphe, he had asked her to marry him.

"Hack—"

"Don't say no. Don't say anything. Just listen. We love each other, right?"

"Right."

"We get along."

"Yes."

"We love being with each other."

"It's all true."

"It's ten years. You know I won't hurt her. I've made up my mind, Jane. I'm in a marriage that benefits no one."

"Your daughters," she said, as she always did.

"I can handle my daughters."

"Hack, you can't 'handle' your daughters. They're not cops in your command. They won't say, 'Yes, sir,' when you tell them you're leaving their mother for someone else. They're your daughters, not your subordinates."

"They'll understand. They'll like you. It'll take a while for a divorce to come through. When you and I get together, it won't be a shock."

"I'll always be Daddy's whore."

"Jane." He closed his eyes briefly, as though to recover from the shock of the word.

"I don't want to—"

"Jane, you are not . . . you have never been . . . I can't believe you would use that word to describe yourself. Is that the reason you've always been so reluctant to consider marriage?"

She wished she had an answer to that. "Partly."

"What's the other part?" His voice reflected irritation, as though it were all getting away from him.

"I don't know. There's something about marriage. . . ."

"Are we committed to each other now?"

"Of course we are."

"Then I fail to see . . ."

She smiled. "You're sounding like a cop."

"I am a cop. I want to live with you, Jane. I want us to have a whole life together."

The waiter approached the table with a tray of blue cheeses. Jane made several choices, Hack a few more. The interlude defused the tension.

"I'm a real blue lover," he said, and she knew he wanted to put an end to the discussion, at least for the moment.

The blues were wonderful, each with a bite that left a memory. When dinner was over, they walked on the Champs-Elysées, away from the Étoile, toward the distant Place de lá Concorde. They passed Metro stations and taxis, but he did not move to take one or the other.

"I want you to think about this, Jane," he said after a silence. "It's important to me."

She didn't answer. He had never put anything that way to her. Their ten years had been largely devoid of the kind of arguments that people living together fell into, and she liked that. They lived to please each other, to enjoy each other, to integrate their lives so that each one was better than a life without the other. Why could she not go that last step? And how important was it to him that she do so?

She felt a fluttering of fear. Was it possible that he wanted marriage more than he wanted her? Was her reticence, her reluctance, her downright refusal a deal-breaker? In the ten years they had loved each other, that thought had never occurred to her.

At the hotel he made an excuse for not making love to her. It was a good excuse—he was tired and had eaten too much—but it scared her. She wanted to talk to him about it, but she was afraid to bring it up. This was not the first time they had discussed marriage, but it was the first time he had stated so firmly that he wanted to leave his wife, that he was prepared to leave her, and was ready to marry Jane.

They flew back without mentioning. At the airport, he kissed her and put her in the first taxi. "Think about it," he said before he closed the door, knowing she would understand the reference.

That was an order she had no difficulty following.

*   *   *

"So what happened last night?" Smithson said as he walked in on Friday morning.

"Something interesting," Jane said.

"Finally."

She told him about the Fitzhugh apartment and the Fitzhugh widow.

"Marble bathroom," Smithson said. "My wife would give anything for that."

"Here's his name, the hospital, and the date of death." She handed it to MacHovec.

He picked up the phone and a minute later was arguing with someone about how long it would take to check out the records. "I understand your difficulty," he said, "but I need this right away. I don't want to have to go up there with a warrant." He sat listening, making motions with his head. Then he gave his phone number and hung up. "Half an hour, she tells me. What else you got?"

"Just find everything you can about him. And I'll make a call, too." She called Ron Delancey.

"Still working on that case?" he said. "They'll have the Second Avenue subway done by the time you find your perp."

"That's what I'm afraid of. Tell me, you ever hear of a Transit cop named Garrett Fitzhugh?"

"Fitzhugh, yeah. I think he died, Jane, several years ago. He was out on terminal leave for a long time."

"What do you know about him?"

"He was a sergeant last I saw him, but I think he was studying for the lieutenant's exam. I don't know if he ever took it. You want to point me in the direction you're going?"

"I visited his widow last night. Her apartment is furnished like a palace and she's dressed like a queen."

"Gotcha. You think he was the guy who did the big job."

"Either that or something like it. The guy I'm looking for was alive Tuesday night of this week."

"Then Fitzhugh's not your man."

"I thought he might have faked his death."

Delancey laughed. "You're reaching. Maybe you can do

that if you blow up a building, but it's pretty hard in a New York hospital."

"OK. If you think of anything, let me know, like if he's connected to the big one. I should be home tonight."

MacHovec's phone rang and he picked up, talked to the hospital source, and got off the phone. "They're faxing the death certificate. If Fitzhugh was the mastermind of the big trick, that wasn't him up in Queens on Monday night."

"Then let's find another sergeant."

Smithson took off with his list. MacHovec got back to his calls. Jane made more calls, took more notes, never feeling as though she had hit the jackpot. The chances were that Fitzhugh was dead and had been dirty, although not involved in the truck thefts. He had obviously lived carefully enough that no one had suspected him of being on the take until now.

She kept coming back to John Beasely. Finally, she walked over to McElroy's office.

"Come in. Got something?"

She told him about the Fitzhugh apartment.

"But he's dead," McElroy said.

"Right. And I'm wondering about Lieutenant Beasely."

"Let's leave him alone. The inspector's pretty sure he's clean."

"Suppose I went up and talked to his wife."

The lieutenant took a deep breath. "What are you planning to ask her?"

"Just about Micah Anthony, their friendship. I won't ask anything about her husband. I'd like to see their apartment."

She could see McElroy didn't like it. "OK. Give it a try. And don't agitate."

"Thanks, Loot."

Before leaving, she called Beasely's number. A woman answered and Jane hung up. In the background she had heard a child's voice, so the Beaselys had a youngster. She told MacHovec where she was going. He showed her Fitzhugh's death certificate. The cause of death was colon cancer, as the widow had said. And the home address was the one Jane had visited the night before. That much, at least, had been true.

[42]

SHE TOOK THE subway uptown, changing for the Broadway line. The train was nearly empty, a few older people, a few men who should have been at work, and assorted others. She got off at One Hundred Forty-fifth Street, one stop north of City College. As she walked, she found the pay phone the calls to the Farrar number had come from. Then she sped up and went directly to the building where the Beaselys lived.

Like many buildings on the block, it was a fine old brownstone converted into several apartments. The Beaselys were on the third floor, and a woman called from inside to find out who had rung.

"Det. Jane Bauer, NYPD."

The door flew open. "Is my husband—"

"Your husband's fine, Mrs. Beasely. I'm sorry to have upset you."

The woman put a hand over her chest, as though to calm herself. She looked at Jane's ID, then said, "Come in."

"I'm investigating an old case," Jane said as they walked from the foyer into the living room. A small boy came out of a bedroom and looked up at Jane with big brown eyes.

"Go back to your room and play," his mother said. "OK?"

He nodded and turned around, sneaking a peek as he retraced his steps to the bedroom.

"He's a handful," Mrs. Beasely said.

Jane smiled.

"You said an old case?"

"The murder of Micah Anthony."

"Micah. Yes. Sit down. I was just in the middle of cleaning up." Her hair was pulled back in a ponytail, and she was wearing jeans and a man's blue shirt.

The room looked pretty clean and well furnished. "It's a lovely apartment," Jane said, picking a chair.

"We were lucky to find it. John's parents live nearby, and his mother looks after the kids sometimes."

"How close were you to Detective Anthony?" Jane asked.

"John was very close. They grew up together. I met him when we were going out. And I became friendly with Melodie after we all married."

"Are you still friends?"

"We're friends but we don't see each other much. We're here and she's on Staten Island. For a long time, she didn't really want to go out, although we asked her to join us." A slightly different take from that of Mrs. Appleby.

"Were they getting along at the time of Detective Anthony's death?"

"They always got along. Why are you asking? She was distraught when Micah died. He was young, she was pregnant, they'd just bought a house—it was a nightmare."

"How did you hear about his death?"

"John called me."

"Was he working that night?"

"Yes. He was a sergeant then, and I think he was doing four-to-twelves."

"Detective Anthony was murdered after midnight."

Mrs. Beasely looked confused. "I don't know. I was sleeping and the phone rang. It was John, and he said something terrible had happened and he couldn't come home. He had to go to Micah's apartment. Maybe he was working midnight to eight. It was a long time ago."

The little boy called her and she jumped up and dashed into his bedroom. Jane stood and took a close look around the room. The furniture was good stuff. The rug was Chinese with soft blues in the design. Jane walked to the window, which looked out over the street. A car drove by, then nothing. It was a quiet place to live, not a druggie in sight.

"Sorry."

Jane turned around. "This is a lovely location."

"We're quite happy here. The kids can walk to school and the neighbors are nice."

"How long have you lived here?"

"Almost seven years. We've been restoring the apartment slowly. It's a big job but a worthwhile payoff. Can I ask why you're here? I mean, talking to me?"

"My team has been assigned the Micah Anthony homicide and we're interviewing people who weren't originally interviewed."

"What for? What do you expect to learn that could possibly be useful?"

"You never know until you ask the question," Jane said. "Did you go to the wake or the funeral?"

"We went to everything. I stayed over at Melodie's apartment. She wouldn't leave it. I slept on a couch in the living room and heard her cry all night." Mrs. Beasely's face looked infinitely sad. "You're a cop. You know what those times are like."

Jane asked to use the bathroom, and Mrs. Beasely walked her to it. Like Mrs. Fitzhugh's the night before, this one was elegant and expensive, with top-of-the-line plumbing, if not marble. When she left, she glanced over at the kitchen.

"You have a beautiful kitchen," she said, admiring the stainless-steel refrigerator and sink, the large stove, the tile floor. "It looks professional."

"What was here when we moved in was falling apart. We decided to do it right. We don't have a dining room, so this is where we sit down to dinner when we entertain. I'm a good cook and I love every minute I spend here."

"Thanks for your help, Mrs. Beasely. Just one more question. Do you know Mrs. Appleby's new husband?"

"We've met. We didn't go to the wedding because it was very small and private. But we got to know him and he seems like a good man for her. She deserves a good man."

"I agree with you. Thank you for your time."

Smithson had not returned from his interviews, so Jane briefed McElroy and MacHovec in the lieutenant's office.

"That kitchen costs what I earn in a year," she said. "Everything stainless steel, indirect lighting around the counter, a gorgeous tile floor. The dining table is what my Salvation Army table pretends to be."

"Without bullet holes," McElroy said.

"So far."

"So he's on the take, too," MacHovec said.

"Not necessarily," the lieutenant put in, eager to stop the characterization before it got out of hand. "He's got parents; she's got parents. They could all have chipped in. All you're telling me is that they've spent money on the apartment. Maybe they got it cheap."

"And her story about how her husband told her about Anthony's death doesn't jive with Mrs. Appleby's story."

"It's been ten years," McElroy said.

"All I'm saying is, we shouldn't drop Beasely as a suspect."

"We're not dropping him. We're working around him."

They went back to their office.

"Graves doesn't want it to be Beasely," MacHovec said. "Opens a can of worms."

"If Beasely did it, I want his ass."

"If Beasely did it, we'll get him."

"You talk to anyone that needs interviewing?"

"The best of them are iffy. Without looking at their bank accounts, I can't put a star next to any name." He passed her several sheets of paper.

From their addresses, none of them lived in obviously expensive neighborhoods, but then, neither did Fitzhugh. "I'm going to lunch. If Warren comes back, tell him to wait for me before he takes off again."

*   *   *

Smithson was eating a sandwich at his desk when Jane returned. "No flashing lights," he said. "Everybody's a no or a maybe. MacHovec says you went up to Beasely's place."

She told him about it.

"Marble bathrooms and stainless-steel kitchens. How do these guys get away with it?"

"Beasely didn't pay for it out of his salary. I couldn't ask directly; the lieutenant would have killed me."

Smithson put a Five in the typewriter and started banging.

Jane swiveled toward MacHovec. "Here's what I want. Every course that Fitzhugh, Beasely, your favorites, and Warren's favorites took. Like studying for the sergeant's exam. See if there are overlaps. If it was Fitzhugh, maybe he had a pal who took over when he went on leave. Look into the districts they served in, who served with them. If it wasn't Fitzhugh over in Queens on Tuesday night, maybe it was Beasely or one of these other guys filling in for him. And I want photos of Beasely and Fitzhugh and everybody's favorites."

MacHovec looked at his watch. "I'll do what I can but I may not be able to go through all the stuff."

"Just print it out and leave it for me. I'll take it home tonight." She read page after page as they flew out of the printer, finding nothing useful.

When the typewriter was free, Jane sat down to do her Fives. A few minutes into the first one, Annie showed up at the door.

"Detective Bauer, the inspector wants to see you. I have to warn you: He's not in a good mood."

"Thanks, Annie."

"That for going up to Beasely's?" Smithson asked.

"Can't be anything else." She left the Five in the typewriter.

McElroy was already in the inspector's office. He glanced at her briefly, then looked away.

"Where did you go this morning, Detective Bauer?" Graves asked.

"To the Beaselys' apartment."

"I made it clear we were not considering him a suspect."

"I found no Fives on Mrs. Beasely in the Anthony file. I thought it might be helpful to hear her version of what happened the night Micah Anthony was shot."

"And?"

"Her version differs somewhat from Mrs. Anthony's. Which is in the file."

"I'm aware of that."

"And the apartment they live in has been expensively renovated. The kitchen alone—"

"I don't care what their kitchen looks like. I don't care what their view is. I want Lieutenant Beasely and his wife and his children treated as though they are not suspects, because they are not Have I made myself clear?"

"Yes, sir."

"There will be no further discussion of Lieutenant Beasely unless I initiate it."

"Yes, sir."

"In case it slipped by you, I am not happy with your behavior."

"Yes, sir."

"You're dismissed."

She returned to the office.

"That was quick," MacHovec said. "Guess he didn't pull any fingernails."

She smiled in spite of herself. "Not yet. That's what's coming when we clear this case."

"You're the optimist," Smithson said. "You think we'll clear it?"

"We have to now. We've gone too far to fail. Beasely's off-limits for discussion. I have some ideas, but I'll keep them to myself. No use taking you guys down with me."

"Graves needs you," Smithson said. "If we pull this out, he'll be throwing rose petals at you."

Rose petals. She sat down at the typewriter and went back to her Fives.

Fifteen minutes later, McElroy walked in. "The inspector got a very angry call from Lieutenant Beasely."

"I'm sorry I put you on the spot, Loot," Jane said. "If

Garrett Fitzhugh is a suspect, John Beasely should be one."

"Keep it to yourself. Inspector Graves has made up his mind on this one."

By the end of the day they had contacted almost all of the four hundred sergeants. Smithson had a few he wanted to interview on Monday; MacHovec had some possibles. Jane kept returning to Beasely and Fitzhugh. MacHovec got her photos of both men plus a few others and she dropped them in her bag. That night she would return to the block where Micah Anthony had been found, the block she and Smithson had canvassed with no success. This time she would show photos and ring doorbells where no one had been home last time. All she needed was one ID to give new life to the investigation.

[43]

SHE WASTED NO time with dinner, stopping at a coffee shop for a sandwich, then getting herself over to Waverly Place to start ringing bells of people who had said they had lived on the block ten years before. If Beasely had told his wife he was working four to twelve the night of the murder, he had an excuse for not being home, and he could have been at the wheel of the vehicle that picked Anthony up in the West Fifties. Anthony would have had no problem getting into his friend's car, whether it was a personal car or a Transit

Police car. Beasely would have known that Anthony had learned something potentially lethal because Charley Farrar would have briefed him after the meeting, but Anthony wouldn't have known what, if anything, Beasely knew. And maybe Sergeant Beasely had a little action going down in the Village.

All of the above was also true of Garrett Fitzhugh. All Jane needed was one ID of one of the photos.

She started her canvass where she and Smithson had started, and watched heads shake as she showed the pictures. Finishing one building, she went down the outside stairs and up the next set, got herself rung in, and walked up to the top floor to start again. A pretty black woman in her mid-thirties answered one door, her hair full of tight braids, wearing big earrings and a large choker at her neck.

"Ms. Hand?"

"Yes?"

"Det. Jane Bauer. We're looking into the murder of a police detective ten years ago. Did you live here then?" The woman had not answered during the last canvass.

"Ten years? Yeah, just about. I was new here."

"Do you recall the murder?"

"I heard about it the next day. I live in the back and I don't hear the street noise."

Jane showed pictures of her partners' favorites with no response. "Does this man look familiar to you?" Jane showed her Fitzhugh.

The woman studied it. "I don't think so."

"How about this man?" She handed her Beasely's picture.

"I've never seen him before."

"Are you sure? Look at it a moment." The answer had come too quickly.

"I'm sure. I'm sorry. I don't know who they are."

"Thanks for your help."

The fifth floor, the fourth, the third, the second. She wanted to hit all the apartments that hadn't answered last time, as well as those that had age-appropriate women, even if they had already talked to them.

Down to the street level, up to the ground floor of the next building, up to the top floor, ring a bell again. She reminded herself, as she always did, that this was police work: knocking on doors, reading grim autopsy reports and the text of interviews with people who had little to say and less time to spare to say it.

"Yes?"

The preliminaries again, the photos, the head shaking. "Sorry I can't help."

The rest of the floor, then down one flight. Doorbell, woman's voice calling, "Coming."

The woman was white, blond, slim, lots of hair, a nice smile. Jane said it all again, then handed her Beasely's photo.

"He doesn't look familiar."

"It was ten years ago. Maybe he came to visit someone in this building."

"I don't think so."

Jane showed her Fitzhugh.

The woman took the picture and held it away from her face. She was about forty, becoming farsighted. "Let me get my glasses." She walked into the apartment and returned wearing oval gold-rimmed glasses. Then she looked closely at the picture of Fitzhugh.

Jane stopped breathing. "Look familiar?"

"I don't know. It's possible I saw him somewhere. When was this again?"

Jane told her.

"Ten years ago. Seems hard to believe I'd remember a face from so long back. Do you know his name?"

"Garrett Fitzhugh."

"Doesn't ring a bell at all. Sorry. He must look like someone at work." She handed the picture back to Jane.

"Maybe you'd like to think about it," Jane said. "I could leave a copy of the picture with you and call you tomorrow."

"I don't think so." She smiled and handed the photo back to Jane. She was a very pretty woman. Ten years ago she would have been thirty and the smile even more radiant.

"Were you single when you moved here?" Jane asked.

"Oh, yes. It was my second apartment after one of those

disastrous roommate deals. I got married a few years ago and we decided to stay. We only have one child so we're able to manage. We both love the Village."

"Thank you, Mrs. Kislav. By the way, what was your name when you were single?"

"Berlnger. Alicia Beringer."

"Thanks for your help."

The rest of the street was routine. No one blinked at the pictures; no one added anything significant. Jane went home. She made some coffee and sat down to look at her notes. The phone rang.

"Jane, it's Ron Delancey."

"What've you got?"

"Gossip. I talked to some guys I knew on the job. They all thought Fitzhugh was a good cop but they all had reservations about him. One guy said Fitz would take a hot stove if it wasn't nailed down, but he didn't know who Fitzhugh's connections were. Another guy said Fitzhugh took expensive vacations."

"How would he know that?"

"Fitzhugh let little things slip, you know, the rain in London, the heat in Rome, that kind of thing. It's not impossible to do on a sergeant's salary, but tongues wagged."

"Anything about his clothes? Jewelry?"

"He wore an expensive watch, said his father-in-law gave it to him. Anyway, that's what I got. Forget about making a case against him, but if you've got other stuff—"

"Right. I really thank you."

"It was fun. Got to talk to some guys I hadn't been in touch with for a while."

"Maybe we'll have dinner."

"Get your man first."

She went back to Alicia Beringer. When she was thirty and single, Garrett Fitzhugh was in his forties, ten or twelve years older than she. Any man would be pleased to have such a pretty young woman open her door to him. No one else in that building admitted to recognizing him, but if he arrived at night and left at night, they would have little opportunity to see him. Few tenants of Jane's old building in the West Eighties had ever noticed Hack.

Maybe Alicia and Fitzhugh had begun an affair when she was living with the roommate, and that had been the cause of the disruption. She needed a place of her own where her intimacy would be completely private.

Jane found the Kislav number and called it. Alicia answered.

"This is Detective Bauer," Jane said. "We spoke earlier this evening."

"Right. Hi."

"Mrs. Kislav, where did you live before you moved to the Village?"

The woman gave an address over on the east side, near Alphabet City. "It wasn't the best neighborhood, but it was what we could afford."

"And what was your roommate's name?"

"Beverly Quick. She's married now. I think her married name is Shaw."

"Do you have an address and phone number for her?"

"Just a moment." Alicia came back and read off an address near Columbia University. "Her husband teaches up there."

"Thanks, Mrs. Kislav."

It was too late to call, too late to visit. If Alicia was protecting Fitzhugh—and she might not know he had died—Beverly might give him up. The next day Jane would find out.

On Saturday morning Jane called the Shaw apartment and a woman answered. She hung up, walked to the subway and rode up to One Hundred Sixteenth Street and Broadway.

The Shaws lived on One Hundred Fourteenth Street between Broadway and Riverside Drive, not far from where the Beretta had been found a couple of weeks before and where she and Hack had met that evening to view the area. Now Jane walked down Broadway and turned right at One Hundred Fourteenth, finding the apartment house quickly. Beverly Shaw was home.

"I don't have much time," the woman said as Jane entered. "I have a meeting and I have to drop my son off at play group."

"This won't take long." She followed the woman into the living room. It looked professorial, one step up from graduate student. Beverly Shaw was physically the opposite of her former roommate. Short, with short, dark, straight hair, and her face was a picture of tension, as though her worries were a permanent burden.

Jane gave her the intro. "Ten or eleven years ago you shared an apartment with Alicia Beringer."

"That's right."

"Why did you split up?"

She let air out of her mouth in a puff. "Alicia had a boyfriend, a married boyfriend, by the way, and his presence drove me crazy. One night they locked me out of the apartment."

"Why is that?"

"They were fucking, that's why. They wanted the apartment to themselves. I was furious."

"I can understand that. What did the boyfriend look like?"

Beverly Shaw seemed flustered. "I never saw him."

"I don't understand."

"I wasn't allowed in the apartment when he was there. Usually, Alicia would tell me in advance that he was coming and I'd make other plans, but it got to be wearing. I lived there, after all. It was my home as much as it was hers." From the sound of her voice, she was arguing her position all over again.

"And you never even got a glance at him?"

"I may have seen him once, when he was leaving and I was coming home. I'm not sure."

Jane handed her Beasely's picture.

"Oh, no, this isn't him. Alicia would never go out with a black man."

Jane gave her Fitzhugh's picture.

"I really don't know. I can't tell you I recognize him. I don't think I've ever seen this man before."

"Would you like to hold on to—"

"I don't think so. I'm in a hurry." She glanced at her watch and passed the photo back to Jane. "I can tell you one thing. I'm pretty sure the man she was seeing was a cop."

"Did she tell you that?"

"She must have. It was probably why she kept him so secret."

"Do you know if he was a Transit cop?"

Beverly Shaw frowned. "Is there a difference?"

"Actually, there isn't, but some people refer to the cops in the subway as Transit cops."

"I don't think that ever came up."

"She ever refer to him by name?"

"She called him 'my honey,' as in, 'My honey's coming over tonight.'"

"Thank you, Mrs. Shaw. You've been very helpful."

Jane sat on the subway turning it all over. She had thought it was Beasely because of his wife's inconsistencies and his closeness to Anthony. But Beverly Shaw's comment that Alicia would not date a black man made her reconsider. Maybe, she thought, it was something Alicia said to point Beverly in the wrong direction. If Beasely had enough money for that kitchen, he might shave a bit off and be nice to a beautiful woman, maybe pay a piece of her rent in the Village so they could do their thing in private.

The same, of course, was true of Fitzhugh. What Jane liked about Beasely was that he was alive. Two cops in Queens had heard his voice. Both had heard Manelli ask if he was the sarge. Whichever it was, if it were one of them, Alicia had had an affair with him, Jane was sure of that. And that fact made him a good suspect for murder.

Her head was abuzz, thinking of all the things she needed to do. First, if they were working today, she wanted to show the photos to the two Transit workers, Garland and Crawford. And she wanted to talk to Defino.

She went to Centre Street and found the phone numbers for Garland and Crawford. Luck was with her. They were both working today. But first she called Defino.

"Yeah, hello."

"Gordon, it's Jane."

"You just saved me from going nuts. What's up?"

"I think I've got the woman who was the sarge's little girl."

"No kidding."

She spelled it out.

"And the roommate's sure it was a cop?"

"She volunteered it. Here's what I'm thinking. Smithson and MacHovec have some guys that are probables. I want to find the Transit workers who were suspects in the big theft and show them pictures. And I'm reading lists to find out if there could have been a connection between Fitzhugh and Beasely."

"Like what?"

"Like maybe they took a class together at John Jay College. Maybe they even went through the Academy together."

"Beasely's much younger, isn't he?"

"Yes, but I don't know when Fitzhugh entered the academy. Maybe this was a second career. Maybe Beasely taught a course that Fitzhugh attended, or the other way around."

"So they get to know each other and get involved in . . . what?"

"The big theft for sure. Maybe Anthony's death too."

"The big theft is easier for me to take."

"Whatever it is, if there's a connection, we've got to find it."

"So tell MacHovec to get his ass in front of the computer."

"He's hardly left it and today's Saturday. Look, I'm going to see these Transit workers. Maybe I can figure this out. If I call—"

"I'll be here, going stir-crazy."

[44]

SHE FOUND GARLAND and sat down with him in an empty office. Jane handed him one photo after another while she kept her eyes glued to his face. He recognized Beasely as a Transit cop but didn't know his name. One of Smithson's possibles, Pete Fasio, evoked a smile and a comment. He stopped at Fitzhugh, saying he hadn't seen him for a while and his name was Fitz something. After that he identified one more sergeant by name, one of MacHovec's choices. Equal opportunity, Jane thought.

She went through the same routine with Crawford. He too recognized Fitzhugh but had nothing to say about him. When she was done, she returned to Centre Street.

She turned on the lights in her office, and in the briefing area and sat down at the computer.

The night before, she had gone through MacHovec's printouts. One sergeant among the possible suspects was in each group of names. The key was to find one other known name, one of the suspects in the big theft, or another sergeant on the list, or anyone whose name had come up in the investigation. Jane was fairly certain that Fitzhugh was their man, although she hadn't discounted Beasely as the mastermind of the big theft and as the sarge in the gun deal. She accepted that Fitzhugh was dead; therefore he had to have had a partner or someone who took his place when he went on medical leave.

She had gone through sheet after sheet, scanning for names. In each class she had marked the possible suspect, then searched for another familiar name, checking them against her master list. She knew that chance might give her some combinations, but every one of them would be investigated. Plenty of cases were solved by chance.

Her phone rang.

"Why is your cell phone off?" Hack asked. "I haven't been able to reach you."

"Sorry. Things have been popping. I turned it off this morning and forgot to turn it back on. How are you?"

"Up to my ears. Sounds like you are, too. What are you doing in the office on Saturday?"

"Working solo. I think I may have nailed the guy who they called 'the sarge.' Trouble is, he's dead."

"I told you to start there first."

She grinned. "But he must have had a partner, and I've been looking through classes and duty rosters all the suspect sergeants were in, to see if some name shows up that rings a bell. Where are you?"

"In a moving vehicle. I may see you soon."

"That sounds good."

"Keep your cell phone on."

"I will."

The lists had eventually yielded a couple of matches, neither of them with Fitzhugh. One of the sergeants was Smithson's, one MacHovec's. They could look at them Monday. No one except Jane Bauer would spend a minute working on a cold case on the weekend.

She booted up the computer and worked her way into classes at the Academy. Fortunately, the class rolls had been put on the computer as far back as Fitzhugh's class. She printed it out, stuffed it in her bag, and went home.

She kept thinking about the case as she walked. Fitzhugh had to be the man at the top. Charley Farrar had been his right-hand man, the fourth man in the crib, but it hadn't been Charley over in Queens on Tuesday night. Fitzhugh had had access to the Second Avenue subway tunnel, had met Charley somehow, maybe even brought in Curtis Morgan, unless Charley had done that. They were a cozy little group that had added Carl Randolph and Salvatore Manelli.

Fitzhugh had to be Alicia Beringer's boyfriend at the time of Anthony's death. If they exhausted every other lead, they would take her to the Six and question her. She would be scared enough to tell them the truth. Or Jane hoped so.

Unless it was Beasely.

And as often happened, it could be none of the above.

She had a light lunch and read the paper, which she had picked up on her way home. Out there was a world of turmoil, not much different from the world she worked in. Three weeks before she had thought they would be lucky to learn anything new, no matter how small, in the case of Micah Anthony, but they had gone so far, learned so much, that she wanted to put an end to it, find the bastard and put him away.

She put the paper down. What was the next step? Then she remembered that she had stuffed something in her bag before leaving Centre Street. She pulled the papers out of her bag, unfolded them, and sat at the table. It was Fitzhugh's class at the Academy, the last group of cops she had a list for. She found Fitzhugh and marked his name. Then she started at the top of the alphabetical list.

The name leaped out at her like a sprung coil. "Holy Mother of God," she whispered. She took a couple of breaths, went to the refrigerator and poured a glass of orange juice and drank it in seconds, thinking what she had to do, whom she had to tell.

She grabbed her bag and went out into the street, walked to a phone booth and called Hack's cell phone.

"Hackett."

"I need to talk to you on a landline."

"Are you all right? You sound—"

"I'm fine. This is very important."

"I need—hold on." She heard him call, "Over there," to someone. "Sorry. I can't call right now; I'm not alone. Will you be home?"

"I'll go home now and wait for your call."

"Half an hour."

She drifted more than walked back to the apartment. I don't want this to be, she thought. I want to go back three giant steps and hand this case over to someone else. The apartment was quiet, one of the advantages of not facing the street. She wanted to call Lisa, her lovely daughter, and listen to college chatter, but there wasn't time. She had to leave the line free for Hack's call.

When the phone rang, she took it in the kitchen and sat down at the table, her eyes grazing the bullet holes and the sheet of paper with one mark on it next to Fitzhugh's name.

"Hello?"

"OK. Tell me what's up."

"Hack, you said a couple of weeks ago, when I first started working the Anthony case, that Harold Bowman had a girlfriend."

"Right."

"Do you know where she lived? Was it in the Village?"

"Let me think. No, I'm sure it wasn't."

"How do you know?"

"Because he told me, or I overheard him telling someone else where he was going. It wasn't the Village, Jane."

"Where was it?"

"I don't remember. But it wasn't the Village. What's going on?"

"I have to think. I don't want to talk about it."

"Can I see you tonight? I've finished all the crap I had to do this week."

"That would be great."

"Six, seven. I'll bring dinner. I miss you."

She smiled. "I'll be waiting."

Garrett Fitzhugh had graduated from the Police Academy with Harold Bowman. They had known each other over thirty years. If this connection held, Bowman was the top guy in the Anthony murder, the gun deal, maybe even the big truck theft. It meant you couldn't believe one word that Lieutenant Bowman claimed he had heard from Micah Anthony on the night of the murder. For all Jane and all the other investigators of this case knew, Anthony may have heard the name Fitzhugh at the crib that night or he had met Charley Farrar for the first time. Maybe Charley had inadvertently dropped the name when he meant to say "the sarge." And when Anthony called Bowman and told him, or when Farrar reported it after the meeting, Bowman knew it was all down the tube and Anthony had to die. Whether Bowman pulled the trigger, or Fitzhugh or Charley Farrar, it was Bowman's order that made it happen.

I can't bear this, she thought. Anthony's life was in his hands from the first day of the operation. Melodie Anthony trusted him so completely. Everyone did, the whole fucking police department.

She wanted to go to Alicia Kislav's apartment and tear her apart. She must have recognized Fitzhugh's picture from a quick accidental encounter. But that was not the way to do it. That was the way to make mistakes that would cost the whole investigation.

The phone rang. She felt dazed, glanced at her watch. "Hello?"

"It wasn't the Village," Hack's voice said. "It was on the east side, Twelfth or Thirteenth Street. Alphabet City."

Her heart skipped a beat. "Thanks, Hack. I'll see you later."

[45]

HACK ARRIVED WITH dinner, wine, and his briefcase. He was casually dressed, a short-sleeved shirt for a warm day. It was almost June.

"I don't like the way you look," he said.

"Harold Bowman was the top man in the gun deal."

"You think he ordered Anthony killed?"

"Or killed him himself." She saw him wince. "He and the dead Transit sergeant that I picked as the top guy went to the Academy together. Last night I found the woman that I think had the affair with Bowman. She lives in an apartment on the block where Anthony's body was found. She stopped when she saw the picture of Fitzhugh—the sergeant—but said she'd never seen him. Her name is Alicia Beringer Kislav and she used to live in Alphabet City with a roommate. They didn't get along because when Alicia's boyfriend came calling, they locked out the roommate. The roommate told me the boyfriend was a cop. So they split up and Alicia took an apartment on Waverly Place."

"And kept seeing the boyfriend."

"Right."

"And you want to kill him."

She nodded. "I've never felt this way about a—about a perp. The man has no decency. How could he call Mrs. Anthony and console her? How could he order a hit on his own detective?"

"It's all about money."

"Not to Micah Anthony, it wasn't."

"Let's have something to eat and we'll talk about it."

"I don't know if I can eat, Hack. I don't know—"

"Let's try some food first. It's a good wine. I think you'll like it."

It was a good wine. She thought maybe she should ask her father for the crystal he had not used since her mother's death. It would be nice to drink from that rather than dime-store glass, although Hack never complained.

They talked about it as they ate, fitting the small pieces into the small gaps, the large into the large.

"How did all the previous teams miss out on the number of men in the crib?" he asked.

"Because Charley Farrar wasn't there when the cops arrived. Charley must have left just after Micah Anthony. He may be the actual killer; I don't know. If it wasn't him, it was the sarge, Fitzhugh, or possibly Bowman himself."

"Harold wouldn't dirty his hands that way. He'd delegate."

"And the three guys that were left kept their discipline. Fitzhugh must have promised them plenty of money if they just kept quiet. That's why he had to pull a big theft, so he could buy their silence."

"And that was the truck theft."

"I think so. Four trucks worth a million dollars. Probably on the high seas by the next morning. Everyone paid well enough that they kept quiet. And enough left over to pay off Farrar, Morgan, Randolph, and Manelli. Not to mention Fitzhugh himself."

"And some small change for Bowman."

"That son of a bitch."

"You know you've only got a circumstantial case against him."

"I've been worrying about that all afternoon. There are going to be phone records that we can trace to him. Charley Farrar must have called him, and he called Charley. And calls between Fitzhugh and Bowman. Maybe Alicia Kislav will admit Bowman was her lover and that she saw Fitzhugh once, waiting in a car outside her apartment.

And Bowman may still have the gun he used to shoot Manelli."

"I think you've got enough for a search warrant, both his office and his home. He may keep a second phone in his desk, maybe even the gun."

"I'll tell McElroy we need a meeting with Graves Monday morning. This isn't going to be good news for Graves."

"That's not your problem."

"I'm too independent for him, Hack."

"Tell me about it." He smiled, and she smiled back. "Can I change the subject?"

"I wish you would."

He went to the foyer and came back with his briefcase. "I have something for you." He reached down deep and pulled out two keys on a round key ring. "These are for you."

She took them, not comprehending.

"They're for my apartment."

"Your what?"

He reached back into the briefcase and took out an envelope, from which he drew a document bound in blue. He laid it on the table facing her. "This is my separation agreement."

She looked at it, then at him, then put it together. "You didn't hear a word I said to you in Paris."

"I heard every word, Jane. I probably memorized that whole conversation, I turned it over so many times. And then I had a talk with myself. I've spent almost my entire career working with people and I'm damned good at it. But when I try to work with the one person who means the most to me, I never get it right. So I decided to do what I knew was right for me, right for my family, and right for you too. I talked to my wife when I got back from Paris and we filed for a separation. Then I got myself an apartment, and I moved in today."

She swallowed, thinking that this was what it was like to be at a loss for words. Finally she said, "How are your daughters taking it?"

"One's OK; one isn't."

That, at least, was honest. She nodded. "Where's your apartment?"

"East of here. In an old renovated factory. It's about the size of this kitchen."

She smiled, feeling a little teary. Hackett the compromiser. Unexpectedly, she felt light. It was done. He had made the break, and they had each other and two apartments.

He covered the hand that lay on top of the separation agreement. "I can take you there. It's pretty clean and I've got a good bed."

"Take me."

They drove in his car, parked a block away, and walked. It was not just old; it had gargoyles and other decorations from a time when buildings were built to be beautiful, not just serviceable. They took the elevator and he used her key to let them in.

It was a small box with a kitchen area that could be closed off, a closet that was actually large, and a bathroom with a stall shower. All the fixtures were new and gleaming. The bed was made in military fashion, tight sheets, square corners, no spread. A table with two chairs was near the kitchen, and a small leather sofa filled in the remaining wall space.

"I love it," she said.

"They call it a one and a half. I've found the half. I'm still looking for the one."

"It's wonderful, Hack. I can't believe this."

"You're not angry."

"I should be." She grinned at him, Harold Bowman and Micah Anthony left behind for the moment as she surveyed the apartment. "I'm not. I feel . . . I'm happy. Why should I feel happy?"

"Because we've done the right thing."

"You did."

"I did, we did, it's the same thing now." He put his arms around her, kissed her, moved his face against hers. "Let's do what we do best. I haven't slept in the bed yet."

[46]

SHE CALLED MCELROY on Sunday afternoon, told him she wanted a meeting first thing Monday morning, and asked if she could invite Defino.

"You got this solved?"

"I think so."

"I'll let the inspector know, and I'll call Detective Defino."

She hoped Graves wouldn't call, because she didn't want to talk about it on the phone. He was probably too annoyed with her to do so, but Defino did, and she told him to be at Centre Street by nine in the morning.

Graves broke into a genuine smile when Defino entered his office. "Detective Defino, it's good to see you. How're you doing?"

"Just fine, sir. It aches a little less every day. It's good to be back, even if it's just for a meeting."

"Well, you're a big part of this. Have a seat."

Graves listened stoically as Jane narrated what she alone knew. The others interjected words of surprise and congratulations. When she was done, Graves asked her and the others to start at the beginning of their investigation and bring him up to the present. She and Defino, with MacHovec's assistance, began; then she, Smithson, and MacHovec continued from the point where Defino was kidnapped.

"What don't we know for sure?" Graves asked at the end.

"Who killed Anthony. It could have been Farrar, Fitzhugh, or Bowman. Also who killed Farrar. It could have been Bowman or Manelli. Bowman had to be the one who killed Manelli because there wasn't anyone else left. Randolph has been at Rikers since Gordon and I saw him three weeks ago.

"Another thing. I don't know for sure that Bowman ordered Farrar to leave the Beretta in Riverside Park. That could have been Charley Farrar's decision. I don't even know if he told Bowman that Randolph had called."

"He had to," Graves said. "Farrar wasn't a decision maker. Maybe he just acted on impulse and left the Beretta. Which could be why Farrar had to go."

"Farrar had to go because Bowman was doing away with the links between himself and the men in the crib," Defino said. "With Farrar gone and Manelli gone, Bowman was untouchable. Even if we offered Randolph a sweet deal, he had nothing to give us. He didn't know who the sarge was, and no one except the sarge knew there was someone else in the hierarchy."

"Farrar knew after the sarge retired. A million-dollar heist and he gave all of it away to keep those guys quiet. One smart thief."

"He gave some of it away," Jane said. "If you saw his apartment, you'd know he kept a good bit for himself."

"Kind of funny," Graves said. "The sarge pulled a bigger heist to keep those guys quiet than they would have ever realized from the sale of the guns."

"But it kept them quiet."

"All right. I'm not with you a hundred percent, but we have to follow this up. We'll need a couple of warrants, and I'd like you to handle those without Annie's intervention. Write me up an application explaining why we have to search Captain Bowman's office and home. We don't need one for his locker; that belongs to the city."

"Just one thing." He looked at Jane, then at the other detectives. "This woman you found who you think was a friend of Bowman. How exactly did you come to her?"

Smithson picked it up. "She lives on the block where Anthony was found. Jane thought the car that dropped him there may have been headed for a familiar location. Even if Bowman wasn't in the car that night, he could have told Fitzhugh or Farrar to go there to get Anthony off the street till they decided what to do with him. Bowman would have had a key, and he could call the girl and tell her to let them in."

"We need her testimony. We need to know she knew Bowman, that Bowman had a key, if he did, and that she got a call from him that night, if she did."

"I'll talk to her this evening," Jane said. "She mentioned that she works. I think we should also check to see whether Fitzhugh or his widow sold or turned in a handgun."

"He wouldn't do that," Smithson said. "Not if he used it for a felony murder."

"Then we need a search warrant for her apartment."

"All right, Detectives. You've got a day's work to do. I want those warrants before four o'clock, so let's get cracking."

Graves hadn't mentioned it, but Jane knew he would have to alert the chief of D's to the situation. From the chief of Detectives' office, word would go to the police commissioner's office and then spiral out to the other super chiefs.

Defino hung around, helping with the wording for the warrants. When Jane and Smithson went over to 100 Centre Street to get them, he took the subway to Queens. The warrants were issued by a judge who was less than pleased to do it, sorrowful that police officers might be implicated in one of the worst killings in department memory.

The plan was to execute the Bowman warrants and the Fitzhugh warrant at nine A.M. Tuesday and take Bowman into custody. Jane and Smithson would be in on the collar, and Defino would make an appearance as well. She put the warrant for Bowman's office in her bag. Detectives from two Queens precinct squads were on their way to pick up the warrant for Bowman's home and for Fitzhugh's apartment.

At six thirty Jane walked over to Alicia Kislav's apartment and rang the bell. This time she had a photo of Harold Bowman along with one of Garrett Fitzhugh.

Alicia opened the door and smiled at her. "Detective Bauer," she said with surprise. "Come in."

"Mrs. Kislav, we have to talk privately."

"I don't know what else there is I can tell you. I answered all your questions the other day."

"I have some new ones."

Alicia left the room to talk to her husband, who looked in at Jane, then left with his son, going into a bedroom at the back of the apartment.

"At the time that you moved into this apartment," Jane began, "you were having a relationship with a man. Can you tell me his name?"

Alicia smiled, looking flustered. "I'm sure I can't remember. I went out with many men before I met my husband."

"I'm sure you did. You're a beautiful woman. But this man caused friction between you and your roommate when you lived in Alphabet City. Tell me his name."

"It could have been that fellow Mark, I forget his last name, or Greg or Will—I really don't know."

Jane put the photo of Bowman on the table in front of them and watched Alicia's face. The eyes teared but nothing else showed. "What's his name?"

Alicia shook her head.

"Mrs. Kislav, if you're not going to cooperate, I think we should take a ride to the station house and continue our conversation there. I'll call for a car." Jane took her cell phone out and opened it.

Alicia's face turned fearful. "That's not necessary," she said. "I remember his name. Harold. Harold Bowman."

"And what did he do for a living?"

"He was a lieutenant on the police force." Her voice had become low and cloudy.

"And did he come to see you in this apartment?"

Alicia nodded.

"Often?"

"Once a week, twice a week."

"Did he have a key?"

"Yes."

"On the night of the murder of the police detective, did he call you?"

"I don't want to talk about it. I can't get into trouble."

"I don't want to get you into trouble, Mrs. Kislav. I wan

to put together what happened that night. Did Lieutenant Bowman call you?"

She nodded.

"What did he say?"

"He said . . ." She was weeping now. "Someone might come by that night, maybe a couple of people. I should let them in. They wouldn't hurt me, they wouldn't do anything, they just needed a place to stay for a while."

"And did they come?"

"No."

"What happened?"

"Nothing happened. I fell asleep and then it was morning and they never came."

"Did you ever tell anyone about that phone call?"

"No one ever asked me, and Harold said to remember that he had never called. It just never happened." She got up and came back with a box of tissues, using two of them rapidly.

"What happened to your relationship with Lieutenant Bowman?"

"It ended soon after that. We loved each other so much. I thought there was a chance that . . . But it ended." She wept silently, a tissue held to her face. A past she had set aside had returned with a jolt.

"Thank you for your candor," Jane said. "You did nothing wrong and you've helped us in our investigation. You will talk to no one about this conversation."

"No, ma'am."

"If you do, you will be interfering in a police investigation."

"I won't tell anyone."

Assuming there was a trial, she would be called for the information she had just given Jane. But that would be later, perhaps as much as a year from then.

Jane went home, told Hack what had happened.

"I ever tell you you're a good detective?" he said.

"You're just buttering me up. We have a good team."

"When are you making the arrest?"

"Tomorrow at nine when we execute the warrants. I hope you'll be there."

"I wouldn't miss it for the world."

47

THEY ARRIVED AT the station house at eight thirty, Jane, Smithson, Defino, and two detectives from the Manhattan South Detective Task Force, accompanied by a clearly confused uniformed captain from the Manhattan South-Borough Office. They kept out of sight, but Jane saw Bowman enter the station house a few minutes after she arrived. It was the last day of his life that he would enter that building, the last day he would exert the authority of a captain.

At nine exactly they moved into the precinct in a group, Jane exhibiting the warrant as they passed the sergeant's desk. The sergeant moved to the phone and she warned him away from it.

Bowman glanced up from his desk as the door of his office opened and Jane walked in, holding the warrant, followed by the entourage.

"Capt. Harold Bowman," she said, "I am arresting you for the murders of Salvatore Manelli, Charles Farrar, and Det. Micah Anthony. You have the right to remain silent." She read off his Miranda rights, then turned to Defino. "Detective Defino, please relieve the captain of his weapon."

As Bowman stood looking from one to another, Defino removed the Glock from Bowman's holster and put it in a bag.

"We have a warrant to search your office," Jane went on, showing it to Bowman, who declined to read it. "May we have the key to your locker?"

Bowman handed it over.

"Thank you," Jane said with a smile. "Please turn around, Captain." When she stood behind him, she cuffed him. "He's all yours, Detective," she said to one of the borough detectives. Then she turned and shook Defino's hand.

The Queens police found a gun in Fitzhugh's apartment that had not appeared on his ten card, the record of guns a police officer owns. His wife said she knew he had an extra, but when the precinct police came for his weapons after his death, that one wasn't on the list, and she didn't mention it. She turned it over willingly and it was sent to be tested by ballistics.

At the same time, a second set of Queens detectives served the warrant at Bowman's house. They found an unregistered Beretta in a closet and took it with them.

The results came back late Tuesday afternoon, Graves having used his influence to rush the ballistics procedure. The gun in Fitzhugh's apartment was the same one that had shot Micah Anthony. That didn't mean Fitzhugh had committed the murder, but if he hadn't, there were only two other people who could have done it, and they were Charley Farrar and Harold Bowman. The other three men in the crib that night would not have had time to get back to the West Fifties after the shooting before the police came to arrest them. The gun had been bagged at the Fitzhugh apartment and prints lifted before it was sent to ballistics. It was possible, although not likely, that the gun had never been used again and had not been cleaned.

The Beretta found in Bowman's house turned out to be the one used to kill Manelli a week earlier. That, at least, tied Bowman to the killing, and to the gang Micah Anthony was working to expose.

At a quiet moment during the hectic afternoon, Jane called Mrs. Appleby.

"I heard," the quiet voice at the other end of the line said. "I'm sorry. I'm very sorry."

"Are you sure, Detective? I'm finding this very hard to accept. Captain Bowman was so kind to me. He seemed so sincere. He's called me almost once a month since Micah was murdered."

"If he didn't pull the trigger, he ordered it. I'm absolutely certain about that."

"Thank you. I don't know what else to say. What kind of a man is he?"

"A man that loves money, Mrs. Appleby."

"It's more than that. I can't talk about it. Thank you for calling. Thank you for doing your job."

Jane called her father after that and told him what had happened.

"Will I see you on the TV tonight?" he asked.

"I don't think so. I'm ducking out when I've got my Fives done."

"This was a big case, Janey. Maybe you'll get another medal."

"Probably not, Dad. And I don't want one for this case. I just want to put it behind me."

Before the day ended, Annie came in and said the inspector wanted to see her first thing in the morning.

"Thanks, Annie." She had been expecting this.

"What's that for?" MacHovec asked.

"I disobeyed a direct order. Tomorrow I get my twenty lashes."

"Fuck him."

Jane smiled. "Thanks, Sean."

When the two men were gone, she picked up her bag and left. It was a beautiful day and she decided to walk home, drink a beer, do nothing. A layer of depression had settled on her. She heard Mrs. Appleby's soft voice in her head: "What kind of a man is he?" The worst, Jane thought. A traitor. She wondered for how long he would go away. The only homicide they had him for was Manelli. He would say Manelli shot Farrar and Farrar shot Micah Anthony. Neither of the guns that ballistics had tested was the one that shot Farrar. Where was that gun?

Bowman's legally owned guns would be tested, too, but Jane didn't think he was stupid enough to use one of them in a homicide. Sooner or later he would be found out. When she got home, she called McElroy and said they needed a warrant to search the automotive shop in Queens. Manelli had never returned to Franklin's apartment after the Defino kidnapping, so Roger's shop was the only place he could have secreted a gun. McElroy said they would take care of it in the morning.

After she changed her clothes, she opened a beer and sat in the living room. The outside light dimmed, but she didn't move to turn on a lamp. When the phone rang, she thought she might not answer it, but changed her mind. It was Hack.

"You want company?"

"You know what? I don't. I need to be alone. It's nothing personal, Hack."

"You don't have to explain."

"I talked to Micah Anthony's wife."

"This must be quite a blow."

"It is. She said something very nice to me. She said, 'Thanks for doing your job.'"

"That is nice."

"I'll talk to you tomorrow."

When the phone rang again, she let the machine take it. It was Flora with congratulations. No one else called. It got dark, the beer long gone. She rinsed the bottle and went to bed.

Wednesday Jane dressed for her meeting with Graves, choosing the black skirt suit and white silk blouse she had bought the year before for an interview with an insurance company she later decided not to work for. She added a pair of gold earrings her mother had treasured.

Annie looked into their office at five to nine. "You look gorgeous," she said, with just enough surprise that Jane wondered how bad she usually looked.

"Thanks. He ready for me?"

"Right now."

Jane walked to the inspector's office. He was busy writing something, but looked up when she entered.

"I don't tolerate insubordinate behavior," Inspector Graves began. "And I don't believe the end justifies the means."

"Yes, sir."

"And you will pay for it." He pushed aside the papers he had been working on, folded his hands, and looked at her directly. "A week's vacation without pay."

"Yes, sir."

"And you will never disobey a legal order again."

"Yes, sir."

"Dismissed."

It sounded like a military order. She left the office, feeling she had won the battle. As Hack had said, she had so much lost time and unused vacation time accumulated, it would cost her nothing. Graves probably knew that but was unable to give her a punishment more severe that would not produce a backlash.

"You still on the job?" MacHovec asked.

"I got a five-day rip."

"Shit, you can do that without feeling it."

"I know."

"You dress up for the boss or you got a hot date after work?"

She grinned at him. "Maybe both. Hide and watch me leave."

"And miss my train?"

She laughed, took the suit jacket off, and hung it up. "You're good, Sean."

They worked up a request for a warrant to search Roger's automotive shop, and Annie got the warrant with no difficulty. News of Harold Bowman's arrest was everywhere.

Jane and Smithson drove over to Queens and met a detective from the One-oh-eight, and the three of them went inside. On the day that Manelli had gone to the Village, they had searched the room he had been sleeping in and turned up nothing. Now they looked in bathrooms and storerooms. They found the gun stashed behind cans of motor oil. They tagged it and bagged it and sent it off to ballistics. It was the make and model that had been used to shoot Charley Farrar.

So far so good. But there was still one loose end. Back or

Centre Street Jane said, "I need something, Sean, if you've got the time."

MacHovec looked at his watch. "Got plenty left."

"I want lists of sergeants who attended Police Academy prep courses for the lieutenant's exam, going back two years before the Micah Anthony killing and ending with eight years ago. Just print out the lists. I'll read them."

He swiveled back to the computer and started his search, printing out one list after the other as he found them and dropping each on her desk. She scanned the first few, finding nothing of interest on page after page, and left the rest for later.

"That's it unless you want to come up to the present," MacHovec said, tossing the last sheaf on her desk.

"This is fine. Thanks, Sean." She stacked the rest to take home and went to see Annie about arranging to give up her lost time. This punishment would eat up hours that had been accumulated and forgotten long ago. The paperwork for handing over the hours indicated that it was an administrative disciplinary matter.

Before she left, she called her old partner, Marty Hoagland, in the Six. "I'm all dressed with nowhere to go," she told him when she finally reached him. "How 'bout I buy you a drink?"

"Are we sneaking around or is this out in the open?"

"Out in the open. We cleared the case."

"I heard. Graves was on the network news last night. Sounded like he and McElroy aced it themselves."

She wasn't surprised. They picked a bar, one of their old favorites, and she took a cab over, having left her walking shoes at home.

"Hey, who stood you up?" Marty said after a hug.

"I had a chat with Graves this morning. Thought dressing like a lady wouldn't hurt. It didn't, but it didn't help either."

"This gonna be a long story?"

"No story at all. I just wanted your company. It's been a while. What are you drinking?"

"My usual."

She went to the bar and got two of his favorite beers.

"This one really hit me," she said as they poured. "Bowman. The guy who held Micah Anthony's life in his hands. I don't often feel murderous."

"Don't say it. Maybe he'll get a stiff sentence."

"The only homicide we can tie him to directly, where he held the gun in his hand and shot, is of a lowlife named Manelli. The other killers are dead."

"Thanks to Bowman."

She nodded. "Tell me about the family, Marty. I want to hear how the kids are doing."

He obliged her and she listened, smiling at the stories. Along the way she got them another round. While she was at the bar, a cop she didn't know tried to pick her up. She grinned at him and walked away with her two bottles.

At six thirty she told Marty to go home. Beth would have a super meal waiting for him. He invited her to join them, as he always did, and she declined, as she always did. She hadn't called Flora back yet, and that had to be done tonight. And she wanted to get into a pair of jeans and sneakers. But seeing him had been the right thing to do. He had lifted her spirits.

[48]

THE CALL TO Flora took longer than Jane had anticipated. Flora wanted all the details Jane could give her about the case. That Bowman had been involved was shocking. More than involved, Jane told her. Probably the mastermind. Finally they made a date for dinner and Jane got off the phone.

In jeans and a cool shirt, she sat with the class lists of prospective lieutenants that MacHovec had pulled that afternoon. What she was looking for—or perhaps hoping not to find—was in the first one after Anthony's death. Sgt. John Beasely and Sgt. Garrett Fitzhugh were in the same prep class. It was the first link she had found between the two men.

She checked the next year's class and found them both again. Perhaps they had taken the exam and not placed high enough; perhaps they had opted not to take it the first year so as to score higher with more preparation.

She called Beasely's district and asked when he was expected for his next tour. Nine the next morning, she was told. That gave her about twelve hours to decide what, if anything, to do.

In the morning she went to Centre Street and told Annie she had some loose ends to tie up. The two lists were in her bag when she went down to the subway to ride to Beasely's district. She was directed to his office and he called for her to come in when she knocked.

"I'm Detective Bauer, Lieutenant," she said.

"Bauer."

"Yes. I visited your wife last week."

"You had no right."

"I had the permission of my lieutenant, sir. Inspector Graves didn't know about it until you called him."

"Why are you here?" He was a tall, handsome man, fit and muscular, very dark skin, a face barely concealing rage.

"I want to know your relationship to the late Sergeant Fitzhugh."

"Who?"

"I think you know who I mean, Lieutenant."

"I had no relationship to him."

"You knew him."

"I did not."

She leaned over and dropped one of the lists on his desk. Two names were circled in red.

"We were in a class together. What does that mean?"

"It's the timing that's interesting. It was after Detective Anthony was murdered and before the big heist in the subway, the four cable trucks. I'm sure you recall that."

"I recall it."

"I have the chronology of the murder, the heist, and the renovation of your kitchen."

"How dare you, Detective. How dare you insinuate that I had anything to do with those events."

"All I want is information, sir. I have no intention of trying to tie you in to the theft."

"I have no information to give you."

Jane dropped the second list on his desk, again with two names circled in red. Beasely glanced at it.

"Then I will have to recommend an investigation." She got up, put her bag over her shoulder, and moved away from the desk.

"Wait a minute," Beasely said. "Maybe I can be of help to you."

Jane took her seat, putting her bag on the chair beside her. "Who masterminded the theft?"

"Fitzhugh."

"Not Bowman?"

"I didn't know there was a relationship between Fitzhugh and Bowman until you arrested him on Tuesday."

"How much did Fitzhugh pay you?"

"I can't answer that."

"What was your part in the theft?"

"I had no part in the theft."

"What did you do to earn the kitchen?"

"I will deny this conversation took place."

"No one will know about it. I need to tie up loose ends. The theft in the subway is connected to the murder of Micah Anthony."

"That's absurd."

"It may seem that way, but it's true. Sergeant Fitzhugh needed money to keep the men involved in the murder quiet. That's where he got it."

From the look on Beasely's face, it was clear he had never made the connection. "Shit," he said softly.

"Yes, sir," Jane said.

"I was essentially a lookout. That's all. Fitzhugh wasn't even clear what was going down, just that he needed someone that night in three different places at three different times, and he would see to it that I was compensated. That's the whole story."

"Thank you, sir." She doubted that that was true. He probably knew much more, but she had most of what she wanted. "Can you give me any names of people involved in the theft?"

"No, I can't. You've gotten all I know." He looked at his watch. "I have work to do, Detective. I'm sure you do, too."

"Yes, sir. Thank you for your time." She didn't retrieve the lists she had put on his desk. They would be something for him to think about when his wife served him dinner that night in their expensive kitchen.

The rest of the case was a mountain of paperwork. If there were no paperwork, there would be no CASE CLOSED stamp; it was as simple as that. Whether Garrett Fitzhugh or Charley Farrar pulled the trigger on Micah Anthony was impossible to determine. Probably both of them were in the car with Anthony that night, and the gun belonged to Fitzhugh, so it was a reasonable assumption that he had done it.

It was likely but not provable that Salvatore Manelli had been the man in the subway who shot Charley Farrar. The gun found in the automotive shop had been the murder weapon, but the team believed Bowman had given the order. Catty Fellows looked at photos of Manelli and Bowman but declined to identify them.

There was no question who had shot Manelli. The way the hierarchy had been organized, it was doubtful Randolph could contribute any meaningful information, although he was considering a plea deal that would reduce his sentence if he copped to the theft of the two hundred twenty-seven guns from the armory.

The question of whose decision it was to leave the Beretta in Riverside Park still rankled. Bowman denied everything and spoke only with an attorney present, giving up almost nothing. Jane believed it was Charley's idea, that Bowman was too smart to do anything like that. But it was just a belief.

Frank Graves walked around with an aura surrounding him. He had cracked the Micah Anthony case. He had done what no one else had been able to do for ten years. In addition, his team had gone a long way toward clearing the case of the huge TA theft.

When all the forensic information had been collected and the Fives were typed, Graves took McElroy and the team out to lunch to thank Smithson for his work. Defino was invited too. It would be summer before he would return to work, but he was feeling better each day, happy to come into Manhattan for a good lunch. Even MacHovec looked spiffed up for the occasion.

That afternoon, Smithson cleared his things out, shook a lot of hands, and went back to his detective squad. The Micah Anthony case was closed.

[49]

THE SUMMER WAS shaping up nicely. Defino would be back soon. Graves was making eye contact with Jane. Jane had arranged to take two whole weeks of vacation in July, one week of that with Lisa, who would fly to New York and stay with her. Jane's father was ecstatic. He would meet his granddaughter and the three of them would tour the city.

Jane planned to spend at least some of the second week with Hack. His apartment was working out well. The air-conditioning alone was worth the price, he told her. Much better than what he had lived with on Long Island for twenty years. On hot nights that would be the place for her to stay, much cooler than her bedroom with a window unit.

But before all that, there was Medal Day.

Medal Day was as beautiful as days in June can be in New York, the sky bright blue and cloudless. John Bauer, dressed in his new summer suit, took the subway to Manhattan and met Jane before the ceremony, which took place in the plaza just west of One PP. He sat in the section reserved for relatives of those receiving awards. He could hardly keep from smiling.

Hack had arranged with the chief of D's months earlier to award the medals, a favor the chief had granted while Hack was still working in the chief's office at One PP. A photograph would come out of the ceremony of him bestowing the medal on Jane, a photo he could hang in his office and look at with pleasure.

The ceremony went flawlessly. Hack was introduced as Chief Dan Hackett, and he proceded to give medals and shake hands. Jane was one of the first, as they were given in alphabetical order. Her happy smile matched his. For a moment, as he shook her hand, she thought he might lean over and kiss her, but he just looked at her, smiling, for her benefit alone.

When it was over, Jane found her father and they hugged. He looked at the medal in its presentation box and read the inscription.

"This is a great day," he said. "I wish your mother was here to appreciate it."

"I'm sure she knows, Dad."

"You're right, Janey. As usual. You look great. I haven't seen you in uniform for years. Fits you real good."

"You look great, too, Dad. That suit is gorgeous. I hope you have lots of opportunities to wear it."

He turned toward the stage, where the bosses in their white shirts were gathered, talking and laughing. "Looks like a fine man," John Bauer said.

"Who's that?"

"That Chief Hackett who gave you the medal."

"He is, Dad, a very fine man. Would you like to meet him?"

"Could I?"

"Sure. Come with me." She took his arm and led him to the stage, feeling the gentle breeze. They walked to the group of bosses and she stopped. "Chief?" she said.

Hack turned, his surprise visible. "Detective Bauer?"

"Yes, sir. My father wanted to meet you, sir. Chief Hackett, my father, John Bauer."

The unflappable Chief Hackett was clearly unprepared for this meeting. "A pleasure to meet you, sir," he said, offering his hand.

"And for me, too."

"You have a wonderful daughter, Mr. Bauer."

"Oh, I knew that the minute I laid eyes on her, Chief, all those years ago. I knew what a treasure I had, and I've never been disappointed."

And then, to Jane's utter disbelief, Hack put his arms around her father and gave him a hug. Then he stood back and smiled at Jane, a smile of pure pleasure. "Thank you," he said. "Thank you for bringing your father to meet me."

The moment ended, and Jane and her father went back down the stairs and started up the aisle.

"Is he the one?" her father asked.

"What do you mean? Which one?"

"The one you kept from your mother and me all these years?"

Stunned, Jane stopped walking and turned to face her father. "Dad."

"I could see," he said. "I could see the way you looked at each other. Is he?"

"Dad, you must never tell a living soul."

"You can trust me, Janey." He was beaming.

"No one. Not even Madeleine. No one in the world."

"My lips are sealed."

"How did you know?"

"Oh, you think I'm old and I don't know what's going on. I knew there had to be someone. You're the most wonderful girl in the world. There had to be a man that loved you, even if you couldn't bring him home."

"You never asked me."

"I knew when the time came, you'd tell me. I figured today was the time. I'm glad he's the one. I'm glad I got to meet him."

She took his arm and they continued their walk. Flora was up ahead, waiting for her, another introduction her father would enjoy. Flora was all smiles, heaping accolades on Jane. The three of them walked out together. Jane asked Flora to join them for lunch, but Flora had an appointment.

"I'm glad I lived to see this day," John Bauer said.

"So am I. Let's go eat."

She had made a reservation at a good restaurant in the Village. They would eat and Jane would take the subway back to the Bronx with him, over his objections. Later in the day her cell phone would ring and a voice would say, "Your place or mine?" and she would make a decision. Right now she was happy to be with this wonderful old guy who had proved he was smarter than a lot of young ones. Sometimes it was good to be surprised.